VERNON OICKLE

EIGHT CROWS

FOR

A

WISH

Eight Crows for a Wish
© 2024 Vernon Oickle

Cover design: Rebekah Wetmore
Editor: Andrew Wetmore

ISBN: 978-1-998149-37-7
First edition April, 2024

2475 Perotte Road
Annapolis County, NS
B0S 1A0

moosehousepress.com
info@moosehousepress.com

We live and work in Mi'kma'ki, the ancestral and unceded territory of the Mi'kmaw people. This territory is covered by the "Treaties of Peace and Friendship" which Mi'kmaw and Wolastoqiyik (Maliseet) people first signed with the British Crown in 1725. The treaties did not deal with surrender of lands and resources but in fact recognized Mi'kmaq and Wolastoqiyik (Maliseet) title and established the rules for what was to be an ongoing relationship between nations. We are all Treaty people.

Also by Vernon Oickle

One Crow Sorrow
Two Crows Joy
Three Crows a Letter
Four Crows a Boy
Five Crows Silver
Six Crows Gold
Seven Crows a Secret Yet To Be Told

Life and Death after Billy
Friends & Neighbours: a collection of stories from the Liverpool Advance
Busted: Nova Scotia's War on Drugs
Queens County
Ghost Stories of the Maritimes (volumes 1 and 2)
Dancing with the Dead
Great Canadian Ghost Stories Volume II (co-author)
Disasters of Atlantic Canada: stories of courage and chaos
Canada's Haunted Coast: true ghost stories of the Maritimes
The Editor's Diary: the first 13 years
Angels Here Among Us
Red Sky at Night
South Shore Facts and Folklore
I'm Movin' On: the life and legacy of Hank Snow
Beaches of Lunenburg-Queens
Nova Scotia Outstanding Outhouse Reader
Red Coat Brigade
Ghost Stories of Nova Scotia
Kiss the Cod!
Strange Nova Scotia
Newfoundland and Labrador Outrageous Outhouse Reader
Where Evil Dwells
How to talk Nova Scotian: the Bluenoser's book of slang
The Nova Scotia Book of Lists
My Nova Scotia Home
We Love Nova Scotia: a people's portrait
More Ghost Stories of Nova Scotia
Queens County: a history in pictures
The Second Movement: Nova Scotia's outrageous outhouse reader No. 2
So you think you KNOW Nova Scotia?
Forerunners: Harbingers of Death in Nova Scotia

One crow sorrow, two crows joy;
three crows a letter, four crows a boy;
five crows silver, six crows gold;
seven crows a secret yet to be told;
eight crows for a wish;
nine crows for a kiss;
ten crows for a time of joyous bliss.
eleven crows for good health;
twelve crows for improved wealth;
thirteen crows beware for it's the devil himself.

- One version of a common
Nova Scotian folk rhyme

This book is dedicated to these loyal fans
who are an important part of this journey:

Alicia • Andrea • Andy • Andrew • Angela • Ann • Anne • Amy • Barb •
Barbara • Bet • Billy • Bob • Bonnie • Brandy • Brenda • Brian • Carol •
Caroline • Carolyn • Carrie • Cathie • Catherine • Charity • Cheryl G. •
Cheryl K. • Christine • Chrystal • Cindy • Claire • Colby • Corinna •
Daphne • Dan • Darlene • Debi • Debbie • Dee • Diane • Dianne • Donna •
Dwayne • Eddie • Elaine • Eric • Florence • Gail • Gretchen • Heather •
Helen • Holly • Ian • Jacqueline • Jan • Janet • Jeff • Jennifer • Jill • Joan •
Joanne • Joyce • Judi • Judy • Karen • Kathy • Kellen • Kelly • Kelsey •
Kevin • Kim • Kym • Laura • Laurie • Linda • Lori • Lisa • Lucy • Lynn •
Marci • Mark • Martin • Michelle • Mike • Monica • Nancy • Natasha •
Nicole • Nora • Norma • Pam • Patricia • Paul • Peggy • Phyllis • Rhonda
• Robert • Roberta • Ron • Sandra • Sara • Sheila • Sharon • Shelley •
Sophia • Sue • Susan • Tammy • Terry • Tessa • Vivian • Wendy • Yvonne

This is a work of fiction. The author has created the characters, conversations, interactions, and events; and any resemblance of any character to any real person is coincidental.

Eight Crows for a Wish

Eight Crows for a Wish

Prologue

The crows have watched over this town for almost three centuries and, during that time, they have seen many mysterious events go down.

Murder. Rape. Physical assault. Disappearances. Marriages. Births. Miracles.

Through it all, the black sentinels have stood guard, remaining steadfast in their mission, and intervening when and where necessary. But above everything else they have had to do, they have observed.

It has been quiet in recent years. All has been as it should be.

But things can change quickly in this town, without warning, and seemingly without reason or cause. Logic and reality do not always exist in this place.

Such is the case today, for they sense a disturbance that may require their intercession. It appears that the one they seek has suddenly appeared in their midst. They know it is a sign that the universe is now off kilter.

All is not what it should be and the chosen one is surely to be tested yet again.

They feel the turbulence and anticipate they will soon have to act, but, for the present, they will wait, and they will watch.

Ever ready to act when required, they are the eight and they will use their power to protect the chosen one.

That is their mission.

1: A stranger on the rocks

July 2

The crows swoop and glide on the humid summer air, catching the currents as their sleek black feathers shimmer a purplish-green iridescent hue when the sunlight reflects from them. The powerful birds appear to be oblivious to her existence, but she is certain they see her.

A marvel of nature, she thinks, while carefully watching where she places her feet on the rocky shoreline. *So much beauty and grace yet also very powerful—and cunning.*

She takes a deep breath, her mind racing over the turmoil in her personal life over the past few months. It felt as though her world had been turned upside down. But, vowing to shake off the crap that has consumed her in recent weeks, she is determined to put all the drama behind her.

How did I get here? she wonders, her senses on overdrive, soaking up her surroundings—the sights, the sounds and even the smells defuse the tension and help her to relax. This is her happy place.

No matter what happened, she thinks, *I have got to pull it together. It is time to move on.*

She loves visiting this place. It reminds her of the times she spent here as a child, exploring with her parents and siblings. As she remembers, she thinks that an early summertime walk is just what she needs to clear her head.

This is a big day for her. In fact, her entire future rests on what happens in the coming hours, and she knows that she has to be one hundred percent focused on the presentation she has to give. If she blows this, all her past work could be in jeopardy.

Lost in her thoughts, she jumps when her phone rings.

Jesus. She exhales, reaches into her jeans pocket, and pulls out the sleek, wafer-thin cell phone. "Great." She sighs, scanning the screen. *Just what I need this morning.*

Taking a deep breath to steel her nerves, she puts on a smile and answers. "Hey you," she says, trying not to sound put off by the unwelcome intrusion. She cherishes the solitude of this shoreline, and any unexpected interruptions cause her great angst.

"Hey, yourself," the male caller answers. "Just checking in to make sure everything is on track for this morning, and to remind you that things start at nine, sharp. I am sure you remember how important it is that you be here on time."

"Yes, Isaac. I promise that I will be at the office in time for the virtual conference," says the petite woman with the long, fly away black hair. The early summer breeze blowing in from the harbour tosses the strands around so that it looks like her hair has a life of its own. "I get it. I know how important this presentation is to everyone. I don't need you to call and remind me."

"Well," Isaac says, "I *hope* you get it. We need you at the top of your game, as there's a lot riding on this meeting. We can't have a repeat of the last time when you didn't show up. The board of directors was not impressed."

Pushing the long black strands back behind her ears, she takes a deep breath. "Don't worry, Isaac. I said I would be there, and I will."

"Will you? Really? It wouldn't the first time you've left me hanging."

"That again?" She rolls her eyes even though she knows he can't see her. "So I missed a date. Are you going to hold that against me forever?"

"A date? You drive me crazy. I'm incensed at how easily you disregard my feelings. I just can't get over how readily you dismiss the effect your actions have on other people. Are you forgetting? It has been more than once."

"Come on, Isaac. Do you really want to get into all of that right now? Besides, let's not forget that you are no angel." Hoping to change the subject, she quickly asks, "Are all the holograms ready for the presentation?"

"Yes, they have been ready for a week, and I have reviewed them several times. I'm sure they are good to go. We have covered all the bases. I just need you here by my side."

He sighs. "Are you one hundred percent certain I can I count on you?"

"Jesus. Will you just let it go, Isaac? You can count on me. I understand how important this call is. I know that we need this funding to continue our research, and if the university doesn't see results, then they could pull the plug on us."

"Where are you anyway?" he asks. "I swear that I hear seagulls in the background."

"Just taking a little walk before the meeting," she tells him, taking in the panoramic view of the Atlantic Ocean that this vantage point offers. *This never grows old*, she thinks.

She inhales the fresh, salty air. "I needed to clear my head."

"Okay, but please don't be late. I know how easily you can get side-tracked."

"I told you I would be there, and I will be," she tries to assure him and thinks, *This is getting a little tedious, Isaac.* "Please don't worry so much."

"You know I can't help myself, especially when it comes to something this important."

She half-smiles and is about to come back with a snappy retort when a mysterious object lying on the rocks ahead of her catches her attention.

What is that? she wonders. "Just a second, Isaac. I want to check something out."

"What is it?"

Whatever it is, it looks like a person. "Isaac, I am going to have to call you back."

"What? Why?"

"Like I said, I just want to check something. I'll call you back in a few minutes."

"Don't you dare hang up on me."

She immediately disconnects the call and slips her phone into her back pocket. *I was done anyway,* she thinks

Approaching the motionless figure, long and slender with chestnut-coloured hair, she sees that the "thing" on the rocks is a man. She fears the worst.

"Mister," she says.

Kneeling on the gravel, she gives him a gentle nudge, hoping he will open his eyes. When he doesn't respond, she wonders if he's dead.

"Mister, can you hear me? Are you okay?"

She has lived in this town her entire life and doesn't recognize him as anyone from around here.

He's still breathing, she thinks, placing her ear on his chest. *Thank God.*

His clothes are wet. He's clearly badly injured, yet he somehow managed to make it this far up over the rocks.

"That looks pretty nasty," she says, noticing the large gash on the man's right forearm that's bleeding profusely. "I think you'll need some stitches in that."

What happened to you? What in the hell are you doing here? Studying his motionless form, his chest slowly rising and falling to confirm he's still alive, she wonders, *Who are you?*

Scanning his badly battered body and then checking along the shore for any boats or for signs of anyone else in the nearby vicinity, she mutters, "I wonder where you came from."

Did someone attack you and throw you into the water? she wonders, pulling her cell phone from her pocket and preparing to dial 911.

"No," the man blurts out, reaching for her as he suddenly opens his eyes and tries to sit up. "Please don't," he says, and she can tell he's having trouble speaking.

She gently pushes him back down to the ground. "Just stay there and be still, mister. You could be badly injured. I need to get you an ambulance."

"No," he says again, trying to push her hands away from him. "I don't need an ambulance."

"Please stop moving around. You could have internal injuries." Becoming more forceful, she adds, "Can you tell me who you are? What is your name?"

The man considers her questions, then says, his voice nothing more than a whisper, "Honestly, I don't know."

"You don't know? That's interesting," she observes. "Do you know where you are or where you came from?"

He then shakes his head. "No. I have no idea," he says, speaking so softly she has to strain to hear his words.

"So, either you won't tell me who you are or you can't tell me," she says. "Either way, I think you need to see a doctor."

"I am fine," he tells her, moving into a sitting position. "See?" he says. "I can get up."

She nods. "Just don't try to stand up."

"Why?"

"Because I told you not to. I can see you're injured, and you obviously need medical attention. I will call my father. He will know what to do."

"How will he know what to do?" The man makes as if to stand up, then settles back. "I'll just sit here for a few more minutes until the blood finds its way back to my head."

"Because he's a doctor and maybe you will listen to him."

"You are pushy, aren't you?"

"That's what they tell me." She grins.

"Well, you should believe them."

She chuckles. "What would you know about me?"

"Clearly, I don't know very much," he answers. Scanning his surroundings, he asks, "Can you tell me where I am?"

"Liverpool," she answers, pointing toward the opposite shore. "Just go around the head over there, and you'll be right in the bay. The town is right there, on both sides of the harbour."

"Really?" He seems surprised. "As in Liverpool, Nova Scotia?"

"Indeed." She nods. "My hometown. I was born and raised here. I came back to work here after I finished university. So, if you can't remember anything, how can you remember the town is in Nova Scotia?"

"I have no idea. I just know it."

"Does the town mean something to you?"

"Honestly..." he swallows. "I have no idea."

A low-pitched cackling noise cuts through the air, catching their attention. Looking around, they notice that several large crows have perched on the rocks not far from where the man had crawled up on the shore.

"Crows," he says, the word catching in his throat.

"Yes. There are lots of them around this part of the province."

"Can you do me a favour and tell me how many there are?"

She does a quick count. "Eight. There are eight crows in that murder right there."

"Eight?" he whispers. "What does that mean?"

"A wish," she replies. "Eight crows for a wish."

"Right. A wish." He sighs. "You seem to know a lot about crows."

"It's a thing."

"A thing? I see," he studies her face and then adds, "You look awfully familiar to me. Have we met before?"

She shakes her head. "I don't think so, and I am good with faces so I'm pretty sure I would remember you. Besides, let's not forget that you apparently can't remember too much, so maybe it's best not to put a lot of faith in your first impressions. You probably have me confused with someone else you know. I'm sure it will come to you."

"Maybe," he whispers as he continues to scrutinize her features. Finally, he asks, "What did you say your name was?"

"I don't believe I told you," she says with a smile, "but it's Sydney. Dr. Sydney Goodwin."

2: A reunion of sorts

The stranger whom Dr. Sydney Goodwin found on the rocks at the shore takes a deep breath and exhales. He stares at the group of large black birds that has suddenly congregated on the lawn just outside the window of the small, nondescript room where he found himself when he emerged from the darkness.

Eight crows.

He shrugs, watching as the birds prance around on the freshly-mown grass, bobbing their heads, occasionally pausing to glance at him through the window. *What's that all about?*

"Not sure what all of this means, fellas, but I get the feeling you're trying to tell me something," he says, as if the crows can hear him.

"Who is trying to tell you something?" an unfamiliar female voice asks.

Turning his head toward the door, he sees a nurse has entered the room. "Oh," he quickly answers. "No one."

"I see," she replies and approaches him. Her warm smile immediately makes him feel comfortable. He believes this is where the paramedics brought him, although he doesn't know for sure.

"I need to check your blood pressure," she tells him, "if that is okay with you."

"Sure," he stutters, instinctively lifting his left arm to make it easier for the woman to apply the blood pressure cuff. "I guess so." While he has many questions, he feels relaxed around the young woman.

He has no idea how long he's been in this room, but his surroundings and the sudden appearance of a nurse by his bedside confirm that he's in a hospital. The last thing he remembers before he blacked out was talking to a young woman somewhere on a rocky shore of a river. How he got to this place and the identity of the woman who found him remain mysteries him. Furthermore, he still can't remember his name or where he came from.

"How are you feeling, Mr. Doe?" the nurse asks as the blood pressure cuff inflates around the upper portion of his arm and begins to tighten. She can't be any more than thirty years old, if that.

"Mr. Doe? Is that my name?"

"Yes." She smiles and nods. "For now, until we figure out who you really are. Since we don't know your name, we've taken to calling you John Doe."

"Not very original, is it?"

"No, it certainly is not, but that's our standard policy for whenever we have to treat an unidentified stranger."

"Do you get many of those?"

"What? Unidentified strangers?" She shakes her head. "Not really. Actually," she smiles, "you're my first."

"I'm honoured."

"So, how's that memory coming?" the nurse asks. "Any luck remembering your name?"

He shakes his head. "I have no idea who I am. But speaking of names, what do I call you?"

"I'm Jessica," she tells him. "Jessica Young."

"Well, Nurse Jessica Young, it's a pleasure to meet you." He smiles. "How long have I been here? Where's the woman who found me? What's wrong with me? Am I going to be okay? Will my memory come back? Where are my clothes?"

"Wow, Mr. Doe, so many questions. I can't tell you much about how you're doing because the results from your tests have not come back from the lab yet. Once they do, the doctor will be in to see you, but I can tell you that you got here roughly three hours ago."

"Three hours?" He pauses and considers what the nurse just told him. "I don't remember a thing."

"I'm not surprised, as you were unconscious most of the time."

She removes the blood pressure cuff and makes an entry on her digital table. "Your blood pressure is normal, Mr. Doe, so that's a good thing. And your clothes are in the closet. We hung them there so they would dry."

"Where, exactly, is here?"

"You are in the emergency department at the new Queens Memorial Hospital," she tells him.

"The new hospital?"

"Well, it's not exactly new anymore, since it opened about twenty years ago."

"Really? What happened to the old hospital?"

"Oh, they tore that one down once this new place was built. It was just too old to handle any more renovations, but it had a good, long life, so it was time for it to go," the nurse explains. "It served the community well for about ninety years. There's a new condo development on the property now."

"I see," he says. He doesn't remember the old hospital, so he's not really sure how to process the information she just gave him.

"That's quite a gash you have on your right forearm, Mr. Doe. We had to give you eleven stitches to close it up. How does it feel? Any idea how you got it?"

"No." He examines the bandage that covers the wound and flexes his arm. "Not a clue, but it feels okay."

"Maybe you will remember with a little bit of rest." She smiles again. "How's your head? Any pain or headache?"

"No," he answers, closing his eyes and exhaling. "It feels fine. Why?"

"Because it looks like you suffered a major blow to your head during whatever happened to you. Any idea how that happened?"

"No," he says again. "I have no idea."

"Don't worry. I'm sure all your memories will eventually come back to you. It may just take a little time."

"I hope so, because I can't really handle not knowing who I am or how I ended up in this place."

"I am sure it must be difficult, Mr. Doe, but try to relax."

He decides he really likes this woman who seems to sincerely care very much for her patient.

She adds, "Stressing over things won't help you."

"That's easier said than done, Nurse Young." He pauses and then asks, "So, who was that woman who found me? Is she still here?"

"That's Dr. Sydney Goodwin," the nurse says, stepping back from the gurney as if preparing to leave the room. "I think she's still around here somewhere. She's hard to pin down, that one, but the last time I saw her, she was out in the hallway on her phone. I am sure she'll be in to see you just as soon as she can."

"She seems like a nice person."

"She is one of the nicest people I know."

"Have you known her long?"

"Practically my entire life." She chuckles. "We grew up together. Why? Does she mean something to you?"

"No. I mean, I don't think so other than that she's the one who found me. It's just that she seems strangely familiar to me. Like maybe we've met before."

"Sorry, Mr. Doe, that's something you're going to have to discuss with Syd whenever she comes to see you," the nurse tells him adding, "I have more patients to see, so I've got to run, but I'll stop back in a little while to check on you. Maybe by then the doctor will be here with your test results."

"That would be nice," he says as he watches her leave the room.

Very nice person, he thinks, turning back to gaze again at the crows through the window. *Certainly, very pleasant to talk to.*

Seeing the crows are still near, he says, "So fellas, what's happening? I get the feeling that you guys want to tell me something. If only you could talk."

"Hey, mister."

Somehow, he immediately recognizes the voice of the young woman who rescued him from the rocks. She says, "If you're waiting for those crows to talk back to you, I think you'll be waiting a long time."

He turns to face her. "I know, but I just get the weird feeling that, somehow, I'm connected to those black birds. It's very odd."

"You're not the first person in this town who's felt that way," she says, approaching the gurney. "I've been observing the crows around here my whole life and they do have an unusual power or energy that attracts some people to them. It's clear that you have a connection to them. I could see it by the way they gravitated to you down on the shore."

"It's pretty weird," he says, glancing back to observe the eight crows. "How can I find out more about this mysterious connection and what it means?"

"Experience has taught me that when it comes to the crows, you can't rush them," she explains. "They'll reveal their true purpose to you when they're ready, and not before. So, take a deep breath and buckle up, because sometimes, that road can get a little bumpy."

"Great, just what I need." He exhales. "I need answers, not more mysteries."

"Still no luck with the memories?"

He shakes his head. "But I'm hoping you'll have some answers for me."

"Me? Why would I have answers?"

"Well, you are a doctor, aren't you?"

"Yes I am," she says with a chuckle. "But not a medical doctor."

"Seriously?" He looks at her, confused. "What kind of doctor are you?"

"I'm a behavioural ecologist specializing in crows and other corvids," she tells him. "My field of study is ornithology."

He looks at her, confused. "I don't understand."

"Birds." She smiles. "I study bird behaviour."

He laughs. "So when you tell me that you know a thing or two about crows, you really mean it."

She nods. "They have been my life's work."

"Why? What's your fascination with them?"

She considers his question and then answers, "It's something I learned from my father. When I was just a little girl, he would tell me all about the crows and about the special bond he had with them. Of course, I didn't understand it when I was younger and I'm actually not sure I fully understand it now, but I have spent my whole life trying to find out as much about the crows as I can."

"I see."

"Do you?" She looks at him and then says, "You don't have to humour me, but I just love them. They are beautiful birds. They're intelligent, powerful, very sociable, and very protective of each other."

"No, seriously," he says. "I think that it's great that you've devoted your life to such important work. I really do."

"Okay, then. So, how are you feeling now that you've had chance to rest? Any better? I was really worried about you after you blacked out, and that's why I called the ambulance."

"I am feeling fine, but I wish I knew what was happening to me."

"I'm sure the doctor will be along very soon. He'll probably be able to tell you more."

"I hope so, because I want to get out of this place."

"Well," says the tall, middle-aged man with the full head of snow-white hair as he enters the examination room, "I wouldn't be in any rush to do that."

The stranger looks at the man, who is clearly a doctor, and an intense feeling of familiarity washes over him, gripping him and shaking his body. For some reason, he believes he knows this man.

The doctor continues, "I've got your test results here and it looks like you have a concussion, Mr. D—Jesus Christ. It's you. But how?"

3: Anything is possible

"Are you absolutely sure it's him?" Sydney asks her father.

"Yes," the tall, white-haired man replies, his back to her as he stares out the window of his office and onto the grass below, where eight crows have gathered. He observes as the large, black birds prance around, perhaps playing or looking for food. He has long thought their behaviour suggests that they think they own the place.

Perhaps they do, he thinks.

"I am certain," he tells his daughter.

"But how?"

"I have no idea, but I am positive it is him."

"But I thought you told me he died years ago," she says, continuing to probe for answers.

"He did, or at least it was assumed that he died, but they never recovered a body, so we really didn't know for sure. They searched for a long time but couldn't find any trace of him. It was like he just vanished, and that has always bothered me."

"How long ago was that?"

He pauses, breathes deeply, and then answers, his voice raspy. "As of yesterday, July 1, it was thirty-seven years ago."

"Thirty-seven years?" Considering his answer, she then asks, "How is that even possible?"

"Come on, Sydney." He turns to face his daughter. "You know as well as I do that when it comes to the crows around here, anything is possible."

"Well," she says, flopping into one of the plush chairs in the corner of his office where he asks his patients to sit if he has to deliver bad news to them, "I know that to be true and I know that they can do some wondrous things, but I also don't believe that I can accept what you're suggesting."

"Why?" He cocks his right eyebrow. "It's not like we haven't seen other miracles around here. Hell, the fact that I'm even still alive is a miracle in and of itself."

"Come on, Dad, I hardly think that you surviving a few close calls—albeit some wild and nasty ones—is the same thing as what you're implying happened to your mysterious patient."

"Haven't I always told you that when it comes to the crows you have to suspend disbelief? What we think we know to be reality doesn't always turn out to be what's actually happening."

"You have." She nods, becoming pensive. "But this? I'm not sure I can suspend logical thinking long enough to accept this. What makes you think it's even him? How can you be so sure?"

"Granted, it has been a long time since I last saw him, but I would remember him no matter how many years have passed. Besides, did you see that massive wound on his arm?"

She nods.

"Well, I was there when that happened. I saw how he got that cut. He was attacked."

"By whom?"

"By someone who died a long time ago."

"This is insane."

"Is it?"

"Okay, Dad, I can see you're convinced the man in the emergency department is your long-lost friend," Sydney replies.

"Don't patronize me, Sydney." He glares at her. "I am telling you that it's him. I know it is."

"Okay, I believe you. So then, the big question is are you going to tell him?" she asks. "How are you going to explain all of this?"

"My first instinct is to tell him everything," her father answers. "He deserves to know. But I'm not sure that's such a good idea. I mean, the trauma of this news could force him to repress his memories even more than they are now. I'm almost thinking it would be better for him to let his memories emerge on their own. Clearly, he's suffered a major trauma to the head, and another serious shock like this revelation could lead to irreparable physiological damage. I'd be worried that we may lose him forever."

"You're the doctor, Dad, but you have to tell him something. The poor guy looked completely lost and bewildered when you dropped your tablet and rushed out of the room. I could tell he was freaking out, and why wouldn't he? I mean, the doctor just turned and ran away. That wasn't a smart move."

"I know, Sydney. It wasn't my finest minute, that's for sure."

She shrugs.

"You have to understand that was the first time I had laid eyes on him, as Isabel Robbie was the doctor on call when he was brought into the ER," he says. "I was just delivering the test results."

She studies her father's face, and she can see this situation has unnerved him. That concerns her, as it usually takes a lot to fluster him.

"I know you'll do the right thing," she says. "Now, I told him I'd be right back and that was at least fifteen minutes ago. The poor guy is already confused enough that we can't leave him hanging like this. He needs answers."

"I know he does." Her father pauses and gathers his thoughts, then adds, "I need a few more minutes to pull myself together, though. This is tough for me, too."

"I'm sure it is," she says, rising from the chair and approaching her father. Giving him a hug, she adds, "If we've learned one thing over the years about these crows, it's that we can never anticipate what they'll throw at us. Clearly, they think the time has come for you and your friend to reunite, so once you gather your composure you have to go back in there and talk to him."

"But what do I tell him? That the last time he saw me I was only sixteen? How in hell do I explain that? How do I tell him that he saved my life by killing my attackers, who were trying to fulfill a centuries-old vendetta? That he was officially declared dead more than three decades ago? That he hasn't aged one day in all of that time, while the rest of us have moved on? That the world he knew is long gone?"

"I don't know, Dad, but you have to tell him something."

She smiles at him and plants a gentle kiss on his cheek. "You'll think of the appropriate thing to tell him. You're a good doctor and, more than that, you're a good person. You always know the right thing to say."

"Thanks, honey," he says, watching his daughter leave the room.

Turning to observe the eight crows again as they preen and display their beauty, he whispers, "Okay guys. What's your plan? You brought him to me today for a reason, so what do I do with him? I need some help here."

~

"Well, Mr. Whatever-Your-Name-Is," Sydney says as she enters the room where the man known as John Doe is resting. "How are you feeling now?"

"Mostly I'm confused about what just happened. I feel like I'm trapped in a nightmare. Like I'm lost in a thick fog with no one to help me."

Sydney can tell his smile is forced and overlaid with worry. "I'm here to help you."

"Okay, then, I need answers. For starters, can you tell who was that man that just dropped everything and ran out of the room? I think I know him."

"That was the doctor, my father. He just suddenly realized he had forgotten to make an important phone call and wanted to go do it before it was too late."

"I see." He squints at her.

"It was a very important call," she adds.

"So, he just ran out of the room?" He shrugs. "Kind of strange behaviour for a doctor."

"Well, that's just my dad." She smiles. "He can be flighty that way."

"Flighty? I'd say so."

"Let's not be too hasty in our judgments, shall we? Why not just wait until he has chance to come back to see you? I'm sure he will tell you everything he can."

"That's easy for you to say. You're not the one stuck in this freaking bed without a clue as to who you are, where you came from or how in the hell you got here." He pauses and then adds, "I need answers. I can't focus on anything else except who I am. I need to know."

"I understand, and I'm sure he'll be right back. I know he wants to talk to you."

"If you say so."

"I do," she answers with as much assurance as she can muster. "So, tell me, is anything coming back to you? Anything at all."

He shakes his head. "Nothing, except that images of crows and owls and a teenaged boy keep flashing in my head. I don't recognize the boy, but it must mean something, don't you think?"

"I don't know." She shrugs. "I'm not really an expert in the human brain or suppressed memories, but it certainly sounds like something is trying to get out."

"Maybe you don't know much about the human brain, but you are an expert in crows, aren't you?"

"Well, yes, I am and"—she shrugs—"until a few hours ago, I had a job studying them."

He looks at her, puzzled. "What do you mean, 'until a few hours ago'? What happened?"

"Nothing." She shakes her head.

"Come on, Sydney, you can't say something like that and then just drop the subject. What's going on?"

She hesitates for a moment. "I missed an important conference call a few hours ago and jeopardized future funding for our study."

"Oh, I see." He pauses. "Did you miss that call because of me?"

"That's not important."

He nods. "Yes, it is. Please don't tell me that I caused you to miss that call."

"You didn't cause anything. I found someone who was in trouble, and I felt it was my obligation to help him. You. That's all."

"Shit. So now I'm responsible for you losing your job? God-damned. I wish you had just left me on the rocks."

"So you could die there? Come on, mister, that's not my style. When I see someone in trouble, I'm going to help him."

"You better believe her."

It's the voice of her father, who has entered the room. "She's been like that her whole life. She's always looking out for other people, even strangers, and that is one of the things I love about her."

Turning to face the doctor, the man on the gurney answers, "That may be true, but I feel like crap knowing that I was responsible for her problems with whatever funding she was talking about."

"It's okay," Sydney says. "I believe I can work it out with the university president. She is a good person and I'm pretty sure that, when I explain the situation to her, she will understand. As for Isaac, maybe not so much."

"That's no big loss," her father replies.

"Come on, Dad. Not now."

"Sorry, but you know how feel about him."

"Who is Isaac?" the stranger asks.

"No one," Sydney answers. "I'll smooth things over with everyone."

"So, you're pretty sure you won't lose your funding?" the man asks.

"I'll give it a good shot and we'll see how it works out."

"I wish you hadn't sacrificed yourself for me."

"I couldn't help myself." She shrugs. "What you have to understand, mister, is that I'm an empath, so I always have to put other people ahead of myself. I'm just compelled to do it."

"An empath?" He looks puzzled. "What does that mean?"

"As an empath," she explains, "I'm highly intuitive. I can read the energy in a room and I can pick up the vibes that emanate from people with incredible accuracy. I know whether a person or situation is genuine or if something is not what it seems. I can 'hear' what isn't spoken, and my sixth sense for reading people is both a blessing and a curse. I knew instinctively that you needed my help, and not just because of your physical injuries."

"That's a neat trick."

"It's not a trick," the doctor says. "It's a very powerful intuition she has, and that power compels her to help other people. She's always helping other people. It's just who she is."

"I see." Smiling at her, he adds, "Thank you. I think."

She chuckles. "And I think you are welcome."

"So, doctor," the stranger says, turning to Sydney's father. "Can you tell me why I can't remember anything? Can you help me remember who I am?"

Taking a deep breath, the doctor answers, "I can help you, and I can start with telling you who you are."

4: Who am I?

"So, what can you tell me about me?" the stranger asks.

"A lot," the doctor says, pulling up a chair and sitting beside the gurney where the stranger is resting. "But I'm not sure where to start. Honestly, I'm not sure you're going to believe everything I'm about to say, as it's all going to seem pretty far-fetched."

"Way to inspire confidence," John Doe says. Taking a deep breath, he adds, "But I'm sure I can handle whatever you have to say. Why don't you start by telling me what in the hell is wrong with me?"

"Yes, I am sorry about that. You make a good point, and I should know better, but it's overwhelming even for me," the doctor says. Referring to the patient's chart, he continues, "For starters, I can tell you that you don't have any broken bones, so that's a good thing."

"It is, but broken bones aren't really my number one concern right now. I'm more worried about my memory. Why can't I remember any-thing?"

"I was just getting to that. Our tests have confirmed that you have a serious concussion and it's more than likely that the swelling around your brain could be the reason you have lost your memory."

"More than likely?"

"Yes, but we can't say for sure." The doctor pauses, glances at the patient's chart again, and then continues, "When it comes to lost memories such as what you're suffering right now, the brain works in mysterious ways. The amnesia you are experiencing is most likely because of the injury to your head, but it could also be psychological."

"Meaning?"

"Meaning that your memories may be suppressed, not lost. The reason for that could be the result of some major emotional trauma that we don't know about."

The patient sighs, glances out the window to see the eight crows are still there, going about their own business.

Turning back to the doctor, he asks, "Is the loss permanent?"

"Not usually, but considering the amount of swelling around your brain, it is probably going to take some time for things to heal, which means it's likely going to be awhile before you start getting your memory back."

The man nods and considers the doctor's diagnosis. "I see." He sighs. "Well, that's not good."

"It's clear you suffered a major blow to your head," the doctor says. "Any idea how that happened?"

"No. Not a clue," the man answers in little more than a whisper. "I can't remember a god-damned thing and I have to tell you that not knowing who I am is driving me crazy." He eyes the doctor, and then adds, "So when you came into the room a few minutes ago, you said you could tell me who I am, right?"

"I did say that."

The man squints. "So, what are you waiting for? Tell me who I am."

The doctor takes a deep breath. "It's going to be a lot for you take in and I'm concerned that the shock might be too much for you."

"I can handle it," he replies. "Please, just tell me. I need to know who I am."

"I wouldn't be so sure about what you can handle," the doctor says. "I know who you are and I'm not even sure I know how to digest the reality."

"For God's sake, man," the patient snaps, his emotions clearly getting the better of him. "Just get on with it."

"Very well," the doctor nods. "I can tell you that your name is Oliver Lewis. Does that name mean anything to you?"

The man stares at him, then shrugs. "Nope," he whispers. "It doesn't ring any bells."

"It should, because that's who you are. But I'm not surprised you don't remember your name. Your inability to remember such an important detail speaks to the severity of your concussion. Oliver Lewis is a very important name from my past."

"Oh, really? How so?"

"Well," the doctor pauses as if gathering his strength. "Oliver Lewis is the name of the man who saved my life."

"What are you talking about?" The man tries to digest the information. "Where? When? How did I save your life?"

The doctor says, "Right here in this town, but it was a very long time ago. However, there isn't a day that has gone by that I haven't thought about you. Whatever happened to you? Where have you been? How could you have just disappeared? Were you alive? These are questions that have followed me all those years. Truthfully, none of it ever made any sense to me. And now, here you are."

"This is a lot to accept," the man admits. "When you say a very long time ago, exactly how long are you talking about?"

The doctor hesitates for a second, then says, "Thirty-seven years ago."

"What? Come on, doctor, that can't be right."

"You asked for the truth and that's what I'm giving you. Thirty-seven years ago you saved my life, but I looked a lot different than I look now, so that could be part of the reason you don't remember me."

"How young are we talking about?"

"Sixteen."

"Jesus Christ." The man exhales. "This can't be true. I don't believe this."

"It most certainly is true. I wouldn't tell you something like that if it wasn't the truth." He pauses and then adds, "Does the name Alex Good-win mean anything to you?"

After thinking for a few seconds, the patient finally answers, "No."

The doctor nods. "That's my name." Studying the man's reaction, he adds, "I am Alex Goodwin."

"Sorry, but if that's supposed to mean something to me, I hate to tell you it doesn't."

"Perhaps it will come to you in time."

"Let's hope so." The man nods, as if trying to comprehend what he's just heard. "So, if all of this true and I am who you say I am, why did I save your life, Alex Goodwin?"

"What if I told you the crows made you do it? Would you believe me?"

"Not likely." The man studies the doctor, his eyes becoming narrow slits. "I think you're feeding me a lot of bullshit. I don't know what you're trying to prove, but I can't believe it."

"You can believe me when I tell you that the crows compelled you to save me from a man named Myles Merrick and his son, Ozzie, who was actually one of my best friends. It has all got to do with a pact that one of my ancestors made with the crows a few hundred years ago. My family and the Merrick family were destined to destroy each other over past grievances, but the crows intervened and compelled you to save my life. You were lost in the process."

"Lost? I don't understand."

Taking a deep breath, the doctor continues, "While you were in a fight with Myles Merrick, you and he went over a bridge and into the rushing waters of the Mersey River. Merrick died in the fall and his body was eventually recovered, but you—well, they never found you. They searched for a long time. They even sent divers down into the river and scoured the riverbanks, but they never found hide nor hair of you. It was like you had just vanished without a trace."

"Jesus."

"I never gave up hoping that somehow you had managed to survive the fall, but after so many years went by, I finally accepted that I would never see you again. But when I walked into this room a little while ago and saw you in this bed, well, I just lost it."

"How in the hell can this be true?"

"It's all a mystery." The doctor shakes his head. "I really don't know, but my guess is that the eight crows we've been seeing since you crawled out of the water have something to do with it."

"What does eight crows mean?"

"Well, according to the old legend, eight crows mean a wish."

"I still don't get it."

"Honestly, neither do I, but one thing that I've learned after all of these years is that the crows' mission isn't always obvious to discern. We'll work on figuring this out together."

"I'm not sure how to process all of this."

"Here's something else for you to consider. You went missing thirty-seven years ago and I continued to age. But when I look at you, I see the man you were all those years ago. You have not aged a single day."

"I don't understand any of this."

The doctor shakes his head. "I am sure you don't. But how could anyone understand all of this? I have seen the crows do some amazing things over the years but this...well, this seems too fantastic even for them."

The man on the gurney remains quiet for several moments, and then asks, "So now what? If all of what you've told me is true—and I have not yet accepted that it is—then I have a lot of catching up to do."

"The first order of business is for your injuries to heal. When it comes to a concussion, especially a serious one like you've suffered, you can't rush your recovery, or you may find that things will get worse."

"So, what are you saying?"

"We will admit you to the hospital, and you'll stay here for a few days where we can keep a close watch on you. Once the swelling in your brain starts to go down, you will come home with me and stay at our place. Bree will be happy to see you."

"Bree? Who's that?"

"My wife. You actually know her, although it has been thirty-seven years since you've seen each other. It will be a shock for her."

"Can't say her name means anything to me."

The doctor shakes his head. "I'm sure it doesn't. Her full name, back then, was Bree Hamilton. That may give you a few clues for when your memories start to return."

"I hope something helps. Right now I feel like I'm lost in a thick fog."

"I would expect as much. Don't try to rush it. Don't force anything. Just let your memories come to you," the doctor says. "Rest is the best medicine for these types of injuries. And no stress."

"I do have one question."

"What's that?"

"Do owls mean anything to you? Ever since I woke up here in the hospital, I have been seeing these pictures flash through my head. I see crows, which apparently have something to do with why I'm here, and I see a teenaged boy which, according to your explanation, is probably you, but I've also been seeing owls. What does that mean?"

"Interesting that you would remember the owls. Owls were the instruments of Myles Merrick's deadly plot. Those birds were his family's obsession, and he tried to use them to kill me."

"Sounds intense."

"It certainly was. Very intense."

"So why am I remembering them along with the crows and a younger version of you?"

Shaking his head, the doctor says, "I am not sure, but if I had to guess, I would say it probably has something to do with the fact that we, including the crows and owls, were the last things that you saw when you went over the railing and into the water. Or I *hope* that's what it means."

"What are you saying?"

"I hope your sudden reappearance and your memories of the owls aren't an omen that those bloody birds have come back for me after all of these years."

"Would they do that?"

"I don't know, but if they have, then it probably has something to do with that same family feud that's been going on for generations."

"Is there some way of figuring out what that means?"

"The one person who could have helped me find an answer disappeared when you did, but in a different way."

"Who would that be?"

"My aunt, Zoey LaCroix."

Observing the man's reaction, Dr. Goodwin asks, "Does that name mean anything to you?"

The man shakes his head. "I don't know that name at all. Was she someone important to you?"

"Yes, she is my mom's twin sister. Even though she promised she would always be here for me, after the confrontation on the bridge that night, Aunt Zoey just vanished without so much as an explanation."

"What happened to her?"

"She just up and left town," the doctor explains. "I looked for her over the years but could never track her down. It's like she is trying to avoid me, but, honestly, I have no idea if she's even still alive."

"That's harsh."

"Yes, well, that's what she was like. The thing is, she still has a house here in town. It has been sitting empty since she left, but it's still in good shape, so it appears she has been paying someone to take care of the place. They even cut the grass in the summer, but when I asked the land-scape company who is paying for their services, they told me that once a year they receive a money transfer to cover the maintenance costs, but the sender uses a numbered account for the transactions so there is no way to trace it."

"Sounds kind of sketchy."

"It sure does, but that's the way Aunt Zoey functions and honestly, I've given up asking questions about her. I figure if she wants to connect with me, then she'll reach out. I've moved on without her in my life."

"But why would the name mean anything to me?"

"Because you and she were pretty close. I was always under the impression that the two of you were in some kind of romantic relationship."

"If that's the case, then you would think I would remember her, wouldn't you?"

"It might come to you."

"Maybe."

"Okay then," the doctor says, rising from the chair. "I have other patients I must see, and you have to get some rest so your brain can heal. They'll soon move you to another room. You'll be more comfortable once they get you settled in a normal bed."

"Thanks."

As he leaves the room, Alex Goodwin says, "Get some rest. Doctor's orders."

How in hell can I rest after what you've just told me? John Doe thinks.

5: Looking for answers

"Before you start, Isaac," Sydney says as she enters her former boy-friend's well-organized office, "let me just say that I know I screwed up this morning, but I really didn't have any choice."

His obsessive need to have everything in its place was one of his many compulsions that drove her crazy when they were together, as it clashed with her carefree lifestyle. It's not that she's messy or doesn't like things organized; it's just that his meticulous need for organization came across as way too controlling for her liking. Sometimes that rubbed her the wrong way.

This control often caused conflict and usually lead to an argument when she pushed back. When it got too bad, she decided to end the romantic side of their relationship several months ago. But even though it wasn't easy, they have managed to stay involved as business and research partners, at least until this morning.

"I am very sorry about that, but like I said, I had no other choice," she adds, hoping that he will understand how her need to help someone in distress outweighed the urgency of a meeting, even a meeting as important as the one this morning. "Please don't be mad at me. You know I just couldn't walk away from the poor guy."

When he keeps his head buried in his work, ignoring her very presence, she knows he's pissed. She's seen this side of him often enough to know when he's beyond reasoning, but she has to try.

"Come on, Isaac, please look at me," she pleads. "Let's talk this out."

He keeps his eyes focused on his computer screen and whatever documents he's working on. His rigid posture conveys more than any words ever could.

She knows that when he's in one of these moods, the best strategy is to not push the subject, but she'd rather have the argument now and get it over with, instead of letting the issue simmer and fester until it pops like some pus-filled boil.

"Please," she pleads again. "Let's talk about this."

"Don't bother to give me one of your sob stories, Sydney," he finally says, his voice dripping with anger. "I don't want to hear any more of your drawn-out explanations about someone being in trouble. Something always comes up that seems to be more important than what we're doing—more important than us—and honestly, I've had enough."

"You have every right to be angry, but the poor guy was in serious trouble," she tries to reason with his compassionate side. That compassion may not be on display right now, but she knows it's in there; she just has to keep looking without pushing him too hard.

She adds, "He probably would have died if I hadn't stumbled upon him."

"Like I said, I don't want to hear it," he replies, continuing to punch the computer keys. He's hitting them so hard that she wonders what they've done to draw his anger. "You did what you did and now it's over. End of story."

"Come on, Isaac," she says. "Are you telling me you would have walked away if you had found him? I know you wouldn't have done any such thing. You're a better person than that."

"No." His reply is terse. "I would have helped him, but I wouldn't have gone to the hospital with him and I sure as hell would not have stayed there for hours while my career and the careers of three other people were about to be flushed down the god-damned toilet."

"What can I say, Isaac? I felt sorry for the guy. He was alone and couldn't remember anything. He seemed so lost. I couldn't just leave him there."

Positioning herself in front of his desk in an effort to force him to see her, she adds, "Can you look at me, please?"

He raises his eyes and squints at her, his glare so intense that it feels as though it's cutting through her skin. With the corners of his mouth drawn in anger, she can tell she may have crossed a line this time.

"Forget it, Sydney," he says, practically spitting the words at her. "There's nothing you can say that will make this right. You've blown up everything we've been working on for all these years and you've fucked us all in the process. It's over."

"It doesn't have to be over," she replies, telling herself to remain calm in the face of his anger. "I'll call the university president and talk to her right now. We've always had a special relationship. When I explain what happened this morning, I am sure she will totally understand. Just give me a chance. I can make this right."

"The president wasn't the only person on that call," he says, and she can tell he's seething. "The other board members were not very impressed that you left them hanging and I don't blame them for being pissed. They wanted to hear from you, the team leader and chief researcher. Instead, we wasted their time this morning and that's a bad refection on all of us. I know you think you can sweet-talk your way out of anything, but you can't fix this."

"I can."

"No." His words are sharp and cut her to the bone. "You can't and that's that. Like I said, it's over."

She and Isaac met in biology class during her first semester at Dalhousie. They didn't start dating, however, until her second semester in her second year, not because she didn't like him right away, but because she always exercises extreme caution before entering any romantic relationship. Her special gift of being able to feel the emotions of others makes her vulnerable to heartbreak, so she learned at a young age to tread lightly in such matters, especially when forging new friendships.

"I can." She nods. "I'm sure I can make things right."

"Don't bother to try fixing anything on my account," he snaps, focusing his attention back to whatever he's doing on his computer screen.

"Why?"

"Because I'm not staying. I've decided that I can't continue to do this, so I have to leave." His words are sharp, like daggers. "I can't do this anymore, Sydney, because you're driving me crazy. I need something more stable. It's time to move on."

"But I thought you loved studying crows and, more than that, I thought you liked working closely with me."

"Yes, well clearly, it doesn't matter what I liked, does it? What matters is what's happening," he says.

He raises his head, glares at her. The intensity on his face frightens her, even though she is sure he would never do her bodily harm, no matter how angry he is with her. But his boiling anger still causes her to experience real pain.

"Let's just try to calm down," she cautions. Taking a deep breath and offering him a smile, she adds softly, "Before we say or do something that we might regret."

"It's too late to calm down," Isaac counters. "I'm tired of having my life dangling by a thread, always waiting for that thread to break. I can't live like this anymore, so I've accepted a research position in B.C. They've been after me for a while, and I kept putting them off, but not any more. I made my decision this morning after you missed the call. I'm giving you three more weeks so I can help you tie up any loose ends and get things cleaned up around here, then I'm gone."

"Jesus, Isaac, way to blindside me. I know I messed up this morning, but you have to give me the chance to fix things, not just walk away from everything we've worked on for the past four years. You can't do this to me."

"I didn't do anything to you, Sydney. You did it to yourself. And"—he takes a deep breath—"I'm not the only one who's leaving. Skyler and Zachary have also decided to pursue other opportunities. In fact, Zachary is going to B.C. with me. I'm not sure what Skyler is going to do, but she's a good researcher so I have no doubt she'll find something. I'll give her a good reference and I would hope that you would do the same."

"What the hell, Isaac?"

"They are also fed up with this, and you can't really blame them. They are tired of you putting everything else ahead of this study. They have been loyal and hardworking and willing to do whatever we ask of them, but, like me, they've had enough of not knowing when you're going to pull one of your stunts, so they are moving on. And I say, good for them. They need to build up their research experience in a stable environment, so this is what's best for them. I hope you won't stand in their way."

"Fuck you," she fires back. It feels as if her world has just been blown up. "Come on, Isaac, you can't do this."

"You have no one else to blame but yourself."

"All of this because I stopped to help a stranger who washed up on the shore? I had to help him. It was the right thing to do. This isn't fair."

"I'll tell you what isn't fair. It isn't fair to see the team leader piss away a valuable opportunity to secure funding for another three years. You could have just called 911 and then come here once help arrived. It isn't fair that you always do whatever you want to do, everything else be damned." He stares at her, unblinking, and she feels as though he may as well be throwing daggers at her. "That's what isn't fair, and you know I'm right."

She takes a deep breath and exhales. "So, you're done with our research? And we're done?"

"Yes, we are done. Truthfully, we were done a long time ago, you and me. We were just too pigheaded to walk away and I'm blaming both of us for that."

"Where does that leave me? What about the study and all the work we've done here? Are you just willing to let all that go?"

He shrugs. Turning his focus back to his computer screen, he says, "You have three weeks to figure it out, and then I won't be here to help you. So let me know what you want from me and I'll help however I can, but after that you're on your own."

"Can you please stop whatever it is you are doing on your computer and give me your full attention so we can talk this over?" She stares at him, waiting for him to look up. "Please," she says, keeping her anger in check. "Can you do that for me—for us?"

"Why? You don't pay attention to anyone else when they're trying to reach you, so no, I won't stop. I want to get everything done before I leave. I don't want any loose ends when I go."

"Am I a loose end?"

He shakes his head. "Not anymore. I'm over you."

"So your decision is final?"

"Afraid so."

She can sense that he is relieved by his decision.

"I've already given my notice to the landlord that I'll be vacating by the end of the month," he says. "At this point, there is no turning back for me."

She glares at him. "Don't expect me to beg you to stay because I won't do that. I don't want you here if you don't want to be here."

"I am not asking you to do that. I believe this is what's best for both of us. You have wanted to be out of our relationship for a long time so let's just be done with it once and for all."

She's about to answer him when her phone rings. Sliding it from her pocket and glancing at the screen, she sees that it's her uncle Hunter calling.

"Just a second," she says to Isaac, getting out of the chair and moving towards the office door. "I really have to get this. If Uncle Hunter is calling me then it means something must be wrong. You know that he never calls me unless it's a family emergency."

"Sure, go ahead right ahead and get it," Isaac says, glancing back to his computer screen. "We're only talking about our futures here, nothing important."

"Don't do that," she says.

"Don't do what? Ask you to put us ahead of your own needs?" He shrugs. "I would never ask you to do that, so you go right ahead and take your call."

"Jesus Christ," she says, heading into the lab.

I didn't need this today, she thinks, pushing the talk button on her phone. "Hey, Uncle Hunter." She tries to sound chipper. "What's up in your world?"

"Sydney, am I ever glad you answered."

She loves her uncle's deep, gravelly voice. "What's wrong? Did something happen at the store? Are you okay? Aunt Ally? The boys?"

"Just slow down, Sydney. Nothing's happened to anyone. We are all fine, but I've got a strange man here at the store and he claims he knows you."

"Who is it?"

"I have no idea, but he's got brownish hair and a beard, and he's wearing a hospital ID bracelet. He just kind of waltzed in here about ten minutes ago and started acting weird around the staff and customers. I don't know what to do with him. He was babbling something about trying to find out who he was and where he came from. What does that mean?"

"I'm pretty sure I know who he is."

"Should I call the police, Syd?"

"No. No. I don't think he will hurt anyone. What do you want me to do?"

"Well, since he mentioned your name, I thought maybe you could come down to the store and talk to him. If you're too busy, I'll have to call the police and let them take him. Or I suppose I could call your father."

"No, don't do that. I don't know how he got to your store, but I'll be right over. Can you please keep him in sight until I get there?"

"I'll try my best, but please hurry."

She turns off the phone and slips it back into her pocket. She knows she should go back to Isaac and continue their conversation, but, deep down inside, she knows the time for talking has passed.

Shit, she thinks, heading to the exit. *This is not how I saw this day going when I got up.*

6: The mind works in mysterious ways

"Thanks for calling me instead of the police," Sydney says to her uncle upon entering his office at the local supermarket that has been a fixture on the town's Main Street for the past century. Hunter Webster-Henderson purchased Freeman's Foods about twenty-five years ago and rebranded it as Foods Are Us.

It's tough competing against the big box stores that have cornered the market with major markdowns on bulk products, but Hunter has managed to keep pace through special promotions, specialty products and top-notch customer service, something the locals have come to expect and appreciate from his store.

"No problem, Sydney," he says, nodding toward the man sitting on a couch in the corner of the cluttered office. "He hasn't said a peep since I called you."

"Is he okay?"

"I think so. But I don't know anything about him so I can't say for sure. Who is he?"

"Well, Uncle Hunter, he's the man I found washed up on the shore this morning down at the point. Dad says his name is Oliver Lewis," Sydney says. "Does that mean anything to you?"

"Jesus. Oliver Lewis? Are you sure?"

Hunter looks at her, his complexion suddenly fading to white as the blood drains from his head. She can see surprise and shock written all over his face.

"I haven't heard that name in more than thirty years. How in the hell can he be Oliver Lewis?"

"Thirty-seven years, to be exact. Or at least that's what Dad said this morning."

"Shit. I know strange things happen around this town, but this is beyond anything that I've ever heard about. I thought he was dead."

"Actually, Uncle Hunter, I think everyone around here thought he was dead."

"Where has he been all that while," Hunter says, "and why did he suddenly show up after all of these years?"

She shakes her head and says, "I have no idea and Dad doesn't know, either."

"Wow, you have to admit that for a guy who you thought was dead to suddenly appear out of nowhere, that is some pretty weird shit," Hunter says, and Sydney thinks his reaction is in keeping with what she would have expected. He adds, "it is very odd and a little scary."

"I suppose so, but I don't find him particularly scary."

"Well, you usually have good instincts when it comes to people." Hunter smiles at his niece. "So, I trust your intuition. The question is, if he was in the hospital, how in the hell did he get out past security?"

"I have no idea about that, but I called Dad on my way over here and he was surprised to hear that Mr. Lewis had somehow managed to slip out of the hospital. I suspect someone will have to answer for that."

"I suspect you are right," Hunter agrees. "But what's he doing here? Of all places he could have gone, why did he come to my store?"

"And that's another good question. I wish I knew the answer," Sydney says, noticing that the strange man has not moved since she entered her uncle's office. Instead, he remains transfixed on something, as if he's in a trance, staring straight ahead, unblinking. "Maybe he recognized the building and was drawn here?"

"Maybe." Hunter shrugs.

"Think about it, Uncle Hunter. If you suddenly turned up in town after thirty-seven years and just about everything you remember about the place has been changed, wouldn't you be drawn to a building that looks somewhat familiar to you? I mean, today's Main Street is nothing like it was almost four decades ago, so the poor guy must feel lost. But your store hasn't changed much, except for the odd face-lift over the years, so I think it's natural that he would have been drawn here."

"You could be right," Hunter agrees. "So, what are you going to do with him? Are you taking him back to the hospital?"

"No, Dad doesn't want me to do that. He asked me to take him to his place. He was going to call Mom and tell her what was going on, and said he'd meet us there. He thinks that maybe the hospital isn't the best place for Mr. Lewis to recover his memories. He needs to be in a comfortable environment where his brain can rest."

"Do you think that's a good idea, Sydney? Is that safe?" Hunter asks. "You don't really know what he's up to. He's been gone a long time and

God knows why he came back now."

"I don't believe he's dangerous, if that's what you're implying."

"I'm not implying anything, because I don't know anything about him," Hunter says. "But it sounds like you don't know much about him either, so I'm just saying you and my brother should be careful around him."

"If this guy is who Dad says he is, then we've got to take care of him. After all, if this is *the* Oliver Lewis, Dad wouldn't be here if wasn't for him."

"Yeah, well, I don't know about that. That's a lot to accept, but you and your father have to do whatever you think is best," Hunter says. "Do you need me to help you get him to your car?"

She shakes her head. "Thanks for asking but I think I can handle it from here."

"Okay, but I'll be right here if you need me."

"Mr. Lewis?" Sydney says, speaking softly as she approaches the couch where the man is sitting. "Mr. Lewis. Do you remember me?"

He nods but doesn't say anything.

"Are you okay?" she asks, reaching out to take his hand. "Can you come with me, please?"

"Yes," he finally says, his reply so soft it's nothing more than a whisper.

"Okay then," she says, helping him to his feet, as he's still pretty wobbly. She can feel him trembling. "Let's get you to the car."

"No hospital."

"No hospital," she tells him. "I am taking you to my mom and dad's place. Dad is going to meet us there."

"Are you sure about this, Sydney?" Hunter asks again.

"Yes. Dad says this is for the best."

Hunter watches the pair leave his office. "Okay," he says, "but tell your father to call me if he needs anything."

"Will do," she replies. "And thank you for your help."

Helping the man to her car in the lot next to the store, she notices him looking around as if he's checking out his surroundings. His confusion is obvious. She can tell he has no idea where he is.

"You must feel lost and confused, Mr. Lewis. A lot has changed in the nearly forty years that you've been away."

She opens the door for him.

"Has it really been that long?" he asks, sliding into the sleek car.

"If what my dad says is true, then, yes, it has really been that long," she says, closing the door behind him and darting around to the driver's side.

"God-damn," the man says as she settles behind the steering wheel and pulls the seat belt across her slender body. "This is very weird."

"I'm sure it is, Mr. Lewis."

"Do you really have to call me Mr. Lewis?" he asks, glancing around the interior of her vehicle. "They tell me my name is Oliver so I would prefer that. This is a strange looking car," he adds. "What is it?"

"It's an electric car that's totally powered by the sun. I'm sure you haven't seen any of these cars before, but that's all we drive these days. Gas powered vehicles, like the kind you drove back in your day, are no longer permitted. It's all part of the government's effort to protect the environment, but if you ask me, I'd say it was too little, too late."

"Seriously?"

"Yes, seriously." She pushes the start button. The vehicle operates so smoothly that it is nearly impossible to hear its engine running. "Things have changed a lot in forty years, Mr. Lewis, mostly for the better, I hope."

"There's the name thing again. Please don't call me that."

"Sorry, force of habit." She smiles. "I meant Oliver."

"Much better thanks." He pauses. "Can I ask you something?"

"Sure. You can ask me anything. You must have lots of questions."

"What's happened to this place? It's not the town that I think I remember, not that I can remember that much. It's more like instincts than memories. But I do keep getting flashes of a town that looks totally different from this. They are quick images sort of flitting in my head, so I can't tell too much from them, but they sure don't look anything like this."

"No, I am guessing it isn't the same place," she answers, putting the car in drive and exiting the parking lot. "I'll get to that in a minute, but first, I have a question for you." Glancing in his direction, she asks, "How did you end up in my uncle's office at the grocery store?"

"I'm not really sure how I got there. After your dad left my room, I found my clothes in the closet where that nice nurse told me they would be, and once I got dressed, I just walked out of the hospital through the emergency department. I didn't like it there."

"That sounds way too easy. Security or somebody should have stopped you."

"No one bothered me," he says. "It really wasn't difficult. Then I just walked down the street and somehow ended up at the store. It was the only place that sort of looked familiar to me. I just walked in there and I must have looked lost because people started asking me questions. That's when the nice man asked if he could help me. Next thing I knew, there you were."

"That was my uncle, Hunter. Do you remember him? He is Dad's older brother, and he would have probably been around twenty the last time you saw him."

"No, I had no idea who he was."

"I'm sure he's changed a lot in all those years, so that makes sense," Sydney says. "He's married now to a nice woman. His teenage sweetheart. Her name is Ally, and they have two children, nice boys, named Dominic and Dante. Great family. He owns the grocery store and Aunt Ally is the principal of the local elementary school."

"Good for them."

Glancing at the small, designer shops that line the street, he adds, "I don't recognize any of this."

"No, you wouldn't. It's all relatively new. After the waterfront flooded due to the rising oceans, the decision was made to abandon all the buildings down there and move the commercial activity to the town centre. It cost a ton of money, but the government coughed up the cash to help construct these new buildings, and the investment paid off as the development encouraged these new businesses to locate here. They are all mostly specialty shops and galleries aimed at tourists. You know, crafts, antiques and specially lines of clothing, stuff like that. I hear most of the ventures have been very successful."

"I see. And what happened to the older buildings?"

"They demolished the old ones down on the waterfront, but it had to be done because they couldn't use them for anything once they flooded."

Navigating the town streets, she notices that the man sitting to her right is taking in his surroundings, but she can tell he's becoming overwhelmed. "I bet you see a lot of changes."

"I think I do but, to be honest, I'm not sure," he says as she drives through the town square where Oliver used to live. "Actually, this part looks strangely familiar, although I think something is missing."

"Yes, very good. You are very astute."

She slows down the car so he can get a better look. "The old hotel building that you would remember burned down about fifteen years ago, but they've done a nice job cleaning up the lot. Now there's a park on that property and it attracts a lot of families."

"Shame, really."

"Yes, those heritage buildings can never be replaced, but as much as I love and respect the past, I also know that sometimes you just have to embrace the present and move on."

"I guess."

Accelerating again, she says, "Let's get you to my parents' place so you can settle down. Dad should be there by now."

"Thank you for coming to get me."

"It was no problem, Oliver. I'm glad to help." She smiles at him and adds, "You've been through a lot, so I think you need to get some rest. You'll be in good hands with Mom and Dad. They'll take care of you."

"I don't want to be any trouble for them."

"It won't be any trouble," she says, turning down a long driveway lined with red maple trees. A minute later, she declares, "We're here."

Sydney pulls up and parks in front of large, three-level house that's painted beige with dark green trim.

"Oh my God."

"What's wrong? This is my parents' house, where my sisters and I and our younger brother grew up."

She sees that her father's car is also parked in the driveway. "Dad's already here. He'll be able to help with any questions you may have."

"Nothing's wrong, really, or at least I think it's nothing," he says, pointing to the lawn at the right side of the house where eight crows have suddenly landed and are now watching them. "I'm pretty sure that those are the same crows that were outside my window at the hospital."

"It could be them, but you can't really say for sure because there are a lot of crows around this town and they can turn up anywhere, at any time and in various sized groups. But the one thing I know about the crows is that they can always surprise you."

"Isn't it a coincidence that there are eight of them just like there were at the hospital?"

"Not so much." Sydney turns off the car. "They can turn up in any number. Did you know that a group of crows is called a murder?"

He nods as she opens the car door. "Yes, for some strange reason, I knew that. Funny how I can remember something like that, but I couldn't even remember my own name."

"The mind works in mysterious ways, Oliver. Especially when there's an injury involved, but they say eight crows means a wish." She smiles at him and asks, "Did you make a wish?"

"No." He shakes his head. "Or at least, not that I can remember."

7: Meeting again for the first time

"Oliver," Dr. Alex Goodwin says as he greets his daughter and their guest at the front door. Taking the man's arm and gently leading him inside the house, he adds, "Come right in and make yourself comfortable."

"Hey Dad," Sydney says, leaning forward to give her father a quick kiss on the cheek. "Is Mom around?"

"She's in the living room, honey," Alex says.

"Good. I'll let you guys figure things out," she says, slipping past her father and making her way toward the living room. "By the way, Dad, Oliver, and I were just discussing the crows. Seems you have eight visitors outside on your lawn."

"Really? I'm not surprised. You know how mysterious those black birds are. They are unpredictable if nothing else. You just never know when they're going to show up or what they are up to."

"They sure are sneaky. Anyway, he may want to discuss them."

"I'll handle it."

Turning to their guest, Alex says, "Well, Oliver. Come with me into the kitchen and I'll get you something to drink, or perhaps something to eat if you are hungry."

"You have a nice place here," Oliver observes, glancing around as he follows his friend deeper into the house. "Real cozy."

"Thanks," Alex answers. "We like it."

"Lived here long?"

"Nearly thirty years," Alex says. "So, how are you doing? You've had quite an adventure this afternoon. Between sneaking out of the hospital and exploring the town all on your own, you've made your rounds. How did you manage to do that? It should never have been that easy for you get out of there."

"It wasn't hard to slip out," Oliver says. "But I wouldn't really call it an adventure. It was more like a journey into some sort of dark void. I felt lost. In fact, I still feel lost. It's like I'm trapped in a dream that I can't wake up from. And this town has changed from how I remember it, or at least what I *think* I remember, but it's only bits and pieces, really. Just quick flashes in my mind. I can't figure it out."

"Remember, Oliver, you were gone for thirty-seven years, so that's a lot of time and a lot of ground to cover," Alex says, studying his friend's face for any reaction. When he sees nothing, he continues, "I don't know where you were during all that time, but I'm sure our world is a different place today than what you remember."

"God." Oliver exhales. "Just based on what little I've seen and what bits and pieces have come back to me over the past few hours, there's no doubt that things have changed a lot. I really am a stranger here."

"Well, you are not a stranger to us, and you can stay here as long as you like," Alex says. "We'll do whatever we can to fill in the gaps for you."

"That's very generous, Alex, but I really don't want to impose on you and your family."

"Nonsense. Look at this place," Alex answers, glancing around the house. "It's massive. We have a ton of room, more than we'll ever use. The place is practically empty these days. It's just Bree and me here, as well as my mother and her twenty-four-hour nurse, so we have lots of room for one more."

"What about your kids? Sydney said something about her brothers and sisters."

"Two sisters, to be exact. There were three girls—triplets. Sydney, who is the youngest of the three, and then there's Piper and Bailey, in that order going up to the oldest."

"Triplets? That's something."

"It sure is." Alex chuckles, leading Oliver down the brightly lit hallway toward the kitchen. "Bree and I were anticipating one baby and ended up with three. Just imagine our surprise when they arrived."

"I'm sure." Oliver smiles.

"I'm still not sure how that happened. I mean, I know *how* it happened, but I can't figure how two babies could remain undetected throughout all the regular check-ups Bree had during the pregnancy," Alex says. "Only one of the girls ever showed up in the tests. That is a medical anomaly."

He adds, "At least they were all healthy when they were born and, in the end, that's what really matters."

"And you had a son or sons?"

"Yes, we did. One boy, Seth. He's two years younger than the girls."

"Nice family, but none of them live with you?"

"No, they are all out on their own. Seth teaches high school in Halifax. History, so he's doing pretty well for himself. He's married. He and his husband have one child, Elliot. Great kid. As for the girls, Piper still lives right here in town. You will meet her later as she's coming over for dinner."

"I know Sydney is some kind of doctor who studies crows, but what does Piper do?"

"Did you see all of those interesting-looking shops along Main Street?"

He nods. "I didn't recognize any of them, though."

"They weren't there forty years ago," Alex says. "Piper owns a gallery and operates it out of one those shops. We'll have to make sure that you get to see it. She's a very talented painter and displays her work there, along with the works of many other artists. She makes a pretty good living off of it—or I hope she does."

"It sounds like a wonderful place," Oliver says. "What does your other daughter do?"

"Unfortunately, we don't get to see much of Bailey. She works in Ottawa with the Department of National Defence. She has a job in the minister's office that keeps her extremely busy. She's always travelling with the minister. They go all over the world visiting potential hot spots, and when they're in Canada, they crisscross the country, so she's always on the go. She was home last Christmas for a few days, but we haven't seen her since."

"You have a very successful family."

"Yes," he nods, his fatherly pride shining like a beacon on a dark, dreary night. "But it is really a testament to all of their hard work. They made it happen for themselves."

When they reach the kitchen, Alex pulls out a chair at a glass-top oval table and motions for Oliver to sit there. "What can I get you? Perhaps something to drink? Are you hungry? A sandwich maybe or perhaps some fruit? You just name it and I'm sure we have it."

Oliver shakes his head. "Nothing to eat for me, thanks, but I would take a glass of water, if that's no problem. My mouth is really dry, and I can't seem to get enough to drink."

"That's doable," Alex says, retrieving a sleek, crystal-like glass from a cupboard and filling it with water from some kind of oddly-shaped receptacle that looks foreign to Oliver.

"Thanks," Oliver says as Alex gives him the glass.

"You're welcome. Unlike some areas, we still have lots of fresh water around these parts, so we aren't mandated to conserve it as much as we should, not just yet, anyway. But it's getting scarce in some places, and I really think the day is coming when the government is going to order us to conserve," Alex explains. "Major droughts in some parts of the world have made water an expensive commodity in those places, and I don't think this country is too far off from the same thing."

"Really? Who would have ever guessed there would be a water short-age anywhere? Water always seemed so plentiful to me. Guess maybe we took it for granted."

"I guess we did, but we took a lot of things for granted. Over the years, people were warned that conditions were getting bad, but most of the time they—especially the politicians—ignored all the science until it was too late. Now, the world is struggling to survive. It's not a good place, but let's not get bogged down on all of that right now," Alex says. "I'm sure you have lots of questions about this town and probably about the people you knew back then."

Taking a seat in a chair across the table from Oliver, he adds, "You can ask me anything you'd like."

Oliver takes a sip of water and stares at the man with the head of thick, snow-white hair. He's struggling to remember anything about this Alex Goodwin, who claims to be his friend, but his mind won't go there.

He finally says, his words full of confusion, "I wish I knew what to ask you, but the truth is, I really can't remember anything."

"Don't force it, Oliver. Your memories will come back once the swelling around your brain goes down," Alex says. "Drink your water, then we'll get you settled. What you need is some rest. That is the only thing that's going to help with your memories."

"But I don't feel tired and I don't think I can rest. I just feel like I could crawl out of my skin," Oliver says. "What happened to me?"

"Truthfully, my friend," Alex says with a shrug, "I wish I could give you the answers you're looking for, but I have no idea how any of this happened. I thought you died years ago. But I am very happy to see you."

"It's a strange feeling, not knowing who you are or where you belong." Oliver takes another sip of water and studies the man across from him. "And what about those crows? Why do I have the feeling they are follow-ing me?"

"And that's another question that I wish I could answer for you. But if there's one thing I have learned, it's that you can't always figure out their motives. If the crows want something from you, you'll know about it soon enough."

"I hope so because, honestly, they are kind of freaking me out."

"They can have that affect on you, but I've also learned that you cannot let them get into your head. If you let them in, then you'll become obsessed with them and that won't help anything," Alex explains. "Just let them come to you and in time, if they have a plan for you, your role will be revealed. It can take a while, but I've found it's better to let things evolve."

"Easier said than done."

"Oh, trust me, I know what it's like. I've had my own experiences with those birds. I've lived with these crows all around me my entire life. In fact, my best friend when I was younger was a crow named Augustus." Alex pauses, gathers his thoughts and then continues. "He has been gone for a while now, and I miss him very much, but there are always other crows out there. If they have honed in on you, then they have a purpose for you. My best advice to you, Oliver, is to just let it happen."

"I'll try," Oliver says.

He considers the other man's words and then continues. "You mentioned something earlier about your mother living with you. Do I know her?"

"Yes, you do," Alex nods. "Her name is Samantha Henderson. Do you remember that name? She lives with us, along with her live-in care provider, Paula Bethancourt. Paula's only been with us for a few months, but she seems good at her job. She takes very good care of Mom."

Shaking his head, Oliver says, "I can't say the name Samantha Henderson means anything to me."

"That's too bad. You were good friends with her and my other mother, Kate Webster, as well as Kate's brother, Charlie. Do those two names mean anything to you?"

"No, sorry." Oliver shakes his head. "Where are they now?"

"Kate has been gone for many years now," Alex answers, his voice becoming soft as he recalls past events.

"What happened to her?"

"She was killed in a horrific car crash about five years after you went missing. She was driving back home from meetings in Halifax when another driver veered across the centre line and ran into her car, head on. The first responders said she died instantly from her injuries, but I think they just told us that to make it easier on us, especially for my mother."

"I'm sorry, Alex."

"It was a tough time and I don't think that my mother ever got over losing Kate," Alex says. "She was never the same after that accident. When she lost Kate, it was like she lost her entire reason to live."

"How sad." Oliver takes a deep breath and tries to remember the people Alex has just named, but they are a blank. "Can I meet Samantha?"

Alex nods. "We'll make that happen tomorrow, but I wouldn't expect too much from her."

"What do you mean?"

"She has been suffering from dementia for many years now and the disease is in its last stages, so she doesn't remember much from her life. She barely remembers her children and grandchildren. In fact, most of the time, she doesn't even know who I am. She has slowly been slipping away. It has been hard to watch her going through all of that and not being able to help."

Studying the crystal glass on the table, Oliver marvels at the sun sparkling through the clear water. "I bet," he whispers.

"But we've kept her with us because we believe that being around people who love her is the best medicine for her," Alex continues. "Besides, I would do anything for that woman. I owe her everything. She has been a strong influence in my life." He pauses and then adds, "Maybe seeing her will bring back some of your memories."

"I hope so," Oliver says, considering everything he's just heard. "Because right now it's all a blank to me. What about this Charlie character? What's happened to him?"

"Uncle Charlie is still with us," Alex says. "You guys were really good friends. He still lives here in town with his wife, Rebecca, but they've sold their house and live in one of the new condo units in the complex they built on the site of the old hospital. I'll take you to meet him, maybe tomorrow or sometime over the next few days. He will be shocked to see you after all these years, especially since you haven't aged one day since he last saw you—unlike the rest of us."

"Do you think that seeing him will help to bring back some of my memories?"

"Maybe, but I don't know." Alex nods. "But give it time, Oliver. I'm sure it will get better. I promise."

"What will get better?" Sydney asks as she and her mother suddenly enter the kitchen.

Alex smiles at them. "I was just telling Oliver that things will get better and, with time, his memories should start coming back to him." Reaching out to take his wife's hand, he says to the man who, up until a few hours ago, he thought was dead, "Oliver, I would like you to meet my wife. You may remember her as Bree Hamilton."

Slowly rising from the chair, Oliver smiles as the slender brunette slides under Alex's arm and he hugs her tightly. He thinks Sydney is her spitting image.

"Nice to meet you, Oliver," Bree says, extending her right hand. "Or I guess to be precise, I should say, it's nice to meet you again."

"Yes," Oliver stutters, taking her hand. "Nice to meet you, too, and thank you for welcoming me into your lovely home."

"Oh, you are most certainly welcome here and you can stay as long as you need to," Bree says, smiling. "But if you don't mind me saying, you have not aged a single day since the last time I saw you, on the bridge that night when all hell broke loose. How is that even possible?"

"Now, honey," Alex says. "I told you what to expect, so let's not hit him up with a bunch of questions."

"But it's such a shock seeing him standing here. It has to be the crows, right?" she asks. "What other explanation can there be?"

"I don't know, Bree, and we may never know how Oliver got to be here after all of these years, let alone how he has maintained his youth while all of us have aged. It could just be one of those things that we have to accept without ever expecting answers."

"Come on, Dad," Sydney says. "That's not as easy as you make it sound. You have to admit that this is pretty freaky even by crow standards."

"Yes, I will admit that, but we all know that the crows' motives and methods of getting things done are not always as cut and dried as we would like," Alex says. "Now, I think that it's time for Oliver to get some rest."

"Sure thing," Sydney says. "I have to go anyway, as I've got a few fires to put out."

"Fires?" Bree asks. "What's going on, honey?"

"It's nothing to worry about, Mom," Sydney answers, while making her way to the hallway that leads to the front door. "Just work stuff, but I've got to get after it before Isaac tears down my entire world."

"Way to be cryptic, Sydney," Alex says after her.

"Please come back for dinner," Bree adds. "Piper is coming over."

"I'll try, Mom," Sydney calls back, "but I will have to see how things go. Talk later." They hear the door close behind her.

"Gotta love that girl," Alex says with a chuckle. "Her outlook on life is so different from that of her sisters."

"How do you mean?" Oliver asks.

"She's just so carefree and she doesn't get bogged down on things she can't control," Alex says. "We could all learn a lesson or two from her."

"Yes, well, I'd like to see her settle down soon and take things more seriously," Bree observes. "That carefree lifestyle can only take you so far in this world."

"Oh, I don't know about that." Alex smiles at his wife. "I think she's done alright so far."

"Yes, so far, or so it seems. But I worry about her." Bree sighs, then adds as she turns to their guest, "Come, Oliver. Let's show you to your bedroom. It's on the second floor. You'll have your own bathroom and I've put some fresh towels in there so you can get cleaned up. Alex will bring you some clothes. I'd say you two are around the same size, so they should fit."

8: Dead and in the flesh

This feels all wrong, Oliver thinks.

Standing under the shower head as the hot water streams over his aching body, he shudders at the sensation. It wasn't until he felt the hot water hit his bruised flesh that he fully appreciated just how badly he was hurting.

His mind wants to go places, but it's like it's stuck in neutral, unable to gain traction.

I shouldn't be here. How did this happen? How is it even possible?

He feels lost, like he's alone and trapped in a dory set adrift on an angry ocean in the middle of a terrible storm. Desperately yearning to reach an unknown destination, he can't shake the feeling that, as he's riding the churning waters, his fate rests in the hands of someone else.

He trembles at the thought. Whoever is controlling the rudder of this boat also controls his destiny and he has no clue as to who it is or what's coming next.

God damn it, I hate feeling so helpless.

He can sense that a storm is blowing in from somewhere, but he can't see it. He tries to breathe through it but the spinning in his head makes him want to throw up.

Why can't I remember anything about who I was or anything about my life before today? he wonders.

All he knows is the little bit of information that Alex Goodwin has told him.

And that is not much to go on.

I need more.

With his eyes tightly closed, he allows the hot water to caress his face, hoping that it will wash away all his questions and somehow, miraculously, provide him with some answers.

But there are just too many questions.

The biggest question of all, however, is where the hell have I been for thirty-seven years?

That's a long time to lose, he tells himself, and he knows that if it is true, then there is no logical explanation for any of this.

Was I dead? Was I being held captive somewhere?

But where, how, and who was responsible? Someone must know something.

If this Alex Goodwin and I were such good friends, as he says we were, then why can't I remember him? He seems like a nice enough fellow and his family seems very friendly, but I should be able to remember something about him.

As the hot water soothes his physical aches and pains, Oliver plays the events of the last several hours over and over in his mind, rewinding the images and reviewing the conversations he's had and assessing what little information he's gathered. No matter how hard he tries, though, he can't remember anything before Alex's daughter Sydney found him this morning washed up on the rocks. Everything before that is a huge, black void.

"Jesus." He sighs as the timer on the shower suddenly and automatically cuts off the flow of water that has been providing his aching body with some much welcomed relief, even though he wasn't ready for the warm, soothing sensations to end.

While this area of the world has not yet been forced into mandatory rationing of its water supply, he remembers Alex telling him that most people in the region are self-regulating their consumption in an effort to conserve the precious liquid.

Things have really changed in all those years that I've been gone, Oliver thinks.

"Everyone has to do their part," he remembers Alex telling him.

As he steps out of the shower, the cooler air licks at his badly-beaten body, and he cringes at the image in the mirror. The injuries remind him that he's trapped somewhere in a place from which he doesn't see an escape.

Somehow, some way, I've got to get my memories back, he thinks, grabbing a towel and wrapping it around himself while examining the bruises that cover his torso and arms. He has no idea what happened to him, but it's clear from the injuries that the assault was brutal.

"Christ," he whispers. "Looks like I was somebody's punching bag."

"Wonder what the other guy looks like," he muses, trying to find some humour in his current predicament.

Seriously, he shrugs, *this isn't funny. There's no humour in any of this.*

He returns to the bedroom, where Alex has kindly placed some fresh clothes for him.

Now what? he wonders after slipping into a pair of pants that look like jeans but feel strangely odd to him, and a long-sleeved, powder-blue T-shirt that feels so soft against his aching skin that it practically caresses him.

"That feels pretty freaking nice," he says, glancing around the richly-decorated bedroom as if searching for someone that he can talk to. The quietness makes him feel more isolated and alone than he'd like.

Looks like this guy is doing pretty well for himself, Oliver thinks as he sits on the edge of the bed, assimilating the surroundings. The blues, greys and whites make him feel like he's wrapped in a warm embrace.

Nicely done. Someone sure has a knack for decorating, he thinks.

He sighs, wondering what he can do next now that he's all refreshed.

"Seriously, I just can't sit here, doing nothing. Think I'll go check things out," he finally says, as the quietness in the room gets the better of him.

I've got to try and figure this out and I can't do it from this room, he tells himself.

Heading down the brightly-lit hallway that connects all the rooms of the second floor, Oliver admires the tastefully decorated surroundings.

These people definitely have money, he thinks, taking note of the rich décor that includes plush materials, brightly-coloured fabrics and lots of artwork on the walls, that are painted a very light shade of green.

He stops near a bedroom door that's opened just a crack. Even though he knows he shouldn't, he listens, quietly, as the voices of a man and woman spill through the opening.

"So how do you explain how he hasn't aged one single day since we saw him last?" the female voice says. Even though they only spoke briefly, Oliver recognizes the woman as Bree, Alex's wife.

"That's just the thing," Alex answers. "I can't explain any of this. None of it makes any sense. Oliver shouldn't be here after all this time, but clearly something strange is going on that involves him."

"I have to admit, Alex, that his presence in the house scares me more than a little bit," Bree says. "I know you—we—owe him a lot, but I'm not very comfortable with any of this. If he's here without any kind of logical explanation, then it means something nefarious must be up. You, above anyone else, should know how this works. I'm worried, Alex. Very worried about him being here because of what it means."

"I honestly don't think Oliver would ever do anything to harm us," Alex tells his wife. "He's just not made that way."

"How can you be so sure?" she asks. "After all, it has been a long time since you've seen him, and God knows what he's gone through in all of that time. You really don't know him anymore."

"No, I'll concede that thirty-seven years is a long time, and a lot has changed in that period," Alex says. "But I get good vibes around him. Don't forget that Oliver was my protector, and as my protector, he's sworn to uphold the pact that Alexandria made with the crows all those centuries ago. A part of that promise is that the crows will watch over her descendants, especially me as the fiftieth in succession, and all of that suggests that there's a purpose in Oliver's sudden appearance this morning. I believe whatever that reason is will become clear soon enough."

"I know the legend, Alex. How could I ever forget?" Bree says. "We've lived with it our entire lives, but that's just the thing. If Oliver has shown up without warning, then it probably means that trouble is brewing, and maybe we'd be safer to stay away from him. You know, maybe we should keep our distance."

"I don't think it works that way," Alex says. "If Oliver's sudden appearance is a sign that something is coming for us, then it's likely that we're safer being with him."

"But what could be coming for us?" Bree asks. Oliver can sense the distress in her voice. "Should we be worried? And the bigger question is, how can we be so sure that we are safer with him here, or is he the one who is going to attract trouble? Would we be safer with him away from the house and away from our family?"

"I can't be one hundred percent certain, honey," Alex says, "but I'm guessing that if the crows have sent Oliver here because of some sort of danger, then they mean for him to be with us, to watch over us and, yes, even protect us if it comes to that."

"That doesn't make me feel any better, Alex," Bree says, and Oliver can sense that the woman is near tears. He doesn't like it that his presence has made her feel uncomfortable.

But what can I do? he wonders.

Carefully slipping past the bedroom door, Oliver remains in stealth mode and continues down the hallway toward another room, where he hears other people talking. It sounds like two women.

"Come on, Ms. Henderson, I've had enough of your crap for one day. You need to take your medication," he hears one woman say as he inches closer to the open door. "And if you don't open up willingly, I'll put it in your mouth and make you take it."

"I don't want it," he hears the other, more elderly woman respond, her weak voice cracking as she speaks. "It makes me sick."

"Don't be silly," the younger woman says. "The medication is supposed to make you feel better. It's all in your head."

"No," the older woman protests. "I said I don't want it."

"If you don't take this medication right now, I will have to go and get your son," the younger woman threatens. "What do you think he'll do if he finds out that you're not taking your medication? I'll tell you what he'll do. He'll put your wrinkled ass in a home. Is that what you want?"

"No," the older woman cries, her voice cracking with emotion. She speaks so softly Oliver has to strain to hear her words. "I don't want to go in a home."

"Then just take your god-damned medication," the younger woman says, "and stop this freaking foolishness right now. Your son would not be very happy if he knew you behaved like this."

Oliver is no caregiver, but he's sure that's not how this woman should be talking to her elderly charge, especially a woman whose mental acumen seems to be in such a serious state of decline, as Alex explained to him.

I wonder what Alex would think if he knew this is how this woman was treating his mother, Oliver thinks, resisting the urge to burst into the room and tell her she should treat this woman—his long-lost friend—with more dignity and respect. Instead, he continues to listen at the open door.

"I have a son?" the elderly woman asks.

"Yes," the young woman replies. Her lack of patience is painfully clear in her tone. "You have two sons—Alex and Hunter. Alex is a doctor. You live with him and he is the one who hired me to take care of you."

"I don't know who they are."

"Trust me. They know you all too well," the young woman says. "Now, here. Put this god-damned pill in your mouth and take this water. It will relax you and then you can go to sleep. Maybe some sleep will make you less cranky."

"But I don't want to go to sleep," the elderly woman protests and Oliver can tell she's crying. "I'm not tired."

"I don't really care what you want."

Oliver knows he should mind his own business but, taking a deep breath and stepping into the room, he says to the younger woman, "Didn't you hear her? She told you she doesn't want to take the pill."

The caregiver is shocked at the stranger's sudden appearance. "Who the hell are you?" she asks.

Pulling herself up from the slouching position she's been in, the elderly woman turns her head towards the stranger. For the first time, Oliver gets a look at his friend's face.

He hardly recognizes Samantha Henderson, but he knows it is her.

"Oliver Lewis!" she cries out, attempting to get up. "But you are dead."

9: A plan is hatched

"I don't know what you think you heard, Oliver," Alex says, "but I can't have you sneaking around the house, listening to private conversations and making such serious accusations."

They are in Alex's home office, and the young caregiver is sitting on the couch. She sits stoically, head down, not saying a word.

"I'm sorry, Alex," Oliver responds. "But I am positive I heard that woman threatening your mother."

"Or at least that's what you think you heard."

"That's what I heard."

"The thing is, Oliver, when you are dealing with dementia patients you sometimes have to be stern with them," Alex responds. "I'm guessing that's what you heard."

Oliver shakes his head. "It was nothing like that. Your mother was very upset."

"I think it's safe to say that she became even more upset and agitated when a man whom she thought was dead for many, many years suddenly appeared in her bedroom," Alex answers. "I'm sure she must be really confused by that, as we all are."

"Well, yes," Oliver says. "I understand that, but I'm telling you that the conversation I heard was not very pleasant. And maybe I should not have intervened, but I just could not control myself. My instinct was to protect Samantha."

"I can't speak to what you believe you heard, Oliver, because I didn't hear it for myself, but I can tell you that I have known Paula Bethancourt for a while now, and I know her to be very professional, caring and, yes, even stern when she has to be. That's part of the job."

Sensing that he could be crossing another line, Oliver grimaces and says, "So you trust her around your mother?"

"Yes, I do, and until I see something that tells me otherwise, I am going to keep her on, especially now that it looks like the end of life is near,"

Alex says. Oliver can see that this is a difficult conversation for his friend.

"Paula has been very good for my mother and now is not the time to disrupt her care. My mother's condition is very delicate, and any abrupt changes could be very bad for her."

"That is your prerogative."

Alex nods. "The bigger question I have to deal with right now is how do you fit in here? What is your role? As I told you, you are more than welcome to stay with us for as long as you need to, but if you're going to be staying here it is imperative that you get along with Paula and not interfere with her duties. Can you do that?"

"What if I witness something that doesn't sit well with me?"

"Then please tell me about it. I do not want you to confront Paula because the situation may not be as it seems." Alex is blunt. "Let me handle it."

"And what of her?" Oliver asks, motioning toward Paula, the brown-haired, bespectacled woman who has been sitting quietly on the couch as the two men discussed her alleged abuse. "What does she have to say about all of this?"

"Only that she was trying to get my mother to take her medication, which is a very important part of her care," Alex says. "I like her and she provides quality care for my mother so that's all I can ask of her. I hope you understand that my mother's wellbeing is Paula's only priority in this house." He motions to Paula to approach them.

"Okay, Alex," Oliver says. "I have received your message, loud and clear. You have made yourself very clear and I will honour your wishes."

He looks directly at Paula. "I promise, I will keep my distance and let her do her job."

Alex says, "Do you understand, Paula? You and Oliver are not to have any conversations about my mother's care. Those conversations are to be had between you and me or my wife."

"Yes, Dr. Goodwin," the woman says. "I understand."

She turns to Oliver. "I am sorry, Mr. Lewis, for the confusion earlier, but I had no idea who you were."

"Right." Oliver nods, forcing a smile with his senses on full-scale alert. "I'm sorry, too."

"Very well," Alex says. "If we are done here, I have to go and help my wife prepare dinner."

After Paula leaves the office, Oliver asks, "Can I please have one more minute with you, Alex?"

"Sure." He smiles at his friend. "What's up?"

"I just have one more question about your mother, if you don't mind me asking."

"I guess that depends on the question. What is it?"

"I'm wondering what you think of the fact that your mother immediately recognized me without hesitation. Does that not bother you? I mean, after everything you told me about her not being able to remember you and your brother and her grandchildren, I'm curious to know what you think about the sudden flash of pristine memory the second she saw me. There was no hesitation on her part. She immediately knew who I was."

Alex takes a deep breath. "I have to admit that this is rather curious, but when it comes to dementia patients, I have learned that their behaviour can be very unpredictable. While they often can't remember everyday things, like their immediate families or loved ones, or sometimes even their own names, they can often remember things that happened a long time ago and can recognize people from years earlier. It's rather uncanny how that works, and I suspect that's the case with my mother."

"I don't know anything about that," Oliver says with a shrug. "That's your area of expertise. I am no doctor, but that just did not seem like normal behaviour for someone whose memory is as bad you say it is."

"You can't always figure these things out, Oliver, because most of the time, there are no simple answers," Alex says. "This illness is cruel. It can rob people of their very souls and they often become strangers even to those who love them. I can't explain why she would have such vivid memories of you while pretty much forgetting everyone else that's important to her, but for some reason she clearly felt a connection. Maybe that's not such a bad thing."

"Maybe not," Oliver agrees. "Can you use that connection in any way?"

"How?"

"I don't know. But is it possible that you can use me to help stimulate some of her other memories?"

"I suppose that's possible, but I'll have to think about it," Alex cautions. "I don't want to do anything to agitate her any more than I have to. As I said, her condition is very delicate right now."

"Neither do I, but I am happy to help if you think I can. You know I will do anything for her... and you."

"Let me consider it, but in the meantime, please keep your distance from her, as I have asked. Just for the time being. I don't want her to suffer another trauma like what she went through this afternoon. We'll introduce you to her slowly, so that she doesn't become overwhelmed."

Oliver nods. "I don't want to do anything to upset her either. And for what it's worth, Alex, I really am very sorry for what happened earlier. It just seemed to me like she was in distress and I wanted to help."

"I know." Alex smiles. "Now, if that's everything I really must go help Bree prepare dinner."

"Sure thing," Oliver says. "Is it okay if I hang out here in your office for a bit? I just want to regroup."

"No problem. Stay as long as you like."

Pausing at the door, Alex adds, "I don't know what's going on with your sudden appearance, but I want you to know that I really am happy to have you here, Oliver, so don't worry about this afternoon. Everything will be fine. We'll make it work."

"Thanks," Oliver says as he watches his friend leave the room and close the door behind him.

Moving to the window and gazing out upon the beautiful backyard that's awash with an array of colours from the variety of summer plants that dot the property, Oliver thinks the view is breathtaking.

Someone must have a green thumb, he reasons, wondering if Bree and Alex do the work themselves or if they hire someone to do it for them. *Probably have a gardener. I think they can afford it by the looks of this place. Clearly, he's done very well for himself. Good for you, Alex.*

He's suddenly taken aback when he spies a murder of crows that has gathered on the grass just outside the house.

"Eight," he whispers, after doing a quick count. "For a wish." He sighs and wonders, *What wish?*

Watching as the crows prance over the closely manicured grass, he says, "What do you guys have to say about what's happening here? I can't put my finger on it, but something doesn't seem right about any of this. What are you up to?"

"So now you're talking to yourself?"

It's Sydney. Lost in his own head, Oliver hadn't heard her enter the room.

"Jesus," he says, startled. "I guess I am."

"Those crows really have a thing for you."

"Seems that way." He nods, turning to face the young woman who saved his life. "How did you know where I was?"

"Dad said I would find you in here. He also said you might be upset about something that happened this afternoon and he thought maybe you might want to talk about it. Is everything all right? Are you hiding from us?"

"No. Not hiding." Oliver forces a smile. "I just had some thinking to do. So, I guess you heard that I screwed up."

"I heard a little," Sydney says, joining him at the window. "But I think everything is okay, Oliver. And why wouldn't it be? It's a beautiful day. You should really be outside, exploring and getting to know this place better."

"It looks nice, but after what I did today, I don't think I should ever be let outside again."

"Oh, I don't know about all of that that, Oliver."

She smiles and he immediately feels relaxed in her presence. There is something about her that makes him feel connected to her. He can't explain it, but he feels comfortable around this young woman. "Tell me what happened."

"I screwed up big time," he admits. "I basically accused your grandmother's caregiver of abusing her."

"No, I don't think you did, or at least that wasn't the impression I was given."

"I don't know who you talked to, but I wasn't very nice to this Paula Bethancourt. Your father was right to call me out on it."

"Was he? Sounds to me like you were just looking out for my grandmother." Sydney shrugs. "He really can't fault you for that, and I think, once my father has had chance to put things into perspective, he'll come to understand that as well. I wouldn't worry about it."

"Well, I do worry about it because your father and your whole family are being very kind to me, and I would not want to do anything to jeopardize that."

"Trust me, Oliver, you're good here. It's just that my dad is very protective of my grandmother, and he won't stand for anything that might upset her."

Oliver nods. "Clearly, I have to watch what I say."

"Yes, but watching what you say doesn't mean you have to stop watching."

Oliver looks at the young woman. "I don't follow. What do you mean by that?"

"Well Oliver, it's like this," Sydney says, after glancing at the door to make sure no one else has entered the room. "If I'm being perfectly honest, I have never been one hundred percent comfortable with the way Paula Bethancourt treats my grandmother."

"Really? Why?"

""I've seen the way she sometimes handles her, and I've heard the way she speaks to her when she thinks no one else is around."

"Exactly," Oliver says. "That is precisely what I heard. Have you told your father about your suspicions? If you haven't then I think you really should, because he needs to know what is going on."

"I haven't, because right now I can't prove anything. My father is a smart man and he did his research before he hired Paula. He checked her credentials and called all her contacts before he let her anywhere near my grandmother. He was confident that she was well qualified and experienced to take care of my grandmother, so I cannot go to him with accusations unless I have proof of something being out of whack."

"Right." Oliver nods and then asks, "So, now what?"

"Okay, since you and I seem to be on the same page about this, maybe we can help each other."

"How so?"

"You keep your eye on Paula and tell me if you see anything that doesn't sit well with you."

"You want me to be your spy?"

"I guess. Yes, sort of," she answers. "But I don't want you to confront her with anything. That will only make things worse between you and Dad. Instead, keep track of the incidents and tell me if anything happens that doesn't seem right. Once we have some proof, then I'll take it to Dad. That way he won't be able to dismiss it."

"Is this a good idea? What if something serious happens to your grandmother in the meantime?" he asks. "If we wait, it could be too late."

"Jesus, let's hope not. I hear what you're saying but I really think that we have to be discrete about this and build our case," she reasons. "Taking a softer approach with my dad will get us a lot further than just rushing in hot with a bunch of accusations."

"Whatever you think is best," Oliver says, dubiously.

"So, what do you say?" she asks. "Are you willing to help me with this? Do it for my grandmother's sake, if nothing else."

Oliver considers the young woman's proposition and then he nods. "Yes. Of course, I will help you. I have only been here a couple of hours and already I'm afraid for your grandmother. It may seem like a lot of years have gone by—and I guess they have—but something is telling me that I like Samantha Henderson. I believe she was always a good person to me. I believe I liked her very much and I would not be able to live with myself if something happened to her and I thought I could have helped her in some way."

"Good." Sydney smiles. "I am glad to hear that and I am relieved to know that you're here to watch over her."

"I will do what I can."

"That's good enough for me at this point."

"So, what brings you back this evening?" Oliver asks. "Didn't you have some fires to put out or something?"

"Or something, but it seems that blaze is still raging and I'm not sure there's any hope of stopping this fire until it burns itself out," she tells him. "And besides, Mom invited me for dinner. Since I really didn't like the idea of eating alone this evening, I thought why not. Furthermore, I was looking forward to seeing you again and talking some more."

"Really? About what?"

"Why, you, of course."

"Me? What can I tell you that you would possibly find so interesting?"

"A lot of things, like, for instance, what this town was like forty years ago and what my mom and dad were like way back then. You know," she says with a chuckle, "all the juicy stuff, because they don't talk about their pasts very much."

"I'm not sure how much juicy stuff I can tell you—especially with me not being able to remember anything—but I will fill in the blanks as much as I can."

"Awesome," she says. "Should we join the family in the living room? We can wait for dinner there. I think my sister is coming over. You can meet her, if you want to. She's a real piece of work."

Oliver takes a deep breath and steels his nerves. "Sure. Why don't you lead the way?"

Glancing at the crows before he pulls away from the window, he wonders if he's doing the right thing by partnering with Alex's daughter in some kind of undercover operation. *Not sure about all of this, guys,* he thinks. *But it looks like I'm in it now. Let's hope I'm not making a mistake.*

10: The second sister

Following Sydney from Alex's office and into the living room, Oliver feels a sudden cold chill race up his spine. He shivers, unable to shake the feeling that he's being watched.

Jesus, he thinks. *What the hell is that all about?*

Quickly glancing around the brightly painted foyer and running his eyes up the staircase to the second-floor landing, he expects to see someone close by, but he sees nothing.

No one. Maybe I'm just being paranoid. Come on, Oliver. Get out of your head.

Truthfully, though, he thinks he would have rather seen someone checking him out instead of being left with this uneasy feeling that someone is spying on him from the shadows.

"Everything okay, Oliver?" Sydney asks. "Are you looking for something?"

He shakes his head and says, "Not particularly."

"Are you alright?"

"Yes," he manages to stutter, trying to shake off the intense feeling that he's under surveillance.

Quickening his pace to catch up with the young woman, he adds, "Sorry. I was just taking in the beautiful artwork. I don't know much about paintings, but these are pretty impressive. I love the vivid colours, and the attention to detail is amazing."

"Yes, well, that's Piper's handiwork," Sydney says with a dismissive shrug that Oliver thinks is a message in itself. "If you like that sort of thing."

"You don't like her work?"

"I've been exposed to it my whole life, so I guess maybe I'm just tired of hearing about it all the time."

"Right," Oliver answers, deciding not to ask any more questions. "I get that."

"I think you are about to meet my famous sister, because I can hear her in the living room." Sydney says, leading him deeper into the house.

"I do hear a woman's voice," Oliver says.

"Yes, that would be Piper, the second sister," Sydney says. "You can usually hear her before you see her."

"I'm looking forward to meeting her."

"You shouldn't be."

Oliver is surprised by Sydney's not-so-subtle declaration. "Why?" he asks, cautiously as he can see her becoming more tense. "I bet she's a lot like you. She is one of the Goodwin triplets, after all, so you guys must re-semble each other, right? At least a little bit?"

"She's nothing like me," the young woman snaps, just before she and Oliver enter the expansive living room that's filled with fancy, thickly-up-holstered furniture. The intensity in her words leaves little doubt that these two women do not get along. "In fact, she's a real bitch."

Whoa, Oliver thinks. *Sorry I mentioned it.*

He wasn't expecting such a strong reaction from Sydney, and he's not sure what to say, so he decides it's probably best to not say anything at all. He has no desire to be pulled into whatever rivalry exists between the sisters.

"Come on, Oliver," Sydney says, pointing him toward the gathering of plush, beige armchairs near the large, tiled fireplace where Alex and an-other young woman, who looks very familiar to him, are sitting.

He won't say anything to Sydney, but he is taken aback by how much the two women resemble each other, as he expected they might.

"Right behind you," he whispers, keeping close to his guide.

"You sit right there next to Dad," Sydney says, pointing to a chair close to Alex. "I'll just sit right here," she adds, taking a seat on a nearby sofa that's closer to the centre of the room than the other chairs. It's clear to Oliver that she doesn't want to sit anywhere near her sister.

"So, Oliver." Alex smiles as his friend takes a seat. "How are you doing now, my friend?" Avoiding the recent discussions in his office, Alex adds, "I bet you're feeling more relaxed after a little rest and shower. All of this must be very hard on you."

"I'm fine." Oliver smiles and nods. He tries to swallow but his mouth and throat are so dry they are nearly constricted. "All good," he weakly adds, his words nothing more than a whisper.

"Why don't I get you something to drink?" Alex asks. "Beer? Some-thing stronger, perhaps? Or wine? You name it and I'm sure we have it."

"Actually, if it's no bother, Alex, water will just be fine," Oliver says.

"Okay, then. Water it is," Alex says, quickly rising from the chair. "Sydney, why don't you introduce Oliver to your sister? I've filled her in on how he ended up here—or at least on the parts we know."

"If I must," she replies. Nodding to their guest, she says, "Oliver, I would like you to meet my sister, Piper. She's the artist whose paintings you were admiring out in the hallway." Turning to her sister, she adds, "Piper, this is my dad's friend, Oliver Lewis."

"Don't you mean *our* dad's friend?" the other young woman responds, and Oliver is blown away by how much she also sounds like Sydney. The resemblance is uncanny, he thinks—*they are almost exact replicas of each other.*

"It's a pleasure to meet you, Piper," he says, smiling in her direction. He isn't sure if he should get up and shake her hand or not as he doesn't know the proper protocol for this time period, so he decides not to while hoping he doesn't offend her.

"As your sister said, I was admiring your paintings," he continues. "I don't think I know much about art. But your work is amazing. I love your use of colours. Everything is so bright and vivid with great attention to detail. Your brush technique is flawless."

"Thank you, Mr. Lewis," Piper says with a smile. "You may say you don't know much about art, but it sounds like you know more than you let on. Your observations are very astute. Do you paint?"

"Me? Not a chance, except if you mean putting paint on the walls." He chuckles. "That I can do. I bet you've never heard that one before, right?"

"No." She shakes her head. "Never."

He's sure that he saw her roll her eyes. "Sorry. It was my weak attempt at humour. I can't say for sure, because, honestly, I can't remember, but I think I discovered a long time ago that I am really bad at being funny."

"It's all right, Mr. Lewis," she says with a shrug. "That one never gets old."

He can tell she's lying.

"Well, I promise that I will try to refrain from doing it again." He smiles. "And please call me Oliver. I'm still trying to figure out who I am because I'm still new to this body, but I'm sure I would prefer Oliver over Mr. Lewis."

She nods. "As you wish."

"Here you go, my friend," Alex says, offering Oliver a crystal glass full of clear water. "I'd like to say it's fresh from the well, but in this case it's fresh from the bottle. At least it's from a glass bottle, not plastic, so there is that. Good thing about our time period compared to thirty-seven years ago is that plastic water bottles have been phased out. It didn't make sense to me that we were trying to conserve water while dumping plastic bottles into the environment."

"Thanks. If it's wet, then it will be fine, no matter where it came from." Oliver accepts the glass and takes a large gulp. He avoids the plastics discussion as he has no idea what Alex is nattering on about, even though he gets the clear impression that his friend takes environmental issues very seriously.

He welcomes the soothing sensation and immediate relief the water provides. As the cool liquid quenches his thirst, he asks, "Is Bree going to join us? I'd like to get to know her better."

"She'll be out shortly," Alex says. "She's seeing to dinner. We are having her famous stuffed chicken. Actually, it was my mother's favourite recipe. We thought perhaps you would appreciate something familiar from your past, as you often enjoyed dinner at our place when we were younger. Maybe it will bring back a few memories, or let's hope so. But be warned, Bree always prepares way too much food. It's like she's expecting to feed an army. We always have lots of leftovers, so I hope you are hungry."

"I guess I could eat something," Oliver says, although, while he's very thirsty, he doesn't seem to have much of an appetite. He then asks, "What about your mother and her caregiver, Paula? Are they joining us for dinner?"

"No." Alex answers. "Mom always has her meals in her room, as it's less confusing for her and Paula will get something when she's hungry. She usually waits until Mom is settled for the evening before having her dinner. We just let her work on her own schedule. It's easier that way."

"I see," Oliver observes, throwing a worried glance at his friend. He's concerned that his sudden appearance earlier may have been too much for the ailing woman. "Is everything okay, with your mother, I mean?"

Alex nods, offering a reassuring smile. "No worries. She's fine now. All settled down. She's probably already forgotten that you were even in her room."

Piper suddenly speaks up. "I hear you're someone from Dad's past. What's up with that?" She squints at their strange guest. "What's your story, anyway?"

"For God's sake, Piper," Sydney quickly says before Oliver can answer. "Don't be so freaking nosy. Give the poor man a break. He doesn't want to spend the next couple of hours talking about ancient history."

"No Sydney," Oliver says, raising his right hand in hopes of staving off an argument. He doesn't know what's going on between the two sisters, but the tension between them is so tight that he can feel it in the air. "It's all right. I really don't mind talking about it. And besides, maybe talking about it may help to bring back some of my memories."

"See, Sydney," Piper says with a smirk. "He doesn't mind talking about it."

Oliver quickly decides he doesn't like her smugness. *She is nothing like her sister.*

"He says it's all right," Piper continues. "Guess you don't know everything, do you?"

Oliver can tell that Sydney wants to fire back but instead is just glaring at her sister. *And probably biting her tongue*, he thinks.

"Now, girls," Alex says, and Oliver can detect some anger in his voice. "Let's not get into an argument this evening. We have a guest in our home—someone very special to me—so let's just have a nice, quiet family dinner. I'm sure Oliver will tell us whatever he wants us to know when he is ready to talk about it. But let's not inundate him with a bunch of questions. He's still recovering from a serious concussion and a lot of confusion won't be good for him."

"Understood, Dad." Sydney nods.

"Understood," Piper mocks and again her sister glares at her.

"Very mature, Piper," she says, and Oliver wants to jump to Sydney's aid but thinks again. *Better to not get involved, because I have no idea what's really going on here*, he tells himself.

"Girls," Alex says, his voice dripping in anger. "Did you not hear what I just said? You are much too old for this type of nonsense. I should not have to speak to you again. Do you understand?"

"She started it," Piper replies.

"Enough, Piper. Please don't make me cross." Turning to Sydney, he adds, "That goes for both you."

"No worries, Dad," Sydney says, quickly rising from the sofa. "I am going into the kitchen to see if Mom needs any help with dinner."

Watching her sister leave the living room, Piper observes, "She's a little high-strung, that one."

"Piper, no more, please," Alex immediately responds, throwing a sharp glare at his daughter.

"So Oliver," he says, turning to the man he thought was dead until a few hours ago. "Any luck with your memory? Anything come back to you? Any little nuggets at all?"

Oliver shakes his head. "Not really much of anything useful, except that I do continue to have flashes of crows and owls, of all things."

Considering his friend's comment, Alex says, "The crows I understand, but I find it curious that the owls are also coming to you. What are they doing in your memory?"

"That's just the thing. When I see them in my head, the crows and owls are fighting. That makes no sense to me. I know you have a lot of crows around here. In fact, there have been eight of them lurking outside the house all day, but those ones seem pretty calm, almost docile, unlike the ones in my memories."

"What are those ones doing?"

Oliver shivers. "I see them fighting with the owls and there is lots of blood and feathers flying everywhere. Does that happen very often?"

"You mean the crows and owls are fighting? Not so much anymore." Alex shakes his head and adds, "In fact, these days, you hardly ever see any owls around these parts. I haven't seen one for a very long time." He pauses, gathers his thoughts, and then says, "If I'm being honest, I think the last time I saw an owl was probably thirty-seven years ago. That was the last time I saw you, as well."

"Seriously?" Oliver is shocked by that revelation. "That is a major coincidence, don't you think?"

Alex nods. "I do agree. That is pretty suspicious. And why now? I can't help but wonder if your sudden return has something to do with that."

"If you don't mind me asking," Oliver says, "what happened with the owls the last time you saw them?"

Alex hesitates.

"Something wrong, Alex?"

"Well, yes," Alex answers, glancing at his daughter. While Piper and her siblings have all heard the stories and legends about their family's long-running connection to the crows, they are not aware of the circumstances surrounding their father's near-death experience when he was sixteen, and he doesn't have the mindset to get into that with them today. Instead, he says, "It can wait."

"Are you sure?" Oliver asks.

"I am," he replies as Sydney comes back into the room. "Mom wants me to tell you guys that she's about to serve dinner so she would like you all to come into the dining room."

"Thanks, honey," Alex says, jumping to his feet. To Oliver and Piper, who has been listening intently to the exchange between her father and the strange man, he says, "Let's go eat. I'm starving."

"Right behind you," Oliver says, slowly rising from the chair. Thinking about what he's just heard, he is now even more convinced that his being here is not random. He believes the crows have brought him back for a reason.

But why? he wonders, following Alex and Piper to the dining room. *What do they want with me?*

11: After-dinner talk

"Thank you very much for dinner, Bree," Oliver says, leaning back in his chair. "That was delicious. I can't remember the last time I had a meal that tasted so good. In fact," he says with a shrug, "I can't even remember the last meal I had, but I am willing to bet, whatever it was, there's no way it was as delicious as those stuffed chicken breasts."

"You are very welcome, Oliver. I am glad you liked it." Bree nods with an appreciative smile. Aiming a wink at her husband, she adds, "I don't get many compliments these days for my cooking."

"What do you mean?" Alex laughs while rubbing his belly. "I tell you every day how lucky I am."

Bree nods. "Yes, you do." Back to Oliver, she says, "The recipe was one of my mother-in-law's favourites and compliments are always welcome in my house."

"I heard it's an old family favourite," Oliver replies. "That would have been Kate, right?"

"Yes. Kate was a great cook and, for that matter, so is Grandma Sam. That's what the children always called Samantha from when they were young. It's kind of endearing, I think."

Alex chuckles. "I think it must be their way of holding onto their youth for as long as they can. Wish we could all do that, find some way to hang onto our youth, I mean."

"For sure," Oliver agrees.

"What are you talking about, Oliver?" Piper asks, interjecting herself into the conversation. "Doesn't look like you've aged a single day in the past thirty-seven years, not like my mom and dad. While you look like you're still in your prime, they're surely showing their ages."

"Piper Goodwin," Bree speaks up as her daughter's words have clearly hit a nerve. "Are you trying to be funny, young lady? If you are, no one is laughing."

"Come on, honey," Alex says with a chuckle. "Don't be so touchy. She's just making a joke—and an observation. She didn't mean anything by it. Besides, she's not wrong. We are showing our age, but if there's one thing I know, it's that you still look great."

"If you don't mind me saying," Oliver adds, "I think you both look great. There's no way I could ever guess your ages."

"Yeah, well, we're not as young as we used to be, that's for sure," Alex replies. "That's the thing about aging—it doesn't matter how far technology has advanced, you can't slow down the natural cycle of life or the aging process."

"No," Bree says, shaking her head. Oliver can sense the emotion in her voice as she adds, "You certainly can't, and you can't stop the dying process either." She pauses, collecting her thoughts and then adds, "When your time is up, there's not a damned thing you can do about it."

"Seems like Oliver has figured it out," Piper observes. "He doesn't look any worse for the wear even after all of these years."

"For Christ's sake, Piper, what the hell is your problem?" Sydney quickly replies. "This man is a guest in our parents' home and Dad's good friend. You ought to show him a little respect, but then again, you don't know anything about respect."

"Problem?" Piper snaps. "I don't have a problem."

"Yeah, you do."

"Come on, Sydney, unclench your ass. Don't you think it's time to let it go?" Piper answers. "It's been a long time. You should really ask yourself if he is really worth all the energy you're wasting on him. Besides, I thought that you and Isaac had called it quits, romantically, at least, so what was the harm? I was just having a little fun with him."

"Jesus Christ." Sydney rolls her eyes. "You don't have any boundaries, do you? Your total lack of respect for the feelings of other people is just staggering. How do you live with yourself after all the things you've done?"

"Now, girls," Bree interrupts, her face turning blood red. Oliver can see she's about to lose her temper. "This is not the time or place to have that kind of discussion. We have a guest at our dinner table, and he does not want to hear about your dirty laundry. Stop this at once."

"It's never a good time to have any kind of a discussion with Piper," Sydney says. "Because she only sees things the way she wants to see them, and it always has to be her way or no way. She doesn't care how badly she hurts other people just as long as she gets what she wants, so it's fine with me if we just sit here and don't talk to each other. I would be very happy about that."

"Fine with me, too," Piper says, squinting her eyes at her sister. "If that's the way she wants it, I can live with that, too."

"It is," Sydney says and then she adds, "Mom, you sit right there and I'll clear the table for you."

"It's all right, honey," Bree answers. "I can get it."

"No," Sydney says, pushing her chair back from the table while quickly collecting plates and cutlery. "You prepared the meal and it was great. It really was, so the least I can do is clean up for you. Why don't you just sit right there and catch up with Oliver? I am sure you must have lots to talk about."

"But that's not fair," Bree protests. "Why should you be the one to clean up?"

Smiling at her mother, Sydney says, "Because I want to." Taking a deep breath, she adds, "Please just let me do it, okay? It will only take me a few minutes and I really want to keep busy."

"Sure," Piper says, as Sydney heads toward the kitchen with a load of dirty dishes. "Run away and hide. It's what you always do. Heaven forbid that we find a way to talk things out." She continues as her sister walks away, "You know, we're going to have to clear the air at some point."

Sydney resists the urge to respond, exhaling with force and making her way into the kitchen.

"Piper," Alex speaks up on his daughter's behalf, "that will be enough. I've spoken to you once and I am not going to tell you again. Do you understand? Leave your sister alone and let's try to have a civil conversation, shall we? Let's not ruin this evening with an argument."

"Yes, Dad," Piper nods, albeit reluctantly. Oliver can tell this woman likes to argue and she clearly isn't the type to back down from a fight. "I'll try, but it's not easy when she's around. She acts so high and mighty all the time, the great Dr. Sydney Goodwin."

"Just behave," Alex tells her, throwing a glare in her direction. "And watch what you say."

"Okay. Okay," she nods. "Just for you and Mom."

"So," Oliver says in an effort to change the conversation, "what's happened to your family, Bree? I seem to recall that your father is an RCMP officer, correct?"

She nods.

"Funny how I can remember that specific detail," Oliver continues, "but I can't remember his name or anything else about him. Wonder why I can remember something like that when I couldn't even remember my own name."

"Perhaps that's a good sign," Bree says. "Maybe your memory is starting to come back. Even if it's little pieces at a time, it's better than nothing," she adds. "My father was an RCMP officer, and his name is Warren, but he has long since retired from the force. He reached the rank of corporal before he was forced to step down, but" she continues, and Oliver can sense her mood darken, "he didn't have much choice after the incident left him unable to perform many of his duties."

"Incident?" Oliver asks. "What incident? What happened?"

"It has been a few years now, but it was a pretty sad time in this town's history," Alex says. "About twelve years ago, Bree's father and two other officers were caught in a shoot-out with two gunmen who were trying to kidnap the mayor's daughter. It's a good thing the mayor had private security to slow down the would-be kidnappers until the police got there or God only knows what would have happened."

Oliver is shocked at the news. "You would never think anything like that would happen in a small town like this."

"You would think that, wouldn't you? However, as we've seen far too many times, these things can happen anywhere—even in quaint little places like our town," Alex tells him. "But we seem to have more than our fair share of major events like that." Staring at Oliver, he adds, "You and I should know that as well as anyone."

"What do you mean?" Oliver asks. "I don't understand."

Alex hesitates, then says, "It's best that you figure that out on your own. If I tell you anything, that won't help you recover your memories. Your mind can only heal properly if your memories are not influenced by what other people tell you. It's better for you if they come to you organically; that way you will know they are authentic and not embellishments from someone else."

"I guess that makes sense, but that's quite a piece of information to throw at a guy without any context," Oliver replies. He takes a deep breath and then asks, "So, can you at least tell me what happened to everyone involved with the mayor's kid?"

"The two officers who were with Warren were killed at the scene, along with one of the mayor's private security guards. They thwarted the kidnapping and saved the kid, but at a steep cost. Warren was shot twice, in the leg and in the neck. The bullets didn't kill him, but they did cause extensive nerve damage and he was never fully able to regain full use of his left leg. He had no choice but to retire."

"And all of that happened right here?" Oliver can't believe what he's just heard. "Right in this town?"

Alex nods. "A lot has happened in this town while you were gone."

"I guess." Oliver cringes. "Doesn't sound like I would even recognize the town even if I could ever get my memories back." Addressing Bree, he asks, "How is your father doing now?"

"He's doing okay, but it has been a hard struggle. I know we are lucky to still have him after everything he went through, so I am grateful for that. But he is not doing well in retirement. He's always been the kind of person who wanted to work, and he was good at his job, so he's trying to keep himself busy with some woodworking and a few other projects. You know, just trying to keep himself occupied. He and Mom moved to Ontario after Dad retired, as that was where we were from, originally, so I don't see them as often as I would like to. Besides, Dad had to get away from this place, as it held too many bad memories for him."

"That must be difficult."

She nods, and Oliver can see she's upset by the reality of not being with her parents.

"Dad doesn't like to travel much since his injuries, so I go up to visit them for a few weeks at least once a year. I'm going up to see them in October or November. I'm hoping the weather will cool down enough by then, as it's just too hot to go up there during the summer months. Honestly, I don't know how they can stand to live there. The heat waves have gotten worse over the past twenty years, thanks to global warming, but that's another story."

"I am sure you miss them very much," Oliver says. "But, as you say, you are very lucky to have him."

"And my young sister, Lauren, still lives here in town so I see her quite often," Bree adds. "She's married and has two children, a daughter and a son. Lauren's a pharmacist at the local pharmacy on Main Street. Maybe you'll get to meet her soon."

"That would be nice," Oliver says. "I'm not sure where you mean when you say 'the local pharmacy on Main Street' as I am not familiar with this place anymore."

"Well then, I am just going to have to show you around," Piper says, jumping into the conversation. "How about we do it tomorrow morning? I can make myself free after nine and I'm guessing you don't have anything else on your schedule."

"Thanks, but Sydney has already volunteered to show me around starting tomorrow morning," he says, lying to Piper. Her sister has not yet made any such commitment, but even though he has just met Piper, he knows he doesn't like her very much and would rather not be alone with her for any amount of time. "Sorry. Maybe we can do it some other time."

"Sure," she answers, and Oliver can tell she's not happy that he turned down her gesture. It is already clear to him that she likes getting whatever she wants. "I'm sure Sydney can tell you everything you need to know about this town and a whole bunch of other crap that you really don't need to hear from her."

Oliver shrugs. "I'm actually looking forward to it. Again, I am very sorry, but thank you for your kind offer."

"You're right. I think you have a lot to learn," Alex agrees. "This town is nothing like it was when you were around. In fact, this whole world was a different place back then. Everything has changed—a lot."

"Everything?"

Alex nods. "Everything. But it's way too much information for you to digest in a couple of hours, because we don't want to wear you out. I'm sure you'll soon see what I mean."

"I'm fine, really."

"I recommend you take it slowly, Oliver," Alex cautions. "If you try to do too much too quickly, you could have a sensory overload of sorts. We don't know where you've been or what you've been through, and even though we've run tests on you, we still don't really know the full extent of your injuries. As a doctor and as your friend, I suggest that you assimilate the information in small portions. Take it in and then digest it, piece by piece, as it comes to you rather than going out and trying to take it in all at once."

"I'm sure I can handle it."

"I know you like to think that, Oliver, but the human mind is a mysterious thing," Alex says. "You just never know how the brain is going to handle things, so please listen to me. Caution is the best course of action here."

"What are you saying, Dad?" Sydney asks as she returns to the dining room and takes her place at the table. "You want Oliver to take what slowly?" She smiles at their guest. "For some reason, I don't think that's how he's made."

Oliver chuckles. "Listen to this one. She only found me a couple of hours ago and she already thinks she knows me."

"I do know you," Sydney says. "I know you are honest and sincere, and I also know that you really don't know anything about yourself—your past, how you got here or what you're supposed to do here."

"Yup," Oliver says. "That pretty much sums me up quite nicely."

"Well, not exactly," Sydney says, adding, "I don't know what it is, but I can sense that you are here on a mission. You have something very important to do. There is a purpose to all of this."

"A mission?" Alex asks. "What kind of mission?"

Studying Oliver's face, she whispers, "I don't know, but I believe it's a very serious mission. A matter of life and death."

"God Sydney," Piper speaks up. "What kind of bullshit are you feeding this poor guy? You and all your mumbo-jumbo crap. How do you come up with this shit?"

"Piper," Bree scolds her daughter, "please don't speak to your sister like that, not in my house and not ever. You know that, out of all you girls, Sydney has this uncanny ability to tap into people's emotions. If she believes that our friend here has something important to do, then I believe her."

"Of course you do, Mom. You always believe her," Piper responds, pushing herself away from the table. "Thank you for dinner." Forcing a smile, she adds, "It was delicious. Now, if you'll excuse me, I have got to go."

"Come on, Piper, please sit back down," Bree says. "Stay and have some coffee and dessert with us. I've made strawberry-rhubarb crumble, your favourite. It's one of Grandma Sam's recipes."

"No thanks, Mom. Try and save me a slice if you can, and I'll get it tomorrow." Addressing her father, she adds, "Goodnight, Dad. Maybe I'll see you tomorrow."

"Good night, honey. I'll drop by the shop in the morning on my way to do rounds at the hospital. There are a couple of things we need to discuss."

"About what?" she asks.

"It's about the business, but it can wait until tomorrow," Alex tells her.

As she turns to leave, he adds, "Drive carefully, honey."

"Yes, Dad," she replies, leaving the dining room. "I always do."

"There she goes," Alex says as he hears the front door close behind his second daughter. "The whirlwind known as Piper Goodwin."

"That's one way to describe her," Sydney says.

"Please Sydney," Bree says, raising her right hand in protest. "No more tonight. Haven't we had enough of that for one evening?"

"Yes, Mom," Sydney says. "Of course, you are right. I'm sorry. It's just that she brings out the worst in me."

"I know honey." Bree smiles. "She has been like that since you three were little girls." Taking a deep breath, she adds, "I'll call her later to make sure she's okay."

"Now," Oliver says to Sydney, recognizing it's time to change the topic. "What were you saying about me being on a mission? What's that all about?"

"I really wish I knew." She sighs. "All I can tell you for certain is that when I'm around you I get this overwhelming sense of urgency and dread. I can't put my finger on it but I sense that something serious is going to happen and it involves you. Now, do the feelings mean that you are the cause of this event, whatever it is, or are you meant to stop it? I cannot answer that because I just don't have any of the details."

"What can I do to help you get the details you need to form a better picture?"

"Nothing," she tells him. "There is nothing that you can do to help me with this. The truth is that I may never get a better picture than what I have right now." She cringes. "Sorry, but that's all I've got right now."

Alex speaks up. "That's okay. At least we know that Oliver is here for a reason."

"But that's of little help if I don't know what I'm supposed to be doing," Oliver points out.

"Don't be discouraged," Alex tells him. "We know that there has to be something at play here or it's not likely that you would have turned up as you did."

"I suppose you're right," Oliver says. Turning to Sydney, he asks, "Maybe this is a long shot, but can you tell me if the crows play a part in this so-called mission that I appear to be on?"

She hesitates, as if she is afraid to answer his question.

"Come on honey," Alex urges her. "If you can see something then you have to tell us. Oliver needs to know—we all need to know. We can't help him if we don't understand what's going on."

She nods, throwing her glance from her father to Oliver. Taking a deep breath, she says, "I can confirm that the crows do, indeed, play a part in this—eight crows, to be exact."

12: Twisted metal and shattered glass

The bright greenish-blue lights from the digital display embedded in the console of Piper's electric car scream out the time.

"Shit." She sighs, tightly gripping the steering wheel while navigating the curves on the twisty road that will take her home. "12:13," she whispers, even though there is no one else in the vehicle to hear her words.

Didn't realize it was getting so late, she thinks, wishing she had just gone straight home after leaving her parents' place several hours ago. Now it's pitch black and, even though she is an experienced driver as she has had her license since she and her sisters turned eighteen, she still hates driving in the dark.

"But no," she says, scolding herself. "You just had to go the studio, didn't you?"

What was I supposed to do? she asks herself.

"I have got to finish that commission," she says as if preaching to an invisible companion. "The deadline is in a week and it's nowhere near ready for public display. God-damn it. I have already missed three deadlines."

She takes a deep breath, feeling as though the insides of the vehicle are closing in on her. "They will be pissed if I have to tell them again that I need more time."

If I miss this deadline, the hospital foundation board is likely to tell me to take that paining and stick it up my ass.

"I certainly would not blame them," she says, carefully manoeuvring her car around a series of tricky corners and sharp bends in the road where several serious accidents have occurred over the years. She's thankful that at least there's no fog tonight so the visibility isn't as bad as it could be.

I totally understand things from their perspective. It would be so wrong for me to ask for another couple of weeks. I should not even be thinking about asking them and they should not even consider it.

"They won't give it to me. Hell, *I* wouldn't even give it to me."

This is not good. She sighs heavily, griping tightly to the steering wheel, her knuckles turning white. *I can't blame anyone but myself for this mess I'm in. I don't know why this painting is so fucking difficult for me to complete. It's not that complicated, really, and I've done a lot more challenging subjects than this one.*

"Besides, I need the money and they won't give me the second installment until they see the completed work."

Why would they?

"I certainly wouldn't if it was me. I'm sure I haven't inspired much confidence after all the fuck-ups."

What is wrong with you? You have got to get a grip, Piper Goodwin, she thinks, watching as the headlights from an approaching vehicle suddenly come into focus.

"I know that's why Dad is coming by the shop tomorrow," she says as the vehicle passes her. It is moving fast, so fast in fact, that Piper is sure it had exceeded the limit by at least twenty kilometres an hour. "Jesus, buddy," she curses as if the other driver can hear her. "Are you trying to kill someone? Slow the hell down, asshole."

She takes a deep breath and exhales. Her father's impending visit really has her on edge, as she's sure he's coming to confront her about the shop's bleak financial situation. She knows the business is in trouble and she is confident that he knows it as well.

He knows the shop is struggling just to make enough money to stay open. Shit! What the fuck am I going to tell him?

"He is a partner in the business, after all. Supposedly a silent one, or at least that was part of the deal, but he put up a lot of money to help me with this project, so I guess he has a right to ask questions."

She pauses to catch her breath and then continues, "But with this month's rent already due and no money in the account to pay it, I'm sure he's going to ask me what the hell is going on."

He must be so disappointed in me. Hell, I'm disappointed in me. She takes a deep breath, struggling to keep it together. *What is wrong with me? Time to pull my head out of my ass and buckle the hell down, but it's so god-damned hard to focus these days. I've never had that problem before when it came to my paintings so what's going on now?*

"I've let him down, but it won't be the first time and I'm sure it won't be the last time. God-damn it all to hell."

Everyone knows that Piper Goodwin is a failure.

"Yup, a big ole failure." Her eyes squint in anger as she considers her options, which seem very limited to her at the moment.

"Just one big fuck up. Yup, that's me." She pushes the tears from her eyes with the back of her left hand. "But Sydney, well, she is the poster child of success. They ought to write a book about her."

I know the perfect title. They could call it 'Bitch in Disguise.' That would suit her to a T. Little Miss Perfect.

"I bet that book would be a number one bestseller," she says, tapping the brakes as she glides around a corner, dips into a minor gully, and then follows the road up a tiny hill.

I hate this fucking road, she thinks. I should just sell the house and move the fuck away from here, wouldn't they like that? But the market is cold right now and I'd never recoup what I paid for the place. I knew I should have sold a year ago when the market was red-hot, and everything was selling like fucking hotcakes. They were getting good prices for even the smallest, rundown shacks. I waited too god-damned long.

"Story of my life. Wouldn't they all love it if I sold the house and took a major loss? That would be another failure in the books for Piper Goodwin. But I only have myself to blame for this mess. I mean, no one really wanted me to buy this house way out here on the shore, but did I listen?"

No, I did not. There was no fucking way was I going to listen to anyone else. Not a chance. I knew what was best for me and I just had to have a house by the beach so I said fuck you all. It's my money and I am going to buy the house that I want and that's exactly what I did.

"But I'm sorry now that I didn't listen to everyone when they tried to tell me." She pauses, wipes her eyes again and adds, "Why am I so fucking pig-headed? You'd think I would have learned a few things after all of these years. But I had to do it my way and now there's no god-damned way that I'll ever admit that I may have made a huge mistake. No way. I refuse to give Sydney another reason to say 'I told you so.'"

Nope. She shakes her head. *No way. It ain't never gonna happen.*

Picturing Sydney pointing her finger and laughing at her while her entire life goes down the toilet, Piper says, "I don't know what's got up her ass anyway. We used to be so close, but now, I can't stand being anywhere close to her. It's all I can do to keep from punching her in the face."

I get it that she's not happy that I slept with Isaac. Hell, I'd probably be pissed at me, too, if I was her. But it's time for her to get over it. I mean, they had broken up by the time he and I got together.

She sighs and takes a deep breath. *Besides, he's not really worth all the grief. Was she really going to spend the rest of her life with that guy? Was he really the one?*

"If they had still been together and I screwed him, then I would understand why she would be so pissed," she says. "Whatever happened between them wasn't my fault, but she's got to have someone to blame instead of herself. It's called deflecting, but if she'd pull her fucking head out of her ass for just a freaking minute, then maybe she'd see that she isn't so god-damned perfect after all."

Thinking about her sister, Piper shrugs. *Honestly, I just don't get the attraction. What did he see in her in the first place? Ever since we were kids, Sydney has always been so needy. And she's clingy, almost suffocating. How could Isaac even be in a relationship with her, Little Miss Perfect?*

"And honestly, I don't really know what she saw in Isaac. I mean, he's kind of cute, in his own way, and I'll admit that he's pretty good in bed, but in the bigger scheme of things, he's not much of a prize. I certainly wouldn't get tied down to him for the long haul."

Shaking her head, she adds, "He was good for a quick fling, but he's kind of a dick so when you think of it, I was really doing her a favour."

She'll get over it. Once she's had some more time to think about it, she'll see that it's all for the best that they are over. I'm sure she'll come around.

"She always does," Piper says, as the headlights of her car suddenly fall on something up ahead in the middle of the road.

What the hell, she wonders, approaching the large object that's holding its ground near the yellow line despite the traffic that's coming in both directions. *Looks like an animal or something.*

Slowing her speed and inching her car closer, she whispers, "Holy crap. Is that an owl?"

I've never seen one of them around here before. Wonder what it wants, she thinks as she carefully drives past the large nocturnal bird, its yellow eyes blinking as it watches her go by in her sleek, silver car.

"Odd. That's not something you see every day around these parts," she says, gently accelerating once she's sure she is safely past the bird.

If Sydney and I were talking right now, I'd call her. I'm sure she'd find this interesting.

"She's the bird expert. She might know something about owl behaviour," she says as she enters the last series of curves on this road before she reaches her driveway. She has always feared this stretch of the road the most as, in addition to the sharp corners, it passes dangerously close to a steep embankment.

She's heard that, originally, the road was quite a distance back from the cliff, but decades of erosion from the rising ocean water have eaten away at the embankment, making for a dangerous situation.

It's a disaster just waiting to happen and it's about fucking time they move it back even further before the road falls into the ocean, she thinks, tightening her grip on the steering wheel.

Come on, Piper. You have got to pull your shit together. You're just about home, and then you can have a drink.

Keeping her eyes glued to the road ahead, she's passing the steep embankment that falls off to the rocky shores of the Atlantic Ocean at least ten meters below, when a sudden flurry of activity in the middle of the road ahead draws her attention.

What in the bloody hell?

"Jesus," she screams as she tries to avoid the blockage ahead that has suddenly appeared. She hits the brakes and the car swerves, crashes through the metal guard railing and plunges to the rocks below.

"Holy fuck," she cries. "Owls. Someone help me!"

~

"Shit," Sydney screams, feeling like she's suddenly been hit in the head by a sledgehammer. "What the hell was that?"

She's been so wrapped up in her work that three sudden and very loud knocks on her front door not only startle her back to reality but also send a shiver up her spine.

Damn it, she thinks. *That's a good way to give a poor girl a heart attack. This better be important.*

Glancing at her watch she's shocked at the time.

"12:13. Where in the hell did those four hours go?"

That's enough work for tonight, she thinks, quickly closing her laptop. She has been at it since getting back from her parents' house earlier this evening and now it's time for bed. *Not that I'll be able to sleep.*

After Isaac told her earlier today that he was leaving the team, packing up his things and moving to BC in three weeks, she felt compelled to assess the status of their work. She knows she is probably being overly paranoid, but she wants to make sure everything is in order. She doesn't really believe that Isaac would do anything to sabotage all the progress they've made over the past couple of years or to hurt her in any way, but she has to be sure.

You just never know what someone will do when they're pissed, she thinks. *Besides, this is my life's work. I can't take the chance of someone messing with things, not even Isaac just because he's mad at me.*

But this visitor at her front door in the middle of the night has rattled her. She shivers, feeling a sudden wave of coldness wash over her body, racing from her head to her toes. She feels as though she's standing on the edge of a very steep precipice, and someone is about push her off.

"I'm coming," she yells. "Just give me a second."

Making her way to the entry hall, she wonders who could possibly be at her door at this hour of the night. She is alone in her house, so anyone visiting after midnight causes her some concern.

Snapping on the outside light and slowly pulling the flimsy lace curtain back from the door window, she peers outside at the front steps.

"Hmmm," she whispers, glancing around outside. "Who are you? Better still, where in the hell are you?"

Unable to see anyone, Sydney knows that maybe she shouldn't do it, but she has this compelling need to investigate the source of the knocking. She cautiously unlocks the door and opens it just a crack.

"Is someone out here?" she asks, scanning the front doorstep, walkway, and yard. "Anyone?"

Okay, not really sure what game this is, but I really don't like this.

"Hello," she says again, her voice cracking as her anxiety levels begin to climb. "Is anyone out here? Did you want something?"

When no one responds, she opens the door even wider and slowly advances onto the front doorstep.

Maybe this isn't the brightest thing you've ever done, Sydney, she thinks.

She knows that if someone is lurking around outside her house, then she has just made herself vulnerable. But she has never felt threatened in this town, and she most certainly has never felt threatened in her own home so, she is willing to take the chance tonight.

"Is this a prank?" she asks, her voice cracking a little from nerves and the anxiety she's feeling right now. "If someone is out here and you're trying to play a trick on me, I have to tell you, I do not find this funny."

Not one fucking bit.

Moving to the top of the steps, she peers into the darkness of the surrounding neighbourhood, the streetlights sending circles of light to the pavement. As a shiver races up her spine again, she shudders and says, "Please show yourself, whoever you are. If not, I'm going back inside, and if you bother me again, I will call the police."

After waiting several minutes and seeing no one around, she finally says, "Okay. I've had enough of your foolishness. I'm going back inside now. Don't come back, whoever you are, or you'll get more trouble than you're expecting. You've been warned."

Retreating to the safety of her house and closing the front door,

Sydney takes a deep breath. "Jesus, I hate this shit," she whispers, double-checking to make sure the deadbolt is tightly secured.

She thinks, *maybe I just thought I heard someone knocking. That's got to be it. I'm sure it was just my imagination working overtime. Maybe I am more tired than I thought I was.*

Sydney starts down the hallway, heading towards the kitchen to get a drink and to make sure the back door is locked.

Finding Oliver Lewis nearly dead on the rocks this morning, learning that he was her father's long-lost friend, missing her meeting with the university board of directors, blowing her career out of the water and Isaac announcing he was leaving the province in a few weeks—that's a lot of stressors to digest in one day.

Holy fuck. No wonder I'm tense. Time for something to calm my nerves then it's off to bed for you, young lady, she thinks.

She's just about to turn off the hallway light when a loud thud, immediately followed by the unmistakable sound of shattering glass, stop her dead in her tracks.

"Jesus Christ," she screams, quickly spinning around to see that the window in her front door has been shattered and something—she doesn't know exactly what—is lying in a bloody heap on the tiled floor of her entry hallway.

"Jesus. Jesus. Jesus," she whispers when she suddenly realizes that a large brown owl has crashed through the glass and now—with shards of glass spearing its body from the shattered window—it appears to be bleeding to death on her floor.

Holy hell, she thinks, watching as the owl's body spasms several times and then goes limp. She's sure the bird is dead.

Reaching for the phone in her back pants' pocket, she suddenly freezes as an image of her sister, lying amid twisted metal and shattered glass, flashes through her mind. An overwhelming sense of fear and dread grips her body, shaking her to her very core.

Based on the bloodied image of her sister trapped inside the twisted wreck of her car, Sydney concludes there has been an accident, probably on the road Piper would have travelled to get home.

"Oh my God, Piper," she screams.

As her instincts kick into overdrive, she reaches out for help.

Oliver, she thinks.

She doesn't know how, but she believes he will hear her thoughts.

Come quickly. I need your help.

13: Lost in the darkness of his mind

Sleep eludes Oliver.

Instead, his mind races. It takes him to a place that is foreign to him.

In this place, he sees images that he does not recognize.

In this place, he also experiences sensations that feel unusual to him, hears sounds that seem so far away and sees the faces of people that are strangers to him.

But still, at the same time, it all feels oddly familiar.

He knows these things to be real.

How in the hell did I get here? he thinks, his mind racing back over the day's events.

A great deal has happened since Sydney found him sprawled on the rocks this morning. Now he's finding it difficult to gain some perspective on his predicament. He needs something on which to focus if he's going to rebuild his memories.

Instead, it's all just one big blur. The world seems grey and fuzzy, and none of this makes any sense.

He has been lying in the bed for the past couple of hours, just staring up at the ceiling of the darkened guest room where the Goodwins have kindly put him up.

He cannot distinguish anything in the darkness.

Eventually he is able to quiet his mind and calm his nerves. Eventually, he can vanquish the images that have invaded his thoughts.

Finally, as his body is too tired to fight against him, he drifts off to sleep.

But he finds no rest in this sleep, as the thoughts continue to run rampant through his subconscious.

He has no idea where he is. There is only complete darkness in this foreign place.

He is floating, set adrift on a sea of utter blackness.

It is like he's outside of his body and looking down upon a scene that seems oddly familiar, yet it is all so very strange.

The stars and moon have not yet emerged from the darkness. In that way, he knows it is just after dusk, on the cusp of nightfall.

As he floats in the black void of time and space, images slowly begin to emerge. Even though they remain shrouded in a heavy haze, he eventually sees a bridge and hears the unmistakable sounds of a ruckus.

There are people on the bridge. And there are birds. Lots of birds in various shapes, sizes and colours. They are alarmed. They are fighting for their lives.

But mostly he sees lots of the black birds swarming around a boy—a young man. The black birds are trying to protect him.

Who is this?

And there are at least three others on the bridge, but he cannot see their faces. *Who are they?*

The birds are in a frenzy, flying about and flapping their wings, obscuring the faces of those on the bridge.

There is lots of yelling and screaming—too many words for him to clearly distinguish what is being said, but he can hear them, and he knows the exchange to be intense.

Somehow, he knows this to be the scene of a major clash of forces. But he has no idea between who and for what reason they do battle.

Hovering over this place and looking down, he watches as two of them grapple and then tumble over the side of the bridge. He sees them plunge into the water below.

They quickly disappear from sight, swallowed by the water and the complete darkness. They are gone.

He finds it hard to breath.

Within minutes a third person goes over the side, perhaps meeting the fate of the first two who took the plunge.

"Jesus Christ," he cries out as his eyes snap open, a loud crash-bang coupled with shattering glass rousing him out of his trance-like state.

He has no idea how long he has been asleep.

What in the hell just happened?

He feels wet.

But how can that be?

He's in bed and he is nowhere near water. But he is soaked. He can feel the water. It is all around him, swallowing him.

It is as if he is sinking—drowning.

He searches for the surface.

"Oh my God," he whispers, wiping at his face in a feeble attempt to brush away the water.

Gasping for air as he fights his way through the water. He cries for help. "I can't breathe."

He gasps for air.

He bolts upright in the bed, his breathing is laboured.

"Shit," he says, gasping in large gulps of air. "What the hell was that all about?"

As his eyes focus in the darkness he suddenly realizes he is no longer alone. He feels a presence. Someone has entered the room.

Who are you?

"Hello," he whispers between gasps for air. "Is someone there?"

"Oliver Lewis." The voice is that of woman, and she is speaking very softly. He can hardly hear her.

"Who are you?" he asks. "What do you want? How did you get in here?"

"You must go to her at once," the woman says, her words nothing more than a whisper. He strains to hear her speak. "She needs your help. They have taken one of our girls."

"Who needs my help? Who has taken her?" He stutters. "What girls?"

"She needs you," the woman says as he struggles in the darkness to see her identity. "You must go to her at once. She is in pain."

"I know you," Oliver says, trying hard not to panic.

He gasps, his chest feeling tight and heavy as if someone is kneeling on his body. "I know who you are," he whispers. "I know you."

"You must go now, Oliver."

There's something about the way she says his name that provides a clue to her identity. He shudders.

"It *is* you," he finally says. He finds it hard to breath. It's as if he is suf-focating. "How can you be here?"

"Go."

He shakes uncontrollably as if he is a leaf on a nearly-barren tree branch in a violent autumn wind. "I do not understand."

"She is in trouble, Oliver. She needs you."

"Samantha Henderson," he whispers. "What are you doing in my room?"

14: A distress call

Alex is upset over what just happened. That much is very clear to Oliver.

Of course he is, he thinks, unsure if he should say something to comfort his friend.

Instead, he remains quiet. He watches as the man he just met again this morning after thirty-seven years paces back and forth in the living room where they've gathered. However, while Alex has every right to be upset over what just happened with his mother, it is not clear to Oliver if his friend is angry, or who he's even angry with.

Maybe he's just gathering his thoughts, or so Oliver hopes.

"Say something, Alex," Oliver finally pleads. To avoid a collision with his host, Oliver has taken a seat in one of the plush armchairs near the fireplace.

Alex remains silent, quietly pondering the situation.

Uncomfortable, Oliver says, "Please, Alex. It is important for me to know if you are angry with me. While I didn't do anything, I would understand if you were upset. Please talk to me."

Alex stops pacing, stares at him and then takes a deep breath. He finally says, "I honestly don't know what to say, Oliver. I am very confused right now—so confused that I cannot think straight."

Oliver nods. "I am confused, too, and I hate it that this has happened. You must believe me, Alex, that I would never do anything to hurt your mother—never."

"I know that, but my mother's well-being is my utmost concern," Alex says. "I am trying to figure out how this could happen."

"Let's talk this out," Oliver says. "Let's try to figure out what has happened."

"How did my mother got into your room all by herself? That woman has not gotten out of that bed or her wheelchair on her own steam for the past five years yet you are telling me that she managed to get out of the bed, sneak past Paula despite all the monitors and alarms that we have set up in her room, then make her way down the darkened hallway and into your room all on her own and without anyone hearing her?" Alex stares at his friend. "I just don't buy that, Oliver. I can't."

"All I can tell you is that I was asleep—not sleeping very well, but I was asleep nonetheless and when I woke up, there she was, standing at the foot of my bed," Oliver explains. "She scared me half to death. Maybe Paula can tell you something that might help to explain all of this? Surely, she must have heard something."

"I have already spoken to Paula, and she says she did not hear or see a thing. I will be talking to her again, you can be sure of that." Alex takes a deep breath. "But I just don't know what to think about any of this. Between you suddenly showing up this morning and now my mother's strange behaviour, I'm feeling like a bulldozer has hit me. None of this makes any sense."

"The last thing I want to do is to cause you any more problems," Oliver tells his friend. "I wish I could help you figure things out but I'm just as confused as you are. All I can tell you for certain is that when your mother came into the room her words were clear and she knew who I was."

"How is that even remotely possible? She hasn't seen you in almost forty years. There is no way she should remember you."

Oliver takes a deep breath and says, "But she did know me. She knew me by name, and she kept saying something about one of the girls being in trouble. She told me I had to go to her right away." Oliver shakes his head, replaying the recent events. "She insisted that I was the only one who could help."

"What does that even mean, Oliver? What girls?"

"I don't know, and I don't know what I'm supposed to do to help who- ever is in trouble," Oliver says. "I wish I knew, but I think this is somehow all connected to the reason I'm here."

"All of this makes me very uneasy," Alex says, finally taking a chair next to Oliver. Hanging his head and staring at the hardwood floor, he adds, "I suddenly feel like the chicken in the henhouse while the fox stalks me from the outside. I don't feel good about any of this. Something is wrong, Oliver, and I feel threatened, vulnerable."

"It makes me uneasy too." Oliver nods. "And I should tell you that, just before your mother woke me up, I was having some sort of weird dream. Actually, it was more like a nightmare, and it left me feeling really tense and on edge. Now I can't shake this feeling that something bad is going to happen."

"What did you see in this dream?"

"I really couldn't see a whole lot because the images were blurred and it was very dark—almost pitch black. But there were at least four people there and they were all fighting."

"Where did this fight take place?"

"On some kind of bridge."

"A bridge?"

Oliver nods. "A bridge. Why? Is that significant? Does that mean something to you?"

"I don't know. But maybe." Alex pauses, contemplating his next words. "Can you tell me if there were birds involved in this battle, owls and crows?"

Oliver nods again. "There were lots of owls and crows—especially crows. It seemed like there were hundreds of them and they were sort of all flocking around this one young man. It seemed like they were protecting him. I really don't understand what was happening or what it all means, but that's what it looked like."

"Well, my friend," Alex says, staring hard at him as if trying to figure out this man's motives. "That's because you weren't having a dream or a nightmare—what you were experiencing were flashbacks. It appears that some of your memories are finally trying to push their way to the surface."

"Memories?" Oliver whispers. "Memories of what?"

"Memories of something that happened thirty-seven years ago."

Oliver shakes his head and exhales. "I'm confused, Alex. That can't be true."

"It is true." Alex nods, his voice grim but assured. "Those images were memories coming back to you."

"How can you be so sure?"

"Because I was there, Oliver. What you saw was the fight that occurred on the old train bridge that ran over the Mersey River at that time. It happened on the night you disappeared."

"Jesus." Oliver sucks in a mouthful of air, exhales forcefully and then asks, "How can that be?"

"There is more," Alex says, carefully choosing his words.

"More? What more could there possibly be?"

"This may be the most difficult part to believe. The young man that you said you saw, the one all the crows were flocking around and protecting? That boy was me, but I was only sixteen at the time. What you described is exactly what happened that night."

"What are you saying, Alex?"

Looking directly into his friend's eyes he says, "That you were also there that night, and you were one of those two men who were fighting on the bridge."

Quickly trying to assimilate this news, Oliver says, "I was there that night?"

"Yes. You were one of the first two men to go off the bridge during the fight," Alex tells him. "I never saw you again after you toppled over the railing—not until this morning. Imagine my surprise when I saw you."

"Jesus."

"I know it's shocking." Alex nods. "I didn't want to tell you anything about that night because I wanted you to regain your memories without any influence from me, and now it appears that they are coming back to you."

"None of this makes any sense," Oliver says, shaking his head. "How can any of this be true after all this time? How can any of this be real?"

"I don't know, Oliver. I'm just telling you what I know, and that what you experienced tonight were real memories, not a dream."

"God-damn, this is just too much to wrap my head around."

"I hear you," Alex agrees. "I'm just as confused, but now we have to figure out why you've come back after all these years. My guess is that the crows have something to do with it."

"The crows?" Oliver looks at his friend, puzzled. "Do you really think so?"

Alex nods. "These crows can work miracles. I've seen them do some crazy things over the years, and if they have brought you back to me and my family, then there is definitely a reason for it. Something unnatural is at play here and it involves you. I'm pretty sure about that."

"So, if that's the case, how do we figure out what they want me to do?"

"That's just the thing, Oliver: we don't," Alex answers. "Usually, when the crows are involved, they won't just show you what they want. These mysteries have to unfold layer by layer. I would say that whatever it is that's happening is now in motion, and that means we have to be on our toes. We have to watch everything that seems unnatural or out of place."

"You mean unnatural like your long-lost friend suddenly showing up out the blue, with no explanation of how he got here or where he's been?"

"Yes." Alex nods, exhaling with a controlled breath. "Exactly just like that."

Oliver is just about to respond when there is a ringing sound.

"Just a second," Alex says, glancing at the digital display screen on the small, square device that's strapped to his left wrist.

Oliver has been gone for many years and some of the technology he has encountered since his return has been foreign to him. He has never seen anything like the item, but he assumes it is some type of communication's device.

"Who could be calling at this hour of the night?" Alex murmurs, looking at the message on the small screen. "Jesus, it's Sydney. She never calls this late, so I better get this."

Oliver nods.

Pushing the talk button on the device, Alex listens through the small receiver that is hidden behind his left ear as his daughter tells him she needs him to come right away. Oliver cannot hear her words, but he can see the anxiety level rise in his friend's expression.

"What's wrong, honey?" Alex asks, speaking as though his daughter is in the room with him.

"It's Piper," Sydney says. "She needs our help."

"What's happened?"

"I don't know. I've tried calling her several times, but the call goes right to the answering service. However, I know Piper has been in an accident. I could see it. I don't know how serious it is, but I need you to come right away."

"Of course, honey," Alex says. "Where am I going?"

"I can't be one hundred percent sure, but I think you should head towards Piper's house. I am on my way there right now."

"Okay, honey," Alex says. "I am on my way."

"Oh, and Dad, bring Oliver with you."

"Oliver? What do you need him for?"

"I'm not sure, but I just know he needs to come with you."

"Okay," Alex says, nodding to the other man who has been observing the one-sided conversation. "I will also bring your mother. If your sister is in trouble, your mother will need to be there as well. We will leave right away. We'll meet you at Piper's place in about twenty minutes."

"Be careful, Dad," Sydney cautions. "Something strange is happening tonight and you could be in danger."

"We'll be fine honey, but you watch yourself. I will see you very soon."

As Alex disconnects the call, Oliver asks, "What's happened?"

"I don't really know," Alex says as he rises from his chair. "But come with me. Something has happened and the girls need us."

15: Connected

"Come on, Ms. Henderson. Stop this at once," Paula Bethancourt pleads. Her elderly patient has suddenly become agitated and combative, two personality traits the usually docile woman rarely exhibits.

"Please lie back down in bed," Paula insists. "Listen to me. If you keep behaving like this, you're going to get injured and then you'll be in a whole world of hurt."

Taking the older woman by the shoulders and forcing her back down to the mattress, Paula is amazed at Samantha Henderson's strength. But while she may be amazed, she isn't really surprised that the woman's strength nearly matches her own, despite her being more than twice her age and in poor health—mentally, at least.

Paula has been in the personal care business long enough to know that patients in an advanced state of dementia can often exhibit extraordinary strength when they are agitated.

And if there's one thing this old woman is right now, it's agitated, she thinks, quickly ducking to avoid Samantha's flailing arms.

Jesus, she thinks. *That was too close.* She's afraid that if her patient lands one of those blows to her head, it's going to have some sting to it.

"Please, just stop struggling and lie down," Paula begs through clenched teeth. "If you don't settle down, you are going to hurt yourself. Is that what you really want? You'll be in a fine mess if you do that."

"No," the older woman snaps, flailing about in the bed as if she's a rag doll. "I don't want to lie down. You can't make me lie down."

"This is not open for debate, Ms. Henderson," says the tiny-featured woman who has been caring for Samantha Henderson for the past three months. "I am not very happy with you right now, not after what you've just done, so you may not want to push your luck with me. You made me look very bad in front of Dr. Goodwin and that really pisses me off. Trust me. You don't want to make any angrier at you than I am right now."

Struggling as her caregiver attempts to strap her into her bed, Samantha cries, "I said to stop it," she screams, "You are hurting me. Let me go!"

"Not a chance, old woman. Not this time," Paula says, pulling the leather straps tightly around the elderly woman's frail body. The caregiver has told Samantha repeatedly that the straps are necessary to keep her safe because, as Alex agrees, she would likely be injured very badly if she were to fall out of bed.

"Now, just stop fighting me. If you don't, I will have to get help," Paula says. Sighing in disgust, she adds through clenched teeth, "Do you really want me to call reinforcements? Because I will, and maybe they won't be as gentle with you as I'm being."

"No. Don't. Not this time," Samantha cries, trying desperately to push the younger woman away. "I don't like them."

"Well then, just be still and this will be over soon enough."

"Let me go. They are too tight," Samantha pleads, attempting to pull at the straps as Paula puts them into place. Her fingers weak and riddled with arthritis; it is a feeble attempt to get free.

"Not a chance. You fooled me and made me look bad. I will never make that same mistake again," Paula tells her. "I didn't think you could get out of your bed on your own steam but, clearly, I was wrong. You were just pretending to be infirm, weren't you? How else do you explain what you've done. Whatever the case, you will never fool me again, I promise you that."

The straps are standard practice for dementia patients who are known to wander from their beds, but neither Paula nor Alex believed that Samantha would have the strength to pull herself up, let alone stand and walk about all on her own, especially as it appeared that atrophy had set in.

"After that little stunt you just pulled by wandering into that strange man's bedroom, your son told me to make sure you were secured in your bed," Paula says, pulling tightly on the third and final strap.

The elderly woman whimpers and struggles, but the straps are too tight for her to move about. Her eyes are wide like those of an animal about to be slaughtered. "Let me out," she screams.

"Not a chance. Wandering around like that was very dangerous. You could have been badly hurt," Paula says, scolding her patient as a mother would scold an insubordinate child. "Just imagine what would have happened if you had fallen down the stairs. You could have been badly hurt or, even worse; you could have been killed. How do you think your family would have felt about that? Now, just be still and stop the fusing."

"Let me go," Samantha cries. Spurred on by her instincts of self-preservation, she struggles, albeit pointlessly, to break free of her bonds. "I don't like you."

Paula sneers. "I don't care if you like me or not. I am not getting paid for you to like me."

"You are a bitch," Samantha fires back. Frothing at the mouth, she pushes against the straps. "Let me out of here," she pleads. "I don't want to stay here."

"Stop fighting it," Paula jeers. "You aren't going to get away from me again and make me look bad in front of your son—no way."

"You are lying. I don't have a son," Samantha screams as spittle oozes from the corners of her twisted mouth.

"Yes you do. In fact, you have two sons—Dr. Alex Goodwin and his brother, Hunter. You live with Dr. Goodwin and his wife, but you don't see the other son all that much. And I'm not surprised he stays away. Why would he visit such an ungrateful and hateful person like you? You don't treat people very well when they visit, so I guess they figure it would be best just to stay away."

"I don't have any sons," Samantha says. "I don't know who you are talking about, but I want to get out of here."

Fighting against the straps, she screams, "Let me out."

"Not a chance," Paula says, using a key to unlock a small metal cabinet in a corner of the room not far from the woman's bed. "I'm not sure what's got you all riled up this evening, but I'm going to give you something to calm you down."

"No," the elderly woman screams. "Don't."

"Don't make me put a muzzle on you, Ms. Henderson. Because I will if you don't shut up," Paula says, retrieving a needle from the cabinet along with a small vial of Depakote, a sedative for dementia patients. Filling the syringe with the medication she adds, "You need to get some sleep. I promise that you'll feel better once you calm down."

"No," Samantha cries again, struggling under the straps as her caregiver approaches the bed, needle in hand. "I don't want that. Get away from me. I know you are trying to kill me."

"I don't care what you want," Paula sneers while roughly jabbing the needle into the elderly woman's scrawny left arm. "It's what you are going to get. And trust me, my dear, if I was trying to kill you, you would be dead by now—dead, buried and long forgotten."

"Not so hard. It hurts. Please stop," Samantha pleads as her caregiver holds her arm still while the medication flows into her veins and courses through her aging, but apparently not so feeble, body. "My girls are in trouble and I have to help them."

"Your granddaughters?" Paula asks. "I don't know what you're talking about, and I really don't care, but I need you to calm down. This medication will help."

"I need to go to them. They need me," Samantha cries as the medication quickly courses through her tiny body. Its effects are immediate.

"See, you're starting to feel better all ready," Paula says. "Now, just be quiet and relax. You'll feel much better in a few minutes."

"Oliver," Samantha whispers as her body becomes still. "I need you, Oliver," she cries, the tears welling in her eyes. "Somebody please help me."

"No one can hear you, Ms. Webster. They have all left the house. There has been some kind of emergency, so they left me in charge."

Samantha tries to speak, but she can no longer move her mouth. She is trapped, not only in the bed but also inside her own body.

Somebody…anybody…help me, she thinks. *Please help me.*

~

The murder of eight crows remains hidden within the dense foliage of the massive red maple that grows near the Goodwin house. They watch through the bedroom widow, as the younger woman physically restrains the older one.

They can feel the elderly woman's agony. They sense that she is in distress.

The crows would come to the woman's aid if they could get through the double-paned, reinforced window, designed to block the harmful UV rays, but they know any attempt would be futile. They don't like what they have witnessed, but the woman is just beyond their reach.

They are restless, for they know that something more sinister is at play, but for now the large black birds must wait for their opportunity to strike. And that time is close.

The one they need has suddenly appeared in their midst. They know that the forces are now in motion and that the time for action will soon be upon them.

Cocking their heads in unison, the eight crows listen as the light breeze rustles their black feathers. They can feel a shift in the equilibrium. Something has happened and they are needed elsewhere.

Leaving their perches in the maple, the eight black birds take flight, slipping through the warm night air. Silently, they move quickly towards their destination. There is danger and they must answer the call, for they are the lifeblood of this place, they are the bones and the nervous system of this town, they are the glue that holds this family together—they are all connected.

16: Off a cliff

The ominous flashing red and blue lights that suddenly come into view as they turn a sharp corner confirm Alex and Bree's worst fears—there has been a serious accident.

Quickly assessing the cluster of emergency vehicles gathered on side of the road, some of them seemingly balanced precariously close to the edge of the cliff, the couple can clearly see that something has broken through the guardrail.

"Jesus Christ. This doesn't look good," Alex says. Turning to his wife, he says, "Just once I would like for Sydney to be wrong about these things."

"Oh my God, Alex," Bree cries. "This looks bad." She sobs, "Please let Piper be all right. Please let her be alive."

Alex cautiously pulls over to the side of the road, parking his car a safe distance away from the cluster of emergency vehicles and hurried activity. "It looks bad, but let's not jump to conclusions. Let's talk to someone and find out exactly what happened here."

Putting the car in park and turning off the engine, he takes his wife's hand, squeezes it tenderly and adds, "Maybe you should stay here, and I'll go check things out. I'll come back and get you once I know what's going on."

"Not a chance," Bree says, pulling away from him. Releasing the seat belt restraint and pushing open the car door, she says, "If something has happened to one of my girls, there is no way I'm staying here."

"Of course not." Alex nods, releasing his own seat belt restraint. He knew his wife would not accept his suggestion. "What was I thinking?"

"Maybe it's not as serious as it looks," Oliver says from the backseat. "Maybe they dispatched all of these first responders just in case it's bad and they needed backup."

"Maybe," Alex says, trying to remain hopeful. "But this is a bad spot in the road. I don't know why they don't do something about this dangerous zone. Numerous people have been killed here over the years. If Piper's car went off the road at this spot, then she could be seriously hurt."

"Let's try not to jump to any conclusions," Oliver cautions as he releases his own seat belt restraint. "We need facts, so I'll go with you to see what's going on."

"Dad. Mom," Sydney calls as she sees her parents exit their car. "Just stay where you are and I'll come over to you."

"What's going on, Sydney?" Alex asks, hugging his daughter as soon as she gets close. "Is your sister okay?"

"I'm not sure," she says, shaking her head. Fighting to hold back her tears, she takes her mother's hand and explains, "I only got here a few minutes ago and the first responders arrived right behind me. Another driver saw the accident and immediately called 911. The first responders will let us know what's going on."

"Where is your sister?" Bree asks, straining to see Piper's car.

Taking a deep breath in an effort to keep her emotions in check, Sydney says, "You can't see her, Mom. She is still trapped in the car."

"Oh my God," Bree sobs. "Is Piper alive? Can you tell me that much?"

"Honestly, Mom." She shakes her head. "I don't know anything for certain," Sydney says, hugging her mother tightly. "From what I could overhear, it looks like Piper is still breathing. But she appears to be wedged in the wreckage pretty tightly. They will have to cut her out."

She takes a deep breath and adds, "God knows how long that will take."

"What happened?" Alex asks.

"Who knows, Dad? Piper may have lost control of her car for some reason and went off the cliff." Sydney tells her parents. Turning to Oliver, she adds, "I'm glad to see you, Oliver. Thanks for coming."

"I'm not sure what I'm doing here," Oliver answers. "But your father said you asked for me to come. What do you need?"

"I'm not sure," Sydney tells him. "But I just had this strong feeling that you were supposed to be here with the family. Maybe just stand by for now and let's see what happens next."

"I'm here whenever you need me," he tells her. "In the meantime, I think I'll just have a look around."

"When you called a little while ago, you were at your place, weren't you?" Alex asks his daughter.

"Yes, I was home."

"So how did you know about this accident?" he asks. "Did you have one of your visions?"

"Yes," Sydney tells him, speaking softly, her voice shaking with emotion. "It was just a very fast flash of pictures in my head, but I could clearly see that Piper was in trouble. And..." She pauses, reluctant to say anything else for fear of alarming her parents, "Besides the accident, something very strange also happened tonight at my place."

"Something stranger than having a vision of your sister in a car accident?" Bree asks. "Good Lord. I can only imagine what that was."

"Well, Mom, that's just the thing." Sydney shakes her head. "I don't think you could imagine it even if you tried."

Alex squeezes her hand. "Tell us what has you so close to the edge."

Taking a deep breath, she begins, "It all started with three loud knocks on my front door, only when I went to see who in the hell would be stopping by for a visit after midnight, no one was there. I went outside and looked around, but there wasn't a soul anywhere in the vicinity. It was all very creepy."

Bree is alarmed by what she just heard. "You went out in the middle of the night after someone knocked at your door? That's not very smart, Sydney. What if someone had been waiting for you?"

"It was okay, Mom," she assures her mother. "I didn't feel like I was in any kind of danger."

"You didn't *feel* like there was any danger?" Bree answers. "What if your feelings had been wrong this time? What have I told you about taking unnecessary risks?"

Sydney shrugs. "I believed that if there had been a threat, I would have felt it."

"You have got to be more careful, Sydney," Bree tells her daughter. "I've been telling you that for years."

"Yes Mom, I know, but I was fine." She forces a smile and again hugs her mother tightly. "I really believe if I had been in any real danger, I would have sensed it and I would not have opened that door. I promise that I was being very careful."

Alex agrees. "You have to be more cautious, Sydney. I know you've always wanted to be the brave one and you've always been the one to go out on your own, but one of these days your senses may not work."

"Come on, Dad," she replies. "You guys worry way too much about me."

"So, what else happened, Sydney?" Alex asks. "I get the feeling that you are not telling us everything."

She sighs heavily and throws her glance to Oliver as if looking for reinforcements.

Oliver nods to acknowledge that he's there for her if she needs anything.

"There was something else," she says. "And to be honest, it scared the hell out of me."

"What was it?" Alex asks. "Another vision?"

"Worse than a vision." She shivers. "It felt more like a warning."

She pauses, takes a deep breath, and then continues, "I was feeling confused and a little freaked out. I went back into the house, locked the front door and turned off the lights. I was on my way to the kitchen to get a drink when, all of a sudden, something crashed through the door window. It scared the crap out of me."

"Jesus Christ, Sydney," Alex says. "What was it?"

"A large brown owl burst through the window and crashed on the front hallway floor. There was a lot of blood and broken glass everywhere. It died instantly."

"Why would it do that?" Bree asks. "What would compel a living, breathing creature to do something like that? It sounds so violent."

"I don't know, Mom," Sydney says. "But it's like it wanted something."

"Or someone," Alex suggests. "Was it after you?"

"Maybe." Sydney slowly nods. "It was definitely on a mission."

~

A mission? Oliver thinks. *What kind of mission?*

He remembers that in his recent dream or memories—or whatever it is that he has been having—owls have played a prominent role, along with crows.

Why owls, of all things? he wonders, casting his eyes around the stretch of winding road.

I hope the girl will be okay, he thinks, noticing tire marks in the dirt and skid marks on the pavement. *Looks like she hit her brakes pretty hard before going over the edge.*

Noticing a woman standing alone on the shoulder of the road, watching the emergency first responders continue their efforts to free Piper from the wreckage, Oliver decides to find out who she is.

As the red and blue lights reflect off her beige jacket and blondish-brown hair, Oliver carefully approaches her. He takes it slowly as he does not want to cause her any alarm.

"Excuse me, miss," he says, speaking softly as he can see that she is visibly upset. "Are you okay?"

"Yes," the woman answers, turning to face him. "I'm just worried about the young woman down there. It looks like her car hit pretty bad. And the noise it made when it crashed, it was something I don't want to ever hear again. It made my skin crawl."

"You heard it?" Oliver asks.

The woman nods. "And I saw it." Wiping the tears from her eyes with the back of her right hand, she adds, "It was just awful."

"Can you tell me what you saw?"

Studying him, she asks, "Who are you?"

"I am a friend of the family," he answers, motioning toward the Goodwins gathered across the road beside Alex's car. "I came here with them. We are just waiting to hear how Piper is doing."

"I see," the woman says as she glances in the direction he's pointing. "You are friends with Dr. Goodwin?"

"I am." He smiles. "For many years, apparently."

"Apparently?" She studies him. "You don't know?"

"It's a long story, but yes, I've known Dr. Goodwin for a few years," Oliver replies, afraid that he's come across as some kind of freak. "Can you tell me what happened, please, so I can tell my friends?"

He sees the woman take a deep breath before she begins.

"I was heading home," she says, speaking softly, "following a car that was going in the same direction. That car down there," she adds, pointing toward the twisted wreck at the bottom of the cliff. "I just don't know what happened. One minute we were both travelling down the road and then, she hit her brakes, swerved, and went over the cliff. It was terrible."

"Was there another vehicle, or something in the road that may have caused her to lose control of her car?"

She shakes her head and says, "There were no other vehicles besides our two cars. But—" she stops mid-sentence and wipes her eyes.

Oliver decides not to push the woman too hard, but after a moment he asks, "But what? You were going to say something else."

"Sorry. It's just that it's so much to take in. I feel so bad for the young woman. You said her name was Piper?" she finally whispers.

"Yes."

"That's a nice name," the woman says, the tears visible to him. "I wish I could do more to help her."

"Are you the one who called the emergency responders?" Oliver asks.

"Yes," she whispers. "It was just so horrible."

"What was so horrible?" he asks.

"It's like they attacked her car and forced her off the road."

"Who forced her car off the road?"

"It wasn't *who*," she says, shaking her head. "It was owls." She sobs. "There were dozens of owls and I swear to God that they deliberately attacked her car."

Oliver is stunned. "Are you sure it was owls?"

"Yes, I'm sure," the woman answers as the tears streak down her face, reflecting red and blue from the emergency lights. "It was owls and they forced her off the road."

17: Wait and see

The next five and a half hours are among the most difficult that Alex and Bree Goodwin have ever spent.

They are living their worst nightmare and, unable to help their injured daughter, they feel helpless.

While Alex did not directly examine his daughter, a visual examination of her in the ambulance and again as they waited in the ER, confirmed for him that her injuries are serious.

Probably a lot of internal injuries, he thinks, but keeps his observations to himself.

His wife sits in the padded green chair with her face buried in her hands, trying to hide her tears. "Honey, I know it's hard, but you have to calm down," he says. "The doctor will come to see us once she's finished her examination. You can't help Piper if you lose it."

"For God's sake, Alex, this isn't one of your patients we're talking about," she sobs, almost gasping for air. "This is your daughter."

"Come on, Bree. I know you are distraught, but don't take it out on me," he says, pacing the floor in an effort to release the tension that's building in his body. "That won't help Piper in any way."

"It's bad, isn't it?" Bree cries. "You don't have to tell me, Alex. I know it is. She's in serious trouble, isn't she?"

"It's not good," Alex says, "but I haven't examined her, so we should wait to hear from Dr. Robbie before we jump to any conclusions. I have known Isabel Robbie for a long time and she's a sharp doctor. Piper is in very good hands with her."

"I wish you were in there with her," Bree says.

"I'm not allowed into the operating room with her because she's my daughter," Alex explains. "You know that. Hospital policy."

"Screw hospital policy."

Alex reaches out to hug his wife, but she pulls away. "Come on, Bree, you've got to keep it together for Piper's sake."

"Hey Dad," Sydney says, returning to the waiting room with coffee for her parents. "Any news from the operating room yet?"

"Nothing from the doctor yet," Alex replies, forcing a smile at his daughter and the tall, lanky man beside her. "All we can do now is wait, a reality that isn't sitting too well with your mother."

Glancing at her sobbing mother in the green chair, Sydney says, "Come on, Mom. Please try to calm down." Offering her a cup, she adds. "I have brought you some coffee."

"I don't want coffee," Bree answers, keeping her face buried in her hands. "I just want my daughter to be okay."

"She will be all right," Sydney says, speaking softly. Kneeling in front of her mother, she adds, "I know she will make it."

"You know?" Bree asks, raising her head and wiping her eyes. "You know your sister will be okay or you're just saying that to calm me down."

Reaching out to hug her mother, Sydney says, "Listen to me, Mom. Piper is a strong young woman and I know her. She's a lot like me—she *is* me—and if it was me lying on that operating table, I would be fighting like hell for my life. I know that's what Piper is doing. I can feel it. I know she wants to live."

"I'm not so sure," Bree says, her voice just a whisper. "She just seemed so upset when she left the house after dinner. Something is really bothering her and having you two fighting all the time isn't helping." Staring directly into her daughter's eyes, she adds, "You guys have to stop this foolishness. You have to get beyond whatever is tearing you apart. She is your sister, and you need each other."

"It's complicated, Mom."

"Nothing is more complicated than family, Sydney," Bree tells her daughter. "Your sister should be your number one concern right now."

"She is my top priority, but there are things going on that you just don't know about."

"And I don't want to know," Bree cries. "I just want her to wake up and be okay."

"I know, Mom," Sydney whispers, hugging her mother tightly. "I know."

Alex pulls Oliver aside so his wife and daughter can't hear their conversation. "Do you have any theories about what happened?"

"A theory? Yes." Oliver nods. "As for proof, well, that's a different story."

"So, what do you think happened?"

"I think she was attacked."

"Shit." Alex is overwhelmed by his friend's suggestion. "No way. Attacked by who?"

"Not by who, but by what."

"What the hell are you saying, Oliver?"

"Well," Oliver begins, after taking a deep breath. "You are not going to believe this, but I think owls forced your daughter off the road."

Alex thinks about Oliver's suggestion. "Are you fucking kidding me?" he finally answers. "Why do you think it was owls?"

"For starters, I talked to a woman at the accident scene who said she saw Piper go over the cliff. She saw a swarm of owls go after your daughter."

"Jesus Christ." Alex feels his knees get weak, as if he's about to faint. "Why owls and why now?"

"Based on what happened with Sydney last night at her house, and then this accident with Piper, it appears they are coming after your family. Which means they are also coming after you."

"Jesus." Alex sighs, he's suddenly feeling dizzy, his legs wobbly. "It has been so long since I've had to worry about owls, but clearly something has them riled up." Studying his friend, he then asks, "Do you suppose this has something to do with why you've showed up here all of a sudden after all these years?"

"I don't know." Oliver says. "But I feel there's a very good chance that there's a connection, and maybe that also explains why I've been having memories that involve owls."

"And crows," Alex quickly adds.

"Yes, the crows. How could I forget them?"

"We can never forget the crows," Alex says, his voice nothing more than a whisper.

Oliver reaches into his back pants' pocket. "I did some looking around while we were at the accident scene, and I found this."

"God-damn," Alex whispers as he inspects the feather that Oliver has pulled from his pocket. "Is this what I think it is?"

"Yes," Oliver nods. "An owl feather. I found it on the shoulder of the road close to where the car went through the guardrail. I would say it came from a rather large bird."

"What's that?" Sydney asks as she approaches the two men. "What have you got there, Oliver?"

"This?" Oliver shows her the feather. "It's just something I picked up from the road this evening."

"Is that an owl feather?" she asks. "Did you get that near the scene of the accident?"

"Yes."

"Let me see it, please."

Handing the feather to Sydney, Oliver says, "I'm not a bird expert—"

"This looks like it came from a great-horned owl," Sydney says, inspecting the brown feather. "It's the largest owl in Nova Scotia, but they are extremely rare in this part of the province."

"I think I know why," Alex observes. "It's because of the crows. They normally keep the owls away. They've been doing it for years."

Sydney says, "This is quite the coincidence, because that's the same kind of owl that came through the window in my door just a few hours ago. And it would have happened around the same time as Piper's accident."

Oliver shakes his head. "This isn't good—not good at all."

"Alex," Bree calls, rising from the chair. "The doctor is coming."

"Dr. and Mrs. Goodwin," Dr. Isabel Robbie says as she enters the waiting room. "Can we talk please?"

"How is she, doctor?" Bree asks as Alex joins his wife. "Is she going to be okay? Is she awake? Can we see her now?"

"Easy honey," Alex says, putting his arm around his wife's shoulder. "Let Isabel talk."

To the doctor, he adds, "Please, just call us Alex and Bree. We've been friends a long time, Isabel, so there is no need to be so formal."

Dr. Robbie nods. "Your daughter is in recovery, but she has a long road ahead of her. She is very heavily sedated, so I'm afraid you won't be able to talk with her for several hours. You can sit with her, though, if you'd like, but she will be unconscious for some time, as we must keep her comfortable and still. We don't want her moving around and breaking open her incisions."

"What was the damage?" Alex asks. "I need you to be honest with us. Please don't sugar coat anything."

"I'm always honest with my patients," she replies with a gentle smile. "Your daughter is one lucky woman to have survived that accident. However, she did sustain many serious injuries."

"How serious?" Alex asks.

"Several internal organs were seriously damaged, including her liver, spleen and kidneys. Her liver suffered a serious wound. As well, there was substantial intracranial and intra-abdominal bleeding. We have stopped all the bleeding and have it under control for now, but the next thirty-six to forty-eight hours will tell us a lot. We need to wait until some of the swelling goes down to see the full of extent of the damage.

We have done what we can for her, but the rest is up to her."

"Oh my God," Bree sobs. "This sounds bad."

Dr. Robbie says, "Modern medicine and doctors can only do so much. You know that, Alex. She's not out of the woods, not by a long shot. She may require additional surgeries, but all we can do for the time being is observe."

"And pray," Bree whispers.

"Another surgery?" Alex asks.

Dr. Robbie nods. "Her spleen was badly damaged, and we may have to remove it if it starts to bleed again."

"Why didn't you just remove it while you had her on the table," Alex asks. "You could have prevented putting her through another surgery."

"Does she need the spleen to live?" Bree asks.

"No. In fact, some people are born without a spleen or need to have it removed because of disease or injury," Dr. Robbie explains. "It's an important part of your immune system, but you can survive without it. However, considering that she's pregnant and still in the first trimester, we thought it best for the baby that we do not remove the organ unless we absolutely have to. The less intrusion right now, the better it will be for your daughter."

"Pregnant?" Sydney asks.

Bree and Alex had been so wrapped up in their conversation with Dr. Robbie that they had failed to notice their daughter had joined them.

"Piper is pregnant? Did you guys know?" Sydney says to her parents. "Did someone not think to tell me about it? I am her sister after all."

18: Stand your ground

As the sun peeks over the horizon to herald the start of a new day, they watch the sleek silver automobile come to a stop in front of the stately Goodwin house.

Hidden amongst the thick leaves of the large red maples that dot the well-kept property, the eight crows—like eight black sentinels—observe the two individuals who remain inside the vehicle even though the engine has been turned off. They can't hear the words the two humans are speaking, but they can sense the conversation is intense.

"Are you sure you are going to be okay to drive home?" Oliver asks.

When she doesn't answer, he continues, "Are you sure you want to be alone in your house considering everything that happened last night? I still think I should come with you just to make sure you're safe. I know everyone would feel better if you weren't alone right now."

"No," Sydney finally says. "It is precisely because of everything that's happened that I want to be alone. I need to think and digest everything that has happened."

"You don't have to be alone to think. I promise that if I come with you, I will be very quiet. You won't even know that I'm around. I just think you need someone close by."

"Thanks Oliver. I appreciate your concern, but I need the alone time," Sydney replies. "I know you're just trying to help but I am sure you've noticed that things have been more than a little strained between me and my sister, so, after what I just heard at the hospital, I won't be good company for anyone."

"I don't want to be good company. I want to be there in case the owls come back and to make sure you're safe," Oliver says. "For whatever reason, it appears the owls have targeted you and your sister. I feel compelled to watch over you."

"Really?" Sydney chuckles, even though she can't find anything funny to laugh about right now. "You feel compelled to watch over me? And to do what, exactly?"

"I don't know." He shakes his head, feeling a little embarrassed. "Protect you, maybe."

"So, you're my protector?"

"Yes." Oliver shrugs. "I guess I am."

"I can handle myself, Oliver," she says. "I don't need anyone to protect me from anyone and I most definitely don't need anyone to protect me from owls. I have been around birds my whole life and I know how to deal with them."

"I'm not sure about that, Sydney. I'm the first one to admit that I don't know anything about birds or owls, but these ones seem different somehow." He takes a deep breath. "Besides, you admitted earlier that you don't know a whole lot about owls, so maybe, if they come back, you're not as prepared to deal with them as you think."

"Different? How so?"

"They seem very aggressive. Besides, you have to agree that their behaviour seems anything but normal. Throwing yourself through a window to certain death and attacking a fast-moving car hardly seems like normal behaviour, does it?"

"No." Sydney shakes her head. "Not really, but even after all of that, I still don't feel like I'm in any danger. So, thank you for being here for me, but I think I'm just going home, have a nice long bath, probably a drink or two or three, and lie down for a bit. I think a couple of hours sleep is exactly what I need. Now, do you remember the pass code that you'll need to unlock the front door? Dad gave it to you when he told us that he and Mom were going to stay there with Piper."

"Yes," Oliver says. "My memories of my past may be lost, but I remember the code. It's 3-9-1-9-6-1, correct?"

"Correct. Do you need me to come in and help you get settled? It's a big house and you were only there for a couple of hours, so you may find it difficult to navigate."

"I think I can manage on my own," he tells her while pulling the latch to open the passenger-side door. "Just because I've lost my memory doesn't mean that I'm infirm."

"I know that." She pauses and then asks, "How are you feeling, by the way?"

"I'm fine," he says, swinging his legs out the door. "But remember, I don't have a phone so you can't call me if you need me for anything."

"It's all good, Oliver," she assures him. "We'll take care of getting you a communicator when I come back to pick you up later. Meanwhile, if I need anything, I will call Dad. He'll know how to reach you."

"Whatever you say, Sydney," he replies, reluctantly closing the car door and watching as she starts the car and drives away.

I don't like this, Oliver thinks as the vehicle's taillights disappear down the long driveway. *I should have gone with her. If something happens to that woman, I will never forgive myself.*

Turing to enter the house, he feels a sudden cold breeze wash over him even though the early morning July air is already hot and humid.

Jesus, he shivers, quickly glancing around the expansive yard that surrounds the Goodwin home. He senses a presence, and he knows he isn't alone.

"You are here, aren't you?" His eyes quickly scan the large red maple trees and sprawling lawn, searching for the crows. "I can't see you because it's too dark and you're black, so you blend right into the surroundings, but I know you're here."

He becomes quiet and listens, beads of sweat breaking out on his forehead.

Where are you? He shivers again.

"What do you want? I know you want something. Are you here to help me or hurt me?"

A sudden rustle of leaves startles him, but he holds his ground as he watches eight large, black crows spring from the branches and land on the ground not far from where he's standing. The birds form a semicircle around him. They seem bold, almost brazen.

Taking a deep breath, Oliver remains in a stare-down with the crows, as he tries to figure out his next move, or maybe their next move, whichever comes first.

The birds remain still. They don't even blink.

It's like they are frozen, he thinks. *They're just staring—watching me. And waiting. But for what?*

Finally, he decides he must say something, but he does not want them to think he's becoming aggressive. He knows he does not want a confrontation with these crows. He fears that, if they feel threatened, they may attack him.

I'd lose that fight. I'm pretty sure of that.

He takes a deep breath and then, with his voice soft and low so that he does not startle the crows says, "So, fellas. I'm not sure what you want from me, but you and I have to find some way to communicate. Unless, by some miracle, you've learned how to talk, we have got to figure something out."

One of the crows—maybe the leader, Oliver wonders—emits a low, guttural cawing sound.

A greeting? Or maybe it's a warning?

Taking one step back from the birds, he thinks, *Maybe he's telling me to back off.*

"Okay," he says, taking another small step backwards. "I'm just trying to be friends here. If you don't want to connect with me, that's just fine. I'll go into the house and that will be that, okay? But if you want me to do something for you, then you have to let me know what it is."

The crows move forward, in unison and Oliver wonders if maybe he should have gone directly into the house after Sydney left instead of engaging with them.

"I'm just going inside now," he finally says as the crows continue to advance, posturing and opening their wings as if they are getting ready to pounce.

Wait, he thinks as he reaches the door. *Maybe that's what you want me to do.*

Turing back to the crows that are now only inches from him, he asks, "Is that what you want? Do you want me to go into the house?"

The lead crow cackles its response, its head bobbing as if it is agreeing.

"Got it," he says, quickly approaching the keypad on the front door lock. "I'm going."

Carefully entering the pass code, Oliver takes a deep breath, then steps inside the house and quickly closes the door behind him. It's dark and quiet inside the house and he feels out of place here, but he is relieved to be out of striking distance.

He exhales, forcefully. *That was pretty intense. I don't want to ever do that again.*

With only Alex's mother, Samantha Henderson, and her caregiver in the house, the quiet is unsettling. He walks down the darkened hallway to the staircase, assuming both women are sleeping.

I don't belong here, he thinks, slowly ascending the stairs to get to his bedroom. *This town. This house.* He takes a deep breath. *This period in time. It's all so strange to me. What am I doing here?*

Reaching the second level landing, he turns toward his bedroom. *Sleep. That is exactly what I need. But after everything that's happened today, especially that run-in with the crows, I don't see how I'll be able to close my eyes, let alone fall asleep.*

He's being careful not to make any noise. The last thing he wants to do is disturb the women, especially Paula Bethancourt.

Maybe I haven't given her a fair shake, but I don't really care for that woman, I don't really know her so I probably shouldn't be so quick to judge, but there is just something about her that I do not like.

As Oliver nears the door to Alex's mother's room, he notices it's open just a crack. He hears some sort of commotion from inside. *What is that? Is that someone crying?*

Leaning in closer to the door, he is sure he hears a woman sobbing.

Samantha?

"Help me," she whimpers. "Oh my God. It hurts. Why won't somebody help me?"

Oliver gingerly pushes the door, opening it just wide enough for him to peek inside.

"Can anyone hear me?" she cries. "I need help. Please help me."

Scanning the room, Oliver gasps at the glowing lights of red, green, and yellow on the various monitors that surround the bed and cast an ominous light in the darkness.

"Jesus Christ," he whispers, slowly moving toward the bed.

Samantha is strapped tightly to the mattress. The scene reminds him of something he's witnessed before, but his memories are still locked tightly in a black void, just out of his reach.

"Help me," Samantha begs, and he thinks it actually sounds like she's crying more so than moaning.

"Who did this to you?" he whispers, sliding closer to the bed and seeing the straps pulled tightly around his friend's aging and frail body— one across her chest, another around her waist to hold her arms down at her side and a third around her legs. "Who did this?"

"Paula," she says, her voice so soft he can hardly hear her.

He's shocked when the elderly woman roles her head toward him and opens her eyes. He can feel her fear.

"Samantha? Can you hear me? Did Paula do this to you?"

"Yes." Her eyes lock on him and he shivers. "Help me," she pleads.

"I am not really sure what I can do," he says, speaking softly. Pulling on the buckle to loosen the strap that goes across her legs, he adds, "But for starters, we can get you out of these things. I think this is going too far."

"It hurts," Samantha cries.

"What hurts?" Oliver asks. "The straps hurt you? Are they too tight?"

"Chest," she sobs. "Too tight."

"Just give me a few seconds to loosen up this buckle," Oliver says fumbling with the strap. "Does Alex know that Paula is doing this to you?"

"Yes, he does."

Oliver is surprised to hear the angry voice of Paula Bethancourt. He has been so busy messing with the straps that he failed to notice Samantha's caregiver had entered the room. "It was his idea."

"Really?" Oliver quickly answers. "And does he know that you make the straps so tight that they hurt his mother and make her cry?"

"They are as tight as they need to be, Mr. Lewis," she answers, approaching the elderly woman's bed. "Now, please back away from my patient and leave this room at once."

"I will not," Oliver says. "You are clearly abusing this poor woman. She's in a lot of pain, maybe even having a hard time breathing."

"No, Mr. Lewis." Paula seizes the buckle from Oliver's hands and secures it back in place. "Please back off. You don't know anything about any of this."

Oliver shoots back, "Tell me why you have to strap a weak, elderly woman to her bed. Tell me why you have to hurt her in the process."

"You only see what you want to see, Mr. Lewis," Paula answers with disdain. "This is for Ms. Henderson's own safety. Now you should leave as I have asked."

"I don't think this is how Alex wants you to treat his mother."

"I am only doing what is necessary, Mr. Lewis. You simply do not understand."

"I can see she's suffering and that's what I understand. That's the only thing that is important to me."

"Do I have to call Dr. Goodwin to get you to leave this room?" Paula asks.

"Go ahead. I'm sure Alex would like to know how badly you are hurting his mother."

"I do not appreciate your accusations," she snaps. "I would never do anything to hurt Ms. Henderson. She is my patient and I care for her."

"I don't think making her cry is any way to take care of your patient."

"I have been doing this type of work for a very long time, and sometimes it becomes necessary to use restraints on dementia patients," she says. "Please leave this room at once. If you don't, I will be forced to take further action."

"Further action?" Oliver is surprised by her choice of words. He studies the tiny-featured woman and asks, "Is that a threat, Paula?"

"It is what it is," she replies. "Now please go before you upset Ms. Henderson more than she already is."

"I am not leaving Samantha with you. I don't trust you."

Taking him by the arm, she pulls Oliver from Samantha's bedside and guides him towards the door. "Like I said, I want you to leave and never come back into this room. Do you understand?"

"Alex will be hearing about this, Paula. He won't be happy about how you are treating his mother."

"I don't care what you tell Dr. Goodwin," she says, closing the door after Oliver enters the hallway.

Oliver hears Samantha crying out. *I should have stayed in there. What the hell is that woman doing to Samantha?*

Backing away from the bedroom door, he wonders, *Was I supposed to see this? Is this why the crows were all worked up? Did they send me here for this reason?*

He sighs heavily and thinks about Samantha Henderson's predicament. *Could they know what's happening in here? Do they believe Samantha is in danger?*

"Jesus," he exhales. "How would they even know?"

19: A gut punch

"Just hold your fucking horses," Isaac Benjamin yells, jumping out of bed and heading to the front door of the two-bedroom apartment he'll be vacating by the end of the month.

"I'm coming, for Christ's sake," he screams as the pounding on the door continues.

Obviously, he thinks, *someone is really pissed. This god-damn well better be important.*

"Jesus," he yells again. "I said I'm coming. Just calm down."

Now that he's broken things off with Sydney Goodwin—both professionally and personally—he's made the decision to leave this town and go far away by taking a new job in British Columbia starting in late August. Despite his feelings for her, the decision wasn't that difficult to make.

Stealing a glimpse at the clock hanging in the living room and seeing it's not even seven o'clock yet, he groans. "I don't know who in the hell you are, but you better have a damned good reason to be pounding on my door at this time of day or else I'll kick your fucking ass."

Peering through the door's peephole, Isaac is surprised to see Sydney standing in the hallway.

What in the hell? He takes a deep breath and stills his nerves as he can see that she's very agitated. *This can't be good.*

He swings the door open to greet his unwanted visitor. He is not in the mood for another fight with his former girlfriend, and especially not this early. "What are you doing here at this hour, Sydney? Do you have any idea what time it is?"

"Something terrible has happened, Isaac, and I wanted you to hear it from me instead of a stranger on the news," she answers. Pushing the loose strands of long black hair back behind her ears, she asks, "May I come in or have I been exiled to the hallway?"

"Sorry," he replies, stepping aside so she can enter the apartment. He can see that she is shaken and has been crying. "Come on in. What is it this time? Someone die or something?"

"Really?" She rolls her eyes at him. "Sarcasm at this hour?"

"Too early? Sorry again, but what's the crisis this time? Did you find another stranger down on the shore?"

"Listen, Isaac," Sydney shoots back, her words a mixture of anger and angst. "I get it that you're pissed at me, but do you have to be a complete asshole about it?"

"You don't even know the half of it," he says, closing the door once Sydney enters the apartment. "You just totally fucked up my life so, yes, I have to be a complete asshole about it."

"Suit yourself."

He's angry. She knows that and accepts responsibility for what happened, but sometimes she'd just like to kick him in the balls and tell him to smarten the fuck up. In truth, she now often questions what she ever saw in him and wishes they had just kept their relationship professional. She knows she made a terrible mistake when she allowed herself to become involved with him on an intimate level.

It was so wrong, she thinks. *It never should have happened but what's done is done.*

"Come on, Sydney." His lips twitch when he's mad. "Just tell me what's going on so that I can grab a shower and get some coffee. I have a long day ahead of me and, now that you've gotten me up so early, I may as well get on with it and try to do something productive. Who needs sleep, anyway?"

"What a dick." She's seething.

"So, did you come here before seven o'clock just to call me names? You have something important to tell me, so what is it? If it's about the study —or us—I've already told you that I am done on both fronts."

"Jesus, Isaac. Get over yourself," she pauses and then, taking a deep breath, adds, "I have some news to tell you. But it has nothing to do with any of our other shit. It's about Piper."

"What about Piper? Did you two have another argument?" he replies, his eyes narrowing to slits conveying his deep anger. "Time for you to grow up, Sydney. Like I told you the last time we argued about this, Piper and I are over. I admitted that we had slept together a couple of times, but you and I had already broken up by the time she and I got together. So, honestly, I don't know what the big deal was."

"Oh, my friend, it's a big deal all right."

"Come on Sydney. Just stop with the bullshit. Just tell me what the fuck you want and then leave."

"I just want to tell you that you may want to reconsider tucking that tiny tail of yours between your legs and scurrying off to BC like a rejected little puppy scolded for peeing on the floor." She steps closer to him and leans into his face, her warm breath brushing his cheeks. "I have news that is going to rock your fucking world."

He leans closer to her in effort to control the situation. "Enough with the drama. Just tell me the news that I can see you're dying to tell me and then I want you to leave me the hell alone."

"Very well. I wanted to be the first to congratulate you." She smirks at him, smug in the idea that she's finally in charge of his destiny. "I wanted to be the first to tell you that you are going to be a daddy, the poor kid."

She can see the news has hit a nerve, and she can't help but smile over the crippling blow she's just delivered.

"What in the fuck are you are you talking about?" He looks dizzy. "You really are fucking crazy."

"That's right. I'm the crazy one," she says. She enjoys watching him squirm and she wants to drive the knife a little deeper. "I just found out a little while ago that Piper is pregnant."

"Holy shit," Isaac says, exhaling with a force. His knees sag. She can see him struggle to regain his composure. "Well, good for her, but what makes you think I am the father?"

"Come on Isaac. I can do the math," she fires back. "Unless Piper was screwing more than one person at the same time—which I highly doubt because, while she may be a bitch, she is not a slut—you are definitely the baby's father."

"Did Piper tell you that?"

"Nope. She didn't have to tell me anything." She pauses and then adds, "Even if she wanted to, she can't talk right now."

His head snaps back. "What do you mean, she can't talk right now?"

She's about to speak, but the words catch in her throat.

Do I really want to tell him about the accident and that Piper almost died? That her life is just hanging by a thread? Shit, maybe this wasn't such a good idea after all.

"Come on Sydney," Isaac pushes, his voice full of anger and concern. "Why can't Piper talk to me right now?"

She blurts it out, "She drove her car off a cliff last night on her way home and now she's in the hospital in critical condition."

"Holy shit."

She suddenly feels sheepish. Despite everything that has happened between them, Piper is still her sister. They may not always get along, but they still have a deep bond and love for each other. She is sure that will never change.

"The doctors have her heavily sedated to help reduce the swelling in her brain, so that's why she can't talk right now."

"Jesus Christ, Sydney. Do you think that maybe you should have led with that piece of news?" he says, leaning back against the door. "Is she going to be all right?"

"They said the next thirty-six to forty-eight hours is going to be the most critical period. Right now, they just don't know for sure."

"And what about the baby? Is the baby okay?"

"I don't think they know. But both Piper and the baby are in a whole lot of trouble right now."

"Holy hell," Isaac says, regaining his balance and making his way to the living room, where he falls into a padded sofa. He fixates on the opposite wall where a collection of crow photos is displayed. "What in the hell happened, Sydney? Do they know what caused the crash?"

She takes a seat beside him. "It looks like something may have forced her off the road."

"Who in the hell would do that?"

She shrugs. "We are waiting to hear from the police about what might have happened."

"So, what now?" he asks, his tone becoming softer, less combative, and in that moment, she actually feels bad for her former boyfriend. "What do I do now?"

"Honestly, Isaac, I don't think there's anything you can do except wait on news, just like the rest of us."

"Should I go to the hospital to be with her?"

Sydney shakes her head. "I don't think you should do that, not right now, anyway. Mom and Dad are there and Seth is on his way from Halifax to be with her. They don't want a lot of people in her room until she comes out of this. Besides, Dad won't be very happy to see you."

"Does he know I'm the father?"

"I don't know but, truthfully, he's never really liked you all that much and he knows that you were with Piper after you and I broke up." Sydney stares at him. "He's a smart man so I'm pretty sure he's figured it out on his own."

Isaac sighs and she can see the tears forming in his eyes. "I never meant to hurt you or Piper."

"It's too late to think about any of that right now, Isaac," she says, suddenly feeling regret for the way she burst in and delivered the news.

"I am sorry, Sydney," he tells her. "I really am."

She sighs. Even if she despises him for what he had done, he really didn't deserve to be treated this way. She forces a smile. "Why don't I make us some coffee and then you can get on to whatever it is you were going to do today? Just don't go the hospital and cause a scene."

"Yes." He nods. "I think I could use a coffee."

"Just sit right there, and I'll bring it to you when it's ready. I think I remember where everything is."

"Thanks."

"You're welcome and Isaac," she pauses and considers her next words. "For what it's worth, I think you will make a great father."

"You think?"

"I do. As far as boyfriends go, you leave a lot to be desired because you can be a jerk sometimes, but I think you have a lot to offer a child. So just take this slowly and see how things play out."

"I appreciate that. I think."

As she heads into the kitchen he asks, "Do you think you and I could ever be friends again?"

She turns back. He seems so small and vulnerable right at that moment. *Be nice Sydney*, she tells herself.

"Honestly, Isaac," she says, "I'm not sure, because you hurt me really bad. But who knows? Maybe when all the dust settles, we can get back on better terms. But for now, I suggest we just worry about Piper and the baby."

He nods. "I understand."

I don't think you do, Sydney thinks as she turns and heads toward the kitchen. *Honestly, I don't think I understand.*

20: Eight crows on a mission

With the early morning sun licking their backs and the warm light bouncing off their black feathers, the eight crows soar high over the town that hugs the banks of the Mersey River. This place is more than just their home; it's also their responsibility.

Most of the town residents, who are just rising to greet the challenges and successes that a new day offers, have no idea that trouble is brewing in their midst, festering like a ripe, pus-filled boil about to pop. They are oblivious to the fact that something dark and sinister has infiltrated the serenity of this place.

But the crows know that the peace they all take for granted could be shattered in a heartbeat.

For hundreds of years, the crows have stood guard over this small, but flourishing community, founded centuries ago and built on the backs of brave men and women who refused to quit even in the face of seemingly-insurmountable odds. As adversity became the order of the day, hard-working people with vision, determination and true grit stepped up to meet the challenge. They refused to quit.

Through it all, the crows have watched and, when necessary, have intervened. And now, they are called upon to step up one more time.

Today, as the hospital comes into sight and they scope out their best vantage point, the eight crows are on a mission. They will observe and learn.

~

Sitting beside the hospital bed where Piper has been lying unconscious for several hours, motionless and hooked up to a variety of tubes and wires, Bree says a silent prayer.

She's not overly religious. But she does not know what else to do, as it appears the doctors have done all they can for her daughter. She feels helpless.

Holding a vigil without being able to intervene is not her usual way of doing things, as she has always helped her children no matter the crisis. Right now, though, as her fragile daughter clings to life, trapped within her broken body, there is nothing else that can be done.

Waiting, she thinks. *That's often the hardest part. Time seems to stop because of the not knowing and the uncertainty of what is going to happen next. If only we could see into the future...*

"Come on, Piper," she whispers, squeezing her daughter's hand. While she isn't sure if her daughter can hear her, she believes that her words will guide Piper back to the land of the living, back to those who love her.

They have to.

"If you can hear me, honey, follow my voice. We're all praying for you to wake up soon. We need you to find your way back to us."

"Bree, honey," Dr. Alex Goodwin says, entering the room with Dr. Isabel Robbie. "Isabel has stopped in to check on Piper."

"Hi, Isabel. I'm happy you're here. When do you think we'll see some changes?" Bree asks, releasing her daughter's hand and pulling back from the bed. Knowing there's no simple answer, she still asks, "When will we know if she's going to be okay?"

"Sorry, Bree, I really can't say right now," Dr. Robbie says, checking the monitors. "All we can do is continue to keep her comfortable and observe her progress."

"I need my daughter to wake up," Bree says, tears dripping from her eyes. "I need her to open her eyes and tell me that she's all right."

"I know this is hard, honey," Alex says, hugging his wife and giving the doctor room to work. "But there is nothing more anyone can do, except hope for the best."

"That's not so easy, Alex," Bree replies. "Piper has always been so strong—a real fighter—but right now she seems so fragile and vulnerable." She sighs heavily and adds, "I'm just not used to seeing her being so helpless."

"Alex," Dr. Robbie says while pushing on Piper's abdomen. "Can you please come here and feel this?"

Alex quickly moves into position and places his hands on his daughter's stomach. He pushes gently. "Jesus. It feels like there is some internal bleeding. Do you think you need to operate again?"

Nodding, Dr. Robbie says, "I think it's the spleen. If it's bleeding again then we are going to have to take it out, but there could be complications."

"The baby?" Bree asks, her voice quivering with emotion. "Is there a risk?"

"I'm afraid so," Dr. Robbie says. "Piper's only in her first trimester, so there's greater risk for the embryo than if she was further along. At this stage, the embryo may not be able to withstand the shock from an operation, so you should be prepared that Piper could lose the baby."

"And what if you don't remove the spleen?" Bree asks.

"Then Piper will bleed out," Alex answers, glancing at his colleague. "I really don't see as you have much choice, Isabel. You have to take it out."

"I'll be as delicate as a I can around the embryo, but as I said you should be prepared for the worst," Dr. Robbie says. "I'll see that the OR is prepped, and we'll be ready to go in about fifteen minutes. This can't wait."

"Okay, Isabel," Alex shakes the doctor's hand. "We know you will do everything you can to save Piper and the baby."

After Dr. Robbie leaves, Bree says, "Is she going to make it, Alex? Because I don't know what I will do if anything happens to her."

"Just think positive, honey," he says, pulling her to him and wrapping his arms around her. "Piper is a fighter. We have to believe in her."

~

Armed with the update, the eight crows spring from their perches within the trees just outside the window of Piper's hospital room. This is not the news they wanted to hear today, but they know that, in this town, tragedy is common.

Wings flapping to catch the breeze, the octet head to the second of three locations they are watching today. At the Goodwin family home, they take their position in the thick maple trees outside the elderly woman's window. From there they can remain hidden while watching the goings-on within the house.

~

"Good morning, Ms. Henderson," Paula Bethancourt says as she enters the older woman's room carrying her breakfast tray. "Let's get you cleaned up and then you can have your breakfast. We have a hard-boiled egg with multi-grain toast, and, to finish it all off, I've made you a fruit smoothie with lots of blueberries. I know that's your favourite. It looks delicious, so I hope you're hungry."

Samantha Henderson, still trapped in the restraints that her caregiver applied last evening, remains quiet. Her head is turned toward the window; she stares blankly at the large, red maple that has stood there for decades.

"Not talking to me this morning? Well, that's all right," Paula says, approaching her patient's bed and slowly removing the straps. "I am taking these off, but if you don't behave yourself, you'll find yourself back in them pretty damned quick. After yesterday, I have had enough of your foolishness to last me for a while."

Samantha turns from the window and stares at the other woman, but says nothing.

"You did have quite the adventure yesterday, didn't you?" Paula says as she begins her patient's sponge bath. "But the thing is, Ms. Henderson, we don't really know anything about your son's house guest—this Mr. Lewis. We really don't know if we can trust him. I mean, who is he anyway?"

Samantha stares blankly at the ceiling as her caregiver removes her nightclothes and washes her upper body.

"Where did he come from? What does he want? Who really knows? So I think it is best if we just stay away from him. You know, just to be on the safe side."

Keeping her voice calm, Paula continues, "Can you do that? Can you please stay away from this guy?"

"Where is my son?" Samantha says. Her words are cold and void of any emotion.

"Dr. Goodwin? He's at the hospital with your granddaughter, who was hurt in a terrible car accident last night. Don't you remember?"

"No, my other son."

"Hunter? I'd guess he's probably at home, getting ready for work at the store. Why do you want him? He doesn't come around very often—not that I blame him for that because you don't treat him very well when he does visit."

"No," Samantha shakes her head, becoming agitated. "The other one."

"You don't have another son, Ms. Henderson. It's just Alex and Hunter."

"No," she replies, her voice now becoming sharp. "My son, Oliver."

"Oliver? As in Oliver Lewis, the man who is staying here with us? He's not your son. I think you are confused, probably because of what happened earlier," Paula says. "He's just a stranger who turned up here yesterday and Dr. Goodwin invited him to stay, but, as far I know, he is no relation to you."

"I want to talk to him."

"Why?"

"I need him."

"I believe he's gone with your other granddaughter, Sydney. I heard him leave about half an hour ago. But you know what? Even if he was here, I wouldn't let you see him."

Samantha trembles, her lips twitching. She finally stutters, "You... bitch."

Paula can see her last comment hit a nerve, so she decides to push further. "What do you want with Mr. Lewis? If you need something, I can get it for you. But he can't help you and I have forbidden him from seeing you."

Her eyes narrowing to slits, Samantha remains silent.

"Pissed at me again, are you? Oh well," Paula says, finishing the bath and helping her patient into clean pyjamas. "That's no skin off of my ass."

Bringing the tray of food to the bed, she adds, "Now, let's have breakfast and you can watch your favourite vintage TV shows. "*The Big Bang Theory* is all ready to play on your screen. Just press the green button. I have a lot of work to do this morning and I don't want you to bother me for a little while."

"No," Samantha screams, grabbing the breakfast tray and hurling it across the room. "I don't want your slops."

"Suit yourself, Ms. Henderson, but you'll be hungry, and you know what? I'm going to make you wait until lunchtime before you get anything else."

Samantha says nothing, but jeers at the younger woman.

"Now, Ms. Henderson," Paula says, raising the side rails on the bed, "I am going to get the bucket and clean up that mess that was your breakfast. I want you to stay in this bed. If I come back and you're not here, I am going to strap you back down and that's where you're going to stay for the rest of the day. Do you understand what I'm saying?"

Samantha refuses to answer.

"You better listen to me, old woman, or, trust me, you will be sorry," Paula says, just before she leaves the bedroom.

~

The crows have been watching these two women for some time now, and they don't like what they have seen. It is their duty to assist if someone in the family is in trouble, but they have no direct access to the elderly woman.

However, they have sent in reinforcements, and they know their choice of protectors will be there for her when she needs him the most.

That time is coming very soon. They are aware that something has changed in their world. They feel the darkness. The oppression is heavy, almost suffocating.

With centuries of knowledge to draw on, along with an uncanny ability to tap into and assess any change in circumstances that may affect the family, the crows are keenly aware that a major threat has emerged, and they must watch over their charges until the danger has been neutralized. They have chosen their protector and he will know what to do.

Confident that the elderly woman is in no immediate danger, they spring from their perches and take flight. They have one more stop to make today. They must be assured that the members of the family are safe, for that is their purpose, their very reason for existence.

Taking refuge in the foliage that surrounds Sydney's quaint, two-level Cape Cod house, the crows watch the young woman and the man who appeared in their midst yesterday.

~

"I don't know what compelled you to come check on me this morning, but I'm glad you did," Oliver says, accepting the cup of coffee that Sydney has made for him.

The pair has chosen to sit on the front veranda of her house that was built in the mid-1900s to enjoy the coolness that lingers in the morning air. "But what made you think I would even be awake? It's still quite early."

"Well..." She smiles over her cup of coffee. "Since you didn't have a phone, I couldn't call you, so I just decided to stop in to see how you were doing. Let's just say I was worried."

He smells the coffee before taking a sip of the hot liquid. He's not sure if he likes it but doesn't say anything to his new friend. "I thought you were going home to get some sleep after you dropped me off."

"I tried, but I couldn't turn off my brain so I thought a drive might clear my head and, for some reason, I felt compelled to drop by and check on you."

"Did it work? The drive I mean." He studies her reaction. "Did it clear your brain?"

"Not really," she says, shaking her head and deciding to leave out the part where she stopped at her former boyfriend's apartment.

"I do need to get a phone or whatever device you guys are using these days to communicate."

Glancing around the front yard, Oliver adds, "You have a really nice place here. I like it. Don't know why I know this, but it looks like it has good bones. Have you lived here long?"

"I bought the house about three years ago," she tells him. "I fell in love with it the first time I saw it, but it does need some work. That's one of the things I like about the place. I can slowly fix it up as I can afford to, but still live here at the same time. It's a great arrangement and saves me some cash in the long run."

"I can help if you'd like."

"You are a contractor?"

He shrugs. "I'm not sure what I am, but, for some reason, I think I can help you."

She nods. "I'll never turn down an offer like that. I can handle a hammer and saw, but it's always good to have an extra set of hands."

"Great. And it will keep me busy while I figure out what I'm supposed to be doing around here." Oliver smiles. "You just tell me what you need done and I'll do what I can."

"Okay then, for starters," she replies, "I need the window in the front door replaced. That owl did a pretty good job on it last night."

"I'll have a look."

"And speaking of that owl, I have to go and clean up the remains of that poor bird. It's still in there on the floor where it landed last night. I didn't have time to clean it up before I rushed off to see what was happening with Piper."

"I'll get that for you," Oliver says. "Just let me finish my coffee first. Didn't know if I liked it, but it's actually pretty good."

"There is no rush," she tells him. "So, Oliver, have any of your memories come back?"

"No, not that I've noticed, but I have been distracted over the past few hours. First there was your sister's accident and then, after you brought me back to your parents' house, I had another run-in with your grandmother's caregiver."

"With Paula? Now what did she do?"

"I think your suspicions about that woman are right on target," he tells her. "You asked me to observe her, and I can tell you that she seems pretty rough with your grandmother."

"How do you mean?"

"It's the way she handles her. It seems to me that your grandmother's body is in a pretty fragile state, so I would think Paula would be very careful with her."

"You would think so."

"Well, she isn't, and did you know that she straps your grandmother to the bed?"

"What? No, I did not know that."

"I saw them last night. She uses three large leather straps. When I called her out on it, she said they are standard practice to keep patients like your grandmother from getting out of bed and hurting themselves. I'm no doctor—at least, I don't think I am—but that doesn't seem right to me. She says your father knows about it. But even if he knows about the straps, he may not know how she's using them."

"Jesus. Well, I will be taking that up with Dad just as soon as I see him."

"It's best to talk to him before something serious happens," Oliver says, finishing his coffee and handing her the cup. "This was very good. I liked it very much."

Rising from the bench he adds, "Now, I'll look at that window for you. Let's make sure it's secured until we get the material to replace it."

~

As the humans disappear inside the house, the eight crows are content that she is safe with him, the one who they have chosen to be their pro-tector.

Spreading their massive wings in tandem, they leave the safety of their perches and soar upward into the cloudless sky, the sun reflecting an iridescent purplish green off their sleek, aerodynamic feathers.

These powerful birds are built for flight, but they are also made for fighting, and they know that a battle is brewing. They will be ready—this will be a fight, not only for their own lives, but also for the lives of the family.

21: Natural enemies

The crows have inhabited these lands for centuries. They have seen threats come and go and, in many cases, they have had to fight them off. But they have defended their ancestral turf against some tough adversaries, and they have persevered through the ages, in the face of some powerful foes.

When it comes to natural enemies, however, none poses a greater threat than the owls. Crows and owls are instinctively at odds, bred to be adversaries. It's in their blood.

Through the powers of a pact the crows had made with a young woman several hundred years earlier, and sometimes with the aid of allies, the crows have managed to keep their enemies at bay, but sometimes the owls feel emboldened to invade the crows' territory. Spurred on by other forces—usually human—the owls will brazenly cross the battle line.

Even today, the crows maintain their vigil. They are always on the lookout for any signs that owls may make a move and lately they have sensed a shift in the universe, a ripple in the air that informs them that something dark is just over the horizon. The recent attacks on members of the family they guard have confirmed their instincts—the owls are on the move.

But why now? And who has summoned them?

If the owls have been mobilized, that means a human is directing them. But who, the crows wonder.

Recognizing the threat, they have called on reinforcements—the protector, the one who has proven his worth in the past. He has returned and, should the owls attack, the single man and the murder of crows will be the first line of defence against the incursion.

~

Removing the black cloth Sydney had draped over the bloody remains of the owl that had crashed through the window of her front door the night before, Oliver studies the carcass. Its lifeless form intrigues him. He marvels at the bird's aerodynamic body, its size and muscular build conveying its true strength.

"I bet you were one mean son-of-a-bitch in your day," he whispers. He believes the large bird would have been a formidable opponent.

Pulling on the gloves that Sydney had provided, he says, "What in hell would have compelled you to throw your body through a glass window and sacrifice yourself like this? Whatever it was, I hope it was worth it."

As Sydney suggested, Oliver plans to take the owl's body out to the compost bin in her backyard. But he's confused because, for some reason, that particular task seems awfully familiar to him. He can't shake the feeling that he has previously done something similar, in another time…in another life.

"Okay big fella," he whispers. "It's time for you to go as I have got to get this mess cleaned up. I guess whatever force compelled you to do this will have to remain a mystery—for now, at least."

With his gloved hands, Oliver carefully slides the carcass onto a shovel and begins to rise from the floor. Suddenly he feels overwhelmed with emotions. Stumbling backwards, the hallway spinning, the walls closing in on him, he struggles to maintain his footing.

"Jesus," he whispers. Backing up against a wall, Oliver drops the shovel and braces himself as he feels his knees becoming weak.

Then everything goes black.

~

"Oliver? Are you alright?"

He recognizes the voice of Sydney Goodwin as she gently shakes him. "Are you okay, Oliver? Can you talk to me?"

He tries to focus on her words. "What?" he gasps, struggling to catch his breath. "What happened?"

"I think you passed out," she says, kneeling to check on his condition. "Are you okay?"

"Yes," he manages to answer after a few seconds. "I'm okay. Just lost my footing for a few seconds."

"Lost your footing? Is that what you think?" She shakes her head. "It did not look like that to me," she replies, slowly helping him back to his feet. "It looked like you just phased out and disappeared into yourself for a few minutes. What happened?"

"Honestly," he tells her, trying to grasp the situation, "I don't know. One minute I was fine and the next thing the whole house is spinning and I'm having a hard time trying to keep my balance. Then everything just went black."

"Come with me," Sydney says, taking his hand. "Come into the kitchen and sit down for a minute. I'll get you some water. It could be that you're dehydrated. It is pretty hot out there and those UV rays are killer at this time of year. Maybe your body's just not used to it."

"Maybe."

He allows his friend to wrap her right arm around his waist and lead him into the kitchen. Observing the surroundings, he whispers, "This is a nice place."

"Thanks," she answers while guiding him to a chair that's beside the table. "Now, I want you to sit right here until I get you some water."

Although he doesn't recognize most of the appliances in the kitchen, he can tell that the area has recently undergone some major renovations.

"I like what you've done in here."

"I like it, too. It's very comfortable." She hands him a tall glass of cold water and he quickly takes a sip.

She takes a seat across the table from him. "The kitchen and main living space were the first areas I tackled when I moved in a few years ago. I did a lot of the work myself, except for the major structural stuff, but I am really happy with how it turned out."

Oliver takes a few more sips of water. "This really hits the spot. I'm starting to feel much better already."

"You are?" She looks at him albeit suspiciously. "You're sure? Maybe I should call Dad and see what he has to say about this. It's not normal for someone to black out like that and, considering your head injury, this could be something serious. You really should have someone look at you."

"No, please don't bother your father," Oliver says, raising his right hand in a gesture of protest. "He has enough to worry about right now. It's just that, for some reason, when I bent down to clean up that mess in the hallway, all the blood suddenly rushed from head, and I got a little dizzy. It was nothing serious."

"How do you know it was nothing serious? Are you a doctor?" She pauses. "Oh, right, you don't know what you are because you can't remember anything."

"Yes, well, about that," Oliver says. "The thing is, while I don't remember too much about myself, I am fairly certain this is not the first time that I've cleaned up bodies of dead owls. It's like that situation out there in the hallway gave me a brief glimpse into my past."

She looks at him incredulously. "What are you talking about? Why in the hell would you have cleaned up dead owls before? And when?"

"I have no idea, but there was something very familiar about the process," he answers, shaking his head. "When I scooped that owl into the shovel, I suddenly had flashes of me doing the same thing before, but I don't know where it was or what happened...or when it was. But it was like I was reliving a moment from my past and I guess it all became too much for me. I think I blacked out because my mind couldn't handle the stress."

"Now that is interesting," Sydney says. "In light of everything that's happened in the last twenty-four hours, that's kind of a major coincidence, don't you think?"

Oliver nods in agreement. "And the thing is, wherever this other incident took place, the flashes were very vivid, so I am sure they are memories of something that actually happened to me."

"Do you think you've had to deal with owls before? I mean, what's their significance? And why are they showing up now?" she asks. "We've never had any problems with owls that I know of. In fact, we haven't seen any owls in these parts in many, many years, which, when you come to think about it, is kind of unusual in itself."

"I have no idea," he answers, but he believes Sydney is correct. All of this seems like more than a coincidence to him. "If I could get all of my memories back, I might be able to answer those questions."

She's about to say something more, when she feels the band on her wrist vibrate, signalling that someone is calling. Quickly slipping the sleek, paper-thin device from her pocket she scans the screen and says, "It's Dad. I should take this because he might have some news about Piper."

Oliver takes another sip of water. He relishes how refreshing the cool liquid feels as it slides down his throat. He remains quiet as Sydney takes the call from her father.

"So," she says after ending the conversation. "Dad says that Piper had to have another surgery this morning and they had to remove her spleen."

"That doesn't sound good. Is she going to be all right?"

"It's just one more thing that she's going to have fight back from," she says. "But Dad says she's doing okay right now and resting comfortably. He wondered if I could come by the hospital to be with my mother for a bit. My brother Seth won't get there until later this morning and Dad has to see his patients. He doesn't want to leave Mom alone right now as she's very upset, so I am going to the hospital to be with her."

"Yes, you should go right away."

"I want you to come with me. Dad told me that Dr. Robbie is on duty this morning and she's the one who examined you yesterday. I think she should have another look at you. The dizzy spell you just experienced might be a sign that something serious is going on with you so I think we should ask her to check you out."

Oliver sighs. "I am fine, Sydney. I think you were right about being dehydrated." Gulping down the last mouthful of water in the glass, he adds, "I feel good right now."

"That may be so, but I think you should still come with me and let Dr. Robbie have a look. You took a nasty blow to the head so there's no telling what's going on. No," she raises her hand to tell him to stop protesting and says, "You are going with me, and that's final."

He smiles and nods. He's only known this woman for about twenty-four hours, but he believes it will be futile to argue with her any further. "Okay." He throws up his hands. "You win. But first, let me get that dead owl out of your entryway. You don't want that thing lying around any longer or it will begin to get pretty ripe in this heat."

She nods. "But I can get it. I've been dealing with birds my whole life and, sadly, I've seen a lot of dead ones. I should probably take this one in for a necropsy. It might tell us what was going on with it, but I don't really have time today to go to the lab so we will have to dispose of it in the bin."

"No," Oliver says, rising from the chair. "Let me get it. I need to get my blood circulating again."

"Okay. Okay, go ahead, then, and let me know if you need anything. We'll leave for the hospital in about fifteen minutes."

~

"Well, Mr. Owl," Oliver says, lifting the lid on the compost bin. "Looks like you've reached your final destination. I don't know what you were trying to do here, but whatever it was, I hope it was worth it because you made a pretty major sacrifice."

Watching the owl's broken body slide from the shovel, leaving behind a bright streak of red, he shivers despite the oppressive humidity. As the bird's feathered remains tumble into the bin and come to rest on a pile of decaying items that he can't identify, Oliver wonders why any living creature could choose to meet such a tragic end.

"Go and meet your maker," he whispers.

Closing the lid, he's about to head back into the house when a series of loud cackling sounds stops him in his tracks.

What the hell, he thinks, quickly scanning the vicinity. The noise has chilled his blood.

He's suddenly left breathless when he spots several large crows in the spruce trees that border the back property.

"Hey, guys," he says, speaking softly. There are eight of them and they all appear to be locked in on him.

What was that Sydney said about eight crows? Something about a wish, whatever that means.

"What gives?" he asks, deciding to hold his ground. He's not sure how, but he knows he should not make any sudden moves toward the crows or the house. Instead, he remains calm and talks to the black birds.

"Do you guys want something from me?" he asks, not really expecting them to answer him.

But one of them does respond with a series of low-pitched guttural caws and cackles.

"I have no idea what you're trying to tell me," Oliver shrugs. "But I get the feeling that you want me to do something for you."

The crow cackles again.

"That's it, isn't it? You want me to do something for you but what? How am I supposed to know what you want me to do if I can't under-stand you? I know you can't talk but we have to find some way to com-municate with each other."

Oliver watches in utter amazement as the eight crows suddenly rise from their perches and glide toward him, but he doesn't feel intimidated by the large birds. Intuitively, he knows not to fear them.

He remains still as they land and surround him. The air crackles with electricity and the nerve endings in his body tingle all over, yet he is not afraid. He feels an immediate connection to them.

One of the crows—the larger one that had been attempting to com-municate with him—takes a position on the lid of the compost bin, only inches away from Oliver.

"Okay, guys, I want you to know that I mean you no harm," Oliver whispers, keeping his voice calm and mellow. "I'm just trying to figure out what in the hell is going on and how I fit into everything."

The crow closest to him caws lightly, its black, beady eyes blinking quickly.

Oliver shakes his head. "I'm sorry, but I don't understand."

The crow caws again and, this time it locks eyes with the human.

Oliver remains still, the breath catching in his throat. He remains quiet as the link between bird and man strengthens.

The stare-down continues for several minutes until Oliver hears a voice calling to him. He recognizes it as Sydney Goodwin's.

"Jesus," he says, blinking wildly and backing away from the compost bin as the crow and its seven brethren quickly leave their perches, wings flapping, and soar upward and then out of sight. "Wow," he whispers. "What in the hell just happened?"

Quickly rushing up to him, Sydney asks, "Are you okay, Oliver? When you hadn't come back, I thought I had better come and check on you just in case you had blacked out again."

"I'm okay," he tells her, shaking his head. Swallowing and gasping for air at the same time, he adds, "I just need to catch my breath."

She pauses, studies his face for a few seconds and then says, "Honestly, Oliver. You don't look okay. What in the hell was that all about?"

Taking him by the arm to make sure he doesn't stumble, she adds, "I have worked with crows my whole life and I have rarely seen them do anything like that before, not with a human. I have never seen them be so brazen that they would get so close to anyone. That was extraordinary."

Oliver takes a few seconds to gather his thoughts, and then says, "I think we should go the hospital now."

"Are you sure you're okay?" she asks. "I mean, that was pretty weird, but also spectacular at the same time. From where I was standing, it was almost like they were communicating with you. Were they?"

Avoiding her question, he heads toward the front of the house. "Come on Sydney," he says. "We don't want to keep your mother waiting too long."

"Oliver," she replies, keeping pace with him. "What aren't you telling me?"

"Nothing," he answers, stepping quickly, "I just think it's time to go. Clearly, I need to see a doctor."

22: Defining the mission

The unexpected and, without a doubt, abnormal interaction with the crows has left Oliver shaken. He feels like he's trapped in a powerful vortex and his entire world—or what he knows of his world—is spinning out of control. Not that he's sure he ever had control.

He may not remember much about his past life, but, thanks to the crows and whatever they did to him this morning, his purpose for being here at this precise time has suddenly come more sharply into focus.

Damn, he thinks while waiting in the examination room for the doctor to return with his latest test results. *I liked it better when I didn't know what the crows wanted from me. Now that I know what they want me to do, I hope I'm ready for the mission.*

Biting his lower lip, he closes his eyes and lies back flat on the gurney. If only he could sleep. He is tired, his body feeling like it has been put through a blender and his mind feeling as though it has been kicked around like a soccer ball. He takes a deep breath, and sighs forcefully.

"Well, Mr. Lewis," Dr. Isabel Robbie says a few minutes later upon entering the room. She is carrying a digital device.

Oliver assumes that the results from the tests he recently underwent are stored on the sleek silver tablet and sits up to hear the news. It is a device he does not recognize; but then again, he doesn't recognize most of the apparatuses he's seen or encountered upon his return from wherever he's been for almost four decades.

"How are you feeling now?" the doctor asks, offering him a friendly smile, and he immediately feels at ease in her presence. He liked her from the first minute he met her yesterday. For some reason, she makes him feel comfortable, like he has been reacquainted with a long-lost friend or family member who he hasn't seen in quite some time.

"Not too bad, I guess," he lies, as he's actually feeling more than a little overwhelmed by his predicament. "But I suppose that actually depends upon what you're about to tell me my tests have revealed."

If he were to be truthful with the doctor, he'd tell her that he's feeling anxious and confused. First the dizzy and fainting spell and then the run-in with the crows, followed by the battery of tests he underwent after Sydney brought him to the hospital has left him feeling drained.

"I haven't had any more dizzy spells so that's a good thing," he adds, while smiling in an effort to put on a brave front. "I think I'll live, doctor."

"That is a very good thing, Mr. Lewis," Dr. Robbie says, making notes on the device as she approaches the examination table. "I have reviewed the results of the tests I ordered, and I am happy to tell you that everything looks perfectly fine at this point. I was worried that perhaps there was some bleeding around the brain, but the scans have not revealed anything that would be reason for concern."

"Thank you doctor," he says with a sigh. "But if everything looks normal, then why would I get dizzy and why would I black out like I did at Sydney's house?"

"There are lots of reasons for that to happen," the doctor answers, taking a seat beside him. "For one thing, your blood pressure is extremely low, so that would account for the dizziness. It also appears your electrolytes and blood sugars are very low as well, so they most likely contributed to the blackout. And of course, this extreme heat doesn't help with any of that. And, dare I ask, did you get any sleep last night?"

"No." He shakes his head. "Maybe an hour at the most."

"Well, that's not good. Extreme exhaustion will also cause you to experience dizziness and you could also black out," Dr. Robbie says. "You suffered a major blow to your head in the accident or whatever caused your injuries, so you need to allow your body to heal. I know you've heard this before, but I'm going to say it again—if you push your body too hard, it will be rebel against you."

"So now what?" he asks.

"Well, normally, after what you've gone through, I would recommend that we keep you in the hospital for a day or two of observation and rest. But considering that you disappeared yesterday before we had chance to treat you, I'm not sure that's really a viable option." She smiles wryly at him, and he immediately feels sheepish for his actions.

She adds, "I don't see any sense in admitting you to hospital if you're just going to run away again. If I admit you today, what guarantee do I have that you will stay put?"

"Yeah." Oliver nods. Casting his eyes to the corner of the room to avoid direct contact with the doctor, he says, "Sorry about that. I appreciate everything that you were doing for me, but I had to get out of this place because I felt like I was smothering, like the walls were closing in on me. I just couldn't breathe."

"Be that as it may, Mr. Lewis, running away from the people who were trying to help you is no way to show your gratitude for what they've done and, certainly, it's no way to get the help you need," she replies. "Now, do you have any further questions before we discuss what happens next?"

"Just one, but it's not about me."

"What is it?" she asks. "Something else bothering you?"

Oliver studies her, searching for the right words, and then says, "Please excuse me if this sounds too bold, Doctor. However, I have been wondering about something since you examined me yesterday and the curiosity is getting the best of me, so now I have got to ask—have we met before? For some reason, you look very familiar to me, and I can't figure out why."

Dr. Robbie shakes her head "You look vaguely familiar to me, too, but I am sure we have not met before yesterday." Pondering his question further, she adds, "I am pretty good with names and faces, so I am positive that if we had met, I would remember it."

Oliver looks her in the eyes and then replies, "It's the strangest thing, but I swear I know you from somewhere. The feeling is just so intense I... I can't explain it."

"Well, you are suffering from a head injury and your memories are all jumbled up, so it is possible that you're just confused," Dr. Robbie explains. "But as I said, I'm positive that our paths have not previously crossed. My memory is fairly intact so I am sure I would remember if we had met."

"Maybe we haven't met, but I swear that I am remembering someone who looks an awful like you," Oliver says. "Do you have siblings, a sister perhaps? Is it possible I could have met her somewhere?"

She shakes her head again. "I do not have any siblings. It has always just been me and my mother."

"And what's your mother's name?"

She hesitates, studies him and then, taking a deep breath, says, "I don't usually share personal information with patients, but for some reason I like you and I feel I can trust you, so I'll tell you. My mother's name is Anna—Dr. Anna Robbie. But she is considerably older than you, so I am sure you wouldn't know her. She's retired now—has been for a number of years—and living in a condo in Halifax."

"Man." Oliver shakes his head. "This is going to kill me. That name doesn't sound familiar to me at all. What about your father? You said it was just you and your mother. He wasn't in the picture?"

"I didn't know my father, and my mother didn't talk about him much when I was growing up," Dr. Robbie says, and Oliver can see that his question has hit a nerve. "All I know is that he just disappeared one day with no explanation. We hardly ever discussed my father, but my mother says he didn't even know that she was pregnant with me when he disappeared. I never met him."

"And what was his name?"

"That's enough questions, Mr. Lewis," Dr. Robbie says abruptly. "Let's get back to the important business. Can I trust you to take better care of yourself if I let you go home today?"

Oliver is about to answer when Dr. Alex Goodwin enters the room.

"No, Isabel," he says, throwing a smile at Oliver. "I don't think you can trust him to look out for himself, and if you try to keep him in the hospital, it's obvious that he's not going to stay put. But you can trust me. I am going to make sure he gets back to my place safe and sound, has a good meal and then goes to bed to get some sleep. I'll give him something to knock him out if I have to."

"I don't know, Alex," Dr. Robbie says. "He doesn't strike me as the type of person who will obey doctor's orders."

"He'll listen to me," Alex says, nodding toward Oliver. "Won't you, Oliver? You will follow my orders, correct? Food and rest is the order of the day for you. No more overexerting yourself until we are sure your body is healed."

"Yes," Oliver reluctantly answers. "I guess so."

"You guess so?" Dr. Robbie asks. "That's not inspiring much confidence in me. It's important that you take care of yourself, or you will relapse. Let's understand that. So please, do yourself a favour, Mr. Lewis. Go home with Dr. Goodwin and follow his directions. Can you do that?"

"He can and he will," Alex assures his colleague.

"Okay, Alex. If that's what you want," Dr. Robbie says. She hands him the digital tablet and adds, "I have other patients to check on, including your daughter, so I am going to leave Mr. Lewis in your care."

"Thank you, Isabel," Alex says. "I'll take it from here."

"Man, Alex," Oliver begins once Dr. Robbie has disappeared. "I'm glad that you showed up. I have something important to tell you. I've had a breakthrough."

"Just a second, Oliver," Alex says, studying his friend's chart on the tablet. He adds, "Isabel isn't wrong. While your tests don't show any major physical injuries, it is very clear that your brain has taken a beating, so you really do need to give it some time to rest or you may cause irreparable damage. If you want to get better, it's important that you follow her advice."

"Yes, Alex, I promise I will follow your orders," Oliver says, growing impatient with his friend's nonchalant reaction to his proclamation that he's had some sort of breakthrough. "I really need to tell you something and it's important that you listen."

"So is your health, Oliver," Alex says, turning to look him in the eyes. "If you don't take care of yourself, you won't be able to help anyone."

Oliver nods. "I promise that I will do everything you tell me to do."

"Good. Now, what's going on that's got you so fired up?" Alex asks. "Have you regained some of your memories?"

"Not so much my memories," Oliver answers. "But I have made a connection with the crows and now I understand what I'm supposed to do."

"I'm listening," Alex says, placing the tablet on a nearby counter and hanging onto his friend's every word. "If the crows have finally reached out to you then this can't be good. I know how they work."

"It's not good. In fact, it's really bad. The crows have told me that you and your family are under attack."

He can see that the news hits his friend hard.

"From whom?"

"It's not a who," Oliver says, his voice becoming low but the tone becoming more urgent. "It's a what."

Alex frowns. "Are you telling me what I think you're telling me? Have those fucking owls returned?"

Oliver nods. "According to the message I got from the crows, the owls are coming after you with deadly intentions."

"God-damn it," Alex says, his voice nothing more than a whisper. "Why now? Why after all these years?"

"Now that is something I can't tell you, but I got the message from the crows loud and clear—I am here to protect you at all costs. Apparently, that is my mission. That is why I'm here."

Alex studies his friend and then slowly says, "That makes sense. You saved me from the owls before, and if those bloody birds are coming after me again, then it stands to reason that the crows have summoned you to do the same thing again. After all, you are—"

"I am your protector," Oliver finishes his friend's sentence. "That means it's my duty to stop the owls from doing whatever it is they are trying to do."

"And what do you think that is?"

"Based on what the crows told me, they are not only trying to kill you, but they want to wipe out your entire family."

"Shit," Alex says, and Oliver can see that his friend is visibly shaken. "I wish Aunt Zoey was here right now. She would know what to do."

"Sorry, Alex, but I don't know this Aunt Zoey you keep talking about. However, whoever she is, something is telling me that she would urge you to pay careful attention to the crows, because they seem to have the answers."

"I have been following the crows my whole life and I know they are always looking out for me," Alex says. "But I have to admit that the sudden arrival of the owls has put me on edge. I'm usually more grounded than I feel right now and I can tell that something has tipped the scale. The mere fact that the crows somehow performed a miracle and brought you back from wherever you were for the past thirty-seven years is reason to be alarmed."

"It does sound pretty far-fetched when you put it like that," Oliver agrees.

"I sense that the earth has tipped off its axis," Alex says, "and is spinning wildly out of control. Everything is uneven, warped almost. I'm very worried about this development."

"I'm worried too, but we have to hold it together and, if we are going to get you through this, we have to help each other," Oliver says. "Maybe if I could regain more of my memories then I would be of more help, but right now, all I've got to go by is my gut, and my instincts are telling me that we have to brace for something major."

Alex nods. "But there is something else that's bothering me."

"And what's that?"

"Well, the last time the owls came after me, they were compelled into action by members of the Merrick family. I always thought that family had been wiped out. But if the owls are back, does it mean that there's a Merrick lurking around here somewhere?"

Oliver shakes his head. "I don't remember the Merrick family so I'm not sure I can help with that question."

"Remember when you told me about that dream you had involving the people fighting on the bridge and I told you that it wasn't a dream and, in fact, you were actually having memories of Myles Merrick and his son Ozzie attacking me?"

Oliver nods. "I remember but I still don't understand because it's all very hazy to me."

"It's a lot to wrap your head around, I know," Alex says. "But that's the family I'm talking about and they, through a centuries-old pact, are in an allegiance with the owls. Together, the Merrick family and the owls have made it their mission to go after members of my family and the crows that protect us."

"Is it possible that the owls are working on their own without any members of this Merrick family being involved?"

"I suppose that's possible," Alex says, "but until we know for sure what we are dealing with, we won't be able to let our guard down. We have to keep the members of my family very close to us and watch them all. If I'm on the owls' radar, then they might try getting to me by going through any one of them."

"With the attacks on Sydney and Piper last night, we've already seen what they will do. It's almost certain that they won't stop at you."

"I'm worried, Oliver," Alex says. "I know what those God-forsaken owls put me through the last time they came after me and I don't want to go through that again, but it bothers me more that any member of my family could be in danger."

23: Targets

Observing the eight crows—some of the largest and blackest birds that he's seen in a long time—through his office window, Alex takes a deep breath and considers everything that has transpired over the past twenty-four hours since Oliver reappeared.

What in the hell is going on around here? he wonders, watching the birds as they pounce over the recently mowed grass. He isn't sure if the crows are playing or if they're here on serious business.

Whatever they're doing out there, I honestly believe they are watching over my family and me. That should give me some comfort, so why do I feel like the walls are closing in on me?

He is certain this tight feeling in his chest is connected to the sudden appearance of the owls. He hasn't thought about them in a very long time, but now he is certain the powerful birds are coming after him and, even more alarming to him, they appear to be coming after his family. That fact pisses him off and frightens him at the same time.

One of the crows chases another over the grass in pursuit of something that Alex cannot distinguish, but he concludes that, whatever it is, it must be something to eat. Smiling at their antics he thinks, *Those birds have insatiable appetites.*

But he also knows the crows will go after their enemies, and that those enemies include anyone or anything that would harm or threaten him. In many ways, he's always been relieved that the crows have been looking out for him his entire life, but in other ways, it has been a curse. He knows he wouldn't have to rely on the crows to protect him if he wasn't surrounded by imminent danger, a danger that is the result of a pact that was forged hundreds of years before he was born.

Still, I'd rather have them on my side than have them as enemies.

Watching their graceful movements as the eight crows, the sunlight bouncing of their ebony feathers, go about their business on the lawn, he thinks their beauty can be deceiving. *I seriously would not want them coming after me.*

Alex has seen the crows in action. He knows how powerful and cunning they can be—and deadly, if they're pushed or threatened. *Tough adversaries, that's for sure.*

He's also seen the owls in action, and he also knows what they are capable of doing. *They are not to be messed with*, he thinks. *It would be foolish not to take them seriously.*

"Nope," he whispers. "I will never do that."

"You will never do what?"

Startled, he spins around to see his daughter standing behind him.

"Sydney! I didn't hear you come in. You scared me half to death. Did you ever thinking of knocking before you enter a room?"

"I would have." She smiles playfully. "But the door was wide open so I didn't figure I needed to knock. If you didn't want anyone to come in, I assumed the door would have been closed."

"Right, of course." Alex sighs. "It's all good, honey. Guess I'm just a little jumpy."

Forcing a smile for his daughter, he asks, "What's happening with your sister? Any news?"

"She's still sleeping, and Mom is still right there by her side."

"As I would expect."

"Seth just arrived, so I wanted to give them some space. I also wanted to check on Oliver. How's he doing?"

"He's okay." Nodding towards a door in the corner of his office, Alex adds, "He's just in the bathroom. He needed to freshen up after we finished with Dr. Robbie so I told him he could use my private washroom."

"Look at you." She smirks. "You doctors are so important that you have your own private washrooms."

"That we are." Alex smiles smugly and shoots his daughter a wink. "We are treated pretty well around here."

"As you should be."

"There are days. Seriously, though, how's your mother holding up?"

"You know Mom. She has her moments but now that Seth is there, I think she's doing better. He brought Elliot with him, so she's in her glory having her grandson to fuss over," Sydney says. "So, did you have any luck reaching Bailey? I'm sure she's too busy to come home, but at least she should know what's going on with Piper."

"She's travelling with the minister out of the country right now—some place overseas—but I did leave a message on her phone for her to call me just as soon as she can," Alex says. "God know where they are or what they're doing, so I don't even know for sure if she received the message."

"I'm sure she will call when she gets chance," Sydney assures her father. Then she asks, "So now, what's the plan?"

"I think I should stick around here at least until Piper wakes up, so I can keep track of how she's doing. I also want to be here for your mother in case something goes wrong, but I'm hoping you can take Oliver back to the house and make sure he gets something to eat and some rest. He's still in recovery so it's important that he takes care of himself, and I don't trust him to do that without someone watching over him."

"I don't know your friend all that well, Dad, but it seems to me that's a tall order."

Alex nods. "But it's important that he follow these orders if he's going to recover from his injuries. I need him to be ready for whatever is coming at us."

His comment catches Sydney by surprise. "That's an ominous thing to say. What do you mean by that?"

He shrugs, realizing that he has said something that he didn't mean to say. He knows his daughter is a sharp one and she'll pick up on even the smallest detail. He quickly says, "Nothing. I'm just on edge worrying about everything that's happened over the past day and a half. It's a lot to take in."

"It sure is but it sounded like a whole lot more than that to me."

"Me too," Oliver adds, entering Alex's office from the washroom. "Alex, I think you should tell your daughter everything. Best that she knows the whole story, don't you think?"

"Really, Oliver?" Alex says, throwing a sharp glance at his friend. He wasn't sure if his daughter could handle the whole story but now, he fears Oliver has forced him into telling her the family secrets.

"Everything?" Sydney asks, eyeing her father closely. "What does Oliver mean by *everything*?"

"Honestly, honey, it's a lot to digest," Alex says. "I'm just not sure this is the right time to get into all of that ancient history."

"Considering everything that's going on around here right now," Oliver says, "don't you think this is the perfect time to lay it all on the table? I've only known your daughter for a day, but I'm pretty sure she can handle the truth."

Sydney speaks up. "I don't know what's going on between you two, but just tell me the big secret once and for all."

Alex exhales with a force. He throws another sharp glare at Oliver, but he knows it's time to let his daughter in on the family secret.

"Okay. Okay," he says, bowing to the pressure. Speaking quickly and efficiently, but not meeting his daughter's eyes, he goes over the feud that has gone on for centuries between the crows and the owls and, by proxy, between the Merrick family and their own.

"For God's sake, Dad," Sydney says. Her agitated reaction is exactly what he was expecting. "Why didn't you say anything about this before?"

"I didn't want you to worry," he says, his voice calm and mellow. He knows his daughter is right and that he should not have kept this information from his children. Trying to sooth the sting, he adds, "Besides, honey, we haven't seen any owls around these parts in a very long time, so it didn't seem like there was anything to worry about."

Oliver adds, "But obviously, they have returned and, clearly, they mean business. It's important that we be ready for them whenever they come after us."

"Are you in danger, Dad?" Sydney asks. "Are we all in danger?"

"I would say there is a great deal of danger for all of us," Alex says. "And truthfully, I think the crows are also worried, and that's why they've brought Oliver back into this."

"So, if I understand this correctly," she replies, glancing at Oliver, "it's his job to protect you?"

"And the family," Alex quickly adds.

"So, what makes him so special that you think he can protect all of us against the evil that you say is compelling the owls?" she asks.

"His role in all of this was determined many years ago by circumstances beyond our control. Besides, I've seen him take on the owls before. I know he can handle this."

Addressing Oliver, Sydney asks, "Does that explain the strange behaviour I saw this morning between you and the crows?"

Oliver shrugs. "I don't remember anything that your father is describing, and I'm still trying to understand all of this myself, but I would say yes. The crows were reaching out to me and, in that moment, we had a definite connection. I can understand how strange that must have looked to you."

"Strange is an understatement," Sydney says. "I've never seen anything like that before. It was amazing and, if I'm being perfectly honest, a little scary."

"Sorry, but I'm still trying to figure it all out," Oliver says.

"I've been around crows since I was born, or so it seems, and I've made them my life's work. I've been fascinated by them ever since I was a child and now it appears there's reason for that. I thought it was just because Dad always seemed so connected to them, but now I understand that connection goes much deeper than I could have ever imagined."

"Yes, Sydney," her father says, "and I'm sorry I kept this from you. But I hope you see that I had my reasons,"

Taking a deep breath, he adds, "I see now I was wrong to do keep these secrets from you. I see that I should have told you and the family about this much sooner than today, but I really thought there was no immediate threat. I thought the owls had been neutralized a long time ago."

"Yeah, well, clearly that didn't happen. So, the bigger question is, what now? If the owls are coming after us, as they appear to be doing, what do we do?"

"At this point," Oliver adds, "it's important to go on the defensive. It's not that I can remember much about the last time your father says that I did battle with the owls, but it seems logical that a good defence is imperative."

"I really think the only thing we can do is try to be aware of what's happening around us," Alex agrees. "We don't know where the attacks are coming from or who is pulling the strings. Someone is rallying the owls and issuing these commands. It's hard to mount an effective offence if you don't know where to direct your efforts."

"So what? We just sit here and wait for them to make the next move?" Sydney asks. "I'm not sure that's the best strategy. My instincts are telling me that whenever someone—or, in this case, something—threatens you, the worst approach is to sit back and wait for them to attack. If we can strike the owls first, maybe we can neutralize them before they come after us."

"The problem is," Alex replies, acknowledging his daughter's perspective, "that we have no idea who is behind these attacks. How do we strike an unseen enemy? Where do we find them?"

"Your father is right, Sydney," Oliver says. "We have to lure them out."

"So, what are you saying?" she asks. "That we use one of us as bait?"

"That might work," Alex agrees. "But if we were to do that, I can assure you, it wouldn't be one of you guys we would be using as bait. It would be me."

"Come on Dad," Sydney protests. "I'm no slouch. I can handle myself around a few birds."

"No," Oliver says, shaking his head. "I don't think you can. You have no idea how formidable those owls can be. Based upon what little bit I can recall, combined with what I've seen happening around here over the past day, I believe the owls will be tough adversaries. It will be misguided to underestimate them."

"There's no doubt about that," Alex says, nodding in agreement. "But the bigger problem that I keep coming back to is the question of who is really behind this. Maybe the owls are acting alone, but I hardly think so. If the owls are in attack mode, it is because someone has called them out. Someone is making this happen and I think the only way to deal with the owl problem is to find whoever is issuing the orders."

"That's a tall order, Dad," Sydney says. "We don't have anything to go on except some sort of ancient family pact that, quite frankly, sounds more like science fiction than fact to me."

"Don't," Alex fires back at his daughter, his tone conveying the seriousness of the situation. "Please, Sydney, don't make light of things you do not understand. These bonds run deep in our family, and they have seen us through some very challenging and difficult times, so don't shrug them off just because you can't understand them."

"Sorry, Dad," she replies. "But you have to admit that it all seems rather fantastical. Maybe if you had told me about this before today, I would have had more time to digest the facts, but right now, honestly, I'm finding it all very difficult to wrap my head around."

"Listen you two," Oliver interrupts. "This is not the time to argue amongst ourselves. If we are going to flush out whoever is behind these attacks and defeat the owls, then we have to be united. We can't afford to show any weakness right now, not with the owls mustering for attack."

"Of course," Alex agrees after considering his friend's observation. "Fighting with each other won't help us deal with the problem."

Sydney nods and adds, "So, like I asked a few minutes ago, what now?"

"I suggest that we stick to our original plan," Alex says. "I will remain here with your mother until we get a better understanding of how Piper is doing. Sydney, you go back home with Oliver and help him get settled down. If he's going to be effective in helping us to neutralize this threat, he needs to get some rest so that he can start to recover. We need him to be at his best if we have any hopes of defeating the owls."

Turning to Oliver, he adds, "I need you to do this. You need to go with Sydney and do as I've asked. You have to let the healing process begin."

"I'm fine," Oliver protests. "You don't have to worry about me."

"No Oliver," Sydney says. "Dad is right. It's clear to me that you need to get some rest, so let's go back to the house and I'll help you get settled. Besides, I want to see how Grandma Sam is doing."

"Grandma Sam?" Alex asks. "What's going on with your grandmother?"

Sydney says, "Nothing. I just meant that I wanted to drop in to say hello."

"Are you sure?" Alex asks, studying his daughter. "I am sensing that there's something more going on than you are telling me. Is everything okay?"

"Yes, Dad. I haven't seen her yet today, but I am guessing everything is fine."

As the band on his wrist beings to vibrate, signalling an incoming call, Alex decides not to press his daughter on the issue. But he will bring it up again at some point when things settle down. If she has concerns, he needs to hear them.

Glancing at the wrist device, Alex says, "That's Bailey finally getting back to me. I better take this. You two get going but watch yourselves and let's keep in touch."

"About that," Oliver says to Sydney as they leave Alex's office. "If I'm going to keep in touch with you and your dad, then I will need to have some kind of communication device."

"For sure," Sydney says. "Let's stop by my office. It's on the way to my parents' house. I'm sure I have a spare communicator there that you can use."

"Perfect," Oliver replies, adding, "For what it's worth, I won't let your grandmother out of my sight. Now that we know the owls are after your entire family, it's possible that Samantha will also be a target. I promise that I won't let anything happen to her."

"Thanks, Oliver." Sydney smiles, walking down the hospital corridor beside her newly-minted friend. "I appreciate that because I must admit this entire situation has me totally freaked out, and I'm not sure what to expect. It's a lot to digest all at once."

"I'm sure it is," Oliver says. "But remember, you are not in this alone. The important thing is to be on your toes. Never let your guard down. Do not make yourself vulnerable. Do not become an easy target, or the owls will recognize your weakness and come after you."

24: So far, so good

"How's she doing?" Alex asks, taking a place next to his wife, where she holds vigil beside their daughter's hospital bed. "I was talking to Isabel about Piper's condition. She told me there wasn't much change but that she's still stable, so that's a good thing."

"I don't know, Alex," Bree whispers. "She hasn't woken up yet and, to me, it looks like she's hardly breathing. I am very scared for her."

"That's normal, honey. They are keeping her sedated because of the pain and to prevent her from moving around too much so that she doesn't aggravate her injuries," he says, taking Bree's hand and squeezing it gently. "It's actually a good thing that she's so still, considering the damage that the accident caused but give it a few more hours and I'm sure she'll start to come around. That's when we'll get a better idea of how she's doing."

"Hi, Dad."

Quickly throwing a glance around the modestly-decorated yet peaceful hospital room, Alex smiles as he makes eye contact with his son, who had arrived while he was seeing to Oliver in the emergency department.

"Seth," he says, reaching out to give his son a hug. "My boy, I am so happy to see you. And I hear Elliot is with you. Where is my grandson?"

"The nice nurse took him down to the cafeteria to get a snack," answers the tall and wiry young man with the dirty blond hair. "Sorry, I can't remember her name."

"That would be Jessica Young. She's very nice," Alex says. "Elliot will have fun with her. She's excellent with children."

"Well, you know Elliot. We no sooner got here when he said he was hungry." Seth chuckles. "He didn't even take time to visit with his grandmother, the little devil."

Alex laughs. "Yup, that sounds like Elliot. Well, no worries. I'll catch up with him later, but I'm relieved that you are here. Sorry it must be under these circumstances."

"Of course, Dad. I'm happy I could come to be with you and mom," Seth says. "Besides, you had to know there was no way I would stay in the city with Piper being in such a serious condition. Is she going to be okay?"

"We hope so," Alex answers with a weak smile. As a doctor he knows it's best to deal with facts, so he adds, "We still don't know the long-term implications, because she suffered some pretty serious internal injuries in the accident. So, for now, unfortunately, it's a waiting game."

"God," Seth says under his breath. "I feel so useless just standing around here. Is there anything I can do?"

"The doctors have done everything they can possibility do for her, so it's in the hands of a higher power, whoever that is," Alex tells his son. "But the important thing is that you're here for your sisters and your mother. They all need your support right now."

"And what about you, Dad?" Seth asks. "Do you need anything?"

Alex takes in a deep breath and exhales forcefully. "Not really," he says. "I just want Piper to be okay and I want my family to be safe. That's all I ask."

"Speaking of family, where did Sydney get to?" Seth asks. "She was here one minute and then she just up and disappeared."

"She will be back shortly. She just had to drive a friend back to our place and then do a couple of errands for me, but she won't be long. I know she's anxious to spend some time with you and Elliot."

Seth nods. "She rushed out of here so quickly when I arrived that we barely had time to say hi to each other."

"It's a hectic time around here," Alex tells him. He's about to elaborate when a knock interrupts the conversation.

"Dr. Goodwin?" It's Isaac Benjamin, Sydney's former boyfriend and research partner.

Stopping just outside the doorway, he says, "Sorry to interrupt you, sir, but can I please come in? I want to find out how Piper is doing."

"This is not a good time right now, Isaac," Alex tells the young man who, he thinks, with his height and dirty blond hair, looks a lot like Seth. They could pass for brothers in the right lighting conditions.

Alex had never really noticed before today, but he thinks there is an uncanny resemblance between the two young men, perhaps because of the subdued light in the room and the added stress of the situation. Regardless, he doesn't want Isaac anywhere near his daughter.

"That's not a good idea." he says. "It would be better for everyone if you came back another time," he says. "Maybe once Piper has had chance to recover."

"Sure, if that's what you think is best. But can you please tell me how she's doing?" Isaac asks, glancing at the motionless young woman in the hospital bed who is hooked up to a series of tubes and wires. "Can you at least tell me that much?"

"I don't want to discuss it right now," Alex replies. "Now, I think you should just leave."

"Oh, for God's sake, Alex," Bree says, interrupting her husband before he can launch in a tirade. "Just let the young man come in for a few minutes. Can't you see that he's worried about Piper?"

Isaac remains stationed halfway in the room and halfway in the corridor, looking lost and confused.

Alex continues, staring directly as Isaac. "It's not good for Piper to have a lot of confusion around her while she's recovering. She needs to concentrate on getting better and that means the best thing you can do for her right now is leave her alone."

"Come on Alex. I don't really think one more person in the room is going to cause that much confusion for Piper," Bree argues, adding, "If you think it's going to be too much for her to allow Isaac to have a quick visit, why don't you step out into the hallway for a few minutes to let this young man come in?"

Glancing from his wife to the visitor, Alex sighs and finally gives in. "Very well. You've got five minutes, young man, and for the record, I'm not going anywhere."

"Thank you, Dr. Goodwin," Isaac answers, cautiously entering the room and slowly making his way toward the bed. "I promise I will be very quiet."

"Don't expect Piper to talk to you," Alex warns. "She is still very heavily sedated so she may not even be aware that you're even in the room."

"Don't worry about him. He's being an overly protective father," Bree says, smiling at Isaac and reaching out to take the young man's hand." She takes a few steps back from the bed to let him get closer. "Come right up here beside her. I am sure Piper will know you're here."

"Thank you, Mrs. Goodwin," he says, his voice hardly a whisper. "I have been very worried about her ever since Sydney told me about the accident."

"You were talking to Sydney about the accident?" Alex asks. "What else did she tell you?"

"She told me that Piper had been seriously injured and that it was touch and go right now," Isaac cautiously answers. "And—"

"And what?" Alex interrupts. "What else did Sydney tell you?"

"For God's sake, Alex. What are you doing?" Bree says sharply. "Don't be so hateful. Can't you see this young man is worried about our daughter?"

"Seriously, Dr. Goodwin," Isaac replies, keeping his voice low and even keeled. "I really didn't come here today to cause any problems. I was just worried about Piper. We are friends and I want to see if she's going to be okay. That's all."

"I think you're more than just friends, aren't you Isaac?" Bree asks, her gentle voice a welcomed alternative to Alex's overbearing tone. "If you're worrying if my husband and I know about you and Piper being together, you don't have to fret. We know."

"Yes, we do," Alex speaks up. "And we don't like it."

"I never said any such a thing," Bree says, her words conveying annoyance with her husband even though her voice remains calm and mellow. "You and Piper are adults, so it is none of our business. And," she smiles, "we also know that Piper is pregnant."

Isaac nods, looking uncertain. "Is the baby okay? Did it survive the accident?"

"The baby is okay, for now," Bree tells him, giving him a gentle hug. Relief washes over Isaac's face. "But there could still be complications. The doctors had to remove Piper's spleen, and they aren't sure how that will impact the baby, or even if it will have any effect. But so far, so good."

"I didn't know she was pregnant," Isaac tells Bree as tears well in his eyes and trickle down his cheeks. "If I had known, I promise I would have done things differently."

"You didn't know Piper was pregnant?" Alex jumps in again. "How could you not have known?"

"Because Piper didn't tell me," Isaac answers. "I mean it's not like we were *trying* to have a baby or anything. It was an accident."

"An accident? These things don't just happen, Isaac," Alex says sharply. "How can two mature, well-educated adults have an accident like that these days? With all the modern birth control methods at your disposal, there is no such thing as an *accident*."

"Come on Alex," Bree says. "Do you think this is really the time and place to have this argument? I thought you were smarter than that. What if Piper can hear you? Do you want her to know how angry you are? It's not a good look for you."

Alex considers his wife's comments and then, talking directly to Isaac, adds, "The clock is ticking, mister. Your five minutes are almost over, so say whatever it is you have to say and then be on your way."

"Thank you, Dr. Goodwin," Isaac says, turning back to Piper. "And thank you, Mrs. Goodwin. I know I've made some mistakes, but I want to be here for Piper and the baby. I hope I have the chance to tell her how I really feel."

"Come on, Isaac," Alex speaks up again. He knows he should bite his tongue, as Bree will not be happy with him if he continues to inflame the situation, but he just can't stop himself. "If you really cared anything for our daughters you would not have treated Sydney so badly."

"You are right," Isaac says, backing away from Piper's bed. Wiping away the tears, he adds, "I did use Sydney badly and I regret that. She didn't deserve to be disrespected like that. She is a very special young woman—they are both very special."

"Where are you going Isaac?" Bree asks. "You don't have to leave. Don't listen to anything Dr. Goodwin says. He's just worried about Piper and doesn't know what he's saying."

"No, Mrs. Goodwin," Isaac says, moving toward the door. "I think it is time for me leave. When Piper wakes up, please let her know that I was here and tell her that she can call me if she wants to see me, or maybe if she just wants to talk. I don't want to pressure her, so I'll wait to hear from her."

When Isaac has left, Bree turns to her husband. "There. See what you've done?"

"What I've done?" Alex is not impressed with his wife's tone. "What about what *he's* done?"

"You just can't let the girls run their own lives, can you? You do remember that they are adults, don't you? They aren't our little girls anymore and we can't take care of them forever."

"Don't start with me," Alex says, raising his right hand to end the conversation. "I don't like that young man for how he treated Sydney in the past, and now he's sunk his claws into Piper. Truthfully, I have never cared much for him, and I have not made any secret about that." He takes a deep breath and adds, "I do not apologize for how I feel."

"I am not asking you to apologize for anything," Bree fires back. "I know you better than to expect an apology from you, and I know that when it comes to protecting your children, you will stand your ground, like the king lion. I respect that, but you'll never admit that maybe you were wrong."

"Okay. Okay you two," Seth says. "Let's stop this right now before we have a full-blown argument or someone says something they might regret.”

"Listen to your son, Alex," Bree says. "He makes a lot of sense. He's a smart man."

"I don't know about all of that," Alex says with a rueful smile, reaching out to hug his wife. "But yes, he is a smart man, and I am sorry if I upset you, but I cannot forgive Isaac, not after what he's done to our girls."

"I just don't think this is the time to make an issue out of it." She returns his hug. "We have enough to deal with right now, so it seems to me that having an argument in the hospital is not the right thing to do."

Alex nods. "You are right about that. But," he takes a deep breath and then adds, "this is not over, not by a long shot."

25: Sending a message

"Shit," Sydney says, approaching the wide-open door of her lab and offices. "Shit. Shit. Shit. This is not good."

"No?" Oliver asks, following closely behind his friend. "This door isn't usually open?"

"No, absolutely not. This door is never left open. Even when there are people here working during the day, the door is always closed and locked for safety reasons," she explains. "You need a passcode to get inside and not too many people know the code; just my crew, the cleaners, security and the building owner. If you don't have the code, then one of us has to let you in."

"Is it possible that the last person here yesterday left the door open?" Oliver asks, cautiously approaching the door. "Maybe it's as simple as someone forgetting to lock up after work."

"Of course, it's possible," Sydney concedes although she is clearly reluctant to place blame on one her colleagues. "But I don't think it's very likely. We've been here for a number of years, and everyone knows the drill. It's second nature to all of us, and I just can't see anyone breaking the protocols now, not after all this time. That just would not be like any of them."

"Everyone makes mistakes, Sydney."

"That is true, but I have come to trust the people I work with. I learned a long time ago, that you have to put your faith in other people. I just can't see one of my staff making such a mistake."

"I understand that desire to trust people," Oliver says. "But I also don't think you should dismiss anything. People—even people we believe we can trust—will sometimes do things that we aren't expecting them to do, so I'm just suggesting that you should keep an open mind. That's all. I am not accusing anyone of anything."

"Right. I get that." She nods. "Let's go inside," she says, slipping through the open door. "I need to check on things."

"Just be careful," Oliver cautions. "We don't know if there's anyone in there, and if there is anyone lurking around inside, we don't know whether they are dangerous. It's not smart to just go barging—damn it."

Seeing that she has entered the office before he can finish his sentence, Oliver shrugs and follows close behind.

Of course, she wouldn't go slowly, he thinks. *What was I thinking?*

"Holy Jesus. Who would do something like this?" Sydney asks, upon entering the large room that has been her base of operations ever since she returned to town several years ago to undertake her crow study. Surveying the damage that's been done in her labs, she swallows, exhales and asks, "Why on earth would anyone trash all of this? What were they looking for?"

"I don't know," Oliver says, slowly making his way into the room that's cluttered with a mess, with electronic devices and computers smashed and strewn all over the grey tiled floor. He notices shards of glass and plastic components all over the place as he thinks the attack was thorough in its destruction. He suggests, "To try to stop you from doing your work or at least to slow you down?"

"I guess so, but why? I mean, honestly, this isn't earth-shattering work we're doing here. It's important to us, for sure, primarily for habitat and species protection, but we are studying crow behaviour here," she explains.

Carefully surveying the damage, she adds in a tight voice. "It's not like we're working on anything like a cure for Bellamy's Disease or a way to solve world hunger caused by the massive droughts. That would be great, mind you, but it's crows, for Christ's sake. It's important, but it's not going to save the world."

"I don't have any idea what Bellamy's Disease is," Oliver replies.

"Let's put it this way," Sydney explains, picking up a tablet from the floor, its screen shattered, and laying the pieces on a nearby counter. "It's not very pleasant, as it attacks the nervous system and literally shuts down your body, one vital organ at a time, until you're dead. It was first detected in Europe about twenty years ago and the first recorded patient was a scientist named John Bellamy. He died five days after it was diagnosed as a new virus. It's a highly contagious disease, and if you get it, let's just say it's a death sentence. It's horrific and, as of today, there are no known cures for it."

"Jesus." Oliver cringes at the thought. "Sounds bad."

"It is bad, and it's killed a lot of people around the world over the past two decades. Thankfully, there haven't been any new cases in Canada for about ten years, so fingers crossed that it stays that way," she says as she continues to survey the damage. "That would be the last thing this country needs right now. Between the current political unrest, economic crisis, water shortages, and environmental disasters sweeping the globe, we don't need another pandemic on our hands. The last one was brutal, and we barely survived it. I think another world-wide shutdown would wipe us out."

"Sounds like the world is in trouble."

"You don't know the half of it."

"It doesn't sound good, but let's get back to this mess," Oliver says, while studying the debris that is strewn all over the room. "I don't know why anyone would do this, but if I had to guess, I would say that someone is trying to send you a message."

"A message?" She considers his suggestion then asks, "A message about what, and who would do that?"

"What about your former boyfriend?" Oliver asks, throwing a glance in her direction. "Would he do something like this?"

"Isaac? No, I don't think so. I can't see why he would destroy everything, because this is his work as much as it is mine, so he would only be hurting himself in the long run. He's too arrogant to destroy his own work. Besides, I don't think Isaac would be that vengeful. It is true that he can be a bastard sometimes, but not to this extent. I really don't see it."

"If you're sure about that, then I don't have any idea who would attack you like this," Oliver answers. "Granted, I don't know that many people around here anymore."

Glancing around, he suddenly realizes there is no paper to be found anywhere in the lab, something he isn't used to. While he's curious about that, he decides it's best not to ask Sydney anything about it right now, as he wants to keep her focused on the task at hand. "Does anyone else have access to your lab?"

"Only our assistants, Skyler and Zachary, but they are good kids and I trust them. There is no way either of them would do anything like this." Shaking her head, she adds, "Although, according to what Isaac told me, they were both really pissed at me for missing the meeting yesterday, because I may have caused the university to pull its funding for our study."

She pauses and considers the possibility that either of her young lab assistants could be responsible for this mess, and then adds, "But, honestly, I just can't see them doing anything like this. I will talk to both of them, though, just to make sure."

"It sounds to me that you like them, Sydney, but you can't really under-estimate what someone would do when they're desperate and pushed against the wall," Oliver observes. "I know that anger is a powerful motivator and can make people do crazy things that seem outside of their normal behaviour. Losing a job could have pushed one of them over the edge."

"That is true, so I will take it up with them," she says reluctantly.

She adds, "I have to discuss a few other things with them as well, including what their plans are, and that's when I will ask them about this. Isaac says they are both planning to leave but I have yet to hear it from either of them."

"Your ex-boyfriend had a lot of influence over this place," Oliver observes.

"Yeah, I guess he did. But we started this journey together when we left university, so it has been his baby as much as it has been mine and we've had equal say in most matters, including supervising the staff."

"Sounds like there are lots of reasons for him to be pissed at you, especially if he blames you for losing your funding and ultimately putting an end to your study," Oliver suggests. "I am willing to bet that some people will do a whole lot worse for a whole lot less."

"I guess." She sighs. "But like I said, I just don't see him doing anything this low to hurt me."

"If you say so, but I would suggest that you start to compile a list of possible suspects who you think might do something like this," Oliver suggests, thinking about what their next steps should be. "The police will want that information."

"Shit. I hadn't even thought about calling the police," Sydney says. "I should report this, shouldn't I?"

Oliver nods. "It may be the only way you'll find out who was responsible for this mess. Why don't you see if you can find that phone you were going to let me use, and then we can get out of here before whoever did this decides to come back and complete the job? We may not want to be here if they do."

"Okay," she agrees, heading toward her office in the left corner of the space, just past the main lab area. Surveying the damage, she adds, "I knew exactly where it was before all of this. It was in my desk along with all our backup files. I want to grab those as well."

"Just take it easy," Oliver cautions. "We don't know if someone has planted anything in here."

"Like what? An explosive?" she says in surprise. "Jesus Christ, Oliver.

Are you suggesting that someone may have planted a bomb in this place? I know I can be hard to get along with at times, but I can't imagine any reason why anyone would want to kill me."

"And right there, Sydney," Oliver says. "That's exactly the kind of thinking we were just talking about in your father's office. If the owls are coming after the family—which we agree they are—then you cannot let your guard down. You have to be on your toes at all times and consider all of the possibilities. I know that planting a bomb sounds extreme, but the point is, you just never know."

"Damn it, Oliver. I don't know if I can do this," she says, reaching her office and discovering that just like the labs, the smaller room has also been ransacked, including her desk. "I am not equipped for any of this."

"Yes you are," he assures her. "You have to be strong because you have no other choice."

"I'm trying....Here it is," she says, fishing into the upper right-hand drawer of her desk which seems untouched for some reason. "I can't believe this is still here, but I found the communicator and it looks like it has not been damaged in the attack,"

She glances down at the desktop. "Holy fucking Christ," she screams. "Oliver, you better see this."

"What is it?" He rushes into her ransacked office. "Are you okay? Are you hurt?"

"I'm fine," she stutters, backing away from the desk and pointing. "But take a look at my desk."

"Jesus Christ," Oliver says, the breath catching in his throat as he scans the top of her oak desk, where he sees a message has been scratched directly into the wood.

I AM COMING FOR YOU

"Holy shit," Oliver says, stepping away from the desk. "Remember what we were just saying about calling the police? Well, I think you should call them right now."

"What in the hell is going on, Oliver?" she asks, her voice cracking with emotion. "Who would do something like that?"

"I will tell you who I think it is. It's whoever is controlling the owls."

"Do you really think so?"

Oliver nods, suddenly noticing that the window on the left side of her office is broken. "Was that done before?" he asks.

She shakes her head. "That's new."

"This is getting serious, Sydney," he says. Approaching the broken window and, seeing what he believes to be blood smeared on the shattered glass, he adds, "I think we should get out of here."

"I can't argue with that idea," she says, quickly stuffing the small communications device into her pocket and then grabbing the backup files from the drawer. Moving closer to her friend, she adds, "I'm ready whenever you are."

"Just a second," Oliver says, kneeling in front of the broken window. "God-damn it." The words catch in his throat. "You should have a look at this. Maybe you can tell me what this is."

She joins him in front of the broken window. "No more surprises, please. I don't think I can handle anything else today."

Directing Sydney to a puddle of blood that has grossly trailed down from the window and pooled on the floor, he points to something that looks like a ball of mangled feathers. "You tell me. What is this?"

"Fuck," Sydney says, exhaling with a force as a powerful tremor rocks her body. She shakes fiercely. "What in the bloody hell happened here?"

"I don't know," he says, scanning the room. "It looks like there was an attack in here. This creature has been torn apart," Oliver observes. "I can see this is a bird of some sort and I think I know what it is, but there's so much blood I can't really tell for sure. What do you think?"

Doing a quick visual examination of the bloodied and feathered carcass that's balled up on the floor under the shattered window, Sydney exhales and tries to talk but her throat is so dry she can hardly speak.

"Just take your time," Oliver says, noticing that his friend is struggling to keep herself together. "I know this is a lot to deal with, but see if you can tell me what kind of bird this is, and then we'll get out of here."

Gasping for air, Sydney calms her nerves and, after swallowing several times, she finally says, "I can't tell what species it is, because of all the blood and glass covering the body, but that's definitely an owl."

"That's what I thought," Oliver replies, taking Sydney by the arm and guiding her to the door. "Let's get the hell out of here, and I mean right now."

"You don't have to tell me twice," she says, moving quickly through the labs.

Several sudden, high-pitched, shrill sounds suddenly echo through the room, causing her to stop dead in her tracks. "What the hell is that?"

"I think I've heard that noise before," Oliver tells her, moving to the door. "Come on. Keep going, Sydney. I'm pretty sure that's the sound of owls, and that means we have to get out of here."

26: Take a deep breath

Sydney remains quiet during the drive back to the Goodwin house. She isn't sure how to process what she and Oliver discovered at her lab and office a few hours earlier.

"Holy God, that was intense," she finally says while guiding her car through the streets that she thinks seem especially busy for this time of day. "I didn't think the police would ever let me go. They had so many questions. They were particularly interested in you, but I didn't tell them much. Just said you were a friend visiting from out of town. Don't know if they bought it or not, but I didn't know what else to tell them without getting into all the stuff about crows and owls and ancient curses. I wasn't ready to tell them about all of that or where you came from, because I'm not really sure what I believe about any of that."

"They were just being thorough," Oliver says. "That's a good thing. I think I knew an RCMP officer once and for some reason I think his name was Corporal Graham or something like that. But I can't remember his first name. Something tells me that maybe it was Craig or Cliff. It came to me while you were talking to the officer. I wonder whatever happened to him?"

He adds, "I can't be sure, but I think I liked him. I wonder if he's even still alive after all of these years. He would probably be pretty old by now."

"I'm not sure who you're talking about," Sydney says, remaining focused on the road. "But I know a lot of people around this town, and I don't know anyone by that name. There is a Julie Graham who lives on the other side of town, but a Craig or Cliff Graham doesn't sound familiar to me."

Oliver shrugs. "I'm probably confused, but maybe we can check into that once we've dealt with this owl problem."

"We can certainly do that, and I'll help you look for him," she agrees. Then she adds, "Speaking of the owls, I've never heard of them being so aggressive. Why would they do something like this? It is not normal behaviour for any living creature to sacrifice itself in such a way. Animals and birds, just like humans, will protect themselves. This, however, is anything but natural."

"It's a lot to digest," Oliver answers, keeping his voice low and calm during the drive as he senses that his friend is struggling to maintain her composure. "I'll confess that I was shocked at how badly that place was trashed. Whoever is trying to send you a message, Sydney, really went out of their way to get it to you."

"Well, it worked. I have never seen anything like that before and I am officially freaked out," she says, flicking on the turn signal just before she makes the right-hand turn in the Goodwin driveway. "I may know a lot about crows, but I know very little about owls. Why in the world would those birds sacrifice themselves? First, one crashed through my door window and now one came through my office window. That seems to be on the extreme side to me."

"It's like someone is compelling them to do it," Oliver suggests as Sydney stops the car in front of her parents' house. Glancing around the yard, he adds, "It will be dark soon, so I suggest that we get inside where we can talk in safety."

"Do you really think the owls would come after us out here in the open?" she asks, switching off the car's engine. "Or are we being overly paranoid? Maybe there is a logical explanation for the owls' behaviour. Maybe they are sick or something. We'll know more once I complete the necropsy on the body from my office."

He nods, considering her suggestion. "But do you think it's really likely that any of this could be natural behaviour, sick or otherwise, considering that on two separate occasions the owls have come after you? And don't forget that, based on an eyewitness account, it's also very likely that the owls forced your sister's car off the road. She's very lucky to be alive."

She exhales forcefully and says, "That's true. I have never seen anything like this."

"I think I have," Oliver replies. "My memories are slowly coming back to me, and even though they're sketchy, I am pretty sure that I have done battle with the owls before—a long time ago. If I am correct, I know them to be cunning and extremely dangerous birds. I believe your father will back me up on my assessment. Regardless, we have to be ready for the next attack, because I am positive that it will come."

"Do you really think so?"

"I do. Now that they have gone into attack mode, I think they will keep on coming. The real challenge for us is to anticipate their next move. Speaking of that, what did your father have to say when you told him about the mess at your lab and office?"

"He's very worried about me, of course. He wanted to come right over but I assured him I was all right with you and that there was nothing he could do. I convinced him to stay at the hospital with Mom and Piper."

"I am sure he's worried about you. That's why it's important that everyone stay on their toes," Oliver says. "Is there any word on how Piper is doing?"

"They still have her heavily sedated and Dad said she is still resting comfortably, which is a good thing. He said Dr. Robbie hopes she'll sleep well through the night and then tomorrow morning, if she's stable, they will start to reduce her sedation. It seems like the worst may be over."

"Let's hope so," Oliver replies. "What about your mom and dad? What are they doing for the night?"

"Dad told me he came back to the house this afternoon and picked up a few things for him and Mom, and to check in on Grandma Sam. He has a small room with a bed at the hospital for when he does rounds overnight. They are going to stay there so Mom can be close to Piper. I think she needs to be there."

"That's a good plan," Oliver agrees. "They should be safe there."

"I was talking to Seth earlier," Sydney continues. "I suggested that he and Elliot should come to spend the night at my place so we can have some time to catch up. I haven't seen him in a while, and I thought they might be safe there."

"I'm not sure they will be safe anywhere until we stop the owls," Oliver observes.

"Yes, well, maybe there will be power in numbers, and I want to keep him close to me."

"You guys could stay here," Oliver suggests, glancing around the yard. "It seems pretty secure."

"Yes," Sydney agrees. "We could and maybe under different circumstances we would, but even though I know you think we'd be safer here; I am just not prepared to disrupt my whole life over this. Besides, I think we will be more comfortable at my house. It's smaller than this place, so it will be easier to keep everyone close, which means that I can keep an eye on things."

"True, but I would be more comfortable if you were here where *I* can keep a close watch on things." Oliver says while scanning the surrounding trees, looking for anything that seems out of the ordinary. He knows it is no good to argue with Sydney. She's a strong-willed person, so she'll do whatever she wants to do. "Let's get inside so we can check on your grandmother. I'm worried about her as well."

As they open the front door to the house, they are surprised to find Paula Bethancourt lurking in the main entry foyer.

"Good afternoon, Sydney," she says quickly. "I was just on my way to the kitchen to prepare dinner for your grandmother when I heard your car pull up. I was just checking to see who it was. Guess I'm a little jumpy with everything that's been going on."

"What's been going on?" Sydney asks. "Something happen here?"

"With Piper, I mean. Your dad was here earlier today and he said your sister was doing better. I'm glad to hear that."

"Yes," Sydney replies through a forced smile. "It seems that she's doing much better. That is a relief."

"It sure is." Paula nods.

"And how is Grandma Sam doing?" Sydney asks.

"She's up in her room, watching her favourite vintage television shows," Paula answers. "Thank God for reruns of *The Big Bang Theory*. I'm sure your grandmother has seen all the episodes at least a thousand times, but she still seems to enjoy them. I'm glad she likes them, but no matter how hard I try, I just can't get anything out of the show. Seems kind of lame to me."

"It's something from an earlier era," Oliver suggests. "Maybe it's something she can identify with."

"I suppose that could be it," Paula replies. Until now, she has ignored him. "But I wouldn't know anything about that as the show was way before my time."

"I don't think I can say the same thing," Oliver says with a smile.

"Are you staying the night, Sydney?" Paula asks. "I can make sure one of the guest rooms is ready for you. I'd be happy to help."

"No," Sydney says. "But thanks anyway. I'm going back to my place. Seth is coming over to spend the night with me."

"But I'll be here," Oliver speaks up. "So, if you need help with anything, just let me know and I'll be happy to lend a hand."

"Thanks," the woman's terse reply is quick. "But I can handle it."

Oliver shrugs. "I was just offering."

"So, Paula," Sydney says. "I know you said you were on your way to make Grandma Sam's dinner, but do you have a few minutes? There's something I want to talk to you about."

"Sure," Paula says, turning and heading into the kitchen. "I can talk while I work. I'm pretty good at multi-tasking. What do you want to talk about?"

"It's about my grandmother," Sydney says as she and Oliver follow the woman into the kitchen.

"What about your grandmother?" Paula asks, going to the fridge and removing a bowl of vegetables. "Is there something wrong?"

"As a matter of fact, there is," Sydney replies, stopping near the stove and watching as the other woman chops up the vegetables. "It has come to my attention that you are using leather straps to restrain her."

"Has it, now?" she responds, turning her sharp gaze on Oliver, who is standing next to Sydney. "I wonder what little birdie told you about that."

"I told her," Oliver speaks up, thinking Sydney has hit a nerve.

"And did you tell her the reason why I use the straps?" Paula asks.

"He did," Sydney jumps in. Addressing Oliver, she adds, "Thanks, but I've got this."

Receiving the message loud and clear, Oliver takes a seat at the kitchen table and resists the urge to speak.

"So, I guess you know that the straps are standard practice of care, used to restrain dementia patients who are prone to wandering, like your grandmother," Paula says. "It's how we keep her from hurting herself. Heaven forbid she should fall down the stairs. How would you feel then? You'd be pissed at me for not doing anything to protect her."

"We would," Sydney says. "But restraining her is one thing. Hurting her in the process is another."

"Who says I am hurting her?"

"I've heard."

"I'm sure you have," Paula says, again throwing sharp looks at Oliver. "This is my job, Sydney. I have been doing this for a very long time and I know what I'm doing. Besides that, Dr. Goodwin knows I'm using the straps and he approves of what must be done."

"He may approve of the normal methods, but I am sure he would not be happy to hear that you are hurting my grandmother in the process."

"So, tell him if you think I'm hurting your grandmother," Paula fires back. "I am not denying that I use the straps, but I would caution you about making any accusations that you cannot prove. You don't want to make me cross at you, Sydney." Staring directly at the young woman she asks, "Do you?"

"It is not my intention to make anyone cross, Paula," Sydney replies, holding her ground. "It's my intention to protect my grandmother and I will see to it that she is not harmed in any way. As for telling my father, I will talk to him, but in due time. For now, though, he has a lot on his plate to deal with."

"Well then, I guess for now I'll just go about my business and make your grandmother's dinner," Paula replies, turning to the stove and dumping the vegetables into a pot of water that's been boiling for the past few minutes. "Because, honestly, Sydney, this is really none of your business. Your father pays my salary, not you. Now, if you will excuse me, I must prepare dinner so your grandmother can eat or the next thing I know you will be accusing me of neglect leading to malnourishment. We can't have that, can we?"

"Come on, Paula. There is no need to become nasty," Sydney says, and Oliver can see her complexion is turning a dark shade of red. He can sense that she's pissed. "I only want to do what's best for my grand-mother."

"Yes, well, what you think you know is best for your grandmother and what is actually best for her are two totally different things," Paula says, her words dripping with anger. "I have work to do and if you have noth-ing better to discuss than my alleged abuse of your grandmother, then I'd like to get after it."

Throwing Sydney and then Oliver another sharp look, she adds, "I do believe we are done here."

Rising from the table, Oliver takes a deep breath and says, "I agree." He motions for Sydney to follow him as he leaves the kitchen.

"Oliver," Sydney says, sprinting down the hallway to catch up with him. "Where are you going? I wasn't done."

"Yes you were. It's very clear that woman is not going to listen to you."

"I'll *make* her listen to me."

Heading to the front door, Oliver says, "No you won't. She has dug in her heels and you are not going to get through to her."

"So now what? Do I give up?"

Oliver opens the front door. "For now. You go home and you wait for Seth. I wish you would reconsider and stay here tonight. But I know you won't change your mind about that, so I want you guys to stay at your place where I'll know you'll be safe from the owls. In the meantime, I'll be here, and I'll watch over Samantha. You have my word on that."

"Jesus, Oliver. What the hell is going on around here?" she asks, and he can see that she is overwhelmed with emotions. "It feels like my world is spinning out of control. None of this shit seems real."

"I know it's a lot to take in, but just take a deep breath and breathe.

172

And Sydney, please promise me you will go right home. No side trips, please."

"I promise that I will go right home."

"I have that phone you gave me, and if anything happens, I will call you right away, now that you've helped me figure out how it works," Oliver says with a smirk. "It's not like anything I've ever used before, but I'm sure I can manage."

"Just remember to put the receiver in your ear and then press the red button when you want to make a call. My number and Dad's numbers are programmed into the phone, so when we answer, you just talk. Got that?"

"Got it. And you call me if anything—no matter how insignificant it seems—happens. Okay?"

"Okay," Sydney says, stepping out of the house onto the front steps and into the waning sunlight as dusk is quickly setting in. "And, Oliver, please take care of Grandma Sam. She is too old and feeble to fend for herself. She needs you."

"I am here." He smiles at her. "I promise I won't let anything happen to her."

27: Flesh and hair and an eyeball

He knows he has burned a lot of bridges in recent months, and he has many regrets for the things he's done, but more than anything right now, Isaac feels lost.

Or more to the point, he thinks, as he ascends the steps that lead to the front door of Sydney's house, *I feel like I'm stuck in a dark void, gasping for air, and searching for an elusive light that will lead me out of this prison. I feel like I'm just hanging on for dear life by the very tips of my fingers.*

"Jesus," he whispers, trying to regain some perspective. "What have I done? What a God-damned mess I've made of everything."

Assessing his current predicament as his mind races over the events of the past year, he sucks in a mouthful of hot, humid air and then exhales forcefully. His stomach tightens and convulses. He feels like he could vomit right here on Sydney's front steps.

"That wouldn't be good," he says, even though there is no one around to hear him.

How in the hell did I get here? he wonders, gasping for air and struggling to maintain his balance. *I'm not really a bad guy, am I?*

He shakes his head as if to answer his own question and wonders if he is losing his mind.

Maybe I am a bad guy, he decides. *But I never started out to be that way. I really thought we had something special, but then it all turned sour.*

He tries to swallow, but his mouth is too dry, void of any spit. Instead, he almost gags.

How in the hell did I let things get so out of hand?

He had a steady relationship with Sydney, and he is sure he loved her very much. He felt they were a good fit until they weren't. But he has been thinking about her a lot over the past twenty-four hours, since he told her he was leaving, and he knows exactly where their relationship went off the rails. He knows their problems revolved around him trying to shape her into something she isn't—the perfect woman.

But she wasn't having any of that shit, and good for her. She was right to push back on me. There was no way she was going to let anyone control her.

In the end, when he couldn't find a way to make her conform to his way of thinking and she could no longer deal with him trying to make her into the person he wanted her to be, they fell apart. He knows he was overbearing in many ways. And he knows he treated her badly. He accepts the truth that he is the one who drove the wedge between them.

She doesn't deserve any of that, and I'm a freaking idiot for treating her so badly. I know that now. Whatever problems she had weren't really all that serious, and nothing I couldn't handle. After all, nobody's perfect. Truthfully, they were my problems, not hers. I wish I could have just figured out some way to live with them and moved on.

He takes a deep breath and rubs his eyes, the tears welling there.

But no, I had to push too hard, and now, here we are. I'm alone and she doesn't even want to speak with me.

"Who can blame her?" he whispers, gently tapping on the door, hoping she'll listen to him.

He hopes she'll understand that he has come to apologize. He doesn't want to argue or make any more accusations. He simply wants to set the record straight in hopes that they can move forward and maybe even be friends again.

"I owe her that much," he says, hoping she'll at least give him the opportunity to get all of this off his chest.

I'm the jerk, after all. I'm the one who called it off with her. I'm the one who slept with her sister and I'm the one who got Piper pregnant, even though she's not the one I really want to be with.

His mind races. He needs to make things right between them.

I'm also the one who just quit his job with big plans to move away. But now, clearly, if I'm going to be a father, I should stay here and do the right thing.

He takes a deep breath and then exhales with a force.

Maybe I was too hasty with that decision. Yes, she pissed me off when she fucked up the meeting yesterday, but was it really bad enough to throw everything away?

"Come on Sydney," he says, knocking on the door a second time. "Please let me in. I just want to talk. I know you are mad at me, and I understand that. You have every right to be angry, but I am not here to argue or fight, I promise so, please, let's just talk."

Maybe if we talk things out, he thinks, *we can figure out some way to get beyond this standoff. Maybe,* he sighs because he knows how stubborn she can be, *but probably not. She's pissed at me, and I understand that. Shit, I'd be pissed at me, too, if I was Sydney.*

He knows it's a long shot that she would ever forgive him. However, he hopes she will at least allow him to come in and talk to her about his current situation. Sydney has always been his sounding board and he believes she can talk him off the proverbial ledge that he feels he's on right now.

"The question remains," he says, even though he is alone, "will she want to help me?"

I want to do the right thing. I want to stay here and be in my baby's life. I want to be a good father, but that can only happen if Piper wants me to hang around. How am I supposed to make that happen when I'm not sure she even likes me all that much?

He sighs, his head swimming. *I think she only slept with me to make her sister mad. Now, here I am stuck in the middle between the two sisters, and it's not a good feeling. I hate it that I may come between them.*

The truth of his situation gives him pause. It's a harsh reality check for someone who is usually in command of his future.

I wouldn't blame Piper—or Sydney—if they told me to fuck off. I would deserve that.

Scanning the front yard as he waits for Sydney to come to the door, it suddenly dawns on him that her car is nowhere in sight.

Idiot, he thinks. *How did I not see that her car isn't here?*

"Shit," he whispers. "Just my freaking luck. I finally get up enough nerve to come and talk to her and she's not even here."

God-damn it, he thinks, spinning on his heel in frustration to leave the front steps. He knows that, considering his current predicament, he may not get this chance again, let alone build up enough nerve to confront her. After all, she's really pissed at him, so she's likely to tell him to go to hell and be done with it.

I wouldn't blame her, but what in the hell do I do now? Should I just wait for her to show up? Should I call her and let her know I'm here? Maybe she'll come home so we can talk or maybe she'll tell me to go fuck myself.

After weighing his options, he decides that calling Sydney is not a good idea and that it's probably best if he just leaves her place.

I'm sure that she doesn't want to talk to me or have anything to do with me, he concludes. *Maybe I should just pack up and leave town right now.*

But what about Piper and the baby? Where does that leave them and me?

"For fuck's sake, Isaac," he whispers as he leaves the front steps. "You've really made a mess of things this time around. What a fucking idiot."

Heading toward his car, he's suddenly stopped in his tracks by a low-pitched screeching noise that cuts through the air, shattering the serenity of Sydney's front yard. The noise gives him goose bumps, cutting to the bone. The piercing sound is unlike anything he's ever heard before.

"What in the hell?" he whispers, quickly throwing his glance around the yard, his eyes scanning the nearby bushes and trees for any sign of activity.

He is sure a bird made the noise. As an ornithologist who has studied bird behaviour for several years, he's familiar with many of the species and he knows how they sound. However, even though he has no doubt this sound was made by a bird, this noise was not immediately familiar to him.

That was not your typical bird call, he thinks, his eyes continuing to roam his surroundings.

"What are you?" He scans his surroundings. "More to the point, where are you?"

A series of barks, whistles, and cries echo through the quite evening air. He shivers. Despite the heat, the noise sends another chill racing through his body, but it confirms his first thought.

"Owls," he whispers. "I'm sure of it."

But where are they? he wonders while scoping out the yard. *And why are they here? There are no owls in this part of the province. Nobody has seen any here for many years.*

"This is very strange," he whispers. "What are you doing here, of all places?"

Sounds like there could be a few of them out there, he thinks. With his curiosity aroused, Isaac is driven to locate the birds.

Instead of getting into his car and driving away, he wanders through the front yard. Listening for more owl sounds, he's drawn closer to the trees that surround Sydney's property. He's anxious to find the elusive birds as he rarely has the opportunity to see owls in the wild.

Reaching a stand of thick pine trees at the outer edge of the property, Isaac pauses and listens. The air is still and the humidity clings to him like a second suit of damp clothes. He moves slowly and purposefully. If the owls are here, he knows they can be easily spooked, so it's essential that he refrain from making any sudden movements or loud noises that might startle them.

"Easy," he whispers, inching closer to the trees, drawn to the spot by a series of high-pitched coos and caws that are clearly coming from this location. It's like he's a moth drawn to a flame. He feels the adrenaline rush through his veins as he's anxious to see the elusive birds. He takes a deep breath. "Easy does it."

He's so intent on catching a glimpse of the owls that he's sure are hidden somewhere in the trees, he doesn't see the attack as it comes from behind.

With powerful talons poised to strike, the large brown owl zeros in on its target and then connects. The owl quickly sinks its razor-sharp talons deep into the back of Isaac's head and, flapping its wings wildly, rips out a large chunk of flesh and hair.

The pain is instant, and the force is so powerful that it propels Isaac forward, causing him to stumble. He falls, face-first, onto the ground, writhing in agony.

"Jesus Christ," he cries out as the blood pours from the gaping wound on the back of his head. His first instinct is to run but he feels dizzy, probably from the shock and the pain.

Quickly flipping over and trying to regain his footing, Isaac is stunned. He doesn't see the second attack, as the massive owl swoops around the treetops and zeros in on the human sprawled and bleeding on the ground.

Screeching loudly, the owl strikes again, finding its mark like a precision missile. With talons grabbing and beak ripping flesh, the powerful bird sinks its claws into the man's face. His flesh is no match against the onslaught. The skin immediately crumples and is ripped away from the bones.

"Fuck," Isaac screams in pain, swatting feverishly at the owl. "What the fuck are you doing?" he yells after the bird. He knows this aggressive behaviour is abnormal for the usually reclusive owl.

"Jesus. Jesus. Jesus," he cries, as the searing pain from his injuries sends shockwaves coursing through his body.

Isaac knows he needs help. He must quickly get back to his car, where he can find refuge from his attacker. Trying to muster enough strength to pull himself back up to his feet, he stumbles and falls back to his knees. The pain from his injuries is too severe.

"Why?" he cries, as the blood pours from his face and head. "Why are you doing this?"

He hears them again, but he can't see them. He knows in his current position he is an easy target.

Quickly throwing his hands up to protect his face, he doesn't see the next wave of attackers as three smaller, but equally powerful and agile owls spring from their perches in the pine trees in a well-planned offensive. The trio had been watching as their larger brother delivered the first blows, rendering their prey weak and vulnerable.

Reaching their target, the smaller owls go to work on Isaac's hands and arms, ripping large chunks of flesh from his bones as the blood pools on the ground, forming a sickly bright red circle around their prey. Like the larger owl before them, the trio knows that the human's vulnerable spot is his face, particularly his eyes. That is their ultimate target.

"Get away from me," Isaac screams, swatting feverishly at the owls. He connects with one of the birds, sending it barrelling into the nearby bushes. But amid such a brutal onslaught, he has no time to celebrate such a small victory.

"Leave me the fuck alone," he pleads. "Get away from me."

With one owl out of commission, the remaining two attackers are relentless. They continue their assault, grabbing large chunks of flesh and clawing at his face as the human howls in pain.

"Why are you doing this?" he cries. "Please leave me alone," he begs, flopping onto his back as the loss of blood leaves him weak.

But the owls are relentless, pecking and snapping at the skin on his arms, hands, and face.

"Jesus Christ," Isaac cries, as he feels the life draining from his body with every drop of blood that he spills. He knows he's in serious trouble and he needs help.

As he frantically fishes for his phone in his back pants' pocket, the two smaller owls suddenly take flight and head to the safety of the pine trees.

Is that it? Isaac wonders. *Are they done? Please let them be done.*

"Please, no more," he cries as a loud and piercing screech breaks the otherwise still evening air. He knows the attack is far from over.

Scanning the sky overhead, he's horrified to see a group of owls moving in his direction. He can't be sure of their number, but he believes there must be at least six of the birds and they are locked in on their target. He knows he is no match for these powerful birds.

"Fuck," he screams as one after the other swoops in and connects with him. He is unable to put up any credible resistance.

The owls are relentless as they rip at Isaac's body, tearing his flesh to shreds, piece by bloody piece.

"Why?" he whispers, as he writhes in agony on the blood-soaked ground. The pain is excruciating. "No more, please!"

As tears stream from his eyes, a large black and while owl takes position on his heaving chest, its beak snapping open and closed, signalling its intentions.

Isaac cringes. He knows this is the final attack.

"Please don't," he begs, attempting to raise whatever is left of his hands to fend off the attack, but the owl moves quickly, snatching Isaac's right eye from its socket and taking flight. The pain is excruciating.

That was the final, fatal blow.

28: A bird in a bush

Taking a deep breath, Sydney reviews the run-in that she and Oliver just had a few minutes earlier with Paula Bethancourt. She is now more convinced than ever that she does not like the middle-aged woman her father hired several months ago to take care of her grandmother. More than that, she doesn't trust her.

She knows that, before he hired Paula, her father did his due diligence. She knows he double-checked her credentials and contacted her references, all of whom had glowing praise for her; but still there is something about the woman that doesn't sit well with Sydney.

I'm not sure what you're up to, Sydney thinks as she makes her way through the town from her parents' house to her own home, *but I just don't get good vibes whenever I'm around you. You may talk a good game, but I'm not buying anything you're selling.*

However, without any concrete evidence to back up her suspicions, she knows that she cannot go to her father with accusations and theories, because he won't listen to anything she says, not without proof. She tried that approach shortly after Paula started working with her grandmother and that got her nowhere except on the receiving end of one of her father's lectures about trust and having faith in other people.

So that didn't go so well, she thinks. *Clearly, if I am going to convince Dad that something is off with that woman, I need to find some kind of evidence. In the meantime, I have to hope that Grandma Sam will be okay.*

While she has no idea why anyone would want to harm her grandmother, it has become clear to Sydney that Paula is a conniving, devious person with something to hide. However, despite her suspicions, she isn't sure if the woman is dangerous.

But I'll never forgive myself if something happens to that dear, sweet woman while I'm trying to uncover the truth. Becoming resolute, Sydney tells herself, *I just can't let that happen.*

She's just about to turn to into her driveway when her phone rings. Quickly glancing at the small display screen in the dashboard of her car, she sees that Seth is calling. She presses the green 'answer' button.

"Hey, brother. What's up? Everything okay with Piper? How are Mom and Dad doing?"

"Hey, yourself," Seth answers and she marvels at how he always sounds so chipper and calm even in the face of adversity.

But then again, she thinks, *while I have always had a tendency to jump to conclusions without considering all the facts, he's always had the ability to hide his stress. And he does it so well. Nice trick if you can figure out how to do that.*

"Everything is pretty much status quo here from when you left a few hours ago," he tells his sister. "Piper is still heavily sedated and resting comfortably, Mom and Elliot are with her, playing games on his tablet, and Dad is off doing rounds somewhere in the hospital. You know him. There's no way he's going to sit still, even when there's a crisis in the family. Keeping busy is the best medicine as far as that man is concerned."

"He could never sit still." Sydney chuckles, recalling their childhood. "That man is in constant motion, a proverbial fireball of energy. I don't know where he gets it from, but I wish I had half of his energy."

"Yeah, right," Seth answers, and she knows he's smiling to himself.

"What?"

"What what?"

"You've got that certain lilt in your voice."

"Lilt? I don't know what you mean."

"Yes, you do. Tell me. What are you getting at?"

"It's nothing, really. I was just thinking how much you were like Dad when it comes to work, that's all."

"No, I'm not."

"Yes, you are. You just don't want to admit it." He chuckles. "But it's okay, Sis. I like you anyway."

"Gee, thanks."

They share a laugh.

"Anyway," Seth says, "I know you were expecting me to be at your place by now. I just wanted to let you know that it's probably going to be another hour, maybe even two, before Elliot and I can get away from the hospital. I was hoping to duck out much earlier so we could hang for a while, but I don't want to leave Mom alone here while Dad's off taking care of his patients. God knows how long he'll be."

"No problem, Seth," she assures him. "Actually, I'm just heading home now and I was starting to think about what we could have for dinner."

"Elliot and I aren't really all that fussy, Sis, so don't go to any trouble on our account."

"That's good," Sydney says with a laugh. "Because I wasn't planning to. I was thinking that we should order a pizza. Would that be okay with you?"

"Sure would. Elliot loves pizza and he doesn't have it very often when we're home, so he will be good with that," Seth says. "But remember, it has to be vegetarian for us."

"I remember," Sydney assures her brother. With a cringe, she adds, "Although I'm not sure how you can eat pizza without pepperoni and cheese on it. Just doesn't seem right to me, but I will make sure to order your favourite."

"Awesome."

"So, Seth," Sydney says, keeping her eyes on the street in front of her, "how do you think everyone is really doing? Is Piper showing any real signs of improvement, or do you think she's in deeper trouble than Dad is letting on? You know him. He would never tell us the facts if he doesn't think we could handle them."

"Honesty, Sis," he says, and she can detect the worry in her brother's voice. He could never lie to her. "Based upon some of the conversations I've overheard between Dad and Dr. Robbie, I think that Piper is still in serious trouble. I don't know for sure, because Dad has not said anything to me specifically, and he's probably not going to because he would not want us to worry, but I think that getting her through the next eight to twelve hours will tell us a lot."

"Shit." Sydney sighs. "If something happens to Piper, that will destroy Mom and Dad. Truthfully, I'm not sure they ever would get over it."

"Don't even go there," Seth cautions his sister. "Let's just take it as it comes. I am trying to remain optimistic."

"Me too," she lies. "One more thing. Did Dad tell you what Bailey said when she called? I know she probably can't come home right now because she's stuck somewhere overseas or something, but surely, she could find a few minutes to check in every so often. It is a family crisis, after all. But I should expect that from her."

"Don't get hung up on her," Seth says. "You know what Bailey is like. She's always put herself and her career ahead of everyone else. That's just the way she is."

"No, I guess you are right. She has always been more important than the rest of us, or at least that's always the impression she tries to give—important in her own mind," Sydney says.

Bailey is the oldest triplet by three and a half minutes, and the girls have always struggled to outdo each other.

She adds, "I guess she will check in when she has the time, or whenever she feels the urge."

"Exactly," Seth says. "Now, I guess I should go back into the room and see how Mom is doing. She probably needs a break from El-liot."

"I don't think so." Sydney chuckles. "I'm sure she is loving every single minute she has with that little boy. She's all about her grand-son. She adores him."

"I know she does and that's the reason I brought him along," Seth says. "I could have left him at home with Preston, but I thought Mom and Dad could use the distraction. And you know what Elliot is like. When he's in the room, he commands your full attention."

"He certainly does," Sydney says. "He's such a whirlwind, but he's so much fun and I'm sure Mom is basking in his company. I'm glad you brought him."

"Sure, he's fun when you're not the one who has to entertain him for twenty-four hours a day."

"You and Preston are such good parents," Sydney tells her brother. "You were made to be a father."

"Do you really think so?"

"Yes." She nods even though she knows he can't see her. "I most certainly do. It's part of your DNA."

"Thanks. I will see you in an hour or maybe two," he says, ending the call.

Flipping on the turn signal, Sydney makes a right-hand turn to leave the main road and enter the driveway to her house just as the phone rings a second time. She sees that it's the phone she gave Oliver to use.

"Oliver? What's wrong?" she quickly asks after pressing the talk button.

"Easy, Sydney, Everything is fine here," Oliver answers. "I was just doing a test call to make sure I knew how to use this fancy communication device. I've never seen anything quite like this before and I wasn't sure I could even make it work."

"Jesus," Sydney says. "You scared the shit out of me. When I saw that number come up, my heart stopped. I immediately thought that something must be wrong at the house."

"Sorry to make you panic," he says. "That wasn't my intention."

"I know it wasn't. That's just me being paranoid," she tells him. "Do you want me to come back to the house? Because I can turn around and come right back if you need me."

"No. Everything seems to be good at the moment. I've stayed clear of Paula ever since you left. I thought it was best to give her space to do her thing, and, as far as I can tell, she got your grandmother her dinner and they are settling into their evening routine," Oliver explains. "I haven't heard much from her in the last few minutes and I'm going to give it a bit more time. Then I'll check on your grandmother."

"I am really worried about Grandma Sam, Oliver," Sydney tells him. "Obviously I can't prove anything, but I know there is something not right about that woman. I have never liked Paula since the day she started working for my family and I simply don't trust her."

"I've just met her, so I don't have a whole lot to go on, but I agree with your assessment," Oliver says. "There is definitely something off about her."

"You'll let me know if something comes up?"

"Without hesitation," Oliver assures his new-found friend. "So, can I ask you something?"

"Sure. What's on your mind?"

"I just want to know how you're doing with all of this. I really wish I could have gone back to your house with you, but I can't be in two places at once and I know you want me to stay here and watch over your grandmother. However, I just don't trust those owls. We don't know what they're up to or where they will strike next, so you must be careful. I cannot emphasize that enough. Be vigilant."

"I'm fine, Oliver, and I won't be alone for very long. Seth and Elliot are coming over in about an hour and they will be here all night, so I'll have them for company."

"That's good, but don't let your guard down. You never know when they'll strike. When you get home, please go directly into the house, and make sure you lock the doors and windows."

"Come on, Oliver. I know how to take care of myself."

"I'm sure you do, but I'm also sure that you have never had to deal with the owls before now. You cannot be too careful as far as they are concerned, especially if they are on a rampage. They are ruthless when they are primed for the attack."

"You are right about that, but I think I can handle a few birds if they come after me."

"Instead of taking them on, it's best if we can keep them at bay, until we figure things out." He pauses and then adds, "But they may have other plans, so promise me you will be careful."

"I am always careful, Oliver."

"Even though I have not known you for every long, Sydney,

something tells me that is not always the case."

"Trust me," she says, pulling into her yard and parking directly behind a vehicle that's stopped in front of her house. "I have to go," she adds. "It looks like I have company."

"I know it's really none of business, but do you mind me asking who's there?"

"It's Isaac's car," she tells him, turning off her own vehicle and quickly scanning the yard in front of her house. She exhales and says, "But it doesn't look like he's in the car and I don't see him outside anywhere. It's very odd."

"Could he be inside?" Oliver asks.

"Not likely. He no longer has a key," she answers. "I made him give it back to me when we broke up."

Oliver pauses and then asks, "Can he be trusted?"

"If you mean do I think he would ever cause me any harm, no, he wouldn't." She shakes her head as if Oliver can see her and adds, "Isaac is a lot of things, but I'm sure he's not dangerous. He would never hurt me, or anyone else, for that matter."

"You can't be too sure with people," Oliver cautions. "Everyone has a dark side, even people whom we think we know. People can snap."

"I'm positive that he's harmless. He plays mental games, for sure, but he is no physical threat to me or anyone else," she tells him. "I am going to check on him. I don't see him anywhere so maybe he's gone around the back of the house."

"I really wish you wouldn't do that, Sydney," Oliver replies. "Why don't you just come back to your parents' house? Once your grandmother is settled down for the night and we're sure everything is all right with her, I'll go back to your house with you we'll check things out together."

"No, Oliver. That's crazy. I'm already here and I can handle this, but thank you very much for your concern," she says just before pressing the button to end the conversation

"Come on, Syd—"

She cuts him off before he can finish his sentence. She understands that Oliver will not be happy with her decision, but the ball of anxiety that's suddenly building in the pit of her stomach confirms that she is right to be worried about Isaac. Something feels off to her and she feels compelled to check on him.

She doesn't believe Isaac would show up at her place and then just walk away, leaving his car here. She knows he is usually more practical and methodical than to do something like that.

That doesn't make any sense, she thinks, while opening her car door and carefully stepping out into the sticky humid evening air. *Where are you?* she wonders.

She's just about to follow the walking path that leads from the front to the back of her house when a sudden flurry of activity under a thick growth of pine trees at one of the furthest corners of her property catches her attention.

What the hell? she wonders, heading toward the trees. Despite Oliver's cautionary words, she decides she must investigate the commotion.

Quickly crossing the lawn and drawing closer to the action, she suddenly stops in her tracks. A number of crows are pouncing around under a patch of alders that is nestled under the pine trees.

Crows, she thinks, trying to count the large, black birds. *That's odd behaviour, even for you guys.*

"What are you guys doing?" she asks as she finishes the count. "Eight. There are eight of you again. That's a pretty popular number these days. What gives?"

While the crows may seem almost oblivious to the human as they go about their business, she knows they are keenly aware of her presence.

"What have you guys got there?" she asks, bending to get a better look under the bush. If she's learned one thing in all her years of working with crows and studying their behaviour, it's that you cannot let them intimidate you. She knows they feast on your fear.

Keeping her tone soft and even, she asks, "Are you playing with something, or did you find something to eat?"

As she draws closer, the crows suddenly stop what they're doing and stare at her, all sixteen beady, black, pellet-like eyes throwing daggers at her.

She shivers. Their glare is intense. She feels it in her bones, and she knows she has to be careful not to frighten them.

It's as if they are trying to protect something, she thinks. *Or maybe they're trying to protect me?*

"Don't worry, fellas, I have no desire to piss you off. I know better than to rile you up," she says, speaking softly while inching even closer. "I promise I'm not going to take it. I just want to get a closer look."

Carefully pushing the alders back, she feels the breath catch in her throat.

"Oh, my God," she whispers. "An owl?"

She can see the large, brown raptor is dead, its blood-soaked carcass balled up in grotesque heap at the crows' feet, but she has no way of telling if the crows killed it or if they found it like that.

"Now where in the hell did you guys find an owl?" she asks. "Did you do this?"

29: Mistaken identity?

Stumbling back from the alder bushes and the eight crows that remain assembled there, Sydney trembles. "What the fucking hell?" she mutters.

She struggles to maintain her balance. Her head is spinning; it feels like the earth is shaking under her feet.

"Owls," she whispers, quickly glancing around the yard and surveying the nearby trees. "This is not good."

She fears that if there is one owl under the bush, then there may be others lurking nearby, watching, and zeroing in on her, getting ready to launch an attack at this very moment. The thought sends goosebumps racing up her arms. She shivers even though the humidity is suffocating.

I have got to get out of here, she thinks, recalling the repeated warnings from her father and Oliver about the owls.

She feels panic building in her stomach. She knows she must get back to the house as quickly as she can, because if there are owls in the vicinity, she believes the house is the only place where she'll be safe.

Turning to run away, she stops suddenly as her eyes are drawn to a stand of thick pine trees, under which it appears that someone is lying on the ground. She feels her heart sink into her stomach and her head spin like it's on a swivel. She struggles to breathe.

"Isaac," she calls out. "Is that you, Isaac?"

Her throat is so dry that the words are hardly a whisper.

"What are you doing out here?" she asks, hoping he will sit up and answer her. But she feels in her gut that something is seriously wrong.

"Isaac," she yells again while rushing toward the form that is stretched out on the grass. "Can you hear me?"

The sight of the bloodied, lifeless body makes her weak in the knees. She swallows several times, her stomach retching as she fights the instinct to vomit.

"Oh my God," she cries. "Oh my God."

Falling to her knees, she stares at what she is certain are Isaac's remains, although his face is so badly mutilated it would be impossible to easily identify him if she didn't know him intimately.

"Jesus, Jesus, Isaac," she sobs as the tears spill from her eyes. "What the hell happened? Who did this to you?"

The grotesque remains of her former boyfriend suggest to her that something powerful tore through his body like a hot knife would cut through butter. It is unlike anything she has ever seen.

She thinks, *Maybe I should ask, what did this?*

Examining the badly mutilated body as well as the blood-soaked ground on which it lay, she feels the air rush from her lungs. Gasping for air, she tries to calm her nerves. Quickly scanning the area, she looks for any clues that might tell her what happened.

"Shit," she says, as she discovers numerous brownish tinged feathers hideously submerged in the red puddles. Fear quickly grips her body.

Assessing his injuries, especially the way that large chunks of flesh have been viciously ripped from the bones, she knows how he died.

"Owls," she cries, wiping away the tears with the back of her right hand as panic erupts, sending her mind racing. "Owls," she whispers through clenched teeth, "did this to you."

Regaining her footing and backing away from the grotesque, bloodied body, Sydney keeps a keen eye out for any incoming attacks. She quickly pulls her phone from her back pants' pocket.

"What were you doing out here, Isaac?" she whispers as she presses the dial button and waits for the call to go through. She has so many questions. "Why didn't you call me before you came here today? What did you want? What were you looking for so far from the house?"

"Hello, Sydney," Oliver says, answering the call on the first ring. "Are you okay or is this a test to make sure I can use this new-fangled phone?"

"No," she sobs. "I am not okay. I'm far from it."

"What's wrong?"

"The owls have attacked."

"The owls? Jesus Christ. When? Are you hurt?"

"It's not me, Oliver. It's Isaac," she sobs, her eyes roaming over the remains of her former boyfriend. "It's awful. The owls have killed him." She shudders. "They literally tore him apart. I have never, in my whole life, seen anything so horrific."

"Isaac?" Oliver asks. "But why on earth would they go after him? He's not a member of the family."

"I don't know, but he's dead and his body is a mess. It was a brutal attack. For God's sake, Oliver, they even ripped out one of his eyes. He must have suffered a lot," she says. "What should I do?"

"Are you someplace safe where the owls can't get at you?"

"No. I'm out in the front yard, where I found Isaac, and there are also eight crows, but I have no idea what they're doing here."

She quickly glances at the black birds that are still near the alders and then adds, "They are keeping their distance, though, so I'm not worried about them. I'm not sure what I should do about Isaac."

"Listen to me, Sydney, the crows won't hurt you. They will protect you but you have to get out of there," Oliver tells her. "You need to take cover as quickly as you can. If the owls are around and they've already attacked Isaac, then there is no doubt that they will come after you. So get back to your house as quickly as you can and stay there."

"What about Isaac? I can't just leave him here like this."

"Didn't you tell me he's dead?"

"Yes," she cries. "He is dead."

"Then you have to go right now. If Isaac is dead, you can't do anything for him," Oliver says. "We will deal with him later, but for right now, you have to protect yourself."

"Okay, okay," Sydney whispers, while struggling to keep her equilibrium. Addressing the remains of her former boyfriend, she adds, "I am sorry, Isaac. You did not deserve this. I will come back for you, I promise."

"Listen to me," Oliver says. "I understand you are upset, but you have got to get out of there right now."

"I'm going," she tells him, breaking into a quick stride that's halfway between running and speed walking. "What should I do once I get to the house? Should I call the police or my dad? Maybe he'll know what to do. He seems to be an expert on all these things."

"Don't worry about calling anyone. Just move it, and when you get to the house, just get inside, and stay there. Are there any rooms that don't have many windows?" Oliver asks. "We've seen how the owls will sacrifice themselves by breaking through the glass. It's likely that they were coming for you and somehow ended up attacking Isaac instead, but if they want you, then windows are not going to stop them."

"Jesus, Oliver," she replies, picking up speed. "You make them sound like monsters. They are only birds."

"They may only be birds, Sydney, but, as you've seen, they can also be killers and they are being controlled by someone with a great deal of power over them, someone who is coming after you," he says. "Is there someplace in the house you can hide where they can't get to you?"

"The guest bedroom only has one small window, so I will go there."

"Great. Good idea," Oliver agrees. "Just make sure you avoid the window. Better still, do you think you can find something to cover up the glass? Use a mattress if you have to, but do whatever you can to keep the bastards from getting inside."

"I'll find something to block it with," she says, heading toward the house as her eyes bounce from one tree to the other and quickly scan the front yard. "I don't see anything Oliver. Maybe the owls aren't even here any longer. Maybe they've left."

"Maybe. But you can't take that chance. They are cunning hunters so just because you can't see them, doesn't mean they aren't around. It's likely that they are stalking you as we speak. Are you close to the house?"

"Almost," she tells Oliver, her heart pounding so fast that she fears it may burst from her chest.

She's just about to her destination when a loud screeching noise suddenly breaks the serenity of the surroundings, sending shivers up her spine. She knows it's an owl.

"Shit."

The urgent tone in Oliver's voice is unmistakable. "What is it, Sydney?"

"There is an owl around here somewhere. I can't see it, but I heard it and it sounds angry."

"Don't stop! Keep running until you get to your house. Go as fast as you can."

"Holy fucking hell," she cries, as a large brown owl suddenly swoops over the roof of her house and heads directly towards her. She knows she is under attack.

There is no mistaking its intentions—the deadly raptor has targeted her. If it weren't so potentially dangerous, she would be amazed by the powerful bird's beauty and grace.

"It's coming after me," she tells Oliver, the fear so strong that she feels like it's choking her.

"Run as hard as you can. Your life depends on it."

The owl's talons are in attack position and its beak is open. Sydney braces for impact. She cringes when she thinks about what the owls did to Isaac and the pain they must have inflicted upon him.

"It's too close. I can't outrun it."

"Come on, Sydney, keep going," Oliver pleads. "Don't stop."

With panic gripping her body, she watches in amazement, and even awe, as the murder of crows suddenly swoops in from behind her and launches a counter-offensive. Meeting the owl in mid-flight, the crows quickly knock the raptor to the ground. The powerful and potentially deadly bird lands with a bone-breaking thud almost directly at her feet, stunned by the aerial assault.

The crows pounce on their prey. It's a flurry of black and brown feathers and streams of blood. Beaks snap and talons rip at feathers and flesh.

"Jesus," she whispers as the owl calls out in distress, its mournful cries begging its brethren for help.

She knows it won't be long before this yard is swarming with owls. Unable to compel her feet to move, she stops dead in her tracks, just a few meters from the safety of her house. She knows the crows have just saved her life.

"Sydney? Sydney?" Oliver says. "Can you hear me? Are you alright?"

When she doesn't answer right away, he says, "Please talk to me, Sydney. What's happening right now?"

Gulping in several large mouthfuls of air, she wills her heart to slow down so she can catch her breath. Finally able to speak, she says, "I am okay. I am almost there."

Glancing as the battle between the brown and black birds reaches its ultimate and bloody conclusion, she adds, "But the owl isn't. The crows have taken it out." She cringes. "It's nasty."

"That's good. The crows will do whatever they can to protect you, but you can't stop, Sydney. You have got to keep going."

"Right," she says, forcing her legs to move and breaking into a steady trot.

Finally reaching the front steps of her house, she adds, "I'm here and I'm going inside right now."

"Good. Lock the door and stay inside. Do not open it for any reason."

"Already done," Sydney says, leaning back against the front door to catch her breath, trying to steady her nerves. "Oliver, what in the bloody hell is going on around here?"

"It's the owls, but it is more than that," he tells her. "Like your father says, this isn't normal behaviour for them. If the owls are becoming so aggressive, it must mean someone, or something is compelling them to attack. We have to figure out who that someone is before it is too late."

"It's already too late," Sydney cries, brushing the tears away. "It's already too late for poor Isaac."

"Yes, I know, and I am really sorry for your loss, but we can't help him now. The best thing we can do for him is to keep you and your family safe."

"If the owls are after members of our family, why would they go after Isaac?"

"That is a good question, Sydney, but, as you can see, those bloody birds can be brutal. Once they hone in on you it's game over," he says. "And they won't stop. Thank God the crows were there to protect you this time."

"Yes, thank God," she says, remembering the condition of Isaac's mutilated body, his face looking like it was put through a meat grinder. She trembles, the knots in her stomach becoming tighter, as if she could vomit right there in the front entrance.

She chokes back the bile that has gathered in her mouth and tries to regain her composure. "Is it possible that the owls mistook Isaac for someone else?"

"I guess that is possible. Why? What are you thinking?"

"You know that Seth was supposed to be at my place by now," Sydney says. "Do you think the owls could have mistaken Isaac for Seth? They are around the same age and build, and I've always thought that they kind of resemble each other. I could see why the owls could have been confused, especially with the sun going down."

"So, you are thinking it was a case of mistaken identity?"

"I am." She nods. "Could that be what really happened?" She cringes at the suggestion. "Is it possible that Seth was the real target?"

"I think that, when it comes to these owls, anything is possible."

"Jesus," Sydney says, exhaling with such force that she feels the strength escape from her body. "What do we do now?"

"You go to the guest room and stay put," Oliver says. "Do not come out and please try to find something to cover up that window. And do not, for any reason whatsoever, come out of that house until you hear from me."

"And you? What are you going to do?"

"I'm going to call your father and ask him to swing by and pick me up," Oliver explains. "He'll want to come over once he hears about everything that has happened. You get to safety."

"I will be fine, Oliver," she assures him, quickly ascending the stairs to the second-floor bedrooms.

"This has gotten serious, Sydney," Oliver says. "Those freaking birds are too close for comfort."

"Agreed," she replies entering the guest bedroom and locking the door behind her. "Please do me another favour, Oliver. Check on Grandma Sam before you come over. I need to know if she's okay. If the owls are also coming after her, there is no way she will be able to protect herself."

"I just checked on her not too long ago, but I will check on her again just as soon as we get off the phone," he assures her. "Now, cover up that window and sit tight. Your father and I will get to you just as soon as we can."

30: Regrouping

"I can't believe Isaac is dead. We just left him there," Sydney sobs, remembering the bloodied body of her former boyfriend sprawled on her front lawn. "It was so vicious, what they did to him. He didn't deserve that."

"No, he did not," her father agrees. "But we had to leave him. We had to get you out of there while we had the chance. We didn't know what the owls would do if we had hung around, but after Oliver called me, I contacted the police and told them what was happening at your place. They said they would dispatch some officers right away to investigate. They are probably there right now, and they'll call us once they've secured the area. I promise you that once we know it's safe, we will go back to your place and see what the police have found. We have to make sure there are no owls lurking around, so it's best to do it in daylight."

By the time Alex and Oliver arrived at Sydney's house, the owls had dispersed. But believing they would come back to complete the attack, Alex felt it was best to bring his daughter back to the Goodwin home. Here, he hopes they will be safe from the enemy for the time being, at least. However, he knows this refuge is a short-term remedy, as the danger will persist until the threat is neutralized. With the owls launching their offensive, they know it's time to come up with a solid plan to protect the family.

"The question is," Dr. Alex Goodwin begins as his long-lost friend, Oliver Lewis, and his daughter, Sydney, gather with him in his home office, "how in the hell do we identify who could be behind these attacks? I believe we can only stop the owls by getting to the mastermind."

"Do you have any theories as to who that might be?" Oliver asks.

"I do," Alex says, his eyes narrowing to thin slivers. Worry is clearly written all over his face. "And the possibilities are reason for us to worry. I have been under the impression for the past thirty-seven years that there are no members of the Merrick family left in these parts. I thought they, along with the owls, were wiped out a long time ago, but, clearly, I was wrong."

"Is it possible for someone other than a Merrick to compel the owls, as you explain it?" Sydney asks. She is sitting on a padded sofa with her legs curled up under her petite body and is wrapped tightly in a blanket.

Despite the oppressive heat and suffocating humidity that have smothered the eastern region of Canada for the past several weeks, she shivers with cold chills. Her father has told her that she's in shock after what happened at her home; experiencing cold chills is part of that.

"I suppose it is possible," Alex says. "But I don't think it's very likely. This grudge feels very personal to me and it's pretty obvious that the attacks are targeted at us. It's regrettable that Isaac fell prey to the owls, but it's likely they were looking for one of us; probably Seth, as you suggested, Sydney."

"How is your son doing?" Oliver asks. "I'm guessing you won't tell him anything about your suspicions?"

"He's fine right now and, no, I certainly will not tell him that it appears he has a target on his back, at least not tonight," Alex answers. "I told him I have something important to take care of here at the house that can't wait. I asked him to remain at the hospital with his mother and sister until he hears from me. I'm pretty sure the owls can't reach them there, so they should be safe for now."

"You're *pretty* sure?" Sydney replies, pulling the blanket tighter around her slender body. She shivers and adds, "Is that really good enough? It's clear that those bastards won't let anything get in their way in order to reach their targets, maybe not even a secure building like a hospital."

"Don't you mean 'their prey'?" Oliver suggests.

Sydney nods as cold chills race up her spine. Oliver's suggestion suddenly makes her feel even more vulnerable, if that's even possible. "Yes. Their prey, because that's exactly what it feels like."

Pointing to her father, she adds, "You're their prey. I'm their prey—the whole family is their prey and none of us is safe anywhere from these god-damned owls until we stop these attacks. We're easy targets because we don't know where they are, who is controlling them or when they're coming for us. We are really at their mercy."

"That is precisely why we have to come up with a plan to figure out who is responsible for these attacks," Alex says. He adds, "I know you're scared, honey. Believe me, I'm scared, too, but I have dealt with these owls once before and I know that the only way to defeat the bastards is to be strategic in our approach."

"Strategic?" she asks. "How? It's impossible to be strategic when you know so little about the enemy."

"It's simple," Alex answers. "I have to make myself an easy target to draw out whoever is behind this."

"You mean sacrifice yourself," Oliver says. He shakes his head and adds, "I can't let you do that, Alex. We can't run the risk of losing you. You're too important."

"You can't *let* me? What do you mean you *can't let me*?"

"It's simple," Oliver explains. "I think we have determined that the crows brought me back here for a reason, and there can be little doubt that reason is to protect you. I cannot let them down by allowing you to paint a target on your back. No"—he shakes his head—"that won't work. We have to find a better way."

"I am not sure there is a better way," Alex says. He adds, "Wouldn't you both agree that our goal is to protect the members of this family?"

"I would." Oliver nods. "Without a doubt. You and your family are my number one concern."

"So would I," Sydney agrees. "But that doesn't mean we have to lose you in the process. Protecting the family means protecting the *entire* family."

"You aren't going to lose me, honey," Alex tells his daughter. "We'll just make it look like I'm an easy target and then, once we draw out the person responsible for all of this, we'll spring a trap and Oliver can take care of them."

"How can you be so sure that we could stop them before they hurt you?" Sydney asks. She shakes her head. "I don't like this. It's too risky and I won't support your plan if it means sacrificing you or anyone else in the process. We must stick together. The owls can't take us all out at once if we stick together."

"I'm not so sure about that," Oliver observes. "I believe the owls are more powerful than we think. It would be a mistake to underestimate them, especially since we don't know who's controlling them."

"I know you are right, Oliver," Alex says. "But what other choice do we have? Right now, I feel like we're all prisoners. Sydney can't go home because the owls are after her there, and I'm afraid to bring the family here because I'm not sure how secure this place is or how we'd even get them here safely...and we'd have to leave Piper there alone. I won't do that. But we just can't sit around and let them hunt us. If we do, they'll just pick us off one at a time."

"Of course not," Oliver agrees. "And I am not suggesting anything like that. However, if we are going to set a trap to lure them out, then *I* have to be the target. I cannot allow any member of your family to put themself in harm's way, and that includes you, Alex."

"Why you?" Sydney asks. "Why should you be the target any more than Dad? I don't like your plan any better than I liked Dad's."

"Because I believe that's my purpose for being here," Oliver answers. "I don't remember much from what happened in the past but, based upon everything Alex has told me, combined with what little bits and pieces that have come back to me, I know my role in all of this is to protect Alex and, by extension, his family."

"So, you are willing to sacrifice yourself to protect us?" Sydney asks. "While that's brave and admirable, it's also stupid. I don't want you to do that for me and I'm sure no one else in the family will want that, either."

Alex shakes his head. "None of us want that, Oliver. Thirty-seven years ago, you threw yourself off that bridge to protect me. I don't think I could live with myself if I knew you did that again for me."

"So, what then?" Oliver asks, staring at his companions. "We have to do something. It's clear the owls are going to keep coming after the family, and the way I see it, you're all sitting ducks. If we don't mount some sort of offensive, then we're giving in to them and they will take advantage of that."

"I know you're right about that, Oliver," Alex says with a sigh, taking a seat on the sofa next to his daughter. "But I think for the time being—for the rest of the night at least—let's just keep safe. Maybe things will look different in the morning and then we can come up with a better plan. Daylight may bring clarity."

Oliver nods. "What are you thinking?"

"I think you and Sydney should stay here where we're reasonably sure it's safe," Alex suggests. "That way, you can also keep an eye on Mom. I can't have anything happen to her in all of this."

"Do you think the owls will come after Grandma Sam?" Sydney asks. "Could they even get to her in here?"

"I can't be sure, but why wouldn't they?" Alex answers, his voice dripping with worry. "In her condition, she would be an easy target for them, and it would be a major victory for the owls, as she is the family's matriarch. If nothing else, it would send a powerful message that none of us are safe."

"If they could get to her, she would be an easy target, there is no doubt about that," Oliver says. "And what about you, Alex? If Sydney and I stay here to be with your mother, what will you do?"

"I will go back to the hospital to be with Bree and the kids," Alex tells him. "I can't leave them without protection, so I have to go to them. We will reconvene here in the morning to chart our next course of action. But our first objective is to get through the night with everyone in one piece."

"Come on, Alex. We just talked about how dangerous the owls are. I can't let you go there alone," Oliver replies, shaking his head. "You might not be safe out there on the road. We know that cars can't stop the owls. Look at what they did to Piper. I'm guessing the owls are watching us right now, and if they see that you are alone, they will surely come after you."

"I don't see as we have any other choice," Alex says. "I need you to stay here to protect Sydney and Mom so you can't come with me. You and Sydney are safe here for the time being, or at least we think you are. We can't move Mom, which means you are all stuck here."

"I don't know about this," Oliver says. "I don't like the idea of separating."

"We are already separated," Alex says. "Half of the family is here, and half are at the hospital. Sydney and Mom have you. I have to be with the others. Someone has to protect them. Who else if not me?"

"I don't like this, Dad," Sydney speaks up. "I agree with Oliver. I know you want to be with Mom, but it's not safe for you to leave the house. Why don't you stay here with us? Mom and the others will be safe at the hospital. You said so yourself."

"I can't be sure about that," Alex tells his daughter. "I promise that I will go directly to the hospital, and we can keep in touch the whole way. I just can't sit here and do nothing while your mother and siblings are over there, all alone. I will never forgive myself if something happens to any of them and I wasn't there to help."

"And what if something happens to you?" she asks.

Shaking his head and offering a reassuring smile to his daughter, he says, "I know you're worried, honey, but I have to go to them."

"Is there no other way?" Sydney asks.

"I don't see one," he answers, smiling at her like he used to do when she was younger, and she was upset or worried about something. He adds, "Oliver, I need you to promise me that you will stay here and take care of Sydney and my mother."

Oliver nods. "You know I will do whatever I have to do to make sure they are safe."

"Okay, then," Alex says, giving his daughter a quick hug and a kiss on the forehead. "It's a plan and it is time for me to go."

31: A murder of crows

Something is wrong—very wrong. The crows know it.

There have been far too many close calls over the past two days, and they don't like it.

When danger is this close, it usually means that someone in the family has narrowly escaped with their life.

They can't have that. Not on their watch.

The eight crows gather on the rooftop of the Goodwin house, their senses sharply honed and on overdrive. They are keenly aware that the enemy has mounted its offensive. The current threat has escalated.

Constantly scanning the surroundings, their sixteen eyes quickly bouncing from tree to tree, the crows understand they are up against a tough adversary, and they know an attack can come at any time and from any direction.

It is how the owls hunt—in the dark, remaining stealth-like. Sometimes, they act alone; other times, they attack as a flock.

This natural standoff between owls and crows has gone on for centuries and, even though the owls have kept their distance for nearly the past four decades, the crows know they have returned with a vengeance.

They also believe they know who is behind the attack, the person who is compelling the owls into such brazen action in crow territory, and if they could tell the humans what they know, they would do so.

They must protect the humans at all costs. They can also give them clues in an effort to guide the humans in their search for answers, but communication is not always so easy.

Instead, the crows bide their time while they mount their defence. If any owl is so brazen that it would dare to come onto crow turf and target those whom they are sworn to watch over, then the feathers will fly.

The owls must know that any intrusion will be met with great resistance, for the crows will lay down their own lives to protect those in their charge. Many of their brethren have done just that in the past.

The owls have crossed a line. This evening's brazen attack against someone close to the family is all the proof that the eight crows need. This battle is escalating and is about to erupt. They know there will be deadly consequences.

Recognizing the danger, the eight have put out a call for reinforcements. Over the next few hours, thousands of crows will converge on this seaside town. They will come. They will fight and they will protect. The crows, no matter how far away they are, will always answer the call.

Meanwhile, until backup arrives, the octet must do everything in their power to ensure the family's safety. That is their top priority. That is their mandate.

Watching from their perch high atop the house, the crows know the lay of the land. This is familiar territory to them. If even one owl were to dare to come at the house, these defenders would know it and they would immediately take out the threat.

Nothing will get past them. Their perimeter is secure.

They will remain at their station until they are compelled to take action, either to defend their charges or to follow them wherever they go. They will also count on the one they have called upon for assistance, the one they know as the protector.

The battle lines have been drawn—again.

Like the passing of time itself, this cycle has played on repeat over the centuries, passing down from one generation to the next. The crows act on instinct, and they strike when threatened.

They sit quietly on the rooftop and watch, their senses on high alert, ever ready to spring into action.

When they see Alex Goodwin leave the house, get into his car and drive away, they know they must follow. Four of the crows immediately take flight. Their eyes constantly scanning the horizon, they will follow him wherever he goes while the other four crows will dutifully remain at their posts, watching and waiting. Should any interlopers come too close, they will be quickly eliminated.

The eight crows know this night has just begun and the battle is far from over.

32: Standing his ground

Alex regrets that he had to lie to Sydney and Oliver about calling the police and about where he was going, but he felt he had no other choice. He knows that if they had any idea of what he intends to do there was no chance they would have allowed him to leave the house.

They would be right to worry, he thinks as he navigates his car through the town's streets, most of which are all but abandoned at this hour of the night, except for a few, late stragglers wandering to or from God knows where.

I know this is not a good idea, but what other choice to do I have? Sometimes you have to do what you have to do.

He sighs, wiping back the tears. *And I have to do this to protect everyone. They've left me no other choice.*

He tries to swallow, but what little saliva he has in his mouth feels like shards of broken glass as it passes through his constricted throat. His mouth is so dry he couldn't spit if his life depended upon it.

This is a long time coming, he thinks, vividly recalling events from many years ago. *If tonight is the night when it all ends, then so be it, just as long as it stops all of this, once and for all.*

He's faced the owls before and he knows the threat is real. He knows that if they have targeted him or members of his family, the powerful raptors will keep coming after them until they get to their prey or they are stopped. He's seen first-hand what they are capable of. They are hunters and killers. They are also cunning and relentless.

He also knows that if the owls are coming after him, that means there is someone out there, hiding in the shadows and controlling them. He believes that it must be a member of the Merrick family.

But who? he wonders, while pressing the talk button on his dashboard phone. Listening as the call rings through, he recalls the events from thirty-seven years earlier.

There is no way that either Myles or Ozzie Merrick is behind these at-

tacks, he tells himself. *Their bodies were recovered, and they were buried thirty-seven years ago. There's no way either of them could be doing this. Or could they?*

He pauses and considers the possibilities.

After all, the crows did bring Oliver back to help me and to protect my family. Why couldn't the owls have done the same thing with Myles or Ozzie? Is that even possible? Do they have that kind of power?

"Maybe," he says aloud even though he is alone in his car. He shivers as he considers the possibility that one of his nemeses has returned from the grave to seek revenge. "Could it really be?"

Hell, I didn't even know the crows could work that kind of miracle until Oliver washed up on the rocks yesterday. He swallows again and he almost chokes on the little bit of saliva in his mouth. *How is that even possible?*

He considers the improbabilities of this entire scenario and then reviews the options that lie before him.

If the crows could do it, then why couldn't the owls do it? he wonders as he hears the call finally connect. *Who says they couldn't? Holy hell, that's a scary thought.*

"Hello," the woman's voice says, and she sounds like she may have been crying.

"Bree, are you okay? Is everything alright?" Alex asks his wife. "Did something happen to Piper?"

He's relieved to hear her voice, but he's also frightened for her, because if she is in the owls' crosshairs, she is in grave danger. He is determined to protect her and their children—no matter the cost. He will do whatever he has to do to keep them all safe from the rampaging owls that have zeroed in on them.

"Oh my God, Alex," she quickly replies, her voice wrought with worry. He wishes he were with her so that he could give her a hug and make her feel safe. "Everything is fine here."

"You sounded upset."

"No, just tired and scared," she tells him. "But I am so happy to hear your voice. I was so worried about you and Sydney. What took you so long to call me? I can't believe what happened to poor Isaac. I feel so badly for him. It's just horrific to hear what happened."

"I know, honey," he answers, keeping his voice steady and mellow, trying to mask his own fear. He knows Bree is very astute and will detect any worry in his voice.

He takes a deep breath and continues, "Yes, we are all doing okay. Sydney is back at the house with Oliver, and I have made her promise that she will stay put until morning. She's pretty shaken up over what happened to Isaac, but she is okay, physically at least."

"I expect that she is very distraught," Bree says. "She has always been good at hiding how she really feels. She's done that ever since she was a little girl. She can read other people like an open book, but she can be very difficult to read at times because she builds barriers around herself. She is very protective of her own emotions."

"Yes, she is, but she can't hide them from me. I can tell she's very up-set," Alex says. "She's going to need some time to pull herself together. I didn't see Isaac's body because it was dark by the time I got to her house, but from what Sydney said, the attack was brutal, so it's a lot for her to deal with."

"I'm sure she must be taking this hard," Bree says. "I know they've had their problems in recent months, but she and Isaac were together for quite a while. As we both know, losing someone you care for is not an easy thing to deal with, especially when it's under such tragic circumstances. She'd never admit it, but I'm sure she still has feelings for Isaac, even after everything that happened between him and her sister."

"She's a tough young woman, but, yes, I can see that she is struggling with it."

"Sometimes people can seem tough but that's often just a façade. She could be falling apart on the inside."

"I don't think that's the case with Sydney," Alex says. "She'll get through this, I'm sure of that. She just needs a little time to come to grips with it."

"Do you have any idea who killed Isaac?" Bree asks. "I know the young man had his problems and you didn't really care for him, but who would want to cause him such harm? He wasn't such a bad guy. I never had any issues with him."

"You always see the good in everyone."

He hasn't told Bree that Isaac was attacked and killed by the owls. He chooses to keep that detail from his wife not because he doesn't think she would believe him, but because he doesn't want her to worry. News that the owls have returned would cause her much grief.

Instead, he told her that Isaac was killed by an unknown assailant, and he brought Sydney back to the house because it wasn't clear if the killer had been after her, or if maybe it had been an unidentified transient and Isaac just happened to be in the wrong place at the wrong time.

"They don't know what happened to Isaac," he lies. "The police are investigating, but I don't think they have any idea what happened."

"I should be with Sydney," Bree says. "I should go to her at once."

He can hear that his wife is struggling to keep it together and he gives her a few seconds to regain her composure.

When she is ready, she asks, "What is happening here, Alex? First Piper is almost killed and now someone kills Isaac at Sydney's house. This doesn't feel like anything random to me. What if Sydney was really the target?"

"I know what it feels like, honey. But believe me, it is all a coincidence. Piper had a freak accident. You know how dangerous that stretch of road can be. There have been a lot of accidents along that section. A lot of people have died there over the years. And the other thing could have been a random act of violence. I don't believe there is anything more to it than that."

While he isn't sure how convincing he sounds, he adds, "It was all a set of freaky circumstances."

"I don't know, Alex. I get a feeling that you aren't telling me everything."

"You have known me a long time, Bree, and you know that if there was something going on that I thought you should know about, I would tell you."

Hoping that his lies are justified, he adds, "I can't keep anything from you."

"That may be true, but I also know that you won't tell me everything if you thought you were protecting me."

"I wouldn't keep anything from you, Bree," he assures her. "So, tell me," he adds, "how is Piper doing?"

"Dr. Robbie was here to check on her just a few minutes ago and she seemed to be encouraged by what she saw," Bree says.

Alex can hear the emotion and relief in her voice.

"She says Piper's vitals are really strong now and that all the internal bleeding seems to be under control, which were both good signs. She wouldn't come right out and tell me, but I got the impression that Dr. Robbie believes our girl might be out of the woods." Bree sighs.

"I am very happy to hear that. And no, Isabel wouldn't come right out and say the danger has passed because she wouldn't want to give you any false hope. We'll know by the morning if she's going to pull through, but it sounds like we're just about there."

"It has been difficult seeing her like this."

"I know, honey," Alex says. He wishes he were there to comfort her. "But it sounds like the worst has passed."

"God willing," Bree whispers.

"Yes, God willing," Alex nods, although he's not sure if God can help in these circumstances.

He then asks, "How are Seth and Elliot doing? I am glad they are there with you."

"Me too," Bree says. "I am happy they are spending the night here at the hospital. They went to your room at the residents' dorm about an hour ago. Elliot is so cute. I just adore him. He thinks he and his father are on holidays. Wouldn't it be great if we were all that young and naive again?"

"I'm not so sure about that," Alex answers. "I didn't have the happiest of childhoods, so I don't know that I would want to go back and relive those parts of my life."

"It wasn't all bad, Alex."

"No," he says, his eyes welling up with tears as he remembers past events. "It wasn't all bad. My mothers were wonderful to me, and I met you way back then, so there were some positives, but there were also many dark times for me, more than I would ever want to relive."

"I know, sweetheart. And I'm sorry if you thought I was making light of those difficult years. I know that you went through hell but in the end, you turned out to be a wonderful human being. You are all that I could ever ask for in a husband and you are the absolute best father the children could ever hope for. You're also a terrific doctor who has helped many people over the years. In the end, I think the light outshone all that darkness in your youth."

"I've tried."

"You've done more than try; you've succeeded," she tells him, her voice providing him with some comfort.

"You're sweet for saying that."

"It's the truth. When are you coming back to the hospital?" she asks. "I thought you were going to be here by now."

Alex hesitates. He hadn't thought about coming up with a viable explanation about where he was.

"I'll be there shortly," he finally says. "I just have an errand to run."

"An errand? What could you possibility need at this time of night?"

"Uh," he stutters. "Paula told me that one of Mom's prescriptions was running low and I need to get it refilled while I have the chance so that she doesn't run out," he says. "I'm on my way to the twenty-four-hour pharmacy right now. Once I have the pills, I'll run them back to Paula at the house. After that, I will come directly to the hospital. It won't take me long."

"That couldn't have waited until the morning?"

"Well, yes, I suppose it could have, but I don't know what the morning will bring, what with the police investigation and all that, so since everyone is safely hunkered down for the night, I thought I'd take advantage of the opportunity," he explains.

"I don't know about you, Dr. Alex Goodwin," she says with a chuckle, and he's relieved that he can finally detect a little lightness in her voice. "You sometimes make me shake my head because of the things you do. Just be careful, okay?"

"Yes, honey. I promise that I will be careful. You should try to get some sleep while you can."

"I'm not tired," she assures him. "And besides, between worrying about Piper and Sydney, there is no way I'm going to get any sleep tonight."

"No, I don't expect you will, but please try. I will see you soon."

"Are you sure you are okay, Alex? You don't sound okay."

"I am fine," he answers, deciding it's time to end the conversation before he says something that might tip her off about what he's really up to. He knows the fallout from what he's about to do will hit her hard and he's afraid that the more he talks to his wife, the more his resolve to do this, will fade way and he'll ultimately lose his nerve. He cannot let that happen.

"Okay, honey, I'm here at the pharmacy," he says, knowing the time has come to say goodbye. His heart is breaking but he knows he must do this. "I have got to go now. I love you very much and I will see you soon."

"I love you too," she whispers.

Pressing the red button on the dashboard phone, Alex sighs heavily. He hates lying to her, but he believes it's for the best and he thinks she bought it.

I hope so, he thinks.

Parking his car and turning off the engine, he stares through the windshield at Sydney's house and, as images of Isaac's badly mutilated body flash through his mind, he wonders what in the hell he's doing here. He lied to Bree about not seeing Isaac's body because he knew she would want more answers than he was prepared to give her at this time. But now, even though there does not appear to be another option available to him, he isn't sure about all of this.

Maybe this wasn't such a good idea after all, he thinks, as he feels the icy fingers of fear grab him by the throat and give him a shake.

"No," he whispers, opening the car door and slowly stepping out into the hot summer night air. He shudders even though he's already sweating because of the thick humidity. *I must do this.*

"I can't put my family in any more danger," he says, stepping onto the grass and carefully moving out onto the open lawn. "It's time to confront you bastards, so let's get this over with."

He isn't sure if the owls are still lurking around here, but something is telling him that they are somewhere in the vicinity. He can feel them watching him, their eyes moving over his body, searching for vulnerable or weak spots. He shivers again at the thought of being their prey.

By all that is holy. He gasps for air as his heart pounds in his chest. *Protect my family.*

"If you want me, you can have me," he says, hoping that whoever is compelling the owls to come after him, will hear his words. "But I want you to promise me that, if it's me you are after, you will leave my family alone. They have done nothing to deserve this. They are no threat to you."

Standing his ground, Alex swallows hard and thinks about his wife and children.

"Just don't go after them again," he whispers, throwing his hands up and closing his eyes as a loud, piercing screech suddenly shatters the humid night air.

He falls to his knees. "If it's me you want, then here I am."

33: Wine and worry

I'm sorry, Isaac, Sydney thinks, wiping her eyes and slowly sipping the red wine she poured after her father left about an hour and a half ago.

She's not sure where she may have heard that red wine can reduce a person's anxiety and help them relax, but so far that piece of advice isn't working for her. It feels like her body is being turned inside out and the pain is excruciating.

Probably should have had something stronger, she tells herself.

"God-damned it," she sighs, thinking about the events of the past two days but mostly those events that transpired earlier tonight.

"What the fuck?" she asks, even though she's alone in the den, as Oliver has gone upstairs to check on Grandma Sam, as she had requested.

While she knows very little about this strange man who washed up on the rocks yesterday morning, she is relieved that he's here with her right now because, for some reason that makes no sense to her, she feels safe having him around. And right now, she needs to feel safe because she's scared. Probably more scared than she's ever been in her entire life.

She cringes when she recalls her former boyfriend's badly-mutilated body lying in the grass under the stately pine trees that border her yard, blood oozing from dozens of open wounds inflicted upon him by the owls. She can only imagine the pain he must have suffered in the on-slaught, and she is horrified by the thought.

Bastards, she thinks, wishing the owls had left him alone, as she really doesn't understand what purpose his death serves them. *You really didn't deserve any of this, Isaac. No one deserves to die that way.*

Her heart breaks for the man who, at one time, she thought she would marry and have a family with. Now, knowing there is no way that the owls could have inflicted so much damage on Isaac's body without also causing him excruciating pain, her heart simply aches for him.

She takes another sip of wine and almost gags as it burns going down her nearly-constricted throat.

"Christ," she says, gulping hard as the taste of the bitter, sour liquid lingers in her mouth. She stifles the urge to vomit.

Coughing as the wine burns its way to her stomach, she adds, "What is it with this shit tonight? I know why I prefer white to red, but come on, Sydney, get a fucking grip. Considering everything that's going on, is the taste of wine really all that important right now?"

Shaking her head, she refocuses on the gruesome death of her former boyfriend. She shudders as she knows he really wasn't the target. She can't stop thinking that if she had been home, the owls would have attacked her or, more to the point, Isaac would still be alive.

But why were you at my place, Isaac? she wonders.

Her thoughts turn to her sister and what Piper will think when she hears of his death. She cringes at the thought.

What did you want, Isaac? Did you want to talk? To apologize? To reconcile?

"After everything that happened between us, it was too late for that," she whispers, staring into the flames of the fire in the fireplace, getting lost in its glowing embers. Despite the oppressive heat on the outside of the house, she shivers with cold chills.

Her father, the doctor, may have told her she was in shock as a result of the earlier events, but she thinks it has more to do with what she believes is still to come, rather than anything that has already happened.

But just because we were never going to get back together doesn't mean I still didn't care for you, Isaac, she thinks. *I still have deep feelings for you, and there is no way you deserved to die like that.*

She's so wrapped up in her thoughts, that the sudden vibrations from the phone in her back pocket nearly cause her to jump out of her skin.

"Jesus," she gasps, quickly retrieving the wafer-thin phone. Seeing that it's her mother calling, she takes a deep breath and answers. *Get a grip, Sydney.*

"Hi Mom," she says after pressing the talk button. The connection is instant. "Everything okay at the hospital? Has something happened to Piper?"

"Hi honey," Bree answers. "No, sweetheart, nothing like that Your sister is resting comfortably, and everything is okay over here. I'm calling to see how you're doing."

"Honestly," she tells her mother, tears welling in her eyes again, "I have been better."

"I am sure you have. Based upon everything your father told me, you must have been terrified by what happened to Isaac," Bree says.

"It was horrific."

"I wanted to come over to be with you, but your father wanted me to stay here at the hospital because he said one of us has to be with your sister in case she wakes up or, heaven forbid, takes a turn for the worse. But it was hard for me, knowing that you're in trouble and I'm not there for you."

"You did the right thing, Mom," Sydney assures her mother. "Piper needs you. And there isn't anything you could have done."

"I could have been there for you, honey," Bree says. "I know that losing someone you love can be very hard."

"I am okay, Mom. I really am." Sydney does not like to lie to her mother, but she knows that if she tells her the truth—that she's breaking apart on the inside—Bree will want to come right over and she believes that would put her in danger. Furthermore, she wants her to stay with Piper, Seth and Elliot.

"Dad and Oliver were here with me, so I'm okay. I know you would have been here if you could have been."

"If you're not sure, honey, just tell me and I'll be right over," Bree says. "I can be there in a few minutes. Seth will be here in case your sister wakes up."

"I am sure," she tells her mother. "I am just sitting here in front of the fire and having a glass of wine. Oliver is upstairs checking on Grandma Sam. God bless him. that man has been a godsend. He may be a stranger to me, but I don't know what I would have done without him over the past twenty-four hours."

"How is your grandmother?"

"I think she's fine, for the time being."

"So that's not an ominous thing to say. What do you mean, *for the time being*?" Bree asks.

"Nothing. It's just that with everything that's going on, I'm worried about her, that's all," Sydney says. "She's sick and she's frail, and she gets easily confused. I don't think she could take too much stress."

"Is there something going on with your grandmother that we should worry about, Sydney?"

Lots, Sydney thinks. "There's just so much confusion going on around here that I don't want Grandma Sam to get caught up in it all."

"Have you talked to your father about your concerns for Grandma Sam? He will want to know if something is bothering you about her. You can't keep this from him."

"He's dealing with a lot right now, but I will talk to him when things calm down," Sydney says.

"Now, speaking of your father, is he there? Can I speak to him, please? I haven't heard from him in over an hour and I've tried calling him several times, but he's not answering his phone."

"No, he's not here," Sydney answers as the tiny hairs on the back of her neck immediately spring to attention. "I haven't heard from him since he left here probably an hour and a half ago. I thought he was at the hospital with you and Piper. That's where he said he was going. Said he had some patients to check on while he was there so, maybe he got hung up with them."

"He's not here, honey," Bree says, her angst so palpable that Sydney can almost feel it over the phone.

"Jesus Christ," Sydney says, her heart suddenly feeling as though it has stopped beating. "This can't be good."

"Oh my God," Bree cries. "Where is he? I don't know what I'll do if he's in some kind of trouble. I can't take any more right now."

"Calm down, Mom," Sydney cautions, trying hard to reign in her own emotions that have suddenly kicked into overdrive. "We don't know that anything has happened to him."

"We also don't know that something *hasn't* happened to him. I am very worried about him."

"I know, Mom. I'm worried about him too," Sydney says, carefully considering what her next course of action should be. "But we cannot jump to conclusions. That won't help him."

"What are we going to do, Sydney? Should I go looking for him?" Bree asks. "Where would I even go to look?"

"No, Mom. You have to stay at the hospital. I will get Oliver and we will go to find Dad," she tells her mother. "He can't have gotten too far. I'm sure he's all right. You know how easily he can get side-tracked."

"I'm not so sure, honey. Now that I think about it, when I talked to him an hour ago he sounded very odd."

"Odd? How do you mean?"

"I really didn't think much about it because he promised me that he was going to come right over to the hospital after he brought back your grandmother's prescription, but he sounded very distant, like he was lost or something."

"What prescription?"

"I don't know, honey. He said it wouldn't take him long but that's been more than an hour ago."

"This is the first I'm hearing anything about a prescription," Sydney says, concluding that her father had other plans when he left the house. She now believes he has deliberately set himself up as a target, just as he said he was going to do. But she can't tell her mother anything about any of that, as she knows that news would send her into a frenzy.

She adds, "I really wasn't expecting him back tonight. I thought he went directly to be with you. What did you mean that he sounded like he was lost?"

"It sounded like he was distracted," Bree says. "You know what your father is like when he sets his mind on something. It's like he's talking to you, but he really isn't part of the conversation."

"I do," Sydney says. "It happens a lot with him."

"Well, that's what it was like. He was there, but he really wasn't there," Bree says. "What do you think he is up to?"

"I'm not sure, but we will find him," Sydney says. "I will get Oliver right now and we'll figure this out."

"Please let me know as soon as you find him," Bree says, and Sydney can sense that her mother is bursting with anxiety.

"I will, Mom, but please try not to worry."

"That's easier said than done, honey," Bree says.

34: Peering into the void

It took some doing, but after stressing to Sydney that someone had to stay at the main house to watch over her grandmother, Oliver was able to convince her to let him be the one to go out and search for Alex, while she stayed behind.

It wasn't easy, as she felt something bad had happened to her father but, as Oliver pointed out, he was better equipped to deal with the owls if they should be present.

"But Oliver," she argued, "I should go with you in case you need backup."

Even though having backup might not be a bad idea, he conceded, it wasn't worth the risk of putting her in harm's way. He convinced her to remain at the house for her own safety and to protect her grandmother, as they don't know if the owls would also come after her.

That young woman is certainly no pushover, he thinks as he heads out on his search for his friend. He's sure that, wherever Alex is, it is very likely that the owls are also present, so he didn't want Sydney anywhere near them.

While it goes against his better judgment to leave Sydney alone at the house with the owls on the hunt, he doesn't see that he has much choice. If, as he believes, Alex has gone and done something that puts himself in the direct line of fire, then he is likely in serious trouble. Oliver fears time could be running out for his friend.

He has no idea where Alex may have gone, but he believes his friend probably went to Sydney's place if, indeed, he is looking to confront the owls. That was their last known location and Oliver decides that's where he would go if he was on a suicide mission.

"Jesus, Alex," Oliver says, while carefully navigating the town streets which mostly seem unfamiliar to him as it's been many years since he's been here. "Why would you do this? I thought we had this all worked out."

He isn't comfortable driving one of these new electric automobiles, with its flashing dashboard lights and fancy gadgets that mean nothing to him, but he has no other choice if he has any hopes of locating Alex. This vehicle is not at all like anything he thinks he remembers, but he's thankful that he had convinced Sydney to show him the basics so that he can at least operate it well enough to get around.

It has been many years since he had driven—he believes—but he feels he can handle it. When he got behind the steering wheel, it seemed as though it was a natural fit. No matter what the car looks like, with its sleek, aerodynamic design, he instinctively knows he can handle it.

This isn't good, Oliver thinks while manoeuvring the car along the often-narrow streets that lead to Sydney's house. He's following the same route that he and Sydney travelled the day before, when she brought him to her place. He's sure the car probably has some sort of built-in navigational device, but he has no idea where to find it or, more to the point, how to use it.

Even though Alex insists he's been here before, Oliver does not recognize anything about the place. However, he is confident that he can get from the Goodwin house to Sydney's place without getting lost.

I have to, he thinks, gripping tightly to the steering wheel. *Alex's life depends on it.*

"Why in the hell would you do this?" he asks, as if he were talking to Alex, the man who he fears has given himself up to the owls, those brown-feathered bastards that have been after him for many years, the result of a centuries' old feud.

He knew the answer to that question before he even asked, but Oliver is determined not to let his friend sacrifice himself. Turning into the driveway that leads to Sydney's house, he prays, *I hope I'm not too late.*

Stopping the car in front the Cape Cod style home that's in complete darkness, Oliver sees Alex's car is parked near the front steps, but he can't tell if his friend is still inside it.

Please be there, Alex, he thinks, slamming the automatic transmission into park and shutting down the car. He feels his breathing intensify and his pulse quicken as an eerie silence immediately fills the car's interior. Willing his heart to slow down, Oliver takes a deep breath and tries to steel his nerves.

"Come on Oliver. You got this," he tells himself, taking another a deep breath. He's worried, as he knows there is no one else in the vicinity to call upon if he should need help.

Get a grip, Oliver. You may be on your own, but you can do this, he tells himself. *Alex needs you.*

While many of his memories remain lost, instinctively Oliver knows his adversaries very well and he appreciates the owls' deadly tactics, for they are known to be skilled hunters...and killers.

He also understands that once he leaves the safety of this vehicle, he will be vulnerable with nowhere to hide. Recalling the images of Isaac's shredded face and bloody body, he shudders.

The poor bastard didn't stand a chance, he thinks. He knows that if he's not careful, he could end up the same way. The thought sends cold chills racing up his spine. *But* he asks himself, *what choice do I have?*

Cautiously opening the car door, Oliver takes a deep breath and shakes off any anxiety that may dampen his reaction time. He knows he must move quickly, because once the owls home in on him, every second will count.

There is no room for error. He knows that once he's in their sights, he's as good as dead. Quickly scanning the surroundings, he shivers at the thought.

Darkness blankets the yard, so he fears the owls could be anywhere, lurking in the shadows and ready to strike him down the minute he leaves the car. He knows he will be an easy target because he won't be able to see an attack coming.

"Steady as she goes, Oliver," he whispers, bracing for an assault that he fears could be coming at any minute.

He takes a deep breath, exhales, and steps out into the humid night air, the oppressive humidity immediately wrapping itself around him like a plush blanket. He suddenly feels as though he is suffocating, like someone has pulled a sack over his head.

This isn't good, Alex. Please tell me you didn't go looking for owls. If you did and you found them, this could be bad—very bad, he thinks as his eyes quickly move across the yard, looking for any sign of owls.

It's difficult for him to see much except for the black outline of the house, nearby shrubs, and surrounding trees. He tries squinting but that doesn't help to improve the visuals.

"God-damn it, Alex," he whispers, stepping toward his friend's car. "I know you think you were doing the right thing by coming here, but why would you do this?"

How do you think Sydney will feel if anything happens to you? he won-ders. *What about Bree and the others? It's my job to handle the owls, not yours. That's what the crows brought me back here to do.*

Oliver slowly inches towards Alex's car. He hopes to find his friend inside, but he isn't surprised to find the vehicle empty.

"Jesus, Alex," Oliver says, exhaling with a force while continuously scanning his surroundings, his senses on high alert. He knows that someone—or something—is watching him, sizing him up. "Where in the fuck are you, you brown feathered bastards?"

Thinking that he may already be too late to save his friend, Oliver slowly moves around to the front of Alex's car, his eyes searching for any signs of owls. The darkness swallows him. He feels alone and vulnerable. He knows that if anything has happened to his friend, then he has failed his mission.

"Are you out there?" he whispers into the darkness, his eyes peering into the void. Even though he can't see them, he knows the owls are watching. "I know you're around here somewhere. I can sense it, but you should know that if you come after me, I will fight back. I won't make this easy for you."

Leaning against the car, Oliver takes a breath, holds it, and closes his eyes. He listens, hoping that his ears can do the work that his eyes are unable to do in such complete darkness.

He hears nothing but silence. There is no breeze, so the trees are docile. Not even the crickets or peppers are singing tonight. It's as if the world has come to a standstill.

"Where are you, Alex?" he whispers in a feeble attempt to connect on some plane of consciousness with his friend. "Please don't let this be the end, not after everything we've been through. I do not want this to be how your story ends—how *our* story ends."

He's about to head toward the towering pine trees, the spot where the owls launched their deadly attack against Isaac Benjamin, when a low, guttural cackling noise gives him pause.

What is that? he wonders, listening carefully as the cawing continues to lure him in.

"That is not an owl," he whispers, cautiously heading toward the front steps of Sydney's house, where he believes the noise originated. "That is definitely a crow."

Stepping carefully in the darkness, Oliver desperately wishes he had a light. It's ironic to him the little things he can remember, but he recalls that back in his day he would have had a flashlight on his phone. He's not sure if the modern communications device Sydney gave him has a flashlight and he doesn't know where to look.

However, light or not, he is confident that if the crows are beckoning for him to come to them, then it must mean there is no immediate threat from the owls. If there were, they would have driven them away.

"Je-s-us," Oliver gasps, the word catching in his throat as he reaches the bottom step, where he sees Alex sprawled, face down on the stairs. It is dark, but as he draws closer, he can see a puddle of blood has formed around the body of his friend.

"Shit," he cries. His immediate thought is that Alex is dead.

With four large crows surrounding Alex like an honour guard, it appears that, after being brutalized by the owls, he had tried to crawl to the front door but, overcome by his injuries, couldn't make it. Oliver assumes the birds were defending his friend against the owls, which, based upon the condition of the motionless man at his feet, had clearly launched an attack and it appears to have been brutal.

"Holy Christ," Oliver cries. He rushes forward and slowly turns his friend over onto his back. "Can you hear me?" He shakes him gently. "Alex? What the hell did you do? This was not the plan."

Squinting in the darkness, Oliver scans his bloodied friend. Because of the gaping wounds to his face which are bleeding profusely, he is not able to tell if Alex is alive.

Driven by instinct, Oliver places two fingers on his friend's neck. He sighs with relief when he detects a very faint pulse. "Thank Christ."

He decides his only option is to get Alex away from any immediate danger.

"And thank you, fellas," he says to the four crows, which, while they have backed away from the two men, remain vigilant, close enough to fend off an attack should the owls return. "I have a pretty good idea that you gave it your best effort, and something tells me that you four birds saved my friend's life."

The crows respond with a series of low-key cawing sounds that Oliver thinks sound oddly similar to cooing.

Oliver pulls his friend into a standing position and then, placing his left arm around the man's waist, slowly guides him to Sydney's car. He's sure she won't mind if her father gets some blood on the interior of her car—*and so what if she does*? he decides. The important thing is to get Alex to safety and to find him some much-needed medical attention.

"Let's get you out of here," he says, as Alex remains unresponsive.

He's sure Alex needs to see a doctor, but since he is no longer familiar with the medical system around this town, Oliver decides he will take his friend back to the Goodwin house, where Sydney is waiting.

She'll know what to do, he thinks.

"Hang in there, Alex," Oliver says, guiding his friend into the car's front seat and pulling the seatbelt snugly around the man's bloodied body. "I'm not sure what you were hoping to accomplish, Alex, but let's hope it worked, because those fucking owls have damn near killed you."

It's a slight movement, but Oliver believes he sees Alex's eyelids flutter in response to his comments, but they did not open. Placing his ear close to Alex's mouth, he is relieved to hear him breathing, albeit ever so lightly.

"At least you're alive," he whispers. *So, there is that.*

Once he's sure that his friend is safely secured in the car, Oliver slams the door and quickly sprints around the vehicle. His hopes to get out of this place quickly are crushed as he runs face-first into the enemy.

"Jesus Christ," he whispers, feeling as though his heart has just skipped a beat.

"Fuck," Oliver says, planting his feet in place on the gravel driveway. Several large and extremely angry-looking owls have formed a line between him and the driver's side door, blocking his escape route.

"God-damn it," he whispers, deciding it's best not to irritate the birds by yelling at them.

He wants to run in the opposite direction, but he wills himself to re-main still. He knows that any sudden movement could send the owls into a frenzy. He is sure they will attack him if they see him as a threat, so for now he stands his ground.

Now what? He wonders, feeling trapped and vulnerable.

He knows that if the owls were to launch an attack, he could put up a good fight, but he accepts that he is no match for this many powerful, cunning and deadly hunters. They could tear him to shreds just as they did Isaac Benjamin.

He's thinking that his only option is to run around the car, get in the back, then climb through to the front seat, but he can't be sure that he would make it.

But he doesn't see any other way.

Taking a deep breath, Oliver is about to make a run for it when four crows—probably the same ones that were guarding Alex on the steps—land on the ground in front of him, forming a barricade between him and the owls.

"What are you doing, fellas?" he whispers, relieved that reinforce-ments have arrived. He exhales, observing how the crows react to him. Clearly, they mean to protect him.

He watches as the crows—their wings spread and beaks snapping—take an offensive posture. Inching toward the owls and calling out a warning, they force the killer birds to retreat. He can hardly believe it, but the crows are clearing a path for him to the car door.

"Thanks, guys," Oliver says, quickly sprinting to the door. "You just saved my life, and maybe Alex's, too."

35: A protector

Gently squeezing Piper's hand, Bree struggles to choke back tears while she holds vigil at her daughter's bedside. She hates seeing her daughter like this, weak, vulnerable, and barely clinging to life.

The vibrant young woman, with her in-your-face attitude and carefree disposition, is usually bubbly and full of life, but in recent weeks, Bree has noticed that her daughter has been pulling away from the family. She has no idea what's been bothering Piper, but Bree promises that if her daughter gets through this ordeal alive, then she will do whatever she can to help Piper deal with her issues.

But first, she thinks, *you've got to fight through this. I need you to be all right.*

"Come on, baby girl. Give it everything you've got," she whispers, her voice trembling with fear—the fear of losing a child. "You can fight through this, honey. I know you can. I've never known you to give up on anything, so don't give up now. You have got to find your way back to us."

She takes a deep breath and exhales with force, then continues, "We are all waiting for you to wake up and talk to us. I know you won't believe this, but we miss your smart-assed comments and your go-screw-yourself attitude. Your father and sisters are very worried about you. And Seth and Elliot have come home to be with you. So come on honey, do it for them."

Brushing the tears from her eyes while digging deep down inside of her body for any hidden reserve of strength that she isn't sure she can find, she pleads, "Please, honey. Do it for me, but, more importantly, do it for yourself. You have so much to live for."

She pauses, carefully considering what to say next, and then continues, her voice hardly a whisper.

"Whatever has been going on with you isn't worth dying over. Whatever it is, you don't have to face this alone. I promise that if you come back to me, I will be with you every step of the way. No matter what you need, I'll be here for you."

As images of her daughter's life flash in her mind like a movie on re-play, Bree relishes the happy memories of the bubbly, effusive, always-smiling little girl that was Piper. She recalls how proud her daughter was when she finished art school and when she sold her first painting. She smiles when she thinks of the fun-filled family gatherings they've enjoyed over the years.

She shudders at the idea that she could lose one of her children. She fights hard to not break down, even though she doesn't believe she could survive such a loss.

Parents are not supposed to outlive their children, she thinks while squeezing her daughter's hand again.

Pulling back and rubbing the tears away, she studies her daughter for any sign that Piper has heard her words. Piper remains unresponsive, almost docile.

This is not a good sign, she thinks. *What I need is a miracle.*

Though she is not an openly religious person, Bree recalls some of the wondrous things that have occurred in this town over the years. There have been many events that defy any logical explanation but, to her, are proof that a powerful force envelops the town.

Now, she prays that same power can work a miracle for her. "I know it's asking a lot," she whispers, watching her daughter's chest slowly rise and fall, "but I will take a miracle and I will do whatever it takes to make that happen."

"You are my life," she whispers as the tears trickle down her cheeks. "If you die, a piece of me will die with you, so you can't let that happen."

She has never felt connected to the crows. That special ability belongs to her husband, and she knows that, through whatever connection they seem to have, the bond runs deep with him. Bree believes the black birds are responsible for many of the mysterious happenings that she has experienced over the years, things that she has witnessed first-hand.

She has seen Alex call upon the crows for help, and the powerful birds have always answered his pleas, rising up to protect him whenever he is threatened.

"Now," she whispers, closing her eyes tightly. "Even though I have never asked you for anything, I am calling upon you for help. One of my children—one of Alex's children—needs you to use whatever power you possess to guide her out of the darkness. She needs your help to bring her home."

Taking a deep breath, she continues, "Even when we can't see you, I know you're always around, so please hear my plea. Please bring Piper back to me—to Alex. He needs his daughter to survive this."

Lost in her thoughts, Bree fails to notice that a large crow has taken a perch on the narrow ledge outside the window of Piper's hospital room. The crow observes the woman as she weeps at her daughter's bedside. It is here to watch and serve, as ordered by the eight. It will also protect the women, should the need arise. With the owls on the prowl, that need could present itself at any moment.

There is a ripple, a tear in the very fabric that surrounds this town, and the crow knows it—all the crows in the murder know it. They sense it and recoil against it, ever ready to fight back, to defend those they are sent to watch over.

Bree can't stop thinking that something evil has washed over this town and seems to have targeted her family. It's a powerful, dark force that she has seen before. She shivers as cold chills race up her spine. This is a nightmare with no obvious way out. She feels lost and confused, as if trapped in limbo between what she knows to be real and what her fears lead her to believe.

So far, Alex has not given her any reasonable explanation as to what is going on, and now, he won't answer his phone, a situation that causes her great concern.

With her emotions on high alert, her nerves are shattered. She cannot shake the overwhelming feeling that her husband is in trouble, hurt and vulnerable, and she is praying that Sydney and Oliver can locate him before time runs out.

"You need to be okay, Alex, because I can't take anything else," she whispers, her mind racing through scenarios, taking her to some of the darkest places she can imagine.

She's lost in this dark void, caught up in her thoughts as a gentle tapping on the hospital window suddenly startles her back to reality.

"Jesus." She exhales, pulled back to the present.

Quickly springing from the chair, Bree spins around and gazes at the window, her breath catching in her throat. "What in the hell?" she whispers.

She isn't sure if she should be relieved or afraid to see the large crow perched on the narrow ledge. She knows that the sudden appearance of a crow usually means that something major is brewing.

"What are you doing here?" she asks, her voice soft and mellow as she slowly approaches the window, being careful not to make any sudden movements that might startle the large, ebony bird.

Even though she doesn't expect an answer, she asks, "Have you come to help me? Are you answering my prayers?" Wiping her eyes, she asks, "Are you here to save Piper?"

The crow freezes in place on the ledge, its beady, pellet-like eyes quickly blinking as if it is trying to communicate with her.

What are you saying? She wonders.

Pressing against the glass, Bree steadies her breathing and watches the crow, marvelling at its magnificent and powerful build. Its beauty is breathtaking. If she didn't know the bird was alive, she'd believe it was a statue.

But she knows the majestic crow is very real, and if the bird has come to her, either it is here to help, or someone has died.

Or is about to, she thinks, blinking back the tears.

"Alex," she whispers, afraid that the crow is a messenger. "Where are you, my love? I need you to be all right."

Bree studies the bird's movements, trying desperately to discern any message its opening and closing beak may be trying to relay to her.

"I don't understand," she says. "What are you trying to tell me?"

As if startled, the crow suddenly moves into protective mode, its wings flapping as if to fend off an unseen attacker. Bree concludes that the crow must sense that danger is nearby. She braces for the worst.

"What is it?" She asks the crow through the glass. "What's wrong?"

The crow moves along the ledge in some sort of defensive manoeuvre. Then Bree watches in horror as a large, brown owl—twice the size of the crow—suddenly swoops in from the darkened sky and strikes the black bird, throwing its body back against the window with a loud thud.

"Oh my God," she cries, and pulls back from the window. She holds her breath as she watches the two powerful creatures battle on the ledge.

Sharp beaks stab at bodies and razor-like talons rip at feathers. Bree has never seen anything like this before.

While the crow is putting up a valiant effort, she fears the owl may be too powerful and large for the smaller bird to overcome this attack. She is sure she has never before seen an owl this large.

"Jesus," Bree cries as blood spatters on the window, leaving ominous red streaks in its wake.

The powerful owl suddenly, springs toward the crow, grabs the flailing black bird in its talons and, holding its smaller foe in a deadly grip, takes flight.

Rushing back to the window, Bree watches as the owl carries its prey off into the night sky. "You poor thing," she cries, bringing her hands to face, knowing that the crow gave up its life for her.

If it was the owl's mission to send a message, then she has heard it, loud and clear.

"What the hell do you want from my family?" she sobs.

Backing away from the window, Bree shudders, not only because of the deadly attack she just witnessed but also because she wonders what the crow was trying to tell her.

"Alex, my love," she whispers. "Please be okay. I need you."

36: Owls on the prowl

With her keen senses kicking into overdrive, Sydney braces for the worst. She cannot shake the feeling that something bad has happened. Her world suddenly feels off kilter, as if she is trapped on a merry-go-round that keeps spinning and spinning. It's a whirlwind of a ride.

After Oliver left to search for her father, she did the only thing she could, trying to reach out to him on a parallel plane. She's always had an uncanny ability to connect with people even when they aren't physically near to her.

Closing her eyes tightly, she lets her mind wander, her thoughts roaming freely into the universe as she reaches out to her father. She can feel his pain. She knows he is in serious trouble.

"Be strong, Dad," she whispers, believing that the omnipotent forces within the universe will allow her words to reach her father. "Keep fighting. Oliver is coming for you."

She's in a deep, trance-like state when the phone rings. She knows it is Oliver even before she looks at the display screen. Pressing the green talk button, she braces for the bad news.

"Oliver," she blurts out before he can say anything. "How's my dad?"

"How did you know I even found him?" Oliver asks. Quickly taking a deep breath, he then says, "He's not good, Sydney. The owls have done a number on him. He's really torn up. He's got some serious wounds and he's bleeding badly. He was unconscious when I found him at your place and he's not responding to me."

"I knew he was hurt," she cries. "Can he talk?"

"No," Oliver answers. "He hasn't said a word. I'm bringing him to you."

"I'll call Dr. Robbie," Sydney says. "With a little luck, maybe she can come right over and see him here at the house. But if not, Paula has medical training. She can probably help."

"Would you trust her to work on him?"

"I might not have a choice, Oliver, if he's as bad as you describe him," she says. "Injured birds I can deal with but humans, well, not so much."

"I get it," Oliver replies. "I promise you that we will get him through this."

"How soon before you get here?"

"About five minutes, I think."

"I'll watch for you," Sydney says.

"Okay, but be careful. The owls are out in full force tonight," Oliver says. "The hateful bastards are everywhere, and they mean business. I was lucky to get away from them. The crows saved us"

"God-damn it, Oliver, why is this happening?" she asks, quickly moving to the front door to watch for the car. "Why are these fucking owls coming after all of us and why now?"

"I don't know. I'm just turning up the driveway. Be ready. We'll have to move quickly."

"I see the headlights," she tells him. "I'll meet you outside."

"No," he blurts out. "Please don't go outside. Just wait in the house until I get there," Oliver says. "We can't be sure if it's safe and I can't handle another victim right now."

With concern for her father driving her decisions, Sidney dismisses Oliver's plea. She switches her phone to communicate through her earpiece and heads out to the front steps.

Outside, she's greeted by an image that takes her breath away.

By all that is holy, she thinks, stumbling as she feels her knees go weak. "Holy shit."

"Sydney? Are you okay?" Oliver asks.

"You were right, Oliver," she finally answers, her voice dripping with fear.

"What's wrong?"

"The owls are here," she says. "There are lots of them...must be hundreds. It's like they're staking out the place; just waiting."

"Where?"

"Everywhere," she cries, backing into the house. "In the trees, on the front yard, in the driveway and even on the front steps. I have never seen anything like this. It's freaking scary, Oliver."

"Jesus Christ," Oliver says. "I had a feeling they'd show up there."

"How are you going to get Dad into the house?"

"That is a very good question," Oliver replies.

She hears the car pull up and stop in front of the house.

"You were right" he says, scanning the yard. "There are a lot of god-damned owls out here."

"Oliver?" Sydney asks from inside the house. "What about a loud noise? Will that scare them away?"

"You are the bird expert, so you tell me," he answers. "Are they afraid of loud noises?"

"I don't know. I am not an expert in owls."

"What else have you got?"

"Just give me a second," she tells him while trying to recall everything she knows about owls.

"We don't have much time. Your father is in serious trouble. He's lost a lot of blood."

"I have an idea," she says, running to the switches that control the outside lights. "How about if we shed some light on the fuckers?"

"Good thinking. We know they don't like the bright light. But it won't scare them off for long; we'll only have a minute or two once you hit that switch. Be ready to open that door, because I'll be coming in hot."

"I'll be ready, Oliver," she tells him.

He takes a deep breath and says, "Okay. Let's do it."

As soon as Sydney turns the switches, the front yard floods with bright light, causing the startled owls to disperse. That's Oliver's cue to move.

While the owls flutter off in search of the darkness that is their refuge, he quickly pushes the car door open and, with as much speed as he can muster, rushes around to the passenger side and throws open that door.

"Come on Alex," he says, quickly releasing the seatbelt and pulling his friend from the blood-soaked front seat. The man is deadweight, but Oliver manages to extricate him in quick order and pull him toward the house.

Oliver reaches the steps and struggles to get his friend up them. But he stops abruptly when he encounters a large, brown owl that has taken a perch at the top step, blocking his pathway to safety. It is clear that this one is not afraid of the light.

"Get out of here, you feathered fucker," Oliver says.

The owl takes an offensive posture, its impressive wingspan illustrating just how large this bird really is. Oliver plants his feet and stands fast.

And the only way to get to the front door is to go through the large owl.

"If you want me, you bastard, then come and get me," Oliver says, making eye contact with the owl and stepping forward.

"I know it's Alex that you really want," Oliver says. "But you will have to go through me first."

"But not today," Sydney says as she suddenly emerges from the house, brandishing a golf club. The club connects with the owl, sending the stunned bird barrelling to the side where it crumples in a ball of feathers.

Sydney drops the club and helps Oliver get her father into the house and into the foyer. "And stay the fuck out of here," she screams at the owls, then slams the door.

"Thank you," Oliver says. "I had no idea what I was going to do. There's no way that owl was going to let me pass."

"Thank Dad for leaving his golf clubs in the front hallway closet even after Mom told him a hundred times to put them somewhere else. I didn't know what else to use."

"It was the perfect weapon," Oliver says, sighing with relief. Then, after catching his breath, asks, "Where do you want me to take your father?"

"Let's put him on the sofa in his office," Sydney says, helping to carry her father down the tiled hallway, leaving a trail of blood in their wake. "I'll get Paula. I don't think he can wait for Dr. Robbie to get here. She wasn't sure when she could get away from the hospital and we can't wait for an ambulance to come and get him."

"No, Oliver agrees. "Waiting is not an option. Your father probably does not have much time left."

"It goes against my better judgment, but if we don't have time to get him to the hospital, Paula is our only choice," Sydney says. "He needs of immediate medical assistance."

37: A long night

"What the hell happened, Sydney?" Paula Bethancourt asks, while carefully cleaning and applying stitches to the gaping wounds on Alex's face, arms, hands, neck, and chest. It appears that any exposed skin surface has been hacked by some sharp instrument.

When Sydney fails to answer, Paula adds, "There are some serious wounds here and some of them are so deep that I can't stop the bleeding. Your father is in a lot of pain, and he should really be at the hospital. I'll try my best to help him, but I'm not a doctor."

"There was no time to take him to the hospital," Sydney finally answers while closely monitoring the woman's actions. "It was obvious that he needed immediate medical attention and you were the closest person I could think of who might be able to help. Please do whatever you can to help him."

Despite her reservations, Sydney is relieved that Paula is here to help because she is a trained nurse and will know what to do to stabilize her father, at least.

"This is serious, Sydney. Are you going to tell me how your father received these wounds?" Paula asks, her hands moving swiftly over Alex's body, jumping from one wound to another. "It's very clear that Dr. Goodwin was attacked. If you want me to help him, I think you owe me an explanation."

Sydney hesitates but finally says, "Yes, of course, you are right." She nods, carefully considering her next words, "As you said, he was attacked."

"God. Who did this?" Paula asks. Her concern for Alex's wellbeing seems genuine to Sydney. "I can't imagine anyone would want to hurt Dr. Goodwin. He's such a nice man."

"He is," Sydney agrees, trying hard to keep her emotions under control. "But it wasn't a 'who' did this." She cringes and then adds, "Owls attacked him."

Paula stops to digest this. "Did you say *owls* did this?" she asks, turning to face the younger woman.

"I did," Sydney confirms with a nod. She chooses to withhold specific details about the attack as she believes Paula only needs to know the basics. The rest, she thinks, is none of her business.

"Where did this happen?"

"It was very close to here," Sydney answers, again remaining guarded about the details. "That's how we ended up here at the house instead of going straight to the hospital."

"That doesn't make any sense. Why on earth would owls attack your father?" Paula probes. "Besides, I didn't know there were any owls in this part of the province. I have not seen any of them around here for years."

"For years?" Sydney asks. The comment seems odd to her. "I thought you only moved here a few months ago when you took the job with my grandmother."

"Did I say years?"

Sydney nods. "You said *years.*"

"Sorry, I meant to say months. I haven't seen any owls around these parts in the months that I've been here. Come to think of it, isn't that a bit unusual, not that owls are easy to spot, are they?"

Sydney takes a deep breath, considering the other woman's explanation. She then says, "This is not a region where you'll find many owls, but for some reason they have shown up here now, and they attacked my father."

"I don't understand," Paula says. "Why would owls attack your father?"

"I don't know," Sydney answers, shaking her head. "But I'm sure Dad will be able to tell us what happened once he regains consciousness."

"Let's hope so." Paula says, pausing to study Sydney. She then shrugs and says, "They are typically shy and docile birds around humans, aren't they?"

"Typically, but it's a long story and I really don't want to get into all of that right now," Sydney says, adding, "You seem to know a few things about owls. What's your interest in them?"

"I'm not really interested in them," Paula says. "I'm kind of a sucker for trivial information. I seem to have all this useless stuff floating around in my head. Whatever I know about owls I must have picked up somewhere along the way and I guess it just stuck with me."

Sydney looks hard at the woman who is helping her father. "Whatever the case, I do want to thank you for your help with Dad. I don't know what we would have done if you had not been here. I could tell his wounds were very serious and with the amount of blood he was losing, I don't think he would have made it to the hospital."

Shrugging, Paula turns her attention back to Alex, who has remained still throughout this entire ordeal, only flinching slightly when she applies the antiseptic or inserts the needle into a few of the larger wounds to make stitches.

"These are some serious cuts, Sydney. Very deep. I'm worried about infection. I really do think you need to get him to the hospital so that he can receive adequate care. He needs to be on an IV drip with antibiotics."

"We'll see how he is in the morning," Sydney says. Fearing that the owls are still waiting to attack, she won't risk moving him tonight or calling an ambulance. "In the meantime, is there anything you can give him to fight off infection?"

"I can give him a shot of antibiotics for right now," Paula replies after considering Sydney's question. "I have some Vancomycin in the medicine cabinet upstairs. I'll go up and get it when I'm done here with the stitches."

"What is Vancomycin?"

"It is the most potent antibiotic ever created," Paula explains. "It is used to fight off a long list of serious infections, especially in the bloodstream and in the skin." Closely examining the wounds, she adds, "I think it's a good idea to give him a shot of that."

"And you just have that kind of medicine lying around here?"

"Your father prescribed it for your grandmother awhile back," Paula explains. "Often, people confined to beds and wheelchairs, like your grandmother has been, develop bedsores, and if they aren't cleaned and treated properly then they can develop serious infections that can be deadly, especially if they get into the bloodstream. As your grandmother's caregiver, I'm constantly looking for that sort of thing. I've had to use it a few times since I've been here, but she's good right now."

Sydney nods. "And what other magic potions do you have stashed away in your medicine chest that you use on my grandmother?"

"Not magic," she answers, her eyes squinting as if she's growing tired of this verbal jousting. "It's medicine. You sound like you don't trust me, Sydney. Is there something you want to say to me?"

"No. Nothing," Sydney says, shaking her head. "I'm just worried about my Dad, that's all."

"That's not how it feels to me."

"I just want my father to be all right," Sydney tells her. "I'm sure you can understand that."

"I do, but remember, you brought him to me. I didn't volunteer to do this," Paula replies. "If you didn't trust me to take care of him, then you should have taken him somewhere else."

"I didn't say that I didn't trust you, Paula. I was curious to learn about what's going on around here with my grandmother, that's all."

Paula sighs again and asks, "Is this really the time to get into all of that again, when I'm trying to save your father's life?"

Sydney is about to respond when Oliver finally speaks up. He has been quietly observing, standing in the background while the two women have worked on Alex. He's also carefully listened to their verbal exchange.

"Sydney," he says, "I think Paula is right. This is not the time to have another major discussion about your grandmother. Let's get your father through this crisis first and then you can take it up with her."

"There's nothing to take up, Mr. Lewis," Paula quickly answers, throwing a glare at him that cuts like a knife. "I don't know what your problem is, but everything was just fine here until you showed up."

Turning to Oliver before he has chance to reply, Sydney says to him, "I was just asking, that's all."

"I know," Oliver says, nodding and motioning for her to come with him. "But let's give Paula some room to work. Let's have a look around to see if our friends are still lurking around."

"God-damn it, Oliver," Sydney says, as the pair leave her father's office and head to the front door.

"Just come with me," Oliver says. "I want to see if the owls are still congregating outside."

"Come on Oliver. "What in the hell gives? I wasn't trying to pick a fight with Paula. I was just talking to her."

"I know, Sydney," he answers, heading down the hallway that leads to the front door. "But I want to talk to you about a few things."

"Such as?"

"For starters, who really has a casual interest in owls unless they're an expert, like yourself, who studies birds? And even then, you admit that you don't know a lot about them. I don't think that's a topic that would interest most average people yet Paula seems to know a great deal about them."

Considering his observation, Sydney takes a deep breath and says, "I did find that curious."

"It's all just very odd, considering everything that has been happening around here. What do you really know about Paula?"

She shrugs. "Only what my father told me."

"Your father is a very astute man, so I am sure he did his due diligence," Oliver says. He then asks, "I'm sure he was very thorough, but is there any way you can dig deeper into her?"

"I'm not sure that I have the computer skills. That type of research was really Isaac's area, and since he's...not here, I'm not sure who to ask for help."

Memories of her former boyfriend nearly bring her to tears. She swallows, takes a deep breath, and pushes her emotions aside, understanding that this is not the time to come undone.

"I wouldn't be much help with that," Oliver says. "I wouldn't even know how to turn on one of your computers. They don't look like anything I remember."

She weighs her options and then adds, her voice trembling with emotion, "Maybe I could ask Seth for help. He might have some ideas on what to do."

"It's worth a shot," Oliver says, pulling back the sheer curtain that covers the front door window and peering outside. Scanning the yard, he adds, "I don't see them. but that doesn't really mean anything."

"Do you think they're gone?"

"If there's one thing we've learned about these bloody owls it's that you can't take anything for granted. They could be hiding anywhere, and they can strike when you least expect it."

"I hate this, Oliver," Sydney says, her body shaking with fear, not so much of the owls—although they scare her, too—but because of the unknown threat that appears to be coming after them. "I feel like I'm boxed into a corner and can't find a way to escape. Why is this happening to my family?"

"We are at war," he tells her. "And it's a war that goes back several centuries. And yes"—he nods—"it is scary, but mostly because of the threats that we can't see, like who is behind all of this."

"This is all too much to take in," she replies, squinting as she speaks. "But I am not going to give into those fuckers. If they want me and my family, the bastards are going to have a fight on their hands."

"We can beat them," Oliver says. "We've done it before and we can do it again, so long as we don't panic. We must keep our wits about us. We must be smart and watch our step."

"Does it seem odd to you that all of this happening right now?" Sydney asks.

"It does, but it's very clear that someone has managed to rile up those birds by stoking a long-smouldering fire. There's really no way yet of knowing who's issuing the orders and calling out the owls."

"If we don't know who is behind this, then what's our next step? How do we protect ourselves from someone we can't identify?"

"We'll wait it out here until morning. Then the first thing we have to do is get your father to the hospital," Oliver says. "I believe Paula is right about that."

"Are we safe in here?" she says, referring to the large Goodwin house. "Can the owls get in?"

Quickly glancing around at the sprawling foyer and winding staircase that leads to the second floor, Oliver nods. "I checked earlier and everything is locked up pretty tight, so there is no way for the owls to get in. I'll watch over things while we wait for daylight, when we can get a better picture of what's going on outside. In the meantime, I think you should get some rest."

"Yeah, right. Like that's going to happen." She shrugs. "I'm not sure if I'll ever sleep again."

38: Where there's smoke

"Oliver," Sydney pleads, trying to wake her friend. "Oliver. What is wrong with you?"

Confused and afraid, she nudges him. It appears to her that he passed out in the chair that has been next to her father's desk for as long as she can remember.

When he doesn't respond, she tries again. "Come on, Oliver. Please wake up," she says, shaking him gently. She has no idea why he blacked out, but she's worried by his lack of response.

"Can you hear me, Oliver?" she pleads. "Please open your eyes."

"What?" he finally answers, his voice raspy and cracking, his throat is dry from the lack of saliva. It takes him a few seconds to regain his composure. "Sydney?" He stutters, "What the hell happened?"

"I'm not really sure," she says, relieved that he's finally talking to her.

She adds, "The last thing I remember is that I was sitting in the chair next to the sofa, watching over Dad and trying to figure out what the hell is going on around here. He seemed to be resting comfortably. I remember sipping from a glass of wine that Paula poured for me, and after that, everything went black."

Shaking his head, Oliver tells her he had a similar experience. "Only I didn't have wine," he points out. "I had a glass of water—and you know what? Paula also got that for me. I remember her saying something about us needing a drink to help us relax."

"What?" Sydney says, shocked by the not-so-subtle innuendo. "Are you really suggesting that Paula could have put something in our drinks to knock us out?"

He shakes his head, and asks, "Would she do something like that?"

"I don't know," Sydney says, rubbing her eyes. She's terrified by the suggestion. "But you know I have felt for a while that Paula is up to something. What other explanation is there for both of us blacking out at the same time?"

Pointing toward Alex, who has remained motionless and quiet Oliver asks, "How's your father doing? Is he okay?"

Quickly checking his pulse and then placing her ear on his chest, Sydney exhales with relief. "Thank Jesus, yes. Whatever Paula gave him really seems to have knocked him out, but he's still breathing, so that's a good thing."

Glancing around the room, she adds, "And speaking of Paula, where is she? I want to know if she drugged us."

"We have to find her and figure out what's going on." He pauses, takes a deep breath, and then adds, "But I see we have friends checking in on us."

"What? Who?"

"Look over there," he tells her, pointing to the window that overlooks the backyard.

Illuminated by the light from the full moon, the crows have gathered in the backyard and in large numbers. Oliver shivers at the ominous sight, but he's also relieved at their presence.

"There must be hundreds of them. If the crows have come in such a large group, then they sense there's real danger in the air."

"Je-s-us." Sydney exhales while slowly moving to the window and gazing upon the backyard. Even though she has studied crows for most of her adult life, she has never heard of anything like this. "Oh my God, Oliver, this is extraordinary. You better come over here and check this out."

"What is it?" he asks, following her to the window.

He swallows and whispers, "Holy shit. I knew there were lots of crows, but I don't think I have ever seen so many gathered in one place all at one time. This is amazing and scary at the same time. You are the crow expert. Have you ever seen anything like this?"

"Never," she says, slowly shaking her head. "Crows are social creatures by nature, but this is very unusual behaviour for them."

"Where do you suppose they all come from?"

"I have no idea, but this is extraordinary," she says, sucking in a large breath of air. "And scary at the same time."

She is struck by the sheer number of crows that have congregated in the yard. Under the bright light of the full moon, they can clearly see that more crows have perched on nearby trees and in shrubs. The large murder of crows blanketing the entire yard has turned the grass into a layer of blackness.

"This is amazing," Sydney whispers as she feels her heartbeat pound faster. "Do you think we are in any danger?"

"Probably, but not from them," he whispers. "They mean us no harm."

Oliver stands motionless, transfixed by the activity in the backyard. To Sydney, it's as though he is in communion with the black birds.

"What are we going to do about them?" she asks, willing herself to remain calm.

"Nothing," he answers. "We are not going to do anything about them because they aren't here to hurt us."

She shakes her head. "What are they doing here?"

"They have been summoned here to protect us," Oliver answers. "More specifically, they have come to watch over your father, and you and the rest of the family."

"Summoned?" His suggestion sends shivers up her spine. "By whom?"

"By whatever force was also responsible for bringing me here," Oliver says, his words deliberate. "The eight crows saw what the owls were up to over the past two days and have called in reinforcements. This army of crows will be our first line of defence against the owls. This battle is far from over. In fact, the fight has yet to begin."

"Je-s-us," Sydney whispers as the breath catches in her throat.

Even just considering the possibility of what Oliver is suggesting leaves her in awe. She's terrified by his observation, but she also knows that, according to local legend, crows have been responsible for many strange happenings in this town over the years, so she adds this latest activity to the growing list of unusual things she's seen and experienced in recent days.

"Why would they do this?" she asks, almost afraid of hearing the answer.

"Because that is their primary objective," Oliver tells her, adding, "That is also my primary objective. It has become very clear this is the reason I have returned after all these years."

"No. You are much more than my father's protector, Oliver," she replies, shaking her head. "You are Dad's friend and"—she pauses, watching the number of crows outside the window continue to grow—"you are also my friend."

"I have one job to do, Sydney," he says, turning from the window to look at her. "And that is to keep you all safe from whatever dark forces are coming after you."

"You have done that, Oliver," she assures him. "Dad is here right now because you faced those fucking owls and rescued him from sure death, at great risk to yourself."

She looks at him and adds, "And you have been at my side through my run-ins with the owls. You are family—you are one of us."

"Be that as it may, we aren't out of the woods just yet. There is still lots to do. I have to figure out who is responsible for the owls attacking and then I have to deal with them."

"Well, that is the big question, isn't it?" She sighs and asks, "Any theories?"

"I have an id—" Oliver stops in mid-sentence. Quickly glancing around the room, he asks, "Do you smell that, Sydney?"

She shudders as the smell seeping into the room becomes overpowering. "Shit," she answers. "Oh my God, Oliver, that's—"

"Smoke."

He sprints to the office door and grabs the handle. "Jesus Christ. It's locked."

"What?" Sydney rushes to the door and tries the handle for herself. "Who would lock the door? It's never locked."

"Paula, that's who."

She is shocked by his sudden proclamation. "Are you serious?"

Oliver nods. "Who else?"

"I believe that Paula is the one behind all of this. I just can't figure out why."

Sydney pushes on the door again, an effort that ends in futility. "When you think of it," she says, "It makes sense."

"It does."

"We have got to get out of here, Oliver," she says, placing her hands on the door and feeling the intense heat. "It feels like the fire is just outside the door so, even if we can get it unlocked, we probably can't get out this way. But this is our only exit."

"Right. Check in your father's desk to see if you can find a key to unlock the door and then we'll see if there is a way past the fire," he tells her. "Are you sure there are no other exits?"

"No, there isn't another way out of this room," she answers, searching through her father's desk. "Dad rarely locks the door even when he's having private conversations in here. I don't even know if there *is* a key. If it's locked, I don't know how Paula did it."

"Well, the door isn't the only way out," he tells her, pointing to the window. "But we have to hurry."

"Jesus Christ, Oliver," Sydney cries. "What about my grandmother?"

Oliver picks up a large pot containing a bright purple orchid that's sitting on the corner of Alex's desk and hurls it through the window. As the glass shatters, he says, "Forget about the key. Let's get your father out of here and then I'll take care of your grandmother."

"What about the owls, Oliver?" Sydney asks, struggling to lift her father's unconscious body from the sofa. "Won't they come after us if we go outside?"

"No," he says, helping to lift Alex and carry him to the shattered window. "The crows will keep them away. That's what they are here to do."

"I wonder where Paula is now?" she asks, struggling to help get her father to safety. In his unconscious state, he's more than she can manage.

"I have no idea, but first let's get your father and grandmother to safety, then we'll worry about finding Paula."

"I have never trusted that woman," Sydney says. "But why would she do all of this? Why would she try to kill us?"

"We will get to the bottom of this once we get everyone safely out of the house," Oliver tells her, leaning Alex's body against his own to take most of the weight. "Once we get him outside, the crows will take care of the rest."

After clearing away the large shards of glass, Oliver climbs up and scrambles through the opening. He then helps Sydney guide her father through the window.

"Easy does it," he says, lifting Alex from the windowsill and—as the black birds scurry out of the way—laying his friend on the grass away the house and the fire.

The crows quickly form a tight, impenetrable circle around his unconscious friend. Nothing—especially not the owls—is going to get to Alex.

"Thank you, guys," Oliver says to the crows.

Dozens of tiny black heads turn to look at him, their tiny pellet-like eyes blinking in unison.

He then helps Sydney climb through the window.

"Is Dad okay?" she asks.

"Yes, he is with the crows," he tells her, helping her to the ground. "He's safe. They won't let anything happen to him."

"What now?" she asks.

"Stay here with your father," he tells her. "If the owls come back, the crows will protect both of you."

"And what are you going to do?"

"I am going around to the front door," Oliver answers. "Since we don't have any keys, I've got to find a way to get back inside the house so that I can get to your grandmother."

"What about Paula? We don't know where she is or what she's up to."

"I'll worry about her when I have to," Oliver says, glancing up toward the second-floor window that is Samantha Henderson's bedroom.

39: There's also the truth

Peering through the tall window beside the front door, Oliver can look directly into the foyer. He can't see any flames, but thick, grey smoke floods the entry to the house. He knows the fire is spreading quickly and it's not a smart move to be thinking about going back inside.

But I have to, he thinks, looking around the yard for something he can use to break the glass. *Sydney is counting on me to save her grandmother and the only way I can do that is to get back in there.*

"This will work," he finally says to no one as he spies a large rock that he is sure must have been strategically placed in Bree's garden by a landscaper. Not only is it aesthetically appealing in the garden but now, he thinks, *it's useful for breaking and entering.*

Smashing the narrow window, Oliver carefully reaches through the opening and, avoiding the shards of glass, finds the lock. Giving it a turn, he is relieved when he hears it click open.

There, he thinks, slowly pushing open the door. *That will do it.*

"Holy hell," he whispers as he cautiously enters the foyer and sees that flames have made their way up the walls and are rapidly spreading to the second floor, while thick smoke is billowing from many of the downstairs rooms. He has no idea where the fire originated, but he believes he knows who started it.

Where are you? he wonders while cautiously stepping through the front door.

He is sure that Paula is still lurking somewhere inside the sprawling house, but his number one concern is getting Samantha out of here before it's too late. He'll worry about Paula later.

Scanning the main staircase through the thick smoke, he knows getting to Samantha's room will not be easy.

"Jesus," he whispers while scoping out the rapidly-advancing flames. "What have you done, Paula?"

Sucking in several large mouthfuls of air and then holding his breath,

Oliver darts from the doorway and sprints up the smoke-covered staircase. His eyes already burning from the fumes and his lungs aching for fresh air, he pushes upward, knowing that he is the only thing that stands between life and death for Samantha Henderson.

It's tough going as the air is heavy with smoke, but after a mad dash, he reaches the second-floor landing.

Thank Jesus, he thinks as he exhales, relieved that he's made it this far. Then he hears someone calling his name.

"Oliver?" It's Sydney's voice calling from below. "Where are you?"

Squinting his burning and watery eyes, he's surprised to see Sydney standing in the doorway.

Damn it, he thinks.

"Just hold it right there," she tells him, inching her way into the smoke-filled foyer. "I'm coming up to help you."

"Don't come any further. It's too dangerous," he yells. "What are you doing here? I thought we agreed that you were going to stay with your father."

"That was *your* plan, Oliver. I think the crows had something else in mind."

"Did you see any owls around out there?"

"No."

"How's your father?"

"He is still unconscious, but he seems pretty stable, and the crows didn't seem like they wanted me to get anywhere close to him," she yells. "So, I thought I should come and help you with Grandma Sam."

"No, Sydney," Oliver yells down to her. "Stop right there. You can't come up here. It's really not safe. We don't know where the fire is, so we don't know how sturdy this floor is or if the roof is going to hold for much longer. Please just go back outside where you'll be safe. I can handle this."

"Okay, Oliver," she reluctantly agrees. "I hear you and I get the message."

"Good. I'll be as fast as I can."

God-damn it, Sydney, he thinks, carefully stepping around the falling debris and avoiding the flames that are now shooting from the walls, *I don't want to have to worry about you right now. Why must you be so pig-headed?*

Memories of his life from thirty-seven years ago flash through his mind. It's not the best timing but he suddenly recalls that, when he was younger, Alex was a lot like his daughter.

A brazen, know-it-all teenager who wouldn't listen to anything that anyone told him, Oliver recalls as he dashes towards the room where he hopes to find Samantha.

Kicking the door open, he braces for the worst, but he stops short when he finds Paula is standing in the middle of the room. She has placed Samantha in her wheelchair. The older woman appears to be unresponsive, and he believes she must be drugged.

"Stop right there," Paula screams. "I am getting out of here and Samantha is coming with me."

"You can't get out this way," he says, glaring at the woman through the smoke that's creeping into the room, making it increasingly difficult to breathe. "It's not safe."

"No, you listen to me, Oliver Lewis," she snaps, placing a large syringe at Samantha's neck. He has no idea what the needle contains, but he believes it's probably something dangerous. He knows that Paula will stop at nothing to get what she wants. "Get out of my way so I can get out of here, or Samantha will suffer the consequences."

"Please don't hurt her," Oliver begs.

Paula holds the syringe tight against the elderly woman's skin. "You know I will."

"Okay. Okay. I'll stay put, but there's too much smoke and flames. You'll never get down those stairs on your own. Let me help you. I'll take Samantha and you can follow me down the stairs."

Extending his hand to her, he adds, "Come with me. I can get you safely out of here."

"You are kidding," she replies. "I would never trust you, Oliver Lewis. You are here to do the crows' bidding, to protect Dr. Goodwin and his family."

"You are right about that, Paula," he says, deciding it's strategic to maintain a civil tone. "But that doesn't mean I can't help to get you to safety. Please let me help. There isn't much time."

"That's not going to happen, Oliver," she shoots back, continuing to hold the syringe tight against the elderly woman's neck. "Why don't you step aside and let me and ole Samantha get out of here?"

"You know I can't do that," he says.

"Why are you doing this, Paula?" he asks. "Why have you attacked Alex and his family? What have they done to deserve this?"

"They've done a lot. These events started many years ago," she tells him. "But I think you already know that.?"

Taking a deep breath and coughing as the smoke invades his lungs,

Oliver slowly nods and says, "I think I do." Staring at her, he adds, "Your name isn't really Paula Bethancourt, is it?"

She sneers and shakes her head.

"Who are you, then?" he asks.

"Come on, Oliver. Take a good, hard look at me," she says. Despite the dire situation they face, she is beaming with happiness. "Don't you know who I am?"

"I'm not sure," he says and shakes his head.

"I was really young the last time you saw me."

Squinting through the smoke, he whispers, "Jesus Christ. Are you...?"

She grins. "The last time you saw me, you would have known me as Dani. My full name is Dannielle, but everyone called me Dani."

"Shit," Oliver says, his breath catching in his throat, his head spinning. "You're Dani Merrick, Myles Merrick's daughter?"

"Good for you, Oliver. Give the man a prize. It took you a while, but you finally figured it out. My brother Ozzie was Alex Goodwin's best friend."

"But how?" Oliver asks, his head feeling like it's about to explode as a flood of memories rush into his brain. "Why?"

"The how is a long story. After you killed my father and brother, I was taken in by a reclusive aunt and uncle who lived in a small village in northern Ontario. My uncle taught me all about the owls and how to command them. They really are very intelligent creatures, and it really is amazing what they will do, once you learn how to connect with them. My family figured that out a long time ago."

"But that was so many years ago. What's with the fake identity? Why all the subterfuge?"

"I made a vow that I would get my revenge on the Goodwins. and so, I laid low for all this time. I learned the way of the owls, knowing that someday I would come back here and find you all," Paula explains.

"My wishes were answered when I saw Alex's advertisement for a live-in personal care worker to look after of his ailing mother. I'm a trained nurse, so I applied, and I got the job. It wasn't all that difficult to convince Dr. Goodwin that I was the person he was looking for."

"Jesus Christ," Oliver says, exhaling with a force, his legs feeling as though they are about to give out on him.

Trying to grasp his own reality, he asks, "Why do all of this? If you knew the legend of the crows and the owls, then you knew that Alex and your brother were destined to do battle. They didn't want to fight each other but they were compelled by their destinies."

"I owe it to my father and brother to get revenge, and I needed to bring balance to my world," she says sharply, squeezing Samantha's throat as if she's deriving some sort of perverted pleasure from the feeble woman's inability to fight back. "It was the owls' turn to win for a change."

"But you haven't won," Oliver shoots back. "Alex and Piper are still alive. All of this has been for nothing."

"Oh, I don't know about that," she says. "Ole Samantha here isn't looking too good right about now, and as for Alex, well…"

"What about Alex?"

"It's simple," she smirks as the flames quickly close in on the room, licking at the painted walls. "While you and Sydney were busy, I gave Dr. Goodwin a large dose of morphine. He should have died by now. He will never recover."

"We'll see."

"Some of us will see," she says. "You, my friend, won't see past the next few minutes. You can't stop what's going to happen."

"Come on Paula. You really don't have to do this. We still have time to get out of here, but we have to go right now," Oliver says.

"I'm not going anywhere with you, Oliver Lewis," she screams, and pushes the wheelchair directly at him.

As he grabs the wheelchair to protect Samantha, Paula slips out the doorway and into the smoke-filled hallway.

Oliver fights his instincts to chase after her. Steering Samantha's wheelchair out of the room and around the flaming debris that's falling everywhere, he heads to the stairway. He plans to take the chair as far as he can then he'll carry her the rest of the way.

"You aren't that big," he says to her. The woman remains unresponsive; a result of whatever drugs Paula has given her. "Surely, I can carry you that far."

"Oliver? Oliver? Can you hear me?" As he reaches the top of the stairway, he recognizes Sydney's voice. "What's going on?"

"I'm okay. I've got your grandmother. Wait for me at the front door."

"What about Paula?" she calls back.

"She was here," he answers. "I'll tell you all about that once I get down there."

"You won't be telling Sydney anything," a woman's voice screams from behind him.

Quickly spinning around, Oliver is shocked to see Paula running towards him. He doesn't have time to avoid her, deciding instead to push the wheelchair out of the way.

"Come on, Paula," he says as she grabs hold of him. "You need to get out. The roof could cave in at any minute."

"It's your turn to pay, Oliver Lewis," the woman screams. She strikes him in the chest with such force that he loses his balance. "You are going to die again and this time the crows won't be able to help you."

"If I am going to die," Oliver snaps, grabbing Paula's arms and stumbling backwards, "you are going with me."

"Oliver?" Sydney screams from the ground floor. "Oliver?" she screams again. "Please be all right. Answer me. Oliver?"

40: Here and gone

"Come on, sis," Seth says, trying to grasp the enormity of his sister's claims. "It's been three days since the fire and investigators have not be able to determine how or where it started."

"I don't care what they say. I am telling you it was her," Sydney insists, not taking her eyes from their father, who is resting in his hospital bed. "I know she set the fire."

"Paula? How can you be so sure it was her?"

"I am one hundred percent positive it was her," Sydney says.

It has been touch and go for Alex over the past few days. When he arrived in hospital, he was suffering from a serious loss of blood and an overdose of morphine. However, after the initial scare and around-the-clock care from Dr. Isabel Robbie, he is now recovering from the injuries he suffered in the owl attack and the resulting 'treatment' he received from his mother's caregiver.

Turning back to her brother, Sydney points out, "Only her name wasn't really Paula. After some digging around, we now know her name was Dannielle Merrick. People called her Dani."

"If you say so," Seth says with a shrug. "I'm just saying that maybe the fire was an accident."

"It wasn't an accident," Sydney insists. "I know how bizarre this sounds to you, but I'm telling you she did it."

"That's a lot to digest, Sydney, even for me," Alex suddenly speaks up. "I just can't believe that she was responsible for all of this," he says. Seth and Sydney focus on him. They had thought he was sleeping.

"Her resume was impeccable, and she came highly recommended," he adds. "I really trusted her."

"I know, Dad. We all did," Sydney says.

"Not all of us," Alex answers, looking directly at his daughter. "You never really trusted her, and it appears you had good reason."

"Okay," she says with a shrug. "Some of us trusted her more than others but the point is, we took her in with the belief that she would take care of Grandma Sam, not target everyone as part of a warped revenge plot."

Alex replies, "Right from the beginning, you tried to tell me that something was off about that woman, and I should have listened to you. You always have such strong instincts about people, but I just didn't want to accept that I could have been wrong."

He pauses to gather his thoughts and then adds, "How could I be so wrong about something that important? I put everyone in so much danger. I am so sorry."

"You can't blame yourself, Dad," Sydney replies. "That woman was devious. She fooled all of us. Now that we know the full story, though, it is clear that she had been planning this attack for a long time."

"Perhaps she was," Alex agrees, "but that doesn't make it any easier to accept that her lies nearly cost us our lives. "And"—he tries to inconspicuously brush away the tears that he's struggling to keep hidden from his children—"it did cost poor Isaac his life. He and I had our problems, but that should never have happened to him."

"You are right about that," Sydney says. Reflecting on the death of her former boyfriend and colleague, she swallows and adds, "He didn't deserve to die in such a brutal way, but it wasn't your fault, Dad."

"No, he did not but that just shows how little regard that woman had for other people," Alex says. "In her mission to get to me, she didn't care who else got hurt."

Trying to digest the bizarre circumstances that surround the past few days, he adds, "It had been a lot of years since I had last seen her, but I remember Dani Merrick as a sweet little girl who used to annoy Ozzie so much that he never wanted to hang out at his place, which is why we were always at my house. She was a good kid, bubbly and full of energy, but she just wanted to be with her older brother and he wanted to get away from her as much as he could. How could she do all of this?"

"Revenge is a powerful motivator," Sydney says. "Once she learned her family's secret and understood the power she had to command the owls, she had all the help she needed to pull off this big plan, and what a plan it was. She managed to fool everyone with her act."

"I still don't think I can buy the idea of her coming after Dad and us," Seth says. "It's so—"

"Hard to believe?" Sydney interrupts. "Well, you can believe it because that's exactly what happened."

"And what about committing murder, Sydney?" Seth asks. "That's taking it to the extreme, don't you think?"

"It may seem extreme, Seth," Alex replies. "But once you understand the secret of the crows and how this pact works, you will better understand everything that has happened around here."

Grimacing as he thinks about what he just said, he adds, "I accept the responsibility for this."

"How so?" Sydney asks.

"Because" Alex replies, "it is my fault for not telling you kids about our connection to the crows when you were younger. I should have told you about our family's secret so that you could have been better prepared in the event something like this were to happen, but, honestly, I really thought the fight was behind us. I didn't want to burden you with any of this. It's a lot for you to carry."

"Clearly, it wasn't behind us, Dad," Sydney says, smiling at her father. "But that's all history. What's really important now is for you and everyone else to get better so that we can move on. We need to put as much distance between us and the past as we can."

"I'm not sure that I can do that," Alex says. "Not after everything that has happened in recent days." Taking a deep breath, he asks, "Where is Oliver? I would really like to talk to him. I have a lot of questions that I'm hoping he can clear up."

"Right," Seth says. Glancing at his sister and then at his father, he adds, "About that."

"Hold it, Seth. Let me tell him," Sydney says.

Seth shrugs. "I'm sure you can explain things better than I can."

"I'm not sure about that," she whispers. "But I was there."

"No, that makes sense," her brother tells her. "Go ahead and tell him."

"Okay," she replies, taking a deep breath and turning to face her father. "The truth is, Dad," Sydney begins, "that, right at the moment, we don't really know where Oliver is."

"What do you mean? Why isn't he here? Please don't tell me he died in the fire along with that woman. I couldn't live with myself knowing that he sacrificed himself for me yet again."

"That's just the thing, Dad. Not only is he not here," Sydney says, "but he isn't anywhere."

"I don't understand." Alex looks at his children. They can see he is confused by her comments. "He has to be somewhere."

"You'd think so, wouldn't you," Sydney says. "But after he and Paula went tumbling over the top step, I thought for sure that he was dead. But he just disappeared. The searchers at the house have recovered the remains of a woman, which are obviously Paula's—or Dani's, to be more precise—but they cannot find anything to suggest that Oliver was even there. But I know he was."

"Jesus," Alex says. "He can't have just up and disappeared. He must have gotten away and gone somewhere. But where? Maybe he's hiding from the owls. The searchers must keep looking for him. He could be injured."

"I don't know what to tell you, Dad," Sydney says. "All I know is what the searchers have told us, and they are positive that they have only recovered the remains of one person, a woman."

"Holy hell," Alex says with a sigh. "How is that even possible?"

"You know how this works better than anyone." She hesitates and then asks, "Do you think this is something the crows could have pulled off? Could they have really brought Oliver here just to save you and the family and then...?"

"Then what?" Seth interrupts. "Make him disappear again into thin air?"

Sydney throws him a sharp glare and he bites off whatever he was going to say next.

After a long moment, Alex nods. "Yes, I believe the crows have the power to do that. And if they knew Paula's identity and that she and the owls were coming after me—after all of us—then I believe they could have summoned Oliver, our protector."

"Come on Dad," Seth says, shaking his head. "You can't really believe this."

"I do believe it," Alex says, reaching out to take his son's hand. "But I understand that this may be impossible for you to accept, as it bends the curve of reality."

"Just a little bit." Seth makes no attempt to hide his skepticism.

Alex continues, "It's a lot, Seth, I get that. But you just don't know what the crows are capable of doing. Bringing Oliver here would be a pretty big move even for them, but I have seen them work some major miracles over the years."

Taking a deep breath, he continues, "It has been clear ever since Sydney found him washed up on the rocks that Oliver was here on a mission. He has always been my protector and I knew when he showed up that he must have a purpose for being here, but I just couldn't figure out what that purpose was."

"This all seems pretty far-fetched," Seth says. "I just can't buy it that crows could resurrect someone from the dead, and then send them back once they're done with him like some piece of garbage. So where does he go? Heaven? Hell? Is there some sort of magical 'crow' world where they send him to wait for his next big mission?"

"It's not like that, Seth. The crows work in mysterious ways," Alex says. "But I know it's asking a lot to expect you to believe such a thing. It defies the laws of nature—of logic—but sometimes, things happen that you cannot easily explain. You're a smart young man, and you have to decide for yourself what you believe, but this could be one of those things that you'll have to accept without fully understanding it."

"No." Seth shakes his head. "I just can't do that. There has to be another, more logical, explanation."

"Does there?" Sydney asks. "After everything I've seen over the past couple of days, I am willing to believe some sort of miracle happened here and that the crows were behind it. I believe we have to be willing to suspend reality."

Speaking directly to her brother, she adds, "I believe miracles can happen."

"On the subject of owls," Alex says, "are they still bothering anyone?"

"Nope," Sydney answers, shaking her head. "There have not been any reports of owls around here since the fire at the house. Whatever happened after Oliver and Paula fell down the stairs seems to have driven them away."

"They probably left because they lost their leader," Alex suggests. "Once that woman was gone, they had no reason to stick around. Their bond was severed."

Seth is about to comment on his father's suggestion when Bree enters the room, closely followed by Dr. Robbie. Sydney takes her brother's hand and squeezes gently.

"Let it go, Seth," she whispers and smiles at him. "Just let it go."

"Right," he says, nodding and stepping back from the bed to make room for his mother and the doctor.

"How's the patient?" Dr. Robbie asks, reviewing Alex's charts on her tablet. "It looks like you're doing better than you were a few days ago, my friend. I was worried about you, but I am relieved to see you are on the road to recovery."

"I feel fine," Alex answers, taking Bree's hand as she approaches the bed. Smiling at her, he says, "I'm ready to get out of here."

"Not so fast, mister," Dr. Robbie says. "Let's give it another day or so just to make sure the morphine is all out of your system. To be perfectly honest with you, Alex, you are one lucky man to be alive. With such a large dosage of morphine, you should have been dead. Whoever gave you that much morphine was definitely trying to kill you."

Alex nods. "I've reviewed the charts but, honestly, I cannot explain how I managed to survive."

With a quick smile, the doctor adds, "Is there anything else I can get for you before I leave? My shift is about to end and I'm getting out of here while I can escape. It has been one hell of a long day and I'm tired." She winks. "We're shorthanded because we're down one doctor. Word has it that he's just lounging around somewhere in the hospital, taking a long break. I hear he's a real slack-ass."

Alex chuckles. "Yup. That'd be me—a real slack-ass. But seriously, Isabel, thank you. I can't think of anything I need right now except for a new house."

"Don't worry about that right now. You and Mom are coming to stay at my house," Sydney tells him. "And you can live there as long as you need to. I have the extra room and I'd love to have the company."

"Thanks, honey," Bree says. "We appreciate that. It's going to take some time to get back on our feet because we lost everything."

"They are only things," Alex says. "They can be replaced. But talking about things that can't be replaced, what about Piper? How is she?"

"She is doing very well," Bree tells him and he can see the sparkle has returned to her eyes, which is a sure sign that his daughter must be out of the woods. "Isabel says the incision has healed nicely."

"What about the baby?" he asks.

"Doing well and has a strong heartbeat," Bree explains. "Isabel says Piper should be able to go home tomorrow. So that's some good news."

"It sure is but I don't think she should go home alone," Alex replies.

"Easy, Dad. That's handled. I'm going to stay with her for a few days," Seth says. "Preston came yesterday and got Elliot. They've gone back to the city so I'm free for at least a week, or until she can take care of herself."

"You guys have managed to get everything cleaned up and organized, haven't you? That's the way to take care of business," Alex says. "What about Mom? How is she doing?"

"Now, that's an interesting story," Sydney says. "It really is a miracle that she's even still with us, but somehow, after Oliver and Paula went down the stairs, Grandma Sam must have regained consciousness and managed to make her way back to her room. Not sure where she got the strength to do that, but that's where the firefighters found her with hardly a scratch on her body. Now that's a miracle."

Fighting to keep back the tears, she adds, "I tried to get up the stairs to get to her, but there was just too much smoke and flames that I had to turn back. There was no way I could get to her."

"That is unbelievable," Seth says. "I just don't see how that is even remotely possible. There's a lot that doesn't sound right about all of that."

"I don't know what to tell you, Seth," Sydney says with a shrug. "But I am very grateful that she's still with us. She is doing fine at the seniors' home, in a respite room. I've been checking on her twice a day and the staff are taking very good care of her. They say she is fitting in very well with the other residents."

"It was the crows," Alex speaks up. His tone is matter of fact. "It's obvious the crows saved her life."

Seth asks, "How could they even get into the house through the flames and smoke? How could they move a full-grown woman in a wheelchair?" He pauses, considers the scenario, and then adds, "I'm sorry, but I just can't accept that."

"Don't question it," Alex says. "Just believe it."

"Dad's right, Seth," Sydney adds as she moves to the window that looks out onto the hospital courtyard. There, amongst the colourful blooms on the many shrubs and flowers that have been planted for the patients to enjoy, she counts eight crows, and she is sure that they have come to watch over the family.

"Just believe and accept that the crows have worked another miracle. I know I do."

Epilogue

An uncomfortable silence floods the room as they meet for their second session since he was brought into the emergency room three days ago, barely breathing, badly battered and unconscious.

They stare across the desk at each other, then Dr. Anna Robbie, after scanning her notes, begins her assessment in a calming tone.

"How are you doing this morning?" she asks, carefully watching the man's reaction.

"Fine," he says, keeping his answer brief, his mood protected.

"Did you rest well?"

"Not really," he answers softly. "I don't sleep much these days."

"Why is that?"

He shakes his head.

"What do you think about when you can't sleep?" she asks.

"I keep reviewing the entire story," he answers, keeping his eyes lowered, almost as if he's ashamed to admit what he thinks about recent events. "Over and over. It's like it's running on repeat."

"It's okay to think about it. The important thing is to keep it in perspective."

"Perspective?" He looks at her and shrugs. "Yes, well, that's easier said than done."

"One step at a time," the doctor says. "In your journey to find yourself, it is important not to rush things. You will get there."

Her assignment today is to determine his mental acumen. In the past, she has worked with patients who struggle with distinguishing what is reality and what is fantasy. She knows that his level of acuity will reveal a great deal about his current thought process, if not his overall mental health.

When dealing with people who are suffering from grand delusions like those this patient is experiencing, it is important to assess his ability to think rationally.

"According to theoretical physicist Carlo Rovelli, time is an illusion," she tells the tall, slender man who is sitting across from her, his messy chestnut-coloured hair, unkempt beard and ill-fitting clothes conveying confusion and disorientation.

He listens, hanging onto her every word.

She recognizes that he is struggling to come to grips with reality—or what he perceives to be real. Speaking softly, she tries to defuse the angst that is physically manifesting in his body.

"I know you have been through a major ordeal, and you want quick answers about what happened to you, but you cannot rush your recovery. You cannot expect answers right away," she tells him. "Time is a funny thing. Again, to quote, Rovelli, 'Our naive perception of its flow doesn't correspond to physical reality'."

"But it does," he replies, his voice devoid of any emotions. "I know what happened to me and, as I've told you several times, I jumped thirty-seven years into the future."

"It may seem that way," Dr. Robbie replies, refusing to show any reaction to his assertion that, on the surface, his story seems absurd. "You suffered a severe blow to your head when you went over the bridge and then you lay on the rocks, exposed to the elements, for three days until the searchers found you. It's really a miracle that you survived. To be honest, the fact that you are still alive is a mystery to all of us."

"The searchers couldn't find me for three days because I wasn't there," he insists. "I've already told you this."

"I'm not surprised that you are confused," she agrees. "The past, present, and future are not as neatly divided as we perceive them to be, especially when our body suffers a major physical trauma such as the one you experienced. In that way, what you believe to be real and what is actually real are all jumbled up in your head."

He shakes his head. "It's not like that."

"What is it like, then?" she asks.

"I know what happened to me and it was all real—very, very real. For starters, thirty-seven years from now, I meet your daughter and, you'll be happy to know, she is a medical doctor. Her name is Isabel. She's very nice, smart, and very good with her patients," he tells her, speaking matter-of-factly. "I can also tell you that, in thirty-seven years, you will be retired and living in a condo in Halifax."

"Interesting story but I don't think so." She shakes her head. "That scenario seems very unlikely for me. However, I understand that in your mind these events can seem very real."

"I'm not going to argue with you about this, Dr. Robbie," he replies. "I know you're the psychiatrist and you're supposed to be the expert on head trauma and injuries, but I also know what I experienced. But I've been to the future, and I've seen what a mess it is. I'm sorry to say that things don't look so great there. Humanity is in deep trouble."

"Okay, so let's say that you did, by some miracle, go to the future, how could that even happen?" the doctor asks. She understands that often, when a patient has such deep-seeded beliefs as this one exhibits it is not smart to argue with him. Instead, she asks, "How could you be physically transported into the future and then return to the present? What allows you to move through time so freely?"

He looks at her, carefully considering what he says next.

"It was the crows," he finally blurts out. "The crows are responsible for everything that happened to me."

"Crows?" She pauses, watching the patient for any signs that he may become agitated. The last thing she needs is for him to become confrontational. When she's sure that he's okay to proceed, she adds, "I just want to be clear. You are telling me that crows transported you to the future and then brought you back to the present? That's your explanation?"

He nods. "Yes. The crows did it."

"I see," Dr. Robbie replies, being careful to keep her own thoughts well-guarded. "Well, that's an interesting theory. Let's just say the crows were responsible, how could they do that?"

"You don't know them," he says. "But they are very powerful. If they wanted me to see what the future looks like, then they could absolutely take me there."

"Okay." She nods. "If that's what you think happened, then we are going to have to dig deeper. We have to try to figure out this strange fascination you have with crows. I'd like to know what this crow connection really means and I'm willing to bet that you'd like to know that as well."

"I know what it means," he says. "And I know the role I play in their plans."

"You have a specific role?"

He nods. "I am the protector."

"I see," Dr. Robbie says, making a note on the pad in front of her.

"Do you?"

"Yes, I do," she assures him. "Please tell me, as the protector, what do you do?"

She sees him hesitate. She's been down this road before with other patients. She knows he's probably thinking that the more he talks, the deeper the hole he's digging for himself. She gives him time to collect his thoughts.

After a moment, he explains, "My main objective is to protect the chosen one."

"The chosen one?" She pauses, careful not to show any judgment, and then asks, "And who is that?"

He takes a deep breath and then says, "Alex Goodwin."

"I see," she answers. "Alex Goodwin is only sixteen years old, isn't he?"

"I guess he is, but his age doesn't matter. The important thing is that Alex is bonded to the crows through a pact made by one of his ancestors several hundred years ago."

"Just so I have this straight, in this construct Alex Goodwin is the chosen one because of an ancient curse and you are his protector. Right?"

"Sort of." He nods. "But it's not a curse, it's a pact between Alex's family and the crows."

"Sorry," she says, regretting that she had been mistaken about such a specific detail. She does not want to put her patient on the defensive by misspeaking anything about his truth. "It is a pact and, because of that pact, your role as protector is to protect the chosen one from...what, exactly?"

"The evil forces that threaten him and the natural balance in the world," he says. "He is all that stands between redemption and obliteration."

His assertion is matter-of-fact, which, she thinks, speaks to how valid this reality seems to him. While she cannot yet determine what is causing such a convergence of realities, she gives her patient credit for hanging on to such specific details.

He adds, "In the future, I also have to protect his family."

"That's a lot to deal with, isn't it? For one man, I mean."

"I guess." He shrugs. "But that's what I am here to do."

"And the crows are behind all of this?"

"Yes," he says, suddenly pulling his slender six-foot-two body from the chair.

"Are you going somewhere?"

"Do you mind if I stretch my legs?" he asks, walking about the office. "It helps me to clear my head if I stand up."

"Feel free to do whatever makes you comfortable. Please tell me about these crows."

"In the future, there are eight of them leading the flock, which, is called a 'murder', in case you didn't know," he says, moving to the window, his strides slow and deliberate.

Neighbouring buildings are easily visible from her office window. Over the rooftops of those buildings, is the harbour, where searchers found him on the rocks three days ago.

"And what does eight crows mean?"

Taking in a deep breath, he answers, "It is eight crows for a wish."

"And did you wish to see the future?"

He nods. "Yes. I believe I did. I was curious to know what the future holds for all of us." He pauses, then shakes his head. "I didn't like it so much."

"No, I can see why you feel that way," Dr. Robbie replies. "It sounds like you had quite an ordeal in the future."

"It was something, that's for sure," he agrees, "I hope things change and that it's not too late for any of us, but based on what I've seen, the future isn't looking very good."

"That's a rather bleak outlook."

"Sorry," he says. "I guess it is." He sighs and asks, "Do you think we can change things that haven't happened yet, or are our futures already determined?"

"I don't know," she says, shaking her head. "But if you believe in fate and destiny, then I suppose the future is already set. While time may be fluid, some believe that we are all set on our life paths from the moment we are born and that our journey has been predetermined, reaching its ultimate destination with our death. The trials and tribulations, the challenges and successes, all part of the greater plan."

"God," he says with a sigh.

"You should be worrying about the present," Dr. Robbie suggests. "Let's concentrate on the things we can control right now, and let the future take care of itself. Let's start with trying to get some answers for you."

"I don't need answers," he says, continuing to peer out the window, his breath fogging up the glass as he exhales. "I need hope."

"We all need hope."

"We most certainly do," he agrees, adding, "Would you mind coming over here to the window? I want to show you something."

"What's going on?" Dr. Robbie asks, joining him by the window. She notices that some of the buildings nearby are in desperate need of major face lifts or, at the very least, a fresh coat of paint.

"What do you see?" she asks.

"Look over there on that rooftop," he says. Pointing to a nearby building that has several apartments on the second floor, above a large pharmacy, he asks, "Do you see them?"

She nods. "I see them. There is a bunch of crows up there."

"There are nine of them, to be exact."

"Nine crows. What does that mean to you, Oliver Lewis?"

After a moment, he answers, "I'm not really sure what it means for me, but according to legend, it's nine crows for a kiss."

Acknowledgements

I want to start by sending a huge shout-out to my loyal and enthusiastic fans. This would not be possible without you, so thank you for being supportive throughout this extraordinary journey.

The release of the eighth book in this series is the continuation of dream that has been many years in the making. It's also very gratifying to know that so many people enjoy these stories. It is my hope that all your wishes come true.

As you can imagine, creating a book is a major undertaking, and while the writing often takes years and is usually done in isolation, there are always numerous people who play a key role in completing the process. It's appropriate, then, to acknowledge a few of those people who helped bring *Eight Crows for a Wish* to fruition.

I must extend my deepest and undying gratitude to publisher Brenda J. Thompson and my extraordinary editor, Andrew Wetmore, for their continued belief and faith in me. They are the driving force behind Moose House Publications and who knows where these books would be without their support? This has been an incredible journey. Thank you for guidance throughout the process.

Thank you as well to my friend and fellow dreamer, Marci Lin Melvin, for her many years of unwavering support, advice, insights and gentle prodding. Her never-give-up attitude, encouragement and creativity played a major role in helping to shape this book. I could not have done it without her. Saying thank you hardly seems like enough, but thank you.

I also wish to extend my deepest gratitude to graphic artist Rebekah Wetmore for the amazing cover design. Capturing the essence of an entire book in one image is no easy assignment, but she delivered a cover so compelling that it is simply stunning. Thank you, Rebekah. You do amazing work.

Another person I must acknowledge is my very talented photographer friend, Heidi Jirotka. To say she is creative and innovate would be an understatement. Thank you, Heidi, for going above and beyond to make me look good. I've said it before, but it must be repeated—you rock!

Another heart-felt thank-you goes to the book sellers and bookstore owners for their unwavering support over the years. Those of us who dare to think we can make it as writers would flounder without the support of such outlets. You are a vital piece of the equation, so I applaud you.

I've saved my last and most heart-felt thank you for my most important supporters, my family, especially my wife, Nancy. She has been my rock through the many years I've been chasing this dream of becoming a published author. She is always the first one to give an insightful word of advice and a gentle criticism when it is needed, and to pick me up when I'm sad or frustrated. To say I could not have done it without her is an understatement. There are not enough words to say how much I appreciate her.

Now that the wish has finally been revealed, stay tuned for *Nine Crows for a Kiss.*

About the author

Vernon Oickle was born and raised in Liverpool, Nova Scotia, where he continues to reside with his wife, Nancy, and their family.

Growing up in a small town in rural Nova Scotia, Vernon always wanted to pursue a career as a newspaper reporter. After completing high school in 1979, he attended Lethbridge Community College. He graduated in 1982 with an honours diploma in Journalism and returned to Liverpool to work at the local newspaper, *The Advance*. His community newspaper career spanned 33 years.

In addition to his long list of newspaper awards and honours, in 2012 Vernon received the Queen Elizabeth II Diamond Jubilee Medal, recognizing his contributions to his community, province and country, and in April 2015 he received a Distinguished Alumni Award (Community Leader) from Lethbridge College. He was inducted into the Atlantic Journalism Awards Hall of Fame in the spring of 2020.

As a testimony to his outstanding career, in 2014 the South Queens Middle School in Liverpool announced the creation of the Vernon Oickle Writer's Award, to be given annually to a student who excels in the art of writing, either fiction or non-fiction.

Eight Crows for a Wish is Vernon's 36th published book.

www.ingramcontent.com/pod-product-compliance
Lightning Source LLC
Chambersburg PA
CBHW060259310726
48976CB00007B/2140